CODE BLUE

By KatLyn

CODE BLUE
A BookEnds Press Publication
PO Box 14513
Gainesville, Florida 32604
1-800-881-3208

Cover design by Sheri
if there_be@hotmail.com

Distribution information may be obtained from:
StarCrossed Productions, Inc.
PO Box 357474
Gainesville, Florida 32635-7474
www.starcrossedproductions.com

Printed in the United States of America

By the Author

Storm Surge

Forthcoming Books

Acceptable Losses

Rip Tide
The Sequel to Storm Surge

Dedication

To some, "family" is a word used to describe a group of people bound together by the complex process of biology, created at conception, and endured through a lifetime. To me, family *is* life, and given a choice, I'd choose the same one I was so very blessed to be received into at birth.

Storm Surge and *Code Blue* would never have been possible without the unconditional love of my family. Dad, Kim, and Eric are a constant flow of love and encouragement in my life. My mom, God rest her soul, is the spirit that constantly lifts me to greater heights. Even in her absence, she shows me the light and brightens my path through the journey we call life.

Denise, my love. No one can truly understand the force behind what love can accomplish if given the chance to flourish. Your tireless efforts to help me, encourage me, and nudge me into writing are what has finally made this book a reality. You have sacrificed more than anyone should have to so that I can live my dream, write my stories, and manage SCP. You have given me strength when I was weak, courage when I was unsure, but most of all you have given me the most precious gift one can ever wish for: your love. You are the beat of my heart, and every breath I take is for you.

This book and all that I am is for my family
Mom, Dad, Kim, Eric, and Denise

Acknowledgments

There are so many people who have encouraged me during the writing of *Code Blue*. It is not possible to thank each one individually, but a few must be acknowledged for their unwavering support and the role each played in making this book a reality.

The KLF group is a constant source of encouragement. During the long journey in writing this book, you have continued to stand by me through thick and thin, and for that I will be forever grateful.

Rad, my friend and colleague, continues to raise the bar on my own expectations. The journey we have embarked upon and where it has already taken us goes far beyond what my eyes or mind ever dreamed possible.

My constant thanks to Lee for her patience while I take even more of Rad's time with work and pontificating the future. Through my writing and SCP, I have found a rare and lifelong friend.

Many thanks go to Karen, Pam, Liz, Bob, Pete, and all the wonderful people that make up BookEnds Press. You take my simple words and dreams, make them into a reality, and go beyond what any author could ever hope for in a publisher. You are truly the best and I am proud to be associated with such a fine organization.

The cover of *Code Blue* is the result of Sheri's genius. She took a simple photograph that I made from the top of Mount Washington, overlooking "The Point" and downtown Pittsburgh, and created a masterpiece that brings life and vision to this story.

Stacia Seaman is one of the most professional, in-depth, and accurate editors I have ever had the pleasure of working with. I know without a doubt when she signs off on a book it is the best it can be.

Thank you, ML, for your help and encouragement throughout the writing of *Code Blue*. Your friendship, stories, maps, and tours of Pittsburgh gave me a true feeling of the city and made it possible for me to get the details as close to perfect as possible.

To everyone who supports and encourages lesbian fiction, the authors who write it, SCP, and the many fine independent bookstores throughout the world: Thank you. You are the ones we write for each day.

CHAPTER ONE

The cold Pittsburgh air sliced through the narrow alleyway between two abandoned buildings on Penn Avenue, sending discarded shards of paper and trash cast off by passersby billowing into the air. The snow had begun to fall heavily an hour earlier, but Logan McGregor didn't seem to notice it or the biting cold as she snapped a pair of latex gloves on her hands and knelt beside the garbage Dumpster where the latest victim had been unceremoniously discarded. This was the fifth murder in as many weeks, and her nerves were wearing thin.

Each time the murderer claimed another victim, the detective could feel the noose tightening around her own neck. The mayor had demanded that a special task force be formed to solve the case—and quickly. Logan knew the pressure wasn't because the community was concerned about the murders, but because the mayor and several influential developers of the Strip District were concerned about how the bad publicity around the case might harm tourism and reduce the amount of money pouring into the recently redeveloped area. As head of the task force, Logan was in the hot seat as she desperately attempted to piece together the puzzle that had stumped the entire Pittsburgh police force for the last five weeks.

She looked down on the tattered body of the latest Jane Doe and immediately recognized the M.O. As with each previous murder, a business card from Langston Development Corporation, imprinted with the name of a top-level corporate executive, had been placed carefully on top of the body. This card carried the name of Christine Langston, the senior vice president of Langston Development and daughter of Christopher Winthrop Langston III.

Langston Development, having purchased several blocks of abandoned and dilapidated buildings along the Strip, had torn them down and rebuilt them so that the new buildings complemented the surviving structures. The Strip District had at one time been one of the most popular areas of the city, but over the years had fallen into a downward economic spiral and been taken over by drug dealers and vagrants. With the renovations, Langston Development had been responsible for the recent growth of businesses along the Strip District, and in an indirect way, for the drop in the crime rate and drug trade that had run rampant along Penn Avenue.

Her investigation was hampered by the fact that C.W. Langston, as well as the other executives, were currently hiding behind closed doors, refusing to be interviewed. The mayor, using his political clout to protect his old friend, refused the requests of the police department to force Langston to cooperate, asserting that the development corporation was as much a victim as those who had been murdered. Unraveling the case would be like walking blindfolded through a maze, and the detective knew many of the dead ends would be conveniently placed political barriers protecting the wealthy Langston family.

Logan knew that she would find that the latest victim had arrived alone at one of the nearby bars and then most likely left the establishment a short time later with a man. All of the previous investigations had followed the same route. The victims, regular patrons of the area clubs and having histories of drug abuse and sporadic employment, had all left willingly with their companion, only to be found brutally murdered a few hours later in a nearby, fairly exposed, location.

Glancing around the area, Logan couldn't help but think that the murderer was taunting her, testing her ability to figure out the next move. Her frustration was growing with each day. As she peeled off her gloves, she made a mental note to canvass the clubs again, this time pressing the managers and staff harder for information, and to have several of the investigative officers dig deeper into the victims' lives.

Logan walked away from the body back into the cold air whipping through the alleyway and took a deep breath, rubbing her temples, which throbbed with the headache she'd had for days. She leaned heavily on the hood of the cruiser, dropping her head and stretching the taut muscles of her neck.

"You know, a little sleep might be just what the doctor ordered."

Logan turned to see Jennifer Phillips, the top crime reporter for the *Pittsburgh Post-Gazette*, looking at her with concern. "No comment, Ms. Phillips, and you know for a fact that I have no use for doctors."

Jennifer raised a thin, dark eyebrow as she eyed the tall, dark-haired detective. "Sometimes, Logan, you can be a real pain in the ass. I don't recall asking you any questions. My concern at this moment is for you— *not* the story."

As she rolled her head from side to side, trying to loosen the tense muscles, the detective silently chastised herself for the verbal attack.

They had been friends for many years, and Logan knew that the reporter would be the last person to take advantage of their friendship in order to get a headline. "Sorry, Jen, I'm just really beat and we have nothing to go on here. I didn't mean to jump on you like that—really."

"Are you done here for the night, or are you going to squeeze in another ten or twelve hours before your next shift?" The reporter's sarcastic tone left little room for misinterpretation.

"I'm done." It had been a while since the two women had spent any time together outside of their jobs, and Logan suddenly felt the need for some good company and a strong drink. "Want to go grab a bite to eat?"

Jennifer couldn't hide her surprise. "Yeah, sure. Just give me a minute to call in and I'll be ready."

Logan dropped down into the cruiser and radioed into dispatch, signing out for the evening. Technically, she should have been off duty eight hours before, but she hadn't felt like going to the dark, lonely structure in which she lived. Home was simply a house; a place where she slept, showered, and occasionally ate, but not the warm, comforting home she once knew. Each time she walked through the door she was hit with the deafening silence echoing within the walls and the unforgettable faint scent of Obsession—the scent of Diane.

Logan was still sitting with the radio microphone in her hand when Jennifer walked up a short while later. "Hey, are you all right?"

Through glazed eyes, Logan looked up into her concerned friend's face. "Yes, I'm fine...um, just tired."

Eyeing the detective intently, Jennifer grew concerned over her friend's despondency. She had witnessed Logan at her best and worst, but during the last few months, the complacency Logan had shrouded herself with had turned into apathy. Apathy for everything in her life except her work. It was almost as if she expected her job to rescue her from the demons that haunted her life—a life that since Diane left had been filled with only darkness.

"Logan? If you'd rather take a rain check on dinner, we can. You look like you need some sleep anyway."

Tucking her long legs into the cruiser, Logan shook her head and looked over toward the body bag that held the latest Jane Doe. "No. After this I won't be able to sleep. I can't remember the last time I ate anyway. Follow me to headquarters and let me get my truck. What do you say to going over to Buskers for a while?"

Shrugging, Jennifer turned toward her car. "Fine. Lead the way, Detective."

Buskers, a jazz café located in the Strip District of Pittsburgh, was known for its upscale menu. It attracted affluent patrons who could afford not only the good food and drinks, but also the works by local artists displayed on the walls. Local jazz musicians entertained the crowd after the dinner rush was over each night, and the melodic sound of a tenor sax floated out onto the sidewalk as the women entered. Looking for a quiet table that would allow them the opportunity to talk, Jennifer took a seat in the far corner while Logan strolled to the bar to order their drinks.

As she glanced around the bar, Jennifer wondered how many of the patrons were aware of the current events taking place on the Strip. The murders had received fairly good press coverage, especially in the past two weeks, but the story never led the evening news and was often buried inside the local crime section of the *Post*. Jennifer suspected this was because of the victims' low economic status. She knew Logan was working day and night on the investigation and probably had one of her renowned gut feelings about the case, but given Logan's current state of mind, she pushed away the thought. Tonight was a night for friendship; the story, she reasoned, could wait until tomorrow.

Dropping into the seat across from Jennifer, Logan set two beers on the table and handed Jennifer a menu she'd picked up at the bar. A few silent moments passed as the women considered their choices. From time to time, Jennifer glanced over toward the detective, and she realized that Logan had been staring blankly at the menu for several minutes. "Hey, kid, talk to me. What's going on in that head of yours?"

Seeing only a look of concern and not the professional interest she expected, Logan took a deep breath and closed her eyes before shaking her head. "Too much is going on in my head, Jen. So much, I can't even begin to sort it out."

Jennifer spoke softly. "Anything I can help with? You know, sometimes it helps just to talk." Seeing Logan's walls quickly rising, Jennifer forced herself to continue. "If it's about the case, I understand if you can't talk about it, but if it's something else, you know I'm always here for you."

The detective's eyes held Jennifer's. Her reply was postponed by the timely appearance, pad in hand, of the waiter. The women placed their orders and as the waiter departed, Logan once again looked across the table at her friend.

"Look, Jen, I know you care, but right now I don't have the time or the energy to think about anything other than this case." Logan could feel the tears welling up in her eyes and looked away, pretending to find interest in something across the room. "I promise, once this is over, we'll talk about Diane. I promise."

CHAPTER TWO

Madison Cavanaugh shut off the lights in her office, closing and locking the door before heading down the quiet hallway toward the physicians' locker room. The last thirty-six hours had been frantic, with numerous MVAs caused by a sudden ice storm that had enveloped the city and that, according to the local weather forecast, would continue for the next few days. With a sigh, the surgeon shoved open the heavy door, walked into the cavernous silence of the room, and headed for her locker. She had been in surgery most of the day, and the fatigue now reverberated through her shoulders.

Turning the combination dial on the lock, she debated forgoing her weekly excursion into the streets, but knew in the end that she would be out there walking, searching...waiting. The overwhelming fatigue would have to wait a few more hours before she would give in to it, slide between the warm sheets of her bed and sleep.

She opened the metal door, dug out her street clothes, and tossed them on the vinyl couch. After removing her scrubs, she pulled on a pair of thermal underwear, followed by a pair of faded jeans and a thick long-sleeved flannel shirt that could not hide the fact that Madison Cavanaugh was a beautiful woman. Tonight, she weaved her long blond hair into a French braid before tucking the silky locks under a well-worn baseball cap. Sitting on the couch, she had just begun tying her Doc Martens when the doors swung open, announcing the entrance of the one person she was hoping to avoid: Angela Kramer.

"Well, there you are, Madi. I've been looking all over for you." Angela's face revealed the air of impatience that was renowned throughout the hospital, primarily among the interns and nurses. Madison was one of only a few people within those walls that Angela Kramer couldn't intimidate, which irritated Angela even more. "Let's go have dinner before you go out on your...charity run, shall we?"

Madison glared at the psychologist before she dropped her head once again and finished tying her shoes. "No, thanks. I'm not hungry and I really need to get going."

Angela could feel her patience wearing thin. "I can't understand why you would rather spend the evening scurrying around the alleyways of the Strip than going to dinner with me, Madi."

Madison could feel the weight of Angela's gaze as she calmly slid her arms through the sleeves of the heavy wool navy-issue coat that had once belonged to her father.

Reaching for the door, Madison turned to face her sometimes-lover. "This program is important to me, Angela. I made a commitment when I agreed to work with Operation Safety Net, and unlike some people, I keep my promises."

She stepped out into the hallway, realizing that she had just closed the door on any future she might have with Angela, and yet for the first time in weeks, she felt the pressure lift from her shoulders. The feisty psychologist, while fun to spend time with in the beginning, had been pressing for a commitment over the past few months. *I have no time in my life for anything or anyone, especially someone as demanding as Angela*, Madison thought to herself as she started down the long hallway leading to the elevator.

Walking toward the exit on the first floor, Madison felt the eyes following her progress. She smiled, knowing that people were trying to decide if she was really Madison Cavanaugh, Mercy Hospital's top orthopedic surgeon, or someone that simply resembled her. She prided herself on the good looks she inherited from her parents and always took extra time to make sure her make-up and hair were perfect before venturing out in public. Tonight, however, she didn't have time to go home and change before going to the Strip for her weekly visits. Besides, she certainly didn't want to be caught alone in the Strip District dressed in the tailored clothes and expensive jewelry that she normally wore.

Bracing herself against the bitter cold, Madison pulled her collar tighter around her neck and walked quickly through the sliding glass doors out of Mercy Hospital and into the dimly lit parking lot. After starting her Pathfinder, she waited for the engine to warm as she studied the majestic building before her, feeling the almost palpable energy contained within in the walls.

As an intern, she had learned to make quick, decisive judgments with confidence. Life-and-death decisions were an everyday occurrence and a part of her job. She had never questioned her skill as a surgeon; it was her skill as a person, a friend, and as a lover that had always given

Madison anguish. After leaving the warm embrace of the hospital's walls to enter the world of everyday life, she could no longer fall back on scientific research to guide her. It was during these times that the doctor wondered if she was truly as together as everyone thought.

Sighing heavily, Madison shifted the Pathfinder into gear and left the parking lot, turning right onto Forbes Avenue. As she crossed town heading toward the Strip District, her mood changed as quickly as the environment. She was no longer the wealthy orthopedic surgeon; now she was simply Ms. Madi, friend and advocate for the homeless and downtrodden of the city.

Madison turned onto Smallman Street, a well-traveled area of the Strip, and parked under a streetlight. Bracing herself against the harsh wind that whipped around the old buildings, she grabbed her bag from the backseat and walked away from the more populated area until she came to a small nondescript alleyway just south of Twenty-seventh Street. She slowed her pace for only a moment to take in her surroundings before making her way toward the glow of a small drum fire in the middle of the alley.

Madison was about a third of the way into the shadowed alley when she felt, more than heard, a presence behind her. Before she could react, a man in tattered, soiled clothes stepped out from behind a garbage bin, blocking her path. Turning, she found two other men blocking her exit.

"Ain't seen no pretty woman in a long time," the man before her said through a smile as he edged closer.

Madison could smell the stench of wine and smoke emanating from his body and noticed that his smile revealed poor oral hygiene and several missing teeth. Holding the man's eyes to show her lack of fear, she edged closer, trying to move past him. "I'm not here to bother you, sir, I just need to find Toby."

As the man sidestepped to block her path once again, his face became dark and defensive. "What the hell you be wanting Toby for?"

Holding her bag up for him to see, Madison once again tried to bypass him, only to be cut off a second time. "I'm a doctor. If you know Toby, you'll also know he was attacked last week. I put four stitches in his cheek and now it's time to remove them." Holding the man's glare, she lifted her chin. "If you would be so kind as to direct me to him, I'll be out of your way in a few minutes."

Before the vagrant could respond, a very large man emerged from the shadows. "Leave Ms. Madi be. She don't mean you no harm."

Pushing her way past the first man, Madison walked toward her rescuer, her 5'7" frame dwarfed by his 6'4" height. Craning her head, Madison looked up into his smiling blue eyes. "How are you, Toby? You ready to get those stitches out?"

"Yes'm." Turning, Toby began to walk back toward the flaming barrel. "Let's get closer to the fire where it's warm. You shouldn't be out here on a night like this, Ms. Madi."

Placing her bag on a relatively clean piece of cardboard, she motioned the large man to sit. "Sure I should, Toby. You don't think I would forget about your stitches, do you?"

With a sheepish smile on his face, Toby looked away. "No, ma'am, I didn't think you forgot me, but it could have waited till it was warmer out here."

"I told you I'd be back tonight, and I keep my promises. Now turn around so I can take a look at your cheek."

Madison knew coming into Operation Safety Net that earning the trust and respect of the neighborhood's homeless would be one of the biggest obstacles she would face. Encountering men like the ones who'd pressured her in the alley had chased off more than a few would-be volunteers over the past few years. She knew the danger of going alone into the alleys, but the need to help trumped her fears. The doctor focused on the one thing she knew she could control: providing a concerned and honest source of medical care to the men and women who called the streets home. Thus, twice a week for the past two years, she had walked the streets, searching and caring.

Madison removed the stitches from Toby's cheek, applied an antiseptic, and covered the wound with a clean bandage. The white gauze almost glowed against Toby's dirty unshaven face, and she knew that before morning it would probably be one more piece of litter. She smiled and lifted Toby's chin with her hand until their eyes met. "You think you can keep that clean for me for a few days?"

"Sure thing, Ms. Madi." After rising to his feet, Toby walked Madison toward the entrance of the alley. As they passed the men she had previously encountered, Toby spoke. "Those goons didn't mess with you, did they?"

"No, Toby, they didn't. They were just protecting their territory." She glanced up at the towering man. "Just like you would do if a strange person had come wandering in here unannounced. Right?"

Smiling down into the warm face, Toby chuckled. "Yes'm, I guess you're right, but if anybody ever messes with you, you just let me know. Okay, Ms. Madi?"

"I will, Toby, and thanks." Madison had just cleared the building and stepped out onto the sidewalk when she felt a strong hand grasp her arm and pull her. The doctor watched in horror as the hand released her and grabbed Toby, forcing his face against the wall. She stood speechless as she watched the scene unfold.

A tall, dark, very muscular woman pressed heavily against Toby's back as she swept his feet apart, keeping him off balance. She had Toby's arm wrenched around his back, his fist pressed between his shoulder blades, causing him to cry out in agony. Her other hand was firmly against his head, pressing his face against the cold brick wall.

"What the fuck are you doing, Toby? Harassing the pretty women again?" The woman's low, menacing growl was full of revulsion and anger.

Toby's shoulders sagged against the building. "I was just walking the lady to her car, Officer."

As she shoved him harder against the wall, the officer's voice became low and dark. "Yeah, I guess that's what you said last year when I caught you trying to rape that student two blocks north of here."

Finally finding her voice, Madison stepped forward. "Officer, he's telling you the truth. Please release him; he did nothing wrong."

Her eyes flared when she saw the blood dripping off Toby's cheek as he turned around. "That's just great, Officer. I just removed the stitches from his cheek and you've managed to barge in and in less than five minutes, reopen the wound. *Thank you* so much for your help."

When she turned around, Logan McGregor looked into the greenest eyes she had ever seen. Had they not been shooting daggers at her, she might have fallen into those pools and drowned.

CHAPTER THREE

The doctor glared at Logan as she shoved her way around the officer. "Jesus, Toby. I'm sorry, but I'm going to have to put the stitches back in."

Taking the large man by the arm, she led him down the sidewalk. Toby shuffled along quietly until they reached the Pathfinder. As she unlatched the back hatch and motioned for him to sit on the open gate, he looked at her in surprise.

"Ms. Madi, I can't sit in your car, ma'am. I'll get it all dirty."

She pulled Toby down beside her on the gate. "Toby, I'm not worried about my car at the moment. My main concern is your face. It's not going to be as easy to suture this time and I'm concerned about it scarring."

A shadow fell across the doctor's shoulder as she prepared a syringe of local anesthetic for Toby's cheek. She scowled. "Don't you think you've caused enough problems for one evening, Officer? You're in my light. Please move."

The detective's eyebrow arched as she looked at the doctor's irritated expression. Her first inclination was to turn and walk away, but something in the blonde's eyes held her there. Inhaling the doctor's faint spicy scent, Logan pulled a Mag-Lite from her back pocket and leaned in to shine the light on Toby's face. "Sorry, Toby, I know it's bright, but the Doc here needs to see."

"S'ok, Officer Mac, I understand." Toby closed his eyes, grimacing as the needle punctured his skin. "Damn, Ms. Madi, I thought that stuff was supposed to stop it from hurting."

The doctor turned back to Logan after capping and dropping the empty syringe into her bag. "Thanks for the light, Officer."

"No problem." Logan watched as the doctor disinfected the wound and replaced the sutures. For the first time, she noticed the doctor's long, slender fingers, which were steady and sure as she gently sutured the wound. Logan noticed the contrast to her own hands as the light shook under her trembling palm.

The doctor glanced up. "I appreciate what you're doing, but can you hold the light a little steadier, Officer?"

Sighing, Logan rested the butt of the light on her shoulder, trying to steady the beam. "Sure, Doc. Sorry, it's a little cold out here tonight." The detective prayed the doctor wouldn't see through the lame excuse she had contrived for her shaking hands. For the first time in what seemed like ages, Logan McGregor found herself nervous as she inched closer to the attractive doctor.

After completing the sutures, the surgeon applied a topical disinfectant to the wound before covering it with a sterile bandage. Resting her hand on Toby's shoulder, she gave him a stern look. "Now, I want you to keep that covered and clean. Okay?" She pulled out several prewrapped bandages from her bag and placed them in his hand. "I'll be back next week to see how this is doing. I'll meet you here, about this same time. Think you can remember?"

"Sure thing, Ms. Madi. I always like seeing you around here." Glancing at Logan, he continued, "There aren't many nice folks come down here to see us street people."

He stood, brushed off the tailgate of the truck, and turned to walk back toward the alley. Halfway there, he yelled back over his shoulder. "You be careful out here, Ms. Madi. And remember what I said. Anybody mess with you, you tell me and I'll take care of'm for ya."

The doctor chuckled as she called back, "I will, Toby. You take care of yourself, and I'll see you next week." With the bag in her hand, the doctor walked down the sidewalk and away from the detective. She sighed, then turned back toward the tall, dark figure. "Thanks for your help, Officer."

The detective stood watching the retreating figure for a few moments before mumbling to herself under her breath and jogging to catch up. She fell into step beside her and they walked a short distance before the doctor stopped and turned toward Logan with questioning eyes. "Is there something I can help you with, Officer—um, I don't think I caught your last name."

"McGregor. Logan McGregor," she responded, instantly regretting her decision to pursue the blonde, but knowing she had been given no alternative. "I, ah, you shouldn't be out here alone, Doc. If you haven't heard, there have been several murders in this area over the last few weeks."

The doctor turned around and walked quickly down the sidewalk. "I appreciate your concern, Officer McGregor, but I hardly think that I fit the profile of the murderer's victims. I don't frequent the bars in this neighborhood, and even if I did, I certainly wouldn't be leaving with a strange man."

She tensed as a strong hand encircled her arm. Turning to face Logan, she was met with a dark scowl. "Will you please remove your hand from my arm, Officer?"

Logan dropped her hand and took a deep breath to calm her rapidly rising temper. "Look, I know we got off to a bad start back there, but it really isn't safe for you to be out here by yourself. Why don't you let me tag along with you until you're done?"

The surgeon couldn't contain a laugh. "Sorry, Officer McGregor, but I think our initial meeting is the very reason *why* you shouldn't tag along with me." Seeing the comprehension in Logan's face, she smiled. "I seriously doubt any of these citizens would allow me within fifty feet of them if they saw you walking along beside me. Sorry, but I think I'll go solo on this one."

Logan thought back over the last hour as she walked to her truck. She couldn't understand why this Ms. Madi had been so rude; she had only been trying to protect her, and Toby *had* been arrested the previous year for attempting to assault a young coed. Of course, Toby had claimed that the young woman had snatched a dollar that a passerby had just given him. The coed had denied the accusation and refused to press charges, so Logan had let the incident drop, but she continued to keep an eye on Toby whenever she was in the neighborhood.

Logan watched with interest as people milled along the Strip. She'd had an unusual feeling all day. Something in her gut told her the murderer was in the area that night and she had decided earlier in the day to drive over, on her own time, to surveil the area. It was while she sat watching the crowd that she'd seen the woman disappear into the alley.

She had seriously thought a drug deal was about to take place and waited for a few minutes before exiting her truck and crossing the street. She was about to ease into the shadows when she'd noticed Toby exiting the alley with the blonde, his hand on her arm. Instantly recalling her previous experience with Toby, Logan's first reaction had been to put distance between him and the woman. It never occurred to her the woman might actually be seeking Toby, much less be a doctor.

As she recalled the incident, Logan could understand the doctor's reaction to the offer to accompany her. "Great, McGregor. You don't even know the woman's name and you've managed to piss her off. Yep, you're a real charmer."

The detective released a sigh of relief when she saw the blond woman turn the corner onto Smallman Street about an hour later. She had unconsciously stopped watching the crowds some time ago and found she was searching every face she saw for signs of the mysteriously attractive woman. She felt her heart race as the doctor climbed into her Pathfinder and pulled out into the late-evening traffic. Pulling her Durango behind the Pathfinder, she followed it, far enough behind not to be noticed.

Madison was suddenly struck by the fatigue she had fought all day as she unlocked the door and entered the house. The foyer lights cast a dim light, and as she walked toward the kitchen she heard the familiar sound of her beloved Labrador sliding through the pet door in the laundry room. Laughing as the overgrown pup's paws failed to gain traction on the slate floor, she knelt down and allowed his cold nose to nuzzle her neck.

"Hey there, big guy. I'll bet you're hungry."

After filling his bowl, she turned toward the refrigerator to pull out some leftover roast for dinner. She placed the plate in the microwave and began walking toward her bedroom to change when she suddenly stopped and turned back to the front door. She slid the security chain home and double-checked the deadbolt as she recalled her uneasy feeling of being followed while driving home.

She shed her clothes as she neared the bathroom and the shower that awaited her. She stepped under the warm water and allowed it to rain down across her shoulders, making the tension of the day release its hold on her body. She washed her hair and bathed in record time, returning to the kitchen ten minutes later to gulp down her dinner under the watchful eye of Femur.

Madison looked down into pleading eyes and shook her head in resignation before tossing him a small piece of roast. The Lab snatched the morsel out of the air and groaned as he sat down in front of her with an expectant look on his face. Slipping down beside him, she laughed as he eased his way into her lap, nudging her hand onto his head as she scratched his ear. She smiled at the memory of the remarkable strides he had made toward a full recovery in the last few months.

When she'd spotted him, he was lying on his side, near death, apparently hit by a passing car. She had stopped with the intention of dropping him off at the veterinarian's office, but after looking into his pleading eyes, she knew they were bound together for a lifetime. She had been adamant about assisting with the surgery to reset and pin his broken femur and had spent the rest of the night sitting beside his cage, anxiously waiting for those dark eyes to open. When, at last, they finally did open, she had gently stroked his head and talked softly to him until his fear dissipated and he once again slept.

Femur's recovery had been a long, hard road for both of them. He spent several weeks in the hospital before coming to his new home. However, once inside, he had claimed Madison's house as his own, and life as the doctor knew it hadn't been the same since. Hours of rehab had taken its toll on both animal and human, but the bond that had been forged with each tear and cry had proven to be unbreakable. Now, as she sat on the floor, Madison knew that the one thing in her life that was a constant was this beautiful animal's love.

Patting his back, she levered herself off the floor and took off in a dead run toward the bedroom. They both made a flying leap for the bed and fell into a friendly wrestling match that, before long, had both tired and breathing hard. As Madison stood and peeled off her clothes, Femur took his usual spot beside the bed. Giving him one last scratch, she slid between the sheets and turned out the light.

The detective watched Madison exit Interstate 79 into Bridgeville and then continued heading west until she came to the next exit. Veering off onto the ramp, she decreased her speed as she neared the traffic light. Making a left turn, she maneuvered the Durango down the entrance ramp and back onto the interstate heading east, back toward the city. A pang of guilt surged through her over trailing the mysterious woman, but her curiosity had been piqued, and before she realized what she was doing, they were well outside the city.

Logan climbed out of the truck and trudged up the steps to her house. Even now, after a year, she still missed seeing Diane's car sitting in the drive next to hers. She locked the door behind her and considered eating a light dinner but discarded the idea as the tension of the day hit her. Exhausted, she headed for the bedroom, tore off her clothes and slid naked between the sheets. Her last memory before falling asleep was of green eyes staring into hers.

The darkness of sleep provided only an occasional respite from the emptiness she felt. That night, though, sleep wasn't a peaceful escape, and Logan's eyes flew open as images of Diane's body flashed through her mind. Bolting upright, she tried to slow her breathing as she tossed the covers back. She stood on shaking legs, and after a moment to steady herself, stumbled to the bathroom. She avoided the mirror as she splashed cold water onto her face as the images once again flashed like a slide show behind her eyes.

Toweling her face, she caught her reflection in the mirror. "It's all your fault, McGregor. If you had just been there for her that one time. Just one fucking time." The fury erupted and she struck out, smashing the reflection in the mirror with her fist. Stunned by her violent reaction, she watched as shards of glass and drops of blood fell haphazardly into the sink.

CHAPTER FOUR

Logan trudged into the investigative headquarters on Penn Circle, feeling the stress and sleeplessness of the long night. After shattering her bathroom mirror, she had started a pot of coffee and gone into her office to review the evidence from her current case. Now, at 7:00 a.m., she was regretting her decision to stay awake. As she dropped her backpack beside the desk, she looked up to find Lieutenant Beaudry standing beside her.

"Lieutenant, what brings you out into the trenches this morning?"

Raising an eyebrow at Logan's obvious bad mood, Lieutenant Beaudry motioned her into his office. Once she sat in one of the hard, government-issue chairs in front of his desk, he asked, "So how is the investigation going, and what happened to your hand?"

Smirking audibly, Logan stared back into his unrevealing eyes. "How do you expect it to be going, Lieutenant? It seems as if my hands have been tied. I'm not allowed to disturb the prestigious Langston family, even though we both know someone in their organization holds the answers to at least some of our questions." Looking down at the bandage wrapped around her knuckles, she hesitated. "Um, as for my hand, I cut it last night on some glass."

Raising an eyebrow at her lieutenant, she added sarcastically, "It's not work related, so don't worry about it."

Beaudry held Logan's stare as he took a deep breath, choosing to ignore her last comment. "Look, Logan, I'm only following orders. Until further notice, the Langstons are off limits. You'll just have to find some other way."

Logan abruptly stood and walked toward the door. As she turned the knob, she looked back at her lieutenant. "I guess it does pay to have friends in high places, doesn't it, Lieutenant? One thing is for sure though: cooperation or not, I'm going to break this case. Let's just hope that when I do it doesn't blow up in your superiors' faces."

The lieutenant watched as the blinds crashed against the slamming door, and rubbed the pain that had begun to pulse behind his temples. He picked up his phone and punched in a number he knew from memory—a number that didn't exist in any interoffice Rolodex. On the third ring, the call was answered by a gruff voice.

"Yeah, it's me. Tell your boss I just talked with McGregor, and she has nothing. Something has to be done about this and soon. This is getting out of hand."

Madison woke to the early morning sun shining through the window. She listened to the birds chirping happily as the sun burned off the cool morning dew. Sliding out of the warm bed, she padded to the kitchen and poured herself a cup of coffee, thankful that she had remembered to set the automatic timer the night before. Femur trotted in behind her and whined as he looked hungrily at his master.

"What? You think I live to feed you, little one?" Scratching his head, she leaned down, gave him a quick kiss, then reached into the cabinet for his food. She watched as Femur devoured his breakfast in a few massive gulps and then trotted to the laundry room, through the pet door, and outside.

She retrieved the newspaper from the front porch and walked back into the kitchen to read the morning news as she ate breakfast. She spread out the paper on the table and froze when she saw the face of Officer Logan McGregor on the front page. Those eyes, those incredible blue eyes, stared back at her from the page, and for a moment Madison thought those firm, full lips were going to speak. *Jesus, Madi, get a grip. She's a cop, for God's sake.* Tossing the paper aside in frustration, Madison stormed out of the room.

Five minutes later she stepped under the warm spray of the shower and was surprised to find her skin tingling from the gentle caress. Knowing the photograph of Logan McGregor had awakened her senses, she hurriedly bathed, trying to push the face into the far reaches of her mind.

At 8:00, just as she had every day for as long as she could remember, she walked into Mercy Hospital, ready to start a fresh day. She greeted Susan, her secretary, as she entered her fifth-floor office and gathered her messages. Just as she was closing the door to her private office, Susan called out to her.

"Doctor? An Officer McGregor came by earlier this morning and said she would like to speak with you sometime this morning. I told her you were in surgery for most of the day but that she could call again this afternoon to check your schedule."

Madison stopped midstride when she heard the officer's name. As she remembered those deep blue eyes staring back at her from the morning paper, a warm rush swept over her. She turned abruptly back to her secretary. "Tell Officer McGregor that I won't have any time today. Maybe she can schedule something for the end of next week." Quickly closing the door, Madison dropped the messages on her desk and walked to the window, staring out at the skyline of downtown Pittsburgh. *What could she possibly want from me?*

Sitting at her desk, she found it hard to concentrate on reading her messages, as the officer's face kept stealing her thoughts. Finally giving up, she headed toward the door. "She probably just wants to harass me some more. Well, Officer McGregor, this time we'll do it on my terms." Madison stormed across the reception area, calling back over her shoulder, "I'll be in the OR most of the morning. If that policewoman calls back, tell her I'm not available."

It took Logan most of the morning to get her anger under control. She knew the lieutenant wasn't being forthright with information, but there wasn't a damn thing she could do about it. She decided that her best chance of gaining any headway would be to start from the beginning. She parked her car in a no-parking zone, tossed her police placard on the dash, and unfolded her long frame from the car. She noticed the glaring looks cast her way as she entered the first bar. She knew these people were no different than most she encountered—detesting the police, yet never hesitating to call when trouble headed their way.

After waiting a few moments for her eyes to adjust to the dark interior, she sauntered over to the bar and took a seat at the end, trying to be as discreet as possible. As the bartender mixed a drink for another patron, Logan took the time to look around the dingy establishment. Years of rowdy patrons full of energy and booze had taken its toll on the furnishings. Cigarette burns were evident on the tables, as was a permanent stickiness to the floor.

She thought about the murders over the past five weeks and wondered about the victims' last thoughts. *Did they know their attacker? Is the killer a regular patron of these establishments?* Her thoughts were interrupted by the bartender's voice.

"What can I get you?"

Logan turned to face him, and as she asked in a low, casual voice to speak with the manager, noticed his body tense.

"I'm the manager. What is it that you want?"

She slid her cards toward him. "I'm Detective Logan McGregor, and I'm re—"

"Look, Detective, I've already given my statement to you people several times. Why don't you go back to your squad room and look it up." The manager tossed the card back at Logan and turned toward the other end of the bar.

Logan struggled to contain her increasing anger. She glared at the retreating figure and elevated her voice just enough to gain everyone's attention. "Fine. Then it looks like I'll just have to come back tonight and start interviewing your patrons."

She smiled when the manager stopped and turned back toward her. "I'm investigating a murder. You may not think it's all that important but the families of those victims, and many others in this community, do. All I'm asking for is ten minutes of your time. If that's too much to ask for from your busy schedule, then I'll be back tonight."

Looking up from her notepad, Logan met his eyes. "So, what's it going to be, Mr. Vanguard, do you talk to me or do I talk to your patrons later tonight?" Logan waited as he called to another employee and then motioned her to his office.

Twenty minutes later, she exited the bar, no more enlightened than when she had entered. Walking swiftly down the sidewalk, she entered the next bar and what she was sure would be another confrontation with yet another manager.

Madison trudged into the physicians' locker room, weary from a long morning in surgery. When she slid the surgical cap from her head, her hair fell out and flowed across her shoulders. She looked up just in time to see Logan McGregor's eyes darken, a primal hunger cascading down her face. Irritated by the intrusion, Madison stepped quickly across the room to her locker. "I thought I had my secretary tell you I wasn't available this afternoon, Officer McGregor."

Turning in her seat on the vinyl couch, Logan watched as Madison retrieved a bag of toiletries from her locker. "I'm sorry, Doctor, but I didn't feel that this could wait until the end of next week. Surely you could spare me ten minutes of your time?"

Sighing audibly, Madison pulled a towel from her locker before turning to face Logan. "All right, Officer, I'll give you ten minutes—and you're buying the coffee, but first I'm taking a shower." Turning,

Madison shoved the door leading to the showers open with her shoulder and escaped, if only for a few minutes, from the imposing officer.

Logan sat watching the door swing shut, wondering how she had managed to irritate the doctor this time. *Just the sight of me irritates her.* Shrugging, Logan stood and walked to the window, then looked out at the parking lot below. "It seems like the high-and-mighty doctors around here didn't get a great view of the skyline."

"Pardon me?"

Logan jerked around to see that someone else, obviously a doctor, had silently entered the room. "Ah, sorry, I was just talking to myself."

The woman's lips curled in a small smile as she continued toward the row of lockers on the far wall. "Well if I were you, I'd be careful what I said about doctors around here. You *are* in the physicians' locker room, you know."

Logan could feel the heat rising in her face and knew that the other woman had overheard her. Adequately chastised, she returned to her place on the couch and began reading over her notes. A few moments later, she was pulled from her thoughts as the woman's voice broke through her concentration.

"I'm sorry, were you talking to me?"

Making a show of looking around the room, the other woman finally settled her eyes on Logan's. "Well, I don't see anyone else in the room, and I try not to talk to myself—aloud, anyway." Seeing Logan's obvious unease, she smiled and waved her hand in the air, dismissing her latest remark. "I said, I haven't seen you around here before. Are you new on staff?"

Seeing the woman's eyes devour her body in one long, lingering look, Logan crossed her arms over her chest, irritated by the obvious display of lust. "No. I'm waiting for someone."

The doctor retrieved her toiletries out of the locker and was about to press through the door to the showers when Madison came from the other side, almost knocking her off balance. "Damn, Madi, what's the rush?"

Madison's eyes swept from Angela to Logan, and then back again to Angela. "Sorry, I'm in a hurry." Glancing at Logan on her way to the locker, she tried to keep some semblance of control in her voice. "Are you ready to go?"

Angela's well-known antagonistic side took over. "Well, Madi, I was wondering if some other more enticing woman had lured you away from me." Once again canvassing Logan's tall, lean frame with her eyes, Angela smiled. "You should have simply told me it was someone tall, dark, and gorgeous. I would have understood. Really."

Madison's eyes pinned Angela with a glare. "Give it a rest, Angela." Cutting a look toward Logan, she barked, "Let's get out of here," and then walked swiftly through the swinging door.

Logan watched silently as Madison shoved the door open and stormed from the room, then looked back at Angela, who smirked as she said, "Well, I guess I'm the unlucky one today. Have fun, but be careful. She can really be a tiger when she wants to be, especially in bed."

Logan swallowed hard, her brain suddenly overloaded with visions she couldn't allow inside her head. She was about to rebut Angela's assumption, but then suddenly remembered Madison's hasty retreat from the room. Knowing the doctor would be on the elevator and gone in a matter of seconds, Logan bolted through the door in search of her.

She caught up with Madison at the elevator and stood silently by the doctor's side, waiting for the doors to open, both women's unease almost palpable. When at last the elevator doors opened, the women stepped forward simultaneously. Their arms bumped together, and both women drew away, the unexpected contact startling both.

Logan recovered first and stepped back to allow Madison to enter the elevator, her arm tingling from the brief touch. The detective followed and stood on the opposite side of the car, placing as many people as possible between them, hoping she could regain her composure by the time they reached the basement.

CHAPTER FIVE

The elevator doors opened, and Logan waited until Madison had cleared the doors before pushing off the wall and exiting the car herself. They walked into the cafeteria and stood in line. Feeling the uncomfortable silence, knowing Angela's behavior was the cause, Madison turned her head to speak and was caught off guard as she found Logan's dark blue eyes peering into hers.

"I...um, I'm sorry for, ah...back there." *Jesus, Cavanaugh, you sound like a babbling idiot.*

The glint in Logan's eyes barely preceded the smile that crossed her lips. "Sounds like you have your hands full with that one."

Madison grunted as she stepped further down the line. "The correct term, Officer, would be *had*. I *had* my hands full with that one." She couldn't help but chuckle as she replayed the scene in her head, remembering the confused look on Logan's face. "Luckily, I got out before she did any irreparable damage to my psyche. With others, I'm afraid, I haven't been so fortunate."

Logan was surprised to find Madison so open about her lifestyle and took some time to digest the information as they made their way through the line.

Madison stirred her drink, then looked at Logan with gleaming eyes. "Remember, you're buying. I have an extra-large double mocha latte and a bagel." Logan shook her head and grinned as she watched Madison saunter away toward a table, purposely bypassing the cashier.

After preparing her own cup of coffee, Logan paid the cashier and made her way through the crowded cafeteria to the table Madison had laid claim to moments before. Sitting down across from the beautiful blonde, Logan took a moment to just look at Madison Cavanaugh as the doctor looked out the window. Too soon, however, Madison's eyes turned back toward her and she no longer saw the teasing gleam that had been so evident a few minutes prior.

"So, Officer McGregor, what is it that's so important that you had to come all the way to Mercy and then sit and wait on me for over an hour?"

Logan retreated into her professional persona as her eyes met Madison's. "It's really quite simple, Doctor. There have been five people murdered along the Strip in as many weeks. I figure he'll strike within the next three nights, what with Friday and Saturday being too crowded to give him any amount of privacy."

She looked out the window, knowing her next words were not going to sit well with the independent and stubborn woman sitting across from her. "From what I understand, you visit the Strip on Mondays and Wednesdays. I'm here to ask you not to go down there tomorrow night."

Madison's eyes bored into Logan's. "You mean to tell me you wasted both of our time to ask me not to do something that is vitally important to this community? I think not, Officer."

She drained her cup and stood, but before she could walk away, Logan's hand circled her wrist. She couldn't help but notice the warm heat emanating from Logan's long fingers as she looked down at the bandaged hand that held on to hers. Her eyes traveled up the long arm, appreciating the taut biceps and firm deltoids, before taking in the dark, silky hair and finally coming to rest in the deep pools of sapphire. Madison found that she was unable to respond as an unfamiliar heat spread throughout her body and paralyzed her.

Logan rose from the table and stood very close, so close that the doctor could feel the heat radiating from her body. Madison's senses were further assaulted as Logan bent close to her ear and whispered, her warm breath teasing her earlobe, "Then let me come with you, Ms. Madi."

Madison closed her eyes and inhaled as the faint scent of soap and what could only be the essence of the mysterious detective further battered her resolve. Her pulse quickened and she feared Logan would feel it under her fingers where they gently gripped her wrist. Tearing herself from the onslaught of emotions, she roughly pulled her hand away, immediately feeling the loss of warmth.

"No! Absolutely not, Officer. I'm going to the Strip tomorrow night just as I have for the last two years. I haven't needed your protection before. I don't need it now."

Logan watched as Madison Cavanaugh turned and bolted from the cafeteria. Sitting down at the table, she looked out the window and wondered to herself why and how the doctor had suddenly gotten under her skin. After finishing her coffee, Logan tossed the cup in the trash on her way out the door. *Fine, Doctor, we'll do it your way. You've just made my job a little more difficult, but one way or another, I intend to see that you're safe tomorrow night.*

Madison reached the relative safety of her office just in time to see Susan locking the exterior door. Struggling with a large bundle of paperwork and her keys, Susan let out a relieved sigh when she saw Madison heading toward her. "Thanks goodness. I wasn't sure if I was going to be able to lock the door. Now that you're here, I don't have to."

Smiling at her energetic but stressed assistant, Madison glanced down at the bundle of papers in Susan's arms. "So, where are you off to with the latest financial statements?"

Looking guilty, Susan peered up at Madison. "Well, I really didn't have anything to do tonight, so I thought I'd just take these reports home and finish them up." Susan began moving around Madison in an attempt to escape the lecture she knew was about to come.

"Hold up there, missy. As I recall, you promised me last week that you were going to quit taking work home with you every night and start going out and having some fun."

Susan could feel the heat rise in her face. "Well, yeah, I did say that, but that was before...um, before—"

Madison cut off Susan's words as she relieved her of the bundle of papers. "No excuses. Tonight, I want you to go out and have a good time." Turning to walk through the door, Madison called back over her shoulder, "And Susan? I don't want to see you here a minute before ten tomorrow morning. Is that clear?"

Backing down the hall, Susan grinned at her boss and gave her a mock salute. "Yes, ma'am. No work, good time, not before ten o'clock. Got it."

With a boisterous laugh, Madison returned the salute. "Now get out of here before that slave-driver boss of yours returns and makes you work some overtime." She entered the reception area, then closed and locked the door behind her. Heading toward her office, she smiled at the thought of Susan's loyalty.

The young woman had worked as her personal assistant for the last three years. Susan's first day on the job was a rainy Tuesday morning in mid-January, and she had arrived ten minutes late for work. Madison, a little perturbed, had let her feelings be known as soon as Susan walked in the door. Susan, in return, had casually looked Madison straight in the eye and replied, "If you are going to be one of those typical self-centered, almighty, holier-than-thou, full of piss and vinegar doctors, please let me know right now so I won't waste my time taking off my coat."

Madison had stood dumbstruck at Susan's fiery appraisal for several minutes before she broke out in laughter. Before long, both women were wiping tears from their eyes and Madison was handing Susan a cup of hot coffee. Since that day, each woman had earned a tremendous level of respect from the other, and Susan had not only become the best assistant Madison had ever had, but a dear friend as well.

Dropping into her chair, Madison tried to look over the financial statements she had confiscated from Susan, but found her mind wandering back over the exchange with Logan. *The nerve of that woman, thinking I would desert my responsibilities just because some psycho is out there.* After several attempts to discern the numbers before her, Madison realized the prospect of getting any work done was negligible. With a frustrated sigh, she threw the financial statements into her briefcase and left the office, deciding that home would be a much better environment for her at the moment.

In the darkness of the truck, Logan could see several blocks north of where she sat in her Durango on Smallman Street. It was a cold night, the temperature barely reaching into the low twenties, but that had done little to quell the bar hoppers from coming out. Her alarm had sounded a little after five that morning and Logan had listened as the weather forecast predicted frigid temperatures and snow flurries for most of the day. She loved her work most of the time, but days like these, when she spent most of her time out on the streets, made her bones ache. *What am I whining about? I'm sitting here in a warm truck while Dr. Ego is out there walking the streets. Damn, that woman is stubborn.*

She had been sitting there for over three hours, waiting and watching for any sign of unusual behavior. Something in her gut told her that this would be the night the murderer struck. She had caught glimpses of Madison several times as she made her way through the alleys along Smallman Street. Luckily for Logan, the good doctor hadn't ventured close enough to spot her sitting there under the streetlight. Logan felt a shiver run the length of her spine and knew it wasn't from the cold air seeping in through the windows but rather from the prospect of Dr. Madison Cavanaugh being out there, alone, amidst the evil that had taken over the Strip.

Running a hand through her silky dark hair, Logan tried to analyze the unnatural attraction—if that was what she could call it—that she felt for the doctor. Her mind told her that it was nothing more than a primal urge, but her body reminded her that no one had ever elicited such sensations and yearnings. *Damn, McGregor, you hate doctors. Couldn't you at least fall for an attorney or something? Anyone with an ego smaller than Texas, for God's sake.*

She kept her eye on the alleyway Madison had walked into twenty minutes before. By Logan's calculations, the doctor usually remained within each alley for ten to fifteen minutes, and the detective was beginning to get a little edgy and had just reached over to get her heavy jacket off the seat when the doctor appeared under the streetlamp. Letting out a breath she hadn't realized she was holding, Logan watched as Madison came walking toward her on the opposite side of the street. She was about halfway down the block when a couple coming out of one of the neighborhood bars waved to her.

As Logan witnessed the interaction, the radiant smile she had glimpsed in the cafeteria the previous day flowed across Madison's face. Madison Cavanaugh was an extremely beautiful woman, and Logan once again felt the familiar heat traveling down the length of her body. The woman hugged Madison and they shared a laugh as the doctor waved good-bye and headed for her car. Logan watched as Madison climbed into her Pathfinder and pulled out into the late-night traffic, turning her attention back to the street only after Madison's taillights disappeared from view.

After turning out the light in the bedroom, Logan lay on her back staring at the ceiling. Absently stroking the bandage on her hand with her thumb, she thought about the long lonely nights she had spent in that bed over the last year. Diane had been gone for twelve months and fourteen days, but to Logan, the pain was still so raw and acute that it seemed just like yesterday.

She was drawn away from her musings as the phone on the nightstand rang. Rolling over, she roughly grabbed the handset and barked, "McGregor." She immediately sat up as her lieutenant's voice came over the line.

"Sorry to wake you, Logan, but our guy just struck again. This time we got lucky, she's still alive. Someone just found a white female, approximately thirty years old, in an alleyway at the corner of Smallman and Twenty-third Street. She's already been transported to Mercy. Head over that way and see what you can find out. Rodgers will meet you there and fill you in on what they have so far."

Logan kicked off the covers as she listened to the few details the lieutenant was able to relay to her. By the time she hung up the phone, she was fully dressed and on her way to the kitchen. Grabbing a soda from the refrigerator, she headed out the door and toward Mercy

Hospital. Luckily, she lived only a short drive away and was running toward the ER entrance five minutes later.

She spotted Rodgers as he came through the doors leading back to the trauma suite. Walking toward him, she saw the grim look on his face and knew before asking that the woman in question was in bad shape. "How is she?"

Rodgers pursed his lips and shook his head. "Well, if she makes it, she's going to have a hell of a long way back." Looking at Logan with a sad smile, he nodded back toward the door. "She put up one hell of a fight, Detective. If we're lucky and the doctors do their job right, the lab might be able to get some good physical evidence off of this one."

Logan took the bag he held out toward her and listened as he detailed the information he had gathered so far. "The woman, Jane S. Richardson, is a white female, thirty-two years old, lives in an apartment over on Van Braam Street. I have some other officers over there now checking out the apartment and trying to locate her next of kin."

Just as Rodgers was completing his commentary, a short, balding doctor in rumpled scrubs walked through the trauma suite doors. "The Richardson family? Anyone here from the Richardson family?"

Logan immediately walked over to the doctor and told him that they were still trying to locate the family of the victim. "Is it possible for me to see her, Doctor?"

The obviously tired doctor frowned and glared at Logan. "No, Detective, you can't. She just regained consciousness and we're about to take her to surgery. Maybe tomorrow."

Taking a deep breath, Logan tried to restrain the anger welling in her gut. "Look, Doctor, I'm not trying to be unreasonable, but this woman is the first lead we've had in this case in the last five weeks. Can you promise me she'll make it through surgery to talk to me tomorrow?" Seeing the uncertain look in his eyes, she went in for the kill shot. "I didn't think so. I'll only ask a couple of questions, and then I'll be on my way."

The overweight doctor muttered under his breath as he motioned Logan through the doors. Walking beside her down the hallway, he outlined the conditions of her visit, pointedly regaining control over the situation. "If she shows any signs of distress from your questions, Detective, you're out. No argument, no discussion, nothing. Is that clear?"

Deciding not to press her luck, Logan nodded and replied between clenched teeth, "Yes, sir, perfectly clear." *Damn doctors, always having to have all the control. No wonder half of them are divorced, separated, screwing around, or somewhere in between.*

The trauma room was about twenty degrees cooler than the waiting room, and the sudden change in temperature caused Logan to shiver. Monitors hanging from the walls and ceiling detailed a variety of bodily functions as thin lines danced across the screens and an audible beep kept perfect rhythm. Walking quietly toward the woman on the gurney, Logan carefully took in every detail that was visible to her. The woman's face was partially obscured from view by a large bandage over her right eye.

Logan unconsciously gasped as the other eye opened to meet hers, and her heart stopped as she looked at a face that had smiled back at her only hours before.

CHAPTER SIX

It was after 3:00 a.m. when Logan reached home. Knowing her senses were still too acute to shut down and sleep, she put on a pot of coffee and headed to the bathroom to take a shower. Twenty minutes later, she was sitting in her office staring at the computer screen, trying to find the one clue that would link all of the murders and the attack from the previous night.

The only thing that connected the victims so far were the business cards carefully placed on each body. The latest attack was a little different in that the victim had fought back so hard that the murderer had fled the scene. Although it had taken a little time, a now-familiar Langston Development business card was found about fifteen feet away from the victim's beaten body. This time the name emblazoned on the card was none other than that of C.W. Langston III.

Logan sat back and looked at the list of Langston Development executives.

Thomas M. Peters, Vice President and Chief Financial Officer

Phillip R. Crafton, Vice President and Director of Human Resources

Lester P. Donovan, Vice President and Director of Real Estate and Acquisitions

Jonathon K. Wilson, Vice President and Director of Community Development

Christine Langston, Senior Vice President and Director of Architectural Design and Construction

C.W. Langston, President and Chief Executive Officer

According to Logan's logic, the previous night's attempt had topped out the list of Langston executives. It struck her as odd that the killer would move up the list instead of down—or was he purposely placing a limit on the individuals he was targeting within the corporation? His actions could be a well-thought-out plan, slowly building up to the one name that was most important to his mission: C.W. Langston III. Now all Logan had to do was figure out where he would go from here. *What's your next move, asshole? Where are you going with this? I have to get into the Langston camp, and soon.*

Looking at the clock, she was surprised to find it was almost 6:00 a.m. She shut down the computer, then went through the kitchen and grabbed a last cup of coffee before heading out the door and back to Mercy Hospital.

Madison had returned home around 11:00 p.m. and spent the next couple of hours at her computer inputting her notes on her night's visit to the Strip and on her clients. After e-mailing her report to the Operation Safety Net head office, she took a long, hot shower and went to bed. Her sleep had been fitful, as dark dreams filled with menacing shadows haunted her unconscious mind. Finally giving up any hope of peaceful sleep around 5:00 a.m., Madison tossed the covers back and sat up on the side of the bed. The only clear face she could remember seeing in her dreams was that of one tall, dark, unbelievably sexy-looking police officer.

Several times during her evening at the Strip, she had felt eyes upon her and looked around trying to locate the source. She had replayed her heated conversation with Logan the day before, and for the first time in the two years she had been walking the Strip, she felt a twinge of nervous tension each time she stepped into the darkness of the alleys. It was unusually busy for a Wednesday night and she had not been able to locate the culprit, if there even was one.

Shaking her head to clear her mind, she stood up and headed for the bathroom, telling herself along the way that her dreams were merely a result of her conversation with Logan McGregor and the thoughts in the back of her mind about the recent killings.

After showering and dressing, Madison sat in her office drinking her morning coffee and reading the paper. She was shocked to read that another attack had indeed occurred along the Strip the previous night. Shivers ran up her spine when she read the address and remembered being in that very alleyway what must have been mere hours or even minutes prior to the attack. As she read further, she was again shaken by the fact that the latest victim was an employee at Mercy, although her name was being withheld pending notification to her family.

Madison picked up the phone and dialed the switchboard at Mercy, only to be put on hold after asking for the ER department. After waiting for over five minutes for the phone to be answered, she slammed down the receiver and headed out the door. Steering her Pathfinder north on Interstate 79 toward the city, she could feel her hands becoming sweaty as a nervousness settled inside her gut at the realization of how close she had possibly come to the murderer.

When she reached the hospital, she quickly found a parking spot and headed toward the doors. As she rounded the corner to her office, her eyes fell on the tall, dark woman leaning heavily against her door. *Jesus, just what I don't need right now.*

Taking a deep breath, Madison walked the length of the hall, aware that Logan's eyes were taking in her every move. She unlocked the door and stepped inside, never acknowledging the detective's presence. As she moved toward her office, Logan stepped over the threshold.

"Good morning to you too, Dr. Cavanaugh."

Madison turned so quickly that she startled the approaching detective. "Officer, I don't think we have anything further to discuss. I will not stop going to the Strip District—or any other place in this city— to care for the homeless, and the sooner you get that through your thick head, the better off we all will be." Running a hand through her blond hair, she glared at Logan. "Now, if you'll excuse me, an employee from this hospital was attacked last night and I'm trying to find out who she is. No one is being very cooperative around here this morning."

She looked into the compassionate eyes of the officer, and her heart skipped a beat. "That's right, you're on this case. You know who it is, don't you?"

Logan turned and closed the outer office door, securing the deadbolt. She walked slowly toward Madison, her eyes never leaving the frightened ones staring back at her. "I think we need to talk. Let's go in your office and sit, all right?"

Suddenly speechless, Madison backed into her office and sat in one of the visitor's chairs in front of her desk. "It's someone I know, isn't it? That's why you're here, right?"

Pulling a chair next to Madison's, Logan sat, dropped her elbows to her knees, and leaned in closer to the doctor. She took a deep breath to prepare herself for the next few moments, then looked into Madison's eyes, praying that her mind had been playing tricks on her the night before. "I need to ask you some questions, and I need you to think about your replies and be as honest with me as you can considering doctor/patient confidentiality issues, okay?"

Madison's eyes searched Logan's for any clues but none were forthcoming. "All right, but you know there are some things I just can't discuss with you."

"I understand and I respect that." Sitting back in the chair, Logan knew her nerves were showing. "I, ah, have to confess, last night I was down at the Strip, watching as you made your rounds." Logan held up her hands when she saw the doctor preparing to respond. "I'll admit it wasn't the most professional thing to do, but I was worried about you being down there by yourself, and since you wouldn't allow me to accompany you...well, you left me little choice."

Rolling her eyes, Madison let out a low growl. "Don't you ever— wait, what has that got to do with the attack?" She had a look of total confusion as she looked deeply into Logan's eyes.

Leaning closer, Logan dropped her voice to a near whisper. "Well, that's why I'm here. That woman you were talking to last night on the sidewalk. What is her name?"

Madison's eyes widened and her hands shook as she absorbed Logan's question. "Oh my God, it's Susan, isn't it? Susan is the woman that was attacked last night."

Reaching out, Logan's gently grasped Madison's hand. "I'm sorry I have to put you through this, Doctor, but is her full name Jane Suzanne Richardson?"

A primal groan escaped Madison's lips as tears cascaded down her cheeks. "Oh God, I was there. I-I didn't know. Oh God...I could have helped her."

Logan gathered the trembling doctor into her arms as the sobs wracked her body. Holding her close, she gently caressed Madison's back, soothing her pain while allowing her the time she needed to cry. As she whispered soothing words into Madison's ear, Logan felt the tension begin to ease from the muscles in her shoulders, until the sobs finally faded into quiet whimpers.

Pulling away and looking into Logan's eyes, embarrassment apparent in her expression, Madison said, "I'm...I'm sorry. This is just such a shock." Standing, she walked to the window, putting distance between Logan and herself. "When I read about the attack in the paper this morning, I knew it was a Mercy employee."

Turning, she faced Logan again, fear once again etched across her face. "I never imagined it to be Susan."

Logan recognized all of the stages: shock, anguish, fear, and anger. It would take time for acceptance to set in, and Logan hoped that when that time came, guilt wouldn't be its escort. She sat quietly, trying to give Madison as much time as she needed to sort through the sudden emotions. Finally, with time running short before she had to be back at the station, Logan spoke. "Doctor, the man Susan was with last night. Did you know him?"

The look of terror that crossed Madison's face and the tears that followed almost made Logan wish she hadn't asked the very important question. She stood and quickly walked to the window, gathering the sobbing woman into her arms. Her breath caught as warm arms circled her waist and held her tight, pressing her breasts against Madison's. She inhaled the spicy scent of Madison's shampoo and felt the soft tresses caress her cheek as her pulse quickened, bringing with it a warm aching heat in her gut.

"It's okay. Susan is going to be okay. She came through surgery last night and is in the ICU now in stable condition. I have a guard posted at her door around the clock and I promise, if I haven't caught this bastard before she is released, I'll have someone assigned to stay with her at home."

Madison's arms tightened around Logan's waist and she tucked her chin into the crook of Logan's neck. "I'm sorry I was so rude to you earlier." She leaned back and lifted her head, looking into the deep pools of blue that were, at that moment, the kindest, most gentle eyes she had ever seen. *God, those eyes are captivating.* "I know this has to be hard on you too. I really didn't mean to be so uncooperative." Allowing a small laugh to escape her throat, she rolled her eyes and smiled at Logan. "I, um, I guess I can be a little stubborn sometimes."

"Damn, where's my tape recorder when I need it?" All Logan wanted to do at that moment was lean down a few inches and capture the doctor's warm, full lips with her own. Instead, she pulled back, putting some much-needed space between them before she stepped out of her professional role and acted like a hormonal adolescent. Dropping her hands to her side, she smiled at Madison's heartfelt apology. "It's okay. Why don't you go wash your face and then we can go up and see how Susan is doing this morning."

Nodding, Madison wiped the last of the tears from her cheeks before walking into the bathroom adjoining her office. Turning as she closed the door, she looked at Logan, still standing by the window and gazing out at the sunrise. "Thank you, Logan."

Logan turned, but all she saw was a closed door. *You have it bad, McGregor, but you have to get over this. The good doctor is now way too close to this case.* As she waited for Madison to finish in the bathroom, she dug her cell phone out from the back pocket of her chinos. Waiting patiently for the connection to be made, she again turned to look out at the new day. *Maybe this one will be a lucky one for this case.*

By the time the lieutenant came on the line, Logan had regained her sense of focus. "Hey, I'm with Dr. Cavanaugh. The woman that was attacked last night is her assistant. I'm taking her down to see Ms. Richardson now, and then we're coming into the station. See if Carlos can round up Picasso for me to do the sketch." She turned as Madison walked out of the bathroom and smiled at her refreshed appearance. *Damn, she does look good.* "Huh? What, Lieutenant? Yes, sure. We'll see you in a while."

Raising an eyebrow in Logan's direction, Madison continued toward the desk to retrieve her coat, slipping the heavy garment over her shoulders. "Did I hear you say we'll see you soon?" Casting Logan a suspicious look, she picked up her backpack and they headed out to see Susan. "Just where are *we* going, Detective?"

Grinning, Logan nudged Madison with her elbow. "Hey! You finally got it right, Doctor."

"Excuse me?"

Logan couldn't stop her silly grin. "You got it right. You called me detective." Seeing the look of understanding cross the doctor's face made her smile even brighter, but it quickly turned into a pained look as Madison playfully punched her on the arm.

Laughing at Logan's expression, Madison couldn't help but tease her a little more. "Oh, you wimp. Here I thought you were a big, tough cop." Growing serious, she continued, "Now, you never did tell me where we are supposed to be going after I see Susan."

"Oh, that. Well, I need for you to come down to the station with me for a while. I need to get your official statement as to what you saw last night, and I also have a sketch artist lined up to see if we can get some sort of composite of the man you saw with Ms. Richardson." Pressing the elevator call button, Logan turned to Madison. "Will you be able to come down with me after you've visited with Susan?"

Madison's eyes turned dark and brooding. "Of course. I'll do anything to get the maniac that did this to her." Realizing how she must sound to Logan, she stopped, taking hold of Logan's arm and turning the detective toward her.

"Detective, it's not just Susan that concerns me. It's everyone out there on the streets at night. Black, white, male, female, those going home to a nice warm bed, and those huddling in the dark alleyways covered with only a dirty piece of cardboard. This man is a threat to everyone." Realizing that Logan was closely watching her, Madison dropped her hand from Logan's arm and looked away. "I guess you must think I have a sermon about every subject, huh?"

Logan gently touched Madison's shoulder. "No. However, I do think you are a very passionate woman. I...ah, I mean, well, you feel passionate about the things you believe in." Logan could feel the heat rise in her face, which only worsened when Madison bit her bottom lip in an attempt to stop her grin.

Luckily for Logan, the doors to the elevator opened and she quickly escaped into the crowded car. Behind her, Madison chuckled and whispered, "My, you do turn a very nice shade of red, Detective." Looking up into the shocked, yet smiling eyes, she continued, "Do you do that often, Detective?"

Clearing her throat, Logan smiled back. "Actually, no, but for some reason you do tend to bring out the worst in me. And by the way, you can drop the formality. It's Logan, okay?"

An eyebrow raised as the two women looked into each other's eyes. Madison finally broke the stare as she became aware of the warm heat spreading through her body. Taking a deep breath, she smiled up into Logan's deep blue eyes. "Okay, Logan, but before we head down to your office, we're stopping for breakfast. I'm starving." The doors opened and Madison started walking out, then stopped and glanced back over her shoulder as another grin spread across her face. "Also, since you're monopolizing my morning, you're buying again."

Shaking her head at being duped by the doctor once again, Logan followed Madison out of the elevator and down the hallway to the doors leading to the intensive care unit. She pulled the door open and motioned for Madison to precede her into the ICU. As Madison passed, she gave Logan a quick glance and a small smile, the anticipation and fear of seeing her friend and assistant apparent on her face. Falling into step beside the doctor, Logan knew the next few minutes were going to be very difficult for Madison, and she intended to stay beside her every step of the way.

CHAPTER SEVEN

Madison hesitated at the door to Susan's room, thinking of the hundreds of times she had walked into rooms similar to it. This time, the monitors and every diminutive sound took on a new meaning for her, because this time the person lying in the bed was as close to family as Madison could claim anyone to be. Looking at Susan lying there, vulnerable and in pain, brought a torrent of emotions from deep within Madison's heart. Unconsciously taking a step back, she felt her body press into Logan's, then felt warm, gentle hands softly caress her shoulders. As she leaned her head back against Logan's strong chest, she felt a warm breath whisper in her ear.

"You can do this, Madison. She needs you to be strong for her now." Her hand found Logan's and for a brief moment they shared a tender touch, each reassuring and encouraging the other. Madison slowly walked into the room and to the bed, taking Susan's hand gently in her own. Tired, pained eyes opened and looked into hers. A slight smile crossed Susan's split lips, and with a small whisper, she immediately brought a smile to her boss and friend's face.

"Please don't tell me you're here to get on my ass for being late to work."

Tears streamed down Madison's face as the pent-up emotion overwhelmed her. "I am so sorry. I wish—"

Wincing as she shook her head, Susan cut off Madison's words. "No, you had no idea. I didn't either, so please don't blame yourself, Madi. Promise me."

Logan stood just inside the door, watching the tender exchange between the two women. Once she felt secure that Madison would be okay, she silently backed out of the room to talk to the guard sitting in the hall. "How's it going, James? Were there any unusual people hanging around the halls during the night?"

The uniformed officer stood up, almost at attention, which made Logan a little uneasy. She knew her reputation in the department was one demanding respect, but it still left her feeling uncomfortable. "At ease, James. I'm not your CO, for God's sake. Chill out and just give me your report."

Logan listened as James recounted almost every minute of his shift, emphasizing several times that he had never left his post during the night. He knew carelessness was one transgression Logan would never forgive—or forget. The night had been a quiet one, just as Logan had suspected. The murderer most likely had learned of Susan's survival, as had the rest of the city, from the morning edition of the *Pittsburgh Post-Gazette*.

A smile crossed her face as she envisioned his shock at discovering that his latest victim was safely ensconced in protective custody at Mercy Hospital. Logan hoped that the unexpected news would throw him out of sync, causing him to make mistakes that would lead her right to his doorstep. Hopefully, Madison and Susan could provide her with an adequate description of the man. Logan was certain of one thing: she needed a hit on this one if she was to have any chance of stopping this maniac before he struck again.

She glanced down the hall as another uniformed officer entered to take over James's post. After taking his name and making sure he understood the importance of not leaving his post, she asked him to tell the doctor that she would be back in ten minutes. As she walked down the hallway, she suddenly felt the fatigue from the last few weeks, and the lack of sleep from the previous night, hit her.

Coming out of Susan's room a few minutes later, Madison found Logan gone and felt a sudden sense of uneasiness at being away from the detective's commanding presence. After being advised by the guard that Logan would be back shortly, she walked over to the nurses' station and pulled Susan's chart, sitting down at the desk to review her friend's condition for herself. She felt completely helpless to facilitate Susan's recovery, her broken ankle and wrist having been set the previous night by the surgeon on call and her other injuries not requiring an orthopedist. The only thing she knew she could do was make sure her friend was getting the best care Mercy Hospital could provide. Locating and recognizing the admitting physician's name, she quickly punched in the pager number, left a short message, and waited for the return call.

Madison was on the phone when Logan returned a few minutes later with two large coffees. Sitting one of the cups in front of Madison, she was met with a glowing smile and a mouthed "thank you." The doctor held up one finger, indicating that she would be off soon, and Logan took the time to ease back into Susan's room for a moment.

Fearful eyes opened as she entered, and Logan immediately introduced herself as the detective that had spoken to her the previous night in the emergency room. Seeing the look of recognition appear on Susan's face, she eased a little closer to the bed. "I know you're tired, Ms. Richardson, but as soon as you feel up to it I need to get your official statement. Do you think you might like to try sometime later this afternoon?"

"You were in here a few minutes ago with Madi." It was more a statement than a question, but Logan nodded in confirmation. "Are you a friend of hers or are you just working the case?"

Logan felt uneasy being asked such personal questions, but felt it necessary to be as honest as possible. "Sort of and yes, I am the primary on the case."

"I see." Susan's eyes traveled to the ceiling, a single tear escaping her eye. "Would you do me a favor, Detective?"

Looking a little confused, Logan nodded and stepped even closer to the bed. "Sure, if I can, Ms. Richardson. What do you need?"

Pinning Logan with her eyes, Susan said, "I want you to keep a close eye on Madi for me. You know she also saw that guy last night. She's in as much danger as I am."

Logan's heart raced as the realization of what Susan had said hit home with her. Of course Logan knew that Madison had seen the perp, but with all that had happened since, she hadn't fully comprehended the danger Madison would be in. "I promise Dr. Cavanaugh will be well taken care of. You just concentrate on getting better."

Madison walked into the room just as Logan finished talking and saw the serious looks on both women's faces. "Hey, you two, no heavy stuff right now. Doctor's orders." Leaning down, she placed a kiss on Susan's forehead. "You get some sleep. I'll be back after lunch to check on you again, okay?" Turning to Logan, she smiled before heading toward the door. "And you, Detective, still owe me breakfast. Come on, I'm starving." She walked out of the room, leaving Logan standing there smiling.

Damn, she sure does know how to make an exit. Logan promised Susan that she would be back later in the afternoon with a stenographer and a sketch artist, then turned to catch up with the spitfire doctor.

The two women walked from the hospital to a small restaurant several blocks north. The ease with which they spoke pleasantly surprised both women, given their earlier meetings. Logan asked about

Operation Safety Net and the services that were offered to the community. Watching Madison's eyes as she extolled the program's virtues made Logan realize that any attempt to dissuade her from venturing into the Strip District would be a waste of breath.

Madison finally slowed and she looked up to see Logan smiling down at her. "What?" *God, those eyes are beautiful. Too bad she's a cop, I could really get lost in those pools of blue.*

Laughing, Logan shrugged and opened the door to the restaurant, stepping back and allowing Madison to enter. "Nothing. I was just thinking that now I understand why you got so mad the other day when I asked you not to go down to the Strip." Seeing the look of comprehension flash across her companion's face, Logan winked at her. "I'm surprised you didn't deck me."

Shaking her head, Madison couldn't help but smile. "As well you should be." She turned and headed for a table, leaving Logan once again standing there, watching her back and the sensual sway of her hips as she strolled across the room.

Breakfast was pleasant and unhurried as the women continued to learn about each other. Logan was astonished to see how much the doctor could eat, her meal consisting of eggs, bacon, muffins, fruit, juice, and enough coffee to overdose any novice caffeine addict. Looking up from the feast spread before her, Madison was met with teasing eyes once again. Feigning annoyance, she growled. "Do you always stare at your breakfast companions?"

Scratching her head, not sure of how she should respond, Logan took a moment to study Madison's face. Seeing a small hint of laughter behind the green eyes, she leaned in and, snaring a piece of bacon off Madison's plate, popped it in her mouth. "Um, no. However, as of late, my breakfast companions have tended to be slow eaters, preferring to savor their food rather than inhaling it." The confused look on Madison's face made Logan laugh. "I guess Cat Chow just demands to be slowly relished and enjoyed to the fullest." She watched as an eyebrow slowly crept skyward and a snarl formed on the other woman's lips.

"Well, I can see that you have a lot to learn about me, Detective." Allowing a slow, seductive smile to cross her face, Madison reached across the table and picked a ripe strawberry off Logan's plate. Slipping it between her lips, she bit into the juicy fruit and watched as Logan swallowed hard, lips parting slightly as Logan's tongue slowly slid across her bottom lip. "In everything I do, I give my all. Life is too short not to be experienced completely—and passionately."

Logan's heart raced and her palms became damp as she tried unsuccessfully to control the images flickering at mach speed through her mind. She felt a warm surge of heat flow through her body and knew that it was apparent on her face. With a shaky hand, she lifted a glass of juice to her lips and eagerly drank the cool liquid, hoping it would extinguish the fire burning between her legs.

Madison enjoyed watching Logan's obvious struggle. Crossing her arms across her chest, once again raising her eyebrow and gently biting her bottom lip, she smiled. "Checkmate."

Somehow, Logan managed not to spew juice across the table as she laughed boisterously. Flashing a mock glare at Madison, she said, "Oh, no, you did not." Wiping her mouth with a napkin, she scowled. "As they say, Doctor, paybacks are a bitch."

Catching the eye of the waitress, Madison signaled for the check before turning back toward her pouting companion. "I think I can handle you, Detective, so you'd better be careful if you want to dance with me."

The waitress walking to the table prevented any response from Logan. When the waitress attempted to hand Madison the check, she grinned and stood. "Nope. She's buying." Winking at the waitress, she headed toward the restroom, knowing that the tall, dark, very sexy detective was watching her every step.

Although the sun was bright, the air was crisp, and Madison dug her hands deep into her pockets for warmth. Looking at Madison, Logan thought she looked more like one of the coeds from nearby Duquesne University than a surgeon from Mercy Hospital. As they walked along the quiet street, slowly making their way back to the hospital, the detective suddenly felt the hair stand up on the back of her neck. Looking around, she tried to locate the unseen threat while easing a little closer to Madison.

Feeling an arm brush hers, Madison looked up, seeing a dark, serious scowl on the detective's face. "What's going on?"

Placing her hand on the doctor's elbow, Logan led Madison into a nearby bookstore, not stopping until they were safely hidden behind a tall book rack. Her eyes left no room for argument. "Stay here and don't move. I'll be back in a minute."

Walking toward the front of the store, Logan peered out of the window, looking for any unusual movement. All she could see were people walking in all directions, book bags or packages in hand, heading to unknown destinations. After several minutes, she released a frustrated sigh and turned, only to feel Madison's body collide with hers. Grabbing Madison's arm, Logan again led her back to the safety of the book racks. "I thought I told you to stay put."

Huffing, Madison rolled her eyes. "I didn't want to stay back there. What's the matter, anyway?"

Feeling her temper rise, Logan tried taking several deep breaths before responding. The last thing she wanted to do was frighten Madison, but the doctor had to understand that she was involved in a murder case and possibly in grave danger. Looking around the store, she leaned closer to the doctor, her lips mere inches from the other woman's ears. "Look, I don't know if you realize it or not, but you saw the murderer's face last night, Doctor. Do you think for a moment that he doesn't remember that?" She forced the anger out of her voice. "Do you think he's not going to try and find you? And stop you too?"

Leading the shaking woman to a chair in the back of the store, Logan knelt beside Madison, gently taking her hand into her own. Her thumb made soft, gentle circles around Madison's knuckles as she waited for her breathing to calm. "I'm sorry that all of this had to happen to you and to Susan, but now we have to deal with it as best we can." Logan's other hand massaged Madison's calf as she looked into the doctor's tear-filled eyes.

"I may be a little paranoid right now, but I'm not taking any chances with you. We're still several blocks from the hospital. Will you please stay here while I call for a squad car to take us back?" Getting a nod from the doctor, Logan stood and walked toward the curious manager at the front counter. After showing him her badge, she asked to use the phone and called to request the car. As she walked back to where Madison was sitting, she noticed someone sitting a few yards away, partially hidden behind an open newspaper. She had an urge to walk over and peer over the paper, but instead strolled back to where Madison was sitting, perfectly composed, just as she knew she would be.

The two women walked closer to the front of the store and waited. A police cruiser stopped next to the curb a few minutes later and Logan hurried the doctor out the door and into the waiting car. As they drove off, Logan turned around and looked out the back window. What she saw stunned her. A man rushed from the store and stood on the sidewalk, watching as they drove away. In her gut, Logan knew that the man on the sidewalk was the same man that was behind the newspaper. Turning in her seat to face Madison, Logan placed one hand on the doctor's shoulder. "Are you all right?"

The doctor nodded, still afraid to speak as they made their way toward the hospital. The rest of the ride passed in silence as each woman was lost in her own nightmarish thoughts of what could have been and what was left to come.

CHAPTER EIGHT

The cruiser stopped outside the front entrance of Mercy. Logan exited the car first, looking in all directions for any signs of trouble before holding out her hand. As Madison grasped it, Logan thought how nicely they fit together and found herself holding on much longer than needed. Quickly walking into the lobby, she immediately led Madison to the bank of elevators and pressed the call button, wanting to check in with the guard and alert him to the latest developments. The silence was almost palpable as they rode to the third floor.

When the doors opened, Logan stepped out and waited for Madison to follow. As they walked through the outer doors to the ICU, a frown crossed Logan's face.

"Logan? What's wrong?" Madison could see the detective's jaw clench, causing the muscles in her cheek to twitch. She had to jog to keep up as the tall detective lengthened her stride and quickened her pace.

Stopping outside Susan's door, Logan glanced inside, then turned toward Madison. "Why don't you go ahead and see how she's feeling? I'll be back in a few minutes."

Nodding, Madison eased into the room, knowing that it was not the time to question the detective further. The doctor's main concern was Susan; she wondered if she should have her transferred to another hospital outside the city as soon as her condition allowed. She made a mental note to ask Susan's primary physician. Until then, she knew that everything that could be done to assure Susan's safety was being taken care of by Logan.

She stepped quietly across the floor, but Susan awoke and gave Madison a weak smile. "Hey there," Madison said. "I thought you would be sound asleep by now. Do you need something to help you out? Are you in any pain? Well, of course you are. What am I thinking?"

"Madi?" Susan couldn't get a word in. "Madi?" The doctor fell silent as Susan rolled her eyes. "Will you please sit down? You're going to drive me crazy. Don't you have some work to do or something?"

Sitting in the chair beside the bed, Madison absentmindedly ran a hand through her hair. "Okay. Sorry, and no. It's Thursday, remember? I don't have office hours today."

Susan tried to sit up in the bed but before she could even raise her head, Madison was once again fussing over her. "Madi, I'm going to call the nurse on you in about three seconds if you don't sit down." Properly chastised, Madison sat down crossing her arms across her chest while pursing her lips in a faux pout.

"Don't you have some volunteer work or something you can do?" Susan couldn't help but tease, as Madison's pout grew fierce. She had always teased the doctor about being a mother hen to her patients. That morning, though, she was silently thankful to have her dear friend beside her, even if she was about to drive her insane with the endless picking, fluffing, and doting.

The next time Madison came near, Susan reached out with her good hand and gently grasped the doctor's arm. As their eyes met, volumes were spoken and each woman knew the love and the fright the other was trying to hide. "Thank you!" Two whispered words in the midst of a nightmare were all it took for the bond between the two women to grow stronger.

Logan entered the room to see Madison leaning over the bed, holding the injured woman in her arms. Feeling like she was intruding on a private moment, she backed out of the room and headed out of the ICU, seeking an escape and a reprieve for the growing ache and emptiness she suddenly felt in her stomach.

In the basement, she stood in line waiting to pay for two extra-large double mocha lattes and replayed the scene over in her mind. *Okay, maybe they are just friends and it was a touching moment.* The line moved forward and Logan slid the tray a little further down the line. *No, that was not a moment between friends. There is something more going on between those two.* She paid the cashier and began her journey back toward the ICU.

Pressing the call button for the elevator, she leaned against the wall, the images still flooding her mind. *All right, then, if there is something between them, why was Susan Richardson out with a man—a stranger— last night at the Strip?* The elevator doors opened and Logan stepped into the car. On the ride up, she continued the internal argument with herself. *If there isn't anything between them, then what did I just see?*

By the time the elevator deposited the detective back onto the third floor, she had decided that it didn't matter what was going on between the other women. Either way, she wasn't about to become involved with anyone, especially a doctor.

Stepping into the room, Logan noticed Madison had moved to the chair beside the bed and was talking quietly with Susan. Logan walked in and handed Madison a cup of coffee, then gave Susan an apologetic look. "Sorry I didn't bring you one, but I asked the nurse earlier and she said you're not allowed anything until after your tests come back." Looking at Madison, she received a nod of confirmation. "I've got to take care of a little business outside, but I should be ready to go to the station in about ten minutes. Is that okay with you?"

"Sure. Just let me know when you're ready." Madison's eyes held Logan's for a long moment, creating even more confusion in the detective's mind.

Susan and Madison's conversation was interrupted moments later when they heard a menacing voice just outside. Walking toward the door, Madison peered around the opening and stopped short as Logan's profile came into view. A shiver ran up the doctor's spine as she watched the detective's features transform. She heard Logan inform the uniformed officer that he was relieved of his post and thought the acutely controlled detective was even more intimidating than she had been when they first met in the alleyway on Smallman Street a few days earlier.

"I don't really care if you do piss in your pants, Officer. You never, ever, walk away from your post on my cases." The officer attempted to speak, but was cut short with a single raised finger from the detective. "Not a word. There are no excuses for what you just did."

Running a hand through her hair, Logan pinned the officer with her eyes. "Do you realize that the woman in that bed has seen our Strip District killer up close and personal? That she is one of only two people who can identify this guy?" Not receiving an answer, she moved closer to his face, until she could smell the onions he had just eaten for lunch. "I think I just asked you a question, Officer." The scared policeman nodded, too frightened to speak. "Well, I certainly hope you think about that while you're playing meter mom for the next six months."

Easing closer, Madison watched the officer quickly walk away, most likely surprised to still be standing and probably even more so to still have a job, even if it did mean he was back handing out parking tickets for the next six months.

Turning, Logan spied Madison lurking behind the door. The eyes that had just pinned the officer to the wall relaxed and smiled as Madison eased her way toward the detective. "That was what."

"Excuse me?"

Smiling, Logan stepped closer. "Before, when we got off the elevator and you asked me what? That was it. The officer wasn't at his post."

Madison's eyes reflected her comprehension as she smiled. "Well, I'm certainly happy that you're the detective and I'm only a doctor. I didn't notice."

Laughing, Logan stepped even closer, so close she could smell the scent of Opium filling the electrically charged space between them. Each woman was acutely aware of the other as their auras touched, caressed, begged to be closer. Tearing her gaze from Madison's, Logan looked over the doctor's shoulder toward Susan's room. "Is she all right? No one unusual came in while we were gone, did they?"

Still considering the multiple layers of the detective's personality, Madison replied distractedly, "No, not that she mentioned."

Moving toward the nurses' station, Logan picked up the phone and punched in a number, then turned back to the doctor. "Good. As soon as headquarters sends a replacement for the guard, we'll leave."

"Sure. Fine." Madison stepped back inside the room.

Madison looked around the dull squad room on Central Avenue as she and Logan walked through it on their way to the interview room. She had never been exposed to this aspect of the city's life, nor could she recall ever being inside a police station. Her family had been blessed with enough wealth to keep her safe from the darker side of life, and she sometimes wondered if that sheltered childhood was what had planted the seed within her heart to aid those less fortunate as she grew older.

Madison's father, Malcolm Cavanaugh, was the district attorney in Allegheny County for twenty-three years. Having been re-elected four times, he was planning for the next election and would have most likely won in another landslide in 1983 had he not died of a heart attack while in bed with his mistress. The death of her father was devastating enough for Madison; having to endure the gossip surrounding the circumstances was almost unbearable.

Shaking herself from the memory, Madison glanced around the squad room. *I know she couldn't possibly be here, today, in this building. No wonder I hate cops, when my own father died in the arms of one—the same cop who is now the commander of the major crimes division for the city of Pittsburgh.* Madison felt a gentle hand grasp her arm, pulling bringing her back to the present. "What?"

Logan noticed the faraway look in the doctor's eyes and knew she was thinking about something troublesome. Assuming it was the upcoming interview, she leaned in and spoke softly in Madison's ear.

"Don't look some glum, Doc. I promise I won't pull out the bright lights, whips, and chains." Looking over Madison's shoulder, she saw Picasso in baggy clothes and a two-day beard trudging down the hall toward her. "Come on, let's get the sketch out of the way so I can get the guys out on the streets with a picture, and then I'll take your official statement."

Logan knew the sketch was the most important element in their visit to the precinct. There was very little Madison could tell them about her encounter with the man and Susan, and Logan knew it; she had watched the entire interaction herself. After leading the doctor into the interview room, she waited until Picasso had unpacked his supplies and had begun talking with Madison and intently sketching before she eased out of the room in search of coffee.

Rounding the corner into the break room, Logan ran into her old partner, Wilson Hennessey. They had worked the streets together for almost six years before both officers made changes in their career paths, Logan choosing the major crimes division and Hennessey moving to work narcotics. They had kept in touch, always making time every month or so to have dinner together and catch up on each other's lives. Wilson's wife, Sarah, was a beautiful woman and a successful attorney at one of the city's larger law firms. Logan had always kidded Wilson about being a kept man, and he had always taken it in stride, pleased that there was something in the world that could make Logan McGregor laugh.

"Well, Hen. I haven't seen you around lately. How's the drug business?" Patting his stomach, she laughed and continued to the coffeepot. "I hope you're catching more drug dealers than you are doughnuts, Hen."

"The drug business is going just fine, Mac. I do believe last week my busts outnumbered my doughnuts." Grabbing the newspaper from the table, he sat down on a cracked and faded vinyl couch. "You're getting as bad as Sarah." He thumbed through the sports section, looking for the latest stats on the Steelers. "Between the two of you I never used to get any peace. Thank God all I have to deal with now is junkies and dealers every day."

Logan started a fresh pot of coffee. Sitting down beside Hennessey, she snatched the paper out of his hands and tossed it across the room. "Hey, big guy, you haven't seen me in weeks, so don't think you're going to sit on your ass and read the paper while I'm talking to you. I'm not your wife and I won't put up with that shit from you."

Rolling his eyes, Hennessey sighed. "Okay, Mac, what's on your mind? You never were much for conversation, and if I remember correctly, the times that you were, there was something heavy going on in that pretty head of yours."

A smile threatened to curl her lips as she shook her head, knowing the man beside her probably knew her better than any one else ever had. "Well, it's like this. I'm at a dead end on this Strip District case. The brass has my hands tied and won't let me interview the Langstons. God forbid we should inconvenience the high and mighty of the city, and as of last night we have another victim. This time we were lucky. Although she was viciously beaten, she lived and is now under guard at Mercy. I have another witness with Picasso now, working on a sketch. Other than that I have nothing, and the mayor is going to have my ass if I don't solve this case soon. I need some help, but I need it done quietly. Are you game?"

Hennessey eyed his former partner for a long moment. In all the years they had worked together, he had never seen Logan McGregor doing anything underhanded. He knew if she was playing off the record, there must be a damn good reason. "Sure, Mac, anything you need. You know I'll always have your back."

For the next fifteen minutes, they sat huddled on the couch talking over the situation. Finally, Hennessey stood, stretched his long, not-so-lean form, and yawned. "Well, Mac, I'm going home to sleep on this. I'll give you a call in a couple of days when I have something for you." Without another word, he turned and walked out of the room.

Logan prepared two cups of coffee and then walked back to the interview room. When she crossed the threshold, Madison looked up and Logan could have sworn her heart skipped a beat as the doctor smiled at her. Setting the coffee in front of Madison, she walked behind Picasso to get her first close-up look at the suspect.

Madison had provided a very detailed description of the suspect, which would make Logan's job of finding the man somewhat easier. However, with that knowledge came the undeniable fact that once the suspect saw the picture, he would know for certain that Dr. Madison Cavanaugh had not only seen him, but had paid very close attention. Logan knew that when that happened, he would panic and become desperate, and Madison would be in even more danger than she was already.

A few minutes later Picasso packed up his supplies and promised Logan he would have the composite sketch out on the wire within the hour. Logan gave Madison a few minutes to relax and drink her coffee before calling in one of the other detectives to question her. Logan knew she should do it herself, but since she had watched the scene unfold the previous night, she was afraid she would insert her own memories into Madison's statement.

They were about to begin when the door to the interview room opened and a tall, dark-haired, almost handsome woman entered and walked directly to Madison, extending her hand. "Hello, Dr. Cavanaugh, I'm Loraine Osborne, commander of the major crimes division."

Madison stared, shocked, as the woman stood in front of her, hand outstretched, watching her. It took her a few moments to find her voice. "Commander Osborne, I'm well aware of who you are."

The commander smiled nervously as she dropped her hand, slipping it into her pocket. "Yes, well, I just wanted to come by personally and thank you for taking the time to come down here today."

Logan watched as the scene unfolded and could almost feel the air in the room crackle with electricity. She didn't know the reason, but she could see that it was taking every ounce of the doctor's willpower to control her anger. Deciding the situation needed to be defused, she turned to the other officer. "Are you ready, Troy?"

Nodding, his eyes darted between the three women. "Sure, any time you are."

The commander took her cue from Logan, and with a last glance at Madison, turned to the ever-watchful detective. "Detective McGregor, when you're finished here, I'd like to see you in my office." Glancing at her watch, she looked at Troy Bingham, who was being careful not to stare. "Say...an hour?

"Sure, Chief, I shouldn't be longer than an hour." Turning back toward Madison, Troy smiled, trying to break some of the tension in the room.

Logan walked the commander to the door and then quietly sat at the table, allowing Troy to control the interview. She listened intently, almost as intently as she studied Madison Cavanaugh and the gorgeous features of her face. When the interview was complete and Troy stood up to leave, Logan looked down at her watch, surprised to find almost forty-five minutes had passed. *I could look into those eyes forever.*

She led Madison to the break room and poured another cup of coffee from the half-full pot. After handing it to Madison, she checked her appearance in the mirror. "I shouldn't be but a minute with the commander. I'll be right back. Just make yourself at home, and if you need anything, just ask Troy. He's right outside in the squad room, all right?"

Heading down the long, gunmetal gray hallway, Logan reflected on Madison and the commander's encounter. Her curiosity was soaring, but she knew that it was not the time to be asking questions, especially of Madison Cavanaugh. *I've already dealt with her wrath once—I'm not doing it again.*

CHAPTER NINE

"Sit down, McGregor." Looking up from her paperwork, Loraine Osborne studied the tall, dark detective. On several occasions she'd had the opportunity to work directly with Logan McGregor, but she wasn't able to get a solid handle on what made her mind work. She had never given it much thought, caring only that the detective's solve rate fell within the police department's top five percent.

"Yes, ma'am." Logan sat in one of the visitor's chairs, returning the studious look. "Is there something wrong, Commander?"

Loraine stood, then walked around the desk and closed the door before returning to sit in the chair next to Logan. "No, Detective, nothing is wrong. I haven't had the opportunity to speak with you directly about the Strip District case and thought now would be a good time to go over the details you have so far."

Logan released a silent sigh of relief. On her way to the office, she had worried that the commander was going to criticize her slow progress. Now, though, she saw her as a possible means for assistance. "Actually, Commander, I'm having a difficult time convincing the lieutenant and the deputy chief to let me interview the Langston Development employees."

She carefully watched the commander's eyes for any sign of disapproval. Seeing none, she continued. "I know in my gut that the Langstons have some information that will help with this investigation, but they're hiding behind the mayor's political clout and I need some help."

Loraine bit her bottom lip, taking a moment to sort through the information the detective had just told her. She knew the Langstons were one of the wealthiest families in the city and knew also the political fallout that would ensue if anyone ever crossed them. However, she wouldn't have been in her current position had she followed the path of least resistance. *God knows, I got my first promotion to sergeant as a trade-off for keeping quiet about Malcolm's death.* Returning her gaze to the detective, she nodded and stood, walking to the other side of her desk. She made a note on a legal pad, then sat quietly for a moment, the beat from her pen tapping the desk blotter resonating throughout the room. "I'll see what I can do, Detective. In the meantime, keep me posted on your progress."

Logan stood. "Thank you. I'm sure I'll be in touch soon." She walked from the room and back down the long hallway no more enlightened as to the connection between Madison Cavanaugh and the commander than she'd been before she entered the office. However, the meeting wasn't as unpleasant as she had feared, and she decided it might even help the progress of the slowly progressing investigation.

She stopped by the front desk to check her messages, then went into the squad room to get her backpack before returning to Madison. Entering the break room a few minutes later, she rolled her eyes and couldn't help but laugh as Madison tried to keep up with the questions being asked of her by three overzealous young police officers. She put on her best cop face and stormed into the room.

"Jesus, guys. Can we not have attractive visitors in here without you three embarrassing the entire force with your drooling?" Looking each one of them in the eye, she stepped a little closer and inwardly smiled as they took a step back. "Get out of here and get to work, or in your case, Tommy, go home to your wife."

The three officers apologized and practically fled the room as Logan sat down on the couch beside Madison. "Sorry about that. It seems that with the job also comes an enormous ego and an overwhelming primal compulsion to go forth and conquer."

Lifting an eyebrow, which Logan now regarded as the doctor's trademark sign of surprise, Madison rose and tossed her empty coffee cup into the trash. Turning back toward the detective, she reached for her bag and coat. "Oh, and am I to assume you were able to escape that perilous job malady, Detective?"

Logan was taken by surprise by the comment, temporarily unable to respond as Madison smiled and continued walking away. Jumping up from her seat, Logan took off down the hall, once again in pursuit of the enigmatic doctor. *Jesus, not again.*

As she entered the parking garage, Logan finally found Madison smiling and leaning against the Durango. Tugging the keys from her pocket, she unlocked and opened the passenger door but didn't step aside. Instead, putting on arm on top of the truck, she leaned closer to the beautiful doctor. "Why is it that I always find myself chasing after you, Doctor?"

Madison could feel the heat radiating from the detective's body and inhaled her spicy scent. Feeling her own heartbeat quicken, she boldly returned the intense gaze. "Who knows, Detective, maybe you're on to something." Winking, she slipped under Logan's arm and slid into the passenger seat, leaving the stunned detective standing outside the truck. *What the hell are you doing, Cavanaugh? This ridiculous flirting is going to get you in trouble, big time, if you don't watch it.*

Swallowing hard, Logan closed the door, thinking that if Madison hadn't slipped by her when she had, she would have been receiving an extremely soul-searing kiss at the moment. She slowly walked around the truck. *Yeah right, McGregor. Just what you need, kissing someone right in the middle of the police station garage, and a damn doctor no less.* Sliding into the truck, she pointedly avoided the doctor's eyes and eased into the traffic on Penn Circle. Silently, they rode to Mercy Hospital, both mulling over the obvious attraction they had for each other and the self-imposed barriers that prevented either of them from exploring the possibilities.

As they neared the hospital, Madison directed Logan to the doctors' parking lot. After getting out of the truck, Madison went to her Pathfinder to drop off her briefcase. Logan was about twenty feet from the entrance to the hospital when she heard the doctor calling her name. The look of fear etched across the doctor's face sent Logan into a fast sprint across the parking lot.

Madison was pale and speechless when the detective reached her, and could only point at her truck. The rear tire had been slashed and a Langston Development business card neatly placed under the windshield wiper. Logan used her cell phone to dial the precinct as she led Madison away from the truck. She requested a CSI team, knowing that no fingerprints or physical evidence would be found on or near the car but not wanting to take the chance of missing anything in case the perp had been sloppy in his pursuit of Madison. As they waited for the CSI team to arrive, Logan called upstairs to check on Susan. Speaking directly with the guard, she re-emphasized the importance of not leaving his post and gave him her personal cell phone number in case he needed to reach her.

Madison was leaning against a nearby car, arms hugging her own body in a sign of helpless fear. Once she ended her call, Logan gently lifted the doctor's chin so their eyes met. "I promise you, nothing is going to happen to either you or Susan."

Madison met the confident look from Logan with a weak smile. "You can't promise me that and you know it." Tears sprang to her eyes, and in a moment of sheer terror, the implications of what had happened to her car hit her in the gut as hard as any fist could have and she completely lost all control of her emotions.

Logan gently eased the doctor into her arms, feeling the tremors of fear shaking her body. Madison's arms wrapped around her waist and tears soaked through her shirt, dampening a spot on her chest directly in line with her heart. At that moment, Logan succumbed to the war raging in her soul and accepted that she was quickly falling in love with the woman in her arms. Holding Madison tighter, gently whispering soothing words into her ear, she vowed to protect her, no matter how great the price.

Logan walked Madison up to Susan's room and gave her a cup of coffee before returning to the parking lot to oversee the CSI team. They arrived and spent over two hours going over Madison's car, but in the end, found nothing that they thought would be of any use. They had lifted several sets of fingerprints, but from their location, knew that they most likely belonged to Madison.

While watching the team work, Logan called her lieutenant to request an officer to stay with the doctor overnight.

"I'm sorry, McGregor, but the only other available officer I have on that shift is out with the flu."

Pacing the parking lot, Logan began to feel the tension of the day as it took hold of the muscles in her neck like a vise. "Well, can't you pull someone from another precinct? I can't just leave this woman to her own defenses tonight, Lieutenant."

She could hear a sigh on the other end of the phone. "Sorry, Detective, I guess you'll have to do it yourself if you feel she has to be covered tonight."

Logan's temper flared. "Me? Come on, Lieutenant. This woman lives all the way out near Bridgeville. What if we have another incident tonight? I'd be at least thirty minutes away."

"Well, then, just bring her into town and keep her at your place tonight if you feel it's necessary. Look, I'll see what I can do beginning tomorrow, but for tonight, that's the best you can hope for, McGregor."

Slamming the phone closed, she stormed across the parking lot and headed back toward the hospital, the tense muscles in her neck creating the beginnings of a massive headache. Five minutes later, she entered Susan's room to find her and Madison talking in hushed tones. As Logan moved across the room, she knew that her face told the doctor that the CSI team's efforts had been for naught. "Sorry, but I don't think we were able to get anything of importance from your truck."

Seeing the look of defeat on the doctor's eyes, she gently touched her shoulder and knelt down beside the chair. "They are going to run the prints, but I think they will come back as belonging to you." She gave

Madison's shoulder a gentle squeeze and dipped her head to look into the frightened green eyes. "Hey, come on, look at the bright side; you get stuck with me for the night."

A look of confusion played across the doctor's face. "What?"

Logan shrugged while putting on her best charming grin. "You're stuck with me for the night. We'll go to your house and get a few things and then you're coming home with me. I don't want you staying by yourself tonight, just in case this guy knows where you live."

Running a hand through her long blond hair, Madison sat back in the chair, exasperated. "I can't do that. I have a dog at home that needs taking care of. I can't just dump everything and go running off to hide."

Before Logan could respond, Susan's quiet voice called out to her. "Madi, please. Don't argue with the detective. Stay with her, at least for tonight...for me, please." Seeing her plea weaken the doctor, she looked at Logan for reinforcement. "I'm sure the detective will welcome Femur into her house for one night. Won't you, Detective?"

Logan's eyes widened at the suggestion, but she quickly recovered and forced a smile onto her face. "Sure, Femur is welcome to come along too. He may even be able to teach my cat a few manners along the way."

"Fine. Okay, I'll go, just stop with the directives." Looking between the two women, one tall and strong, the other weak and broken, Madison relented. "Jesus, if I didn't know better I'd swear you two planned this together."

With a wink for Logan, Susan reached out with her good hand and took Madison's. "Thank you, Madi. I don't know what I would do if something happened to you because of me."

Leaning down and placing a light kiss on her friend's forehead, Madison whispered, "I love you, Susan. I promise this will be over soon." Looking up, she pinned Logan McGregor with her eyes. "Won't it, Detective?"

Pulling up in front of Madison's two-story house, Logan let out a quiet whistle. "Nice digs you got here, Doc."

Madison eyed the modern structure made of custom rose-colored brick. "Thank you."

Noticing the doctor's hesitation, Logan decided not to pursue the conversation. "Well, let's gather up your things so we can get back to town. I'm getting hungry, how about you?"

Madison opened the door of the truck and climbed down, heading toward the front door. Logan followed slowly, realizing that her intrusion was most likely unwelcome.

Walking into the open foyer, Logan was struck by the elegant beauty of the doctor's home. The banister and spindles on the staircase leading to the second floor appeared to be hand-turned oak, and Logan surmised that the other woodwork in the house would prove to be custom milled as well.

Madison led her into a comfortable den and turned on the recessed lighting in the ceiling. "Please, have a seat. Would you care for anything to drink?"

Noticing the formal tone in the doctor's voice, Logan could tell she was not accustomed to having a stranger in her private haven. "No thanks, I'm fine."

"Okay, I'll only be a few minutes."

Madison quickly left the room, leaving Logan alone to take in her surroundings. She heard the doctor talking in the background, followed by barks from an obviously happy dog. *Great, I'm sure Clancy is going to love this.* She heard Madison call out and was just about to stand when a blur of fur and tongue raced through the door and leapt onto her lap. Logan's attempt to hold the dog at bay was futile, as was her attempt to shield her face from the excited Lab's tongue.

Racing through the door, Madison stopped short at seeing the tall, muscular detective pinned helplessly under Femur's hefty body. She burst out laughing. "Well, I can see you met Femur." Having mercy on the detective, Madison walked over, and taking the dog by the collar, gently tugged until he released his hold on Logan.

Sitting up and wiping her mouth with the back of her hand, Logan tried unsuccessfully to hide her smile. "Um, yes. He introduced himself."

Madison started to lead the excited Femur from the room and then stopped. She looked at the other woman hesitantly. "Are you sure you really want the two of us barging in on you tonight?"

For the first time all evening, Madison caught a glimpse of the woman beneath the hard façade as Logan stood, walked over, and then knelt beside Femur, stroking his shiny coat. "Of course I am. Although I'm not so sure how eager Femur will be to meet Clancy." Smiling up into the doctor's face, she laughed. "I think he can hold his own with my cat from hell."

Madison groaned and shooed Femur from the room. "Great, a cat with an attitude and a wimpy dog." She looked at the detective with questioning eyes. "It's going to be a long night, isn't it?"

Logan sat down on the couch and interlaced her fingers behind her head before responding in her best cop voice. "I, my dear lady, am a detective sergeant for the Pittsburgh Police Department. I'm fully equipped to handle any situation that may arise."

Rolling her eyes, Madison picked up a pillow from the adjacent chair and tossed it toward Logan. "Whatever. I, for one, am going armed with a good supply of doggie treats and one of his tranquilizers. Just in case."

Catching the pillow with one lightning-quick hand, Logan wrapped her arms around it, hugging it to her chest as Madison walked out of the den. *Okay, McGregor, get a grip, or it is going to be a hell of a long night.*

Twenty minutes later, the two women were on their way back toward the city, Femur sitting in the back smiling, his head stretched over the seat. Madison was turned in her seat stroking his head as she told Logan the story of meeting Femur. "I can't believe that he is so happy after going through all that pain as a pup."

It was apparent to Logan that their devotion to one another was undying. "Maybe having you to help him through it is what gave him such a good outlook on life. Have you ever thought of that?"

After stopping for take-out Chinese for dinner, Logan turned onto Trenton Avenue and glanced at the woman beside her. "Um, my place isn't nearly as, um, nice as yours, but it's warm." For some reason, it was important to Logan for the woman next to her to feel comfortable in her house. *Why? After tonight, she'll never be back. What does it matter if she likes it or not?*

"What?" Pulling herself out of her musing, Logan turned toward Madison. "I'm sorry, I was thinking about something else. What did you say?"

Madison repeated herself, chuckling at the detective's flustered face. "I said, your house is charming." She raised an eyebrow. "Actually, I had you pegged as one of the condo types over near campus."

Still sitting in the truck, Logan reached over and absently scratched Femur's ear. "Nope, not me. I like my privacy too much." As she looked back toward the dark green wood-frame house nestled closely between two others of the same era, she sighed. "Actually, this is a little too crowded for me, but with my job, I have to be close to the precinct, so this is the best it gets."

She got out of the truck, then opened the back door and pulled out Madison's overnight bag. "One day if you're lucky, I'll show you my cabin at Conneaut Lake." *Jeez, why are you going there?*

Logan unlocked the back door of the house and stood back for Madison and Femur to enter. Following behind, she watched the doctor carefully as she took in her surroundings. Femur's nose lifted in the air and the fur on his back stood up as he caught the scent of the resident cat.

Madison knelt down beside the agitated dog and whispered soothing words into his ear. To Logan's amazement, Femur sat back on his haunches and immediately calmed down.

"How do you do that?"

Madison smiled and rose to her feet. "I guess it's my great bedside manner, Detective."

Logan sat their dinner on the counter, then led Madison through the house and down the hall to the guest bedroom. After placing her overnight bag on the foot of the bed, she eased toward the door. "There's a bathroom right through that door. I'm going to get out of these clothes and then I'll meet you back in the kitchen for dinner, okay?"

"Fine, I won't be but a minute myself." Madison watched as Logan shut the door, and then sat heavily on the edge of the bed. For the first time that day she found herself alone, and the events of the day suddenly overwhelmed her. Fighting back the tears that threatened to break through, she went into the bathroom and washed her face.

After changing clothes, she brushed her hair and then headed back toward the kitchen. Passing by an open doorway, she glanced in to see Logan standing in the middle of the room, naked from the waist up. Madison's eyes took in the muscular shoulders and the taut muscles in her back as the detective lifted a T-shirt over her head and slid it over her torso. Madison quickly resumed her trek to the kitchen, thankful that she had not been seen.

They ate dinner at the small bar in the kitchen while talking and learning more about each other's backgrounds. The doctor skirted the issue of family when Logan asked and only vaguely mentioned a brother, Markus, who worked as a graphic designer in Los Angeles. The detective picked up on her hesitancy to speak of her parents and didn't follow that line of conversation, instead focusing on subjects the doctor was more comfortable with.

The rest of the evening was surprisingly comfortable as the women moved to the den after dinner and continued their conversation. Madison sat on the leather couch with Logan on the floor, leaning her back against the other end. She noticed Logan kept frowning and stretching her neck, and finally during a break in the conversation, asked what was wrong.

"Nothing serious." She dismissed the question with a wave of her hand. "I just have a kink in my neck."

Before Logan knew it Madison was on the other end of the couch, one leg on each side of her body pressing against her arms as warm, strong hands took hold of her shoulders. Logan immediately tensed when the doctor started to knead the tense muscles, and her heart began a staccato beat when a warm breath tickled her ear. "Does that feel good?"

"Um..." All she could manage was a groan.

Sensing Logan's uneasiness, Madison whispered in her ear, "Will you relax, Detective. I'm a doctor. I know what I'm doing." Sitting back and putting a little space between them, she continued to work the taut muscles of the detective's shoulders through her T-shirt, remembering how well formed and lean they looked when she had spied the detective in the bedroom earlier in the evening. *Well, if you were a patient I would know what I was doing. But you, Logan McGregor, are not my patient and I definitely don't have a clue about what I'm doing at the moment.*

Madison chose to ignore the warning signals sounding in her head and instead continued massaging the knots out of Logan's neck and back. After a while she felt the muscles release and Logan's shoulders relax, but she continued until her hands had eased to a delicate stroke across the smooth skin of Logan's neck.

Logan had lost herself in the gentle soothing touch and was very close to sleep when she felt a change in the rhythm and pressure on her skin. Her breathing became deeper and a slow, warm sensation overtook her. She knew she had to put some distance between them before she lost all sense of professionalism and seduced the doctor right there in her den. Stretching her neck from side to side, she cleared her throat and slowly turned toward Madison. "Thanks, that really helped my headache."

Madison was fighting her own war with her body and felt the sudden loss of warmth as she pulled her hands away from the detective's neck. She was all too aware that Logan McGregor was sitting between her legs, her arm mere inches from the detective's throbbing heat. Pushing herself back further on the couch, she tried to hide the images passing though her mind and regain some control as she slipped back into her professional persona. "You're welcome. You really should think about getting regular massages. It seems as if you hold a lot of your stress in your shoulder and neck area."

Logan unfolded herself from the floor and stood, looking down at Madison. "Are you ready to go to bed?"

"Sure, whenever you are." Calling Femur, she followed Logan down the hall until they reached the detective's bedroom.

Logan didn't realize how close behind Madison had been following until she turned around and came chest to face with her. Feeling the now-familiar heat rush through her body, she attempted to step back only to be stopped by Femur, who stood solidly behind her. As she inhaled the intoxicating scent of the doctor, Logan had the overpowering urge to lean down and capture the doctor's lips with her own.

Their eyes met and held, each woman afraid to make the first move, equally afraid the other wouldn't. Logan's eyes followed the sensual movement of Madison's tongue as it darted out to moisten the full, wanting lips, and suddenly her resolve was shattered. Slowly, she bent her head, giving the doctor every opportunity to back away, to show her any sign that she was overstepping her boundaries. Sensing none, she moved slowly toward the doctor and watched as Madison's eyes closed in anticipation. Logan's heart pounded in her chest, her mind reeling with emotion as she drew nearer, and just as her lips brushed across Madison's waiting ones, all hell broke loose.

Logan instinctively pushed Madison to the floor, covering the doctor's body with her own. It took several seconds before she realized that the fracas was a result of Femur and Clancy's first meeting. Swearing under her breath, Logan bounded from the floor and rushed into the guest room. Clancy was perilously perched on top of the window valance while Femur frantically jumped and barked. Logan was soon joined by Madison, finally recovered from the shock of being thrown to the floor, who tugged Femur from the room.

Logan carefully climbed onto the bed and placed her foot on the nightstand. She gently retrieved the frightened cat from the valance, noticing its heart was beating double time. "Hmm, you're not such a terror after all, are you, little one?" Cradling the cat in her arms, she walked across the hall and sat her on the bed before closing the door and heading back toward the den in search of Madison and Femur.

When she walked into the den, she noticed the doctor's back was to the door, her head bent near the dog's ear as she whispered. Logan watched as human and animal conversed and was once again stunned by the calming effect Madison's voice had on the dog.

Femur lifted his head, and Madison also looked up. Her eyes met Logan's and held until Madison broke the stare and whispered something into the dog's ear. To Logan's surprise, Femur walked over and sat down in front of her, extending his paw. Logan looked at the dog, then back at his owner, a confused look on her face.

"He's apologizing and wants to shake your hand."

Comprehension dawned and Logan reached down to take the proffered paw, after which she was rewarded with a genuine lick to the face. Laughing, she patted his head, letting him know all was well in the world, before looking back toward Madison. "Well, I have Clancy locked in my room. I think the path is clear if you'd like to try again."

For a moment Madison thought Logan was referring to the kiss, but soon realized that she was referring to retiring for the night. She followed the detective down the hallway to the bedroom. This time, Logan only turned her head and softly said good night before stealing away into her bedroom and closing the door.

In their separate rooms, both woman discarded their clothes and slid between the sheets, relishing the cool relief the material brought to the searing heat of their skin. Turning out the lights, both women lay awake for a long time staring at the ceiling, thinking about what might have been had Femur and Clancy not chosen that moment to introduce themselves.

Rolling over, Logan silently cursed the purring cat at the foot of the bed, as Madison did the snoring dog lying curled on the floor beside her.

CHAPTER TEN

Madison woke to the sound of Femur barking outside. Fighting her way through the fog that had claimed her during the night, she listened as sounds of laughter trickled through the window. She drew back the curtains and peered into the sun-filled backyard, the corners of her mouth lifting in a smile as the detective tossed a Frisbee and Femur caught it midair.

Slipping on her robe, she padded down the hall and into the kitchen, the aroma of fresh coffee catching her attention, luring her forward. She spied the coffeepot on the organized counter next to a neatly handwritten note lying beside a mug letting her know that her hostess and Femur had gone for a walk and would be back soon. The doctor poured herself a mug of coffee and another for the detective, thinking about how nice it felt to wake up to the sounds of laughter.

Madison walked through the sunroom and onto the back deck as she juggled the two hot mugs of coffee. She leaned against the railing, sipping her coffee, she intently watching the other woman play with her dog. *Damn, I could get used to this.*

The blonde had been standing there for a few minutes before Logan looked up and spotted her. "Good morning." The detective trotted over, her shirt damp with good healthy sweat, the sight of which made the tempo of the doctor's heart quicken.

"Good morning to you too." She leaned down to pet Femur's head after handing the dark-haired woman her coffee. "Hey, big guy, it looks like you've made a new friend."

Logan's breath caught in her throat as she tried desperately not to look at the slight parting in Madison's robe that exposed the soft, full curve of her breast. The detective looked away, focusing for a moment on the real reason they were there, at her house, on a beautiful Friday morning before turning back to the alluring woman.

"I heard him moving around in your room when I got up earlier. I was about to go out for a run when I thought he might like to go along." She saw the concerned look in the doctor's eyes and held up her hand before she had a chance to respond. "We decided to take a walk instead. I didn't know if his leg was ready for running yet and I didn't want to take the chance." She scratched the overgrown pup behind the ear. "We were good, so tell Mom to chill out or I won't make breakfast."

As if on cue, Femur looked up at the blonde and released a whining howl, causing both women to break out in laughter.

Logan trotted up the steps of the deck and into the house. "Come on, you two, breakfast awaits."

After dropping Madison at the hospital, the detective sauntered into the squad room and went directly to her desk. As she had expected, the fingerprints on the doctor's Pathfinder came back as Madison's. Several investigators were out re-canvassing all the bars and interviewing witnesses, and after making a few calls to check up on their progress, Logan realized there was nothing else she could do for the day. The one thing she wanted to be doing, interviewing the Langston executives, was still forbidden, so she decided to head back to the hospital. *Now what am I going to do with the good doctor for the rest of the day?*

The detective was halfway out the door when she decided to call Lieutenant Beaudry. To her surprise, she was told that two officers, working twelve-hour shifts starting that evening, had been assigned to protect her witness. Logan felt an unfamiliar feeling of loneliness as she hung up the phone, realizing that the previous night would be the only one the doctor would spend at her house. *Well, this is what you bitched about, isn't it.* Struggling with her emotions as she walked to the truck, she never saw the man standing across the street, lurking in the shadows of a doorway, watching her intently.

The detective arrived at the hospital a little after one o'clock to find a restless and hungry doctor. Smiling at Susan, Logan shook her head and rolled her eyes. "It's a good thing she's a surgeon. I'm not sure any other profession would provide the means to support that appetite she has. Do you?"

Enjoying the easy familiarity between her friend and the detective, Susan joined in. "Well, she keeps me fairly busy. I had to keep a regular surgical schedule lest she starve to death."

The blonde stood and slipped into her coat as she feigned irritation. "Just for that, Detective, you're buying lunch."

The stunned look that crossed Logan's face sent tears to Susan's eyes as she tried not to laugh. "Jeez, Detective, you've done it now."

Snorting, Madison opened the door, and then turned back to the still-stunned woman with a gleam in her eye. "Yep, and if you keep it up, you'll be feeding me for a long time to come." The surgeon made a swift exit, realizing how her comment must have sounded, and missed the look exchanged between her friend and the charming detective.

"Looks like you better hurry, Detective, or the good doctor just might get away."

The detective was halfway out the door when she heard Susan call out her name. Peering back into the room, she saw a sad but encouraging smile on the other woman's face. "You take care of her, okay? She's kind of important to me."

Logan held Susan's gaze for a moment before simply nodding and closing the door.

The day passed more quickly than either woman wanted, and it was after nine when they pulled into Madison's drive. When Logan saw the police cruiser sitting in the drive, the same lonely feeling returned, gripping her gut. She walked over to speak to the officer on duty while Madison took Femur inside the house. When she learned that Officer Patty Freeman was a rookie with the Bridgeville Police Department, the detective released a frustrated sigh. *Great, now I get to baby-sit two people.*

The young officer sat in the police cruiser, returning the investigator's glare with a defiant one of her own. "Detective, I may be a rookie, but I think I can handle a simple guard job." Logan McGregor's reputation as a hard-edged detective was well known, and her superior officer had warned her to tread lightly where the investigator was concerned. "Believe me, I'm not any happier about this assignment than you seem to be, but I can do my job, Detective."

The corners of the detective's lips curled up in a half smile as she regarded the officer. She recalled her similar gusto as a rookie and decided that she had to give the officer the benefit of the doubt. "Okay, fine."

After bidding the rookie good night, Logan turned toward the house, feeling Officer Freeman's eyes on her back as she climbed the steps. The front door was ajar and she realized that the doctor had just assumed that she would come in after speaking with the officer. Easing the door open, she called out as she stepped into the foyer and heard the answer from upstairs.

"I'll only be a minute. There's beer in the refrigerator or if you want something else, just search around."

Logan was standing by the fireplace in the den looking at what she believed was an original Monet when Madison entered a few minutes later. Pretending not to notice the surprised look on the detective's face, she sat down on one end of the couch. "I really had a nice time today, even under the circumstances."

Sitting at the other end of the couch, Logan regarded the other woman intently for a few seconds. "I did too." With an embarrassed chuckle, she looked away. "It's, um, been a while since I just went out and enjoyed myself."

"Well if the tension in your shoulders and neck last night were any indication, I'd say you need to have fun more often." Sitting up on the couch, Madison opened her legs, patting the edge of the couch with her hands. "Come here, let me work on your neck and shoulders again and see if I can work some more of that stress out."

The detective felt as if she had just been gut punched, her breath escaping her as she felt a rush of heat surge through her body.

Seeing the hesitation in Logan's eyes, Madison leaned over and took her arm, tugging her closer. "Come on, I don't bite."

As she settled herself on the floor, Logan felt Madison's legs brush against hers and once again felt the unmistakable ache. *Does she have any idea what she's doing to me?* Gathering her willpower, she leaned back and tried to relax as the doctor's strong, lithe fingers began to work their magic. She closed her eyes and focused on each muscle as the doctor tenderly persuaded them to release, and soon her head was bent forward, allowing Madison full access to her neck and back.

Madison could feel the muscles relax as she carefully tended to each one, paying special attention to those that ran up the back of the detective's neck. A pleasant sensation warmed her own body as she continued working her fingers into the soft flesh, and she closed her eyes, losing herself to the emotions it wrought from within. Unconsciously, she slid her hands along the firm jaw, thumbs tenderly pressing against the muscles as she felt Logan lean back against her legs.

She continued the soft contact as her thumbs moved across high cheekbones to slightly indented temples, and finally to stroke along the strong, powerfully expressive forehead that hinted at deeply hidden and passionately protected emotions. Madison looked down into the face of the woman she was coming to think of not just as her protector, but as a friend. A friend that, at that moment, she desperately wanted to kiss.

Feeling a pause in the tender touch on her forehead, Logan opened her eyes to see a pair of very beautiful, extremely sensual green eyes studying her. Their gaze held for a long moment, volumes racing through each of their minds, as they contemplated the thoughts and desires of the other. Surrendering all sense of control and professional demeanor, Logan slowly lifted her arm, sliding a hand into the doctor's long blond hair, before gently pulling a willing face down to hers.

Madison's head was spinning as she looked into the detective's dark blue eyes. A low moan escaped her throat as Logan's hand slid around her neck, and for a brief moment, her world stopped as those same eyes rested on her lips.

Logan savored the taste of warm, eager lips as the scent of Madison's long blond hair flowed around her like a protective shield. Her breath caught as the doctor's hand cupped her face, pulling them closer, deepening the kiss that was rapidly searing their souls.

Without breaking contact, Logan turned and rose onto her knees. As she wrapped her long, muscular arms around the other woman's waist, a deep primal groan escaped her throat when the doctor gently parted her lips with an exploring tongue.

Trembling hands caressed Madison's back, slowly discovering taut, quivering muscles as both women's breathing deepened and became more uneven. Sliding her hands lower, Logan caressed Madison's small firm hips before continuing on to strong, muscular thighs. She forced herself to slow down, wanting to savor every second. She again cupped Madison's hips in her hands and pulled her closer still, until she heard the doctor gasp as Logan's pelvis pressed into her hot, wet center.

Madison lost all sense of time. Her tongue danced sensually with Logan's in exploration of the newfound silky terrain, and her hips involuntarily thrust forward as the detective's pelvis pressed harder between her legs and her arms tightened around Madison's neck.

The kiss continued until both women were breathless, their need for oxygen forcefully overcoming their desire for each other. Logan, still on her knees, forehead pressed against Madison's, took several deep breaths before opening her eyes, again finding green orbs gazing intently into hers. The doctor, her chest rising and falling in a desperate attempt to replenish the oxygen to her brain, cupped the detective's cheek as her thumb tenderly stroked her full, delicious lips. "Wow."

After kissing Madison's forehead, Logan once again looked into green eyes, dark with yearning. "Do we know what we're doing here?" Before the words were out of her mouth, she felt the other woman tense.

"I didn't mean that the way it sounded." Logan's lips brushed against Madison's before she leaned back, regarding her seriously. "I just need to know that this is what you want and not a result of what has happened in the last twenty-four hours."

Madison closed her eyes and tried to think, but all she could see were the detective's intensely blue orbs as she had pulled her down into that first kiss. The doctor leaned back into the cushions of the couch, needing to put some space between them so she could think, and immediately regretted her movement as her pelvis pressed even harder against Logan's. Fighting her physical desires, she tried to logically contemplate the question. *Is this what I want? God, yes, I want her. Is this a result of Susan's attack? Probably! Do I care? No. Yes.*

Knowing Logan was watching her, she ran a hand through her hair, pushing the long blond locks away from her flushed face. "I...I can't answer that. At least not completely." Her hands were restless, wanting only to resume their gentle caresses and explorations of the other woman's body. "Maybe. Probably. I—oh hell, Logan, I don't know."

Reaching to cup Logan's cheek, she smiled and leaned in, brushing her lips tenderly across Logan's. "I do know that I'm very attracted to you. Even though I've tried to force it to go away."

Logan released a quiet chuckle and moved up onto the couch beside Madison. "Well, Doctor, maybe we should slow this runaway train down a tad then." She lightly lifted the woman's chin with her fingers and looked deeply into the hooded green eyes. "I know, I feel the same attraction. I have from the first time I saw you on Smallman Street." Dipping her head to make sure the blonde could see her face, she continued, "I know I don't want you to do anything you'll regret tomorrow or next week." She leaned forward and gently kissed the doctor's forehead. "Why don't we just take it one day at a time and see what happens, okay?"

Smiling, Madison nodded. "I'd like that."

Both women sat back on the couch, relieved that they had agreed to explore their newly exposed feelings. After a while, Logan nervously stood and held out her hand for Madison. "Walk me to the door?"

Taking the detective's hand, Madison allowed herself to be pulled up into her arms again for another tender kiss. Once they reached the front foyer, Logan turned, and wrapping her arms around the doctor's waist, lowered her lips to warm waiting ones. Both were surprised by how quickly the kiss deepened and their breath grew rapid. Regretfully pulling away, the detective kissed Madison's cheek, sighed into her ear, said good night, and quickly left the house.

Closing the door behind the detective, Madison stood in the foyer, her back against the door, and listened as the sound of Logan's truck faded into the darkness before slowly padding up the stairs to what she knew would be a long, sleepless night.

CHAPTER ELEVEN

M orning was a welcome friend to Logan. Her nights during the past year had been difficult to endure, but this last one had proven to be even more disturbing than usual. She had returned home to an empty house and rather than going to bed, had sat in an old, comfortable chaise lounge in the sunroom, going over the last few hours she had spent with the doctor. The afternoon had been the most relaxing one she'd had in a very long time, and she knew without a doubt that the small blonde was the reason. What Logan couldn't figure out was what she was going to do about the feelings that were stirring within her soul.

Twenty minutes later, while she was sitting at the bar in the kitchen reading the morning edition of the *Post-Gazette* and quietly enjoying her second cup of coffee, the shrill ringing of the phone disturbed the peaceful silence of the house. The detective stared at the phone for two more rings before answering; she had hoped to spend the day cosseted in her house, away from the demons of the night and the realities of the day.

Logan dropped the paper in annoyance and practically snatched the phone off the wall, her voice leaving no doubt that the interruption was an unwelcome one. "McGregor."

"Logan?" The hesitant voice, almost a whisper, shook the detective from her dark mood and brought a gleaming smile to her face.

"Good morning." The gruffness was suddenly gone, replaced by what she would consider in others to be a sappy tone. "Did you sleep well?"

"Well, I've slept better, but, ah, yeah, I guess it was okay."

Logan could sense the hesitation in Madison's voice. Not sure how she should respond, she chose to keep the conversation on safe territory. "How did Officer Freeman work out last night? Did you have any problems?"

"Um, yes, I mean she was fine, and no there weren't any problems." Madison paused for a moment. "You know, I was wondering if you wanted...I mean, if you weren't doing anything today, if you might want to take a drive up to Midland with me. It's such an unusually warm day and, well, I board a couple of horses at a stable up there and, um, I know you said the other day that you liked to ride, and you see if I take one out and not the other I have a jealous horse on my hands...so."

"Yes, that sounds like a great idea. I love to ride." Suddenly, locking herself in the house was the furthest thing from Logan's mind. A smile came to her face and in her voice as she contemplated spending another day in the company of one very attractive doctor. "So how many other hidden pleasures do you harbor, Doctor?" *Jeez, McGregor, that was smooth, very smooth, you schmuck.*

"Well, you'll just have to stick around and find out now, won't you, Detective. Why don't I pick you up around eleven?"

The detective's heart skipped at the sound of the sultry voice, and then she frowned as she considered the prospect of the doctor driving into the city unescorted. "I'll make you a better offer. Why don't I pick you up at eleven? I know a great little café just outside of town where we can have brunch."

"Okay, but on one condition. Brunch is on me."

"Finally! I was beginning to think I was going to have to take out a second mortgage to keep you fed, woman."

Their easy repartee continued for a few more minutes, neither woman wanting to end the conversation. Finally, needing to finish dressing, Logan ended the call and headed to the bedroom, her step much lighter and confident than it was earlier in the morning.

The doctor prided herself on her obsessive qualities, always making sure her appearance was appropriate for the occasion. Normally she would have known exactly what to wear for an afternoon out riding; however, after thirty minutes of changing from one outfit to another, she was frustrated and becoming irritable. *What does it matter? After last night, I'm sure she doesn't want anything more than friendship.*

Finally deciding on the outfit she had put on first, Madison was walking down the curved staircase to the main floor when the doorbell rang. She smiled on observing that it was exactly eleven o'clock. *Why does that not surprise me? The perfectionist cop with perfect timing. What more could I ask for.*

On opening the door, Madison stood pleasantly surprised to see the detective in a pair of form-fitting faded blue jeans and a dark blue shirt that made the color of her eyes even more vibrant. She slowly perused

Logan's body, beginning at the Doc Martens, slowly rising to the slim hips and small waist, the strong muscular torso and broad shoulders. She knew she was making a fool of herself but couldn't tear her eyes away. Finally she looked into silently questioning dark blue eyes that were accented by a single raised eyebrow.

"Am I presentable, Doctor?" The teasing smile that spread across Logan's face rendered the growling inquiry ineffective as she watched Madison's face redden.

"Ahem, um, yes, very. I mean, you look fine, Detective. Come in." Madison stepped back from the doorway, allowing the detective to enter, and couldn't stop herself from noticing how well the tight jeans hugged Logan's small firm buttocks. "I, um, I'm just about ready. Why don't you have a seat and I'll, ah, just get my things."

Logan walked into the den and as she spied the couch, a flood of memories from the previous night ran through her head. She was still standing in the doorway a few moments later, reliving the tender moment they had shared, when Madison came up behind her and spoke.

"Afraid to return to the scene of the crime, Detective?"

Logan turned and found herself facing Madison, the scent of her perfume wrecking havoc on her senses. "Afraid? Not at all, Doctor. I was just savoring the moment." Their eyes held, neither woman willing or able to break the spell; then, in a moment of pure unrestrained need, the detective bent her head closer and captured the warm inviting lips.

Madison's arms circled the detective's slender neck and her fingers intertwined with her dark silky hair as she pulled her closer, her lips parting to accept the detective's warm, probing tongue. Breaths became ragged and heartbeats pounded as what had started as a leisurely kiss became needy with lust.

Logan's hands encircled Madison's waist, then dropped to cup her hips, pulling the doctor closer into her. Knowing the kiss was quickly turning into more than either needed, she pulled away, already aching and hungry for more. "Well, Doctor, if we don't get a move on, those two kids of yours won't be seeing us today."

Releasing a frustrated sigh, Madison nodded, knowing that she had to keep things slow with this mysterious woman. "Um, yes, you're right. We can't keep Steeler and Mercy waiting, now can we?" The doctor closed her eyes and unconsciously licked her lips. "Let's go get some lunch, I'm starving."

Madison treated the detective to brunch, then they traveled on to the Horse Around Stables, just outside of town. The view was breathtaking after they turned off the highway and cleared the trees and the thick green carpeting of pasture spread out before them.

"This is beautiful." Looking out the window, Logan could see nothing but wide-open space as horses ran across the green expanse, enjoying the freedom and safety of their home.

Madison drove farther down the long, winding road through the pastures until they reached the stables. The buildings appeared to be out of a Norman Rockwell painting, with picturesque stables and open fields. As they climbed down from the truck, Logan inhaled the freshest air she had smelt in ages, the subtle scents of grass, wood, and hay filling her senses.

Stepping into the stables, Madison instantly heard Mercy snorting. She ran over to the majestic horse, wrapping her arms around her neck. "Oh, baby, I've missed you." Hearing Steeler snort his own greeting, she quickly walked to the adjacent stall and embraced the other, slightly larger animal, kissing him on the end of his long nose. "I've brought company today, fellas, so we can all go out and have a nice ride together."

Logan stood back, enjoying watching the excited doctor play with her horses.

"You think I'm crazy, don't you?"

Walking over to Madison, Logan stroked Steeler's long neck. "Absolutely not. If I had these two beautiful horses, I'd be running around the stable like a little girl off for her first ride too."

Smacking the detective on the arm, Madison snarled mischievously. "Stop teasing me. It's been a long time since I've seen my babies." Turning back to Steeler, she gave him another tender caress. "I haven't seen them in almost three weeks."

Their conversation was interrupted as Sam, the resident stable master, came walking in. Logan thought he looked like a modern-day Roy Rogers dressed in his chaps and boots, his Stetson sitting low on his brow. The only thing missing was the guitar, but the detective suspected that it wasn't too far away. Madison made the introductions, and soon the horses were saddled and the two women were riding out into one of the vast pastures that made up the ranch.

The doctor led them northwest through the open pastures, then onto a wide, smooth riding trail into the woods. Taking in her surroundings, Logan watched Madison on Mercy in front of her, horse and rider moving together in a synchronous dance that revealed years of companionship. She had never warmed to anyone the way she had to the doctor and couldn't help but smile as she remembered their first few meetings. *Well, she certainly wasn't all warm and cuddly then, now, was she, McGregor?*

Logan's thoughts were broken as the doctor called out to her from ahead. "What did you say?"

Turning in the saddle, Madison regarded Logan curiously. "I've been talking to you for five minutes, Detective. Has the fresh air completely saturated your brain?"

Logan shrugged and grinned innocently as she gently heeled Steeler, urging him to catch up with the doctor and Mercy. "Um, no, I was just enjoying the view."

Shaking her head, Madison chuckled. "Well, just wait. In about five minutes we're going to clear the trees and you'll see one of the reasons I love to come up here so much."

As promised, Logan almost gasped when the embracing shadows of the woods receded to reveal a beautiful lake filled with deep blue, pristine water that reflected the surroundings. "Madi, this is absolutely breathtaking."

The doctor smiled, her heart warming at the sound of her nickname on the detective's lips. Reining in the horses, the women sat for a few moments appreciating the unspoiled landscape before them.

"I didn't know places like this existed any longer."

Madison gently nudged Mercy forward, toward the edge of the lake. "I didn't either until I boarded Mercy and Steeler here. It took me over a year to get them into the stables, but I'm certainly glad I waited. They love it here. So do I."

The women climbed down from the horses. Logan hadn't thought to ask what was inside the saddlebag and was surprised to see that Madison had packed quite a large selection of cheese, crackers, and wine. She had to turn away to keep the doctor from seeing the grin on her face. *Damn, that woman can put some food away.*

Madison handed Logan a blanket and asked her to pick out a spot, then secured the reins and removed the saddles, allowing the horses to roam free. She joined the detective on the blanket in the sun beside the water.

"Aren't you afraid they'll roam away?"

Lying back on the blanket, Madison put her hands under her head and smiled up into the sky, her body warming under the sun's gentle caress. "Nah, they won't go far. They've been out here many times. I hate to tie them to a tree. I guess I feel a little guilty sometimes for not being able to spend more time with them. I mean, they get a lot of attention from Sam, but it's just not the same." She glanced over at the detective. "I look at us being out here as an afternoon adventure for them, too. They'll snoop around for a while, then they'll settle down for a nice rest, just like we are."

Logan stretched her tall frame out on the blanket facing the petite blonde. "I see. I never thought of it that way. Is that why you took off the saddles?"

Madison smiled shyly at Logan, seeing her explanation had hit home. "Yes. I want them to enjoy the outing, too." She turned on her side, tilting her head. "So tell me, why did you decide you wanted to be a cop?"

Logan gave a gruff laugh as she turned her head to look out over the calming water. "It's a long story, but I guess you can say I wasn't really given a choice. It sort of found me."

Madison's eyebrows furrowed. "Did your parents make you go to the academy?"

Logan turned to lie back, tucking her hands beneath her head. "No, nothing quite as simple as that, I'm afraid." She had never told the story to anyone, not even to Wilson Hennessey, and she really didn't know where to start, or even if she wanted to. For some unknown reason, she felt a compelling need to tell Madison about her past, and she found herself in the midst of the story that had changed her life forever. "My brother was murdered when I was seventeen, and the cops in my hometown didn't do too much to investigate his death."

Madison listened quietly, having decided not to ask any questions for fear Logan would shut down.

"My family wasn't very well off financially. Hell, we weren't even able to pay our bills most of the time. The only work my *father* ever did was just enough to buy his next bottle of scotch." Looking over at the doctor, she released a frustrated sigh. "This isn't really very interesting, you know. Isn't there something better we can talk about?"

The pain and anger Logan felt toward her father was almost palpable, and Madison knew that she was embarrassed by her past. The doctor sensed that the detective hadn't told her story to too many others, and she also knew how good an emotional purging could be, so smiling at the other woman, she shook her head. "Nope, too late, you've already captured my undivided attention."

Logan sat up, her face turned so that Madison couldn't see the pain etched across her brow. "Anyway, my mother worked three jobs, trying to keep my brother and I fed and clothed. Richard, my brother, was four years older than me. He and my father would argue all the time because of Pop's drinking, lack of a job and the way he treated my mom."

Taking a deep breath, she focused on calming the anger that was raging in her gut. "Well, Mom had to have an operation, and since we couldn't afford insurance, the doctors refused to operate until we had the money to pay for it. Richard was on a full academic scholarship at the University of Kentucky, and when that happened, he quit college and got a job at a local grocery store to help raise the money."

Madison interrupted for the first time. "The hospital wouldn't allow you to make installment payments?"

Logan snorted. "No. We lived in a relatively small town outside of Lexington, and all the area docs knew my mom. They also knew she was the sole breadwinner in the family. I guess they thought if she were incapacitated, no one would be able to make the payments. You have to remember this was a while back, before the government required hospitals to provide a certain amount of indigent care."

Madison nodded. "Go on."

"Well, anyway, Richard had been working twelve-hour shifts for almost three months and still couldn't raise the money. Mom was getting worse by the day, missing work a lot, and her visits to the clinic were taking almost everything Richard made." Logan prayed the doctor couldn't see her face or the tears forming in her eyes. "It was an endless uphill battle and I think Mom and Richard finally realized that time was running out."

Running a hand through her hair, Logan tried to covertly wipe the tears from her eyes. "One night Mom got really sick, so I called the grocery store to get Richard to come home and found out he no longer worked there. He had quit three weeks before. His boss didn't know where he had gone after he quit and just assumed Richard had gone back to school."

The doctor sat up, easing herself closer to the detective, placing a supportive hand on her shoulder. She needed, in some small way, to let Logan know she was there—listening, not judging, supporting her through the pain.

Leaning into the gentle touch, Logan risked a glance into Madison's eyes. What she saw was not pity or disgust, but understanding and compassion. "When Richard got home late that night, I confronted him. We argued and finally he told me he was running drugs for a local dealer in order to get the money for Mom's surgery. He made me promise not to tell her and he promised that as soon as Mom was better he would return to school and get on with his life."

As Logan looked out over the water, thinking back on that night and the weeks that followed, a tear streaked her angular face. "Three nights later, Richard was shot in what was determined to be a bad drug deal. Although the local cops pretended to investigate, they didn't put too much effort into it, thinking that one more drug dealer dead was better than one more alive."

"You mean they just let it go and did absolutely nothing?"

Logan sighed. "Yeah, they did. Weeks went by and nothing ever happened—no arrests were made, *nada*—so I decided to start doing a little investigating on my own. I went to the dealer Richard worked for and asked him for a job. He knew how desperate we were to get the money for Mom, so he gave it to me. After a couple of months, I had the money and I was beginning to get some answers. A rival gang was responsible for Richard's death. They were trying to put the dealer I was working for out of business. The day Mom had her surgery, I went to the local police and told them what I had been doing and gave them the name of the guy responsible. All they did was laugh and threaten to arrest me."

Madison's face revealed her shock. "You're kidding me, right?"

"I wish I were, but no, they refused to do anything about it. I guess luck was with me, though. I was at the hospital, sitting in the waiting room when this big burly guy walked in and sat down across from me. We started talking, and I found out he was a reporter for the newspaper in Lexington. He was there for his father's surgery. We spent three days talking and getting to know each other and finally I told him what I knew about Richard's death."

Smiling, Logan shook her head. "He couldn't believe that nothing was being done about it either, and for the first time, I thought there might be hope, but a couple of days later he was gone and I was back to square one. I finally got to bring Mom home. Once she was able to take care of herself, I went out and found another job."

Madison ran her thumb gently over the detective's soft hand as she thought about all the pain the detective had lived through. "I guess your father was no help, then."

"My father was an asshole who only cared about one thing, his next drink. No, he was no help at all and continued to sit in that fucking chair every day, drinking and smoking. The only time we heard a word from him was when he ran out of smokes or booze."

Logan tried to calm her anger. "About a month later, this cop comes walking into the fast-food joint I was working at and asks for me. I just knew they had decided to come arrest me for what I had told them earlier, but instead this cop was actually the chief."

A smile flashed across the detective's face. "Supposedly, my newspaper friend had started snooping around and found out that what I told him was true. He called the police chief and threatened to expose the entire story if something wasn't done about it. The chief was there not to arrest me but to ask me for an official statement. Seems no one ever bothered to tell him my story, or so he said. Anyway, they eventually arrested the guy that killed Richard and he is now serving a life sentence upstate."

Madison knew in her gut that she hadn't heard the whole story and she gently caressed the detective's hand, letting her know she was there whenever Logan was ready to continue.

"A few months later, Mom got really sick again and we found out the surgery to remove the tumor came too late. She died a few weeks later."

Logan wiped away the tears that slipped down her cheeks. "After the funeral I went home, packed what I could carry into my backpack, and left. There was no way I was staying in that hellhole with that drunk, so I headed to Lexington. When I got there, I lived off the streets for a while until one day I was walking downtown and saw Jack Silverstein, the reporter from the hospital.

"I stopped him and we started talking. I told him everything that had happened since that day. He took me home with him that night, fed me and gave me a place to sleep, then got me a job in the mailroom at the newspaper the next day. Jack and I kept in touch and one day when we were having lunch in the park, he asked me if I wanted to ride the police beat with one of the crime reporters at the paper. I did, and not too long after that I found myself at the police academy and two years later, here in Pittsburgh."

Madison noticed the detective's small smile but remained quiet as she said, "Actually, Jacko introduced me to the only real friend I've ever had. His niece, Jennifer Phillips, is the crime reporter for the *Post-Gazette* and more often than not a pain in my ass when I'm working a case."

Lifting Logan's chin with her fingers, Madison turned the detective's face toward hers. "I can't believe you had to endure all of that alone, and I'm glad you found Jennifer to help you begin to rebuild your life. I don't think I would have had the strength to do it."

Using her thumb, Madison wiped away a tear that had slipped down the detective's face. "I know you probably thought I would be disgusted by your story, but you're wrong. I'm sorry for what you had to go through, but I'm also amazed at your determination and strength. You should be proud of yourself, Logan, that you beat the odds and turned out to be a good cop."

Smiling into the detective's deep blue eyes, she leaned in and gently placed a kiss on her lips, tasting the salt of her tears. "I know I'm very proud of you. Thank you for telling me your story. I know it was difficult."

A sad smile eased across the detective's face as she regarded the doctor. "I just wish my mom could have known that I escaped from that hellhole. I think she worried about that more than anything else."

Drawing Logan into her arms, Madison held her close and could feel the tension leaving the detective's shoulders. "Oh, I think your mom knows, and I think she is very proud of you too."

Madison lay back on the blanket, pulling Logan with her. They lay there holding each other for a long while until the doctor's stomach released a loud growl. With a chuckle, Logan lifted her head and looked down at the blonde's flat, muscular abdomen. "I think we need to feed the beast soon, or we might not survive the rest of the day."

In an attempt to hide her embarrassment, Madison crawled over to the bag, removing a bottle of wine and some crackers. The detective poured the wine and as she handed a cup to her companion, their eyes met and held. "Thank you." They were two simple words, but words that spoke volumes.

Raising her cup, Madison grinned at the detective. "To new beginnings."

Touching glasses, they drank of the sweet wine, wondering exactly where this new beginning would lead them.

CHAPTER TWELVE

The rest of the day was spent leisurely talking about their lives and jobs. The detective was curious about Madison's family but didn't press the topic when she saw a brooding look cross the doctor's face at the mention of her parents. Logan took the vague answers in stride, deciding that there had already been enough heavy conversations for one day.

They had walked around the lake and were packing up to leave when Logan noticed dark clouds moving in from the west. "Looks like we'd better hurry. Those clouds don't look very friendly."

Following Logan's line of sight, Madison frowned. "I should have known this pleasant weather wouldn't last." She blew out a shrill whistle and watched as Steeler and Mercy trotted over.

"You really have those guys trained well. I would never have believed that you could let them roam free and not be afraid they would wander off, much less have them come when you call them."

"Horses are very intelligent animals, but Steeler and Mercy are special and know they are loved and cared for, so they show their appreciation by being loyal and trustworthy." Madison nuzzled Mercy's neck with her face. "Aren't you, girl?"

Logan cocked her head, her curiosity getting the better of her. "Okay, I give. What's so special about these two, other than the fact you spoil them rotten?"

Chuckling, Madison mounted Mercy and waited for Logan to follow. "I do spoil them, but they deserve it. I got them from a horse rescue organization. They had been removed from a farm in Montana after they were found beaten and half starved. They had been fed molding hay and were severely neglected. Mercy was almost dead when they got her, and Steeler wasn't far behind. When I heard about them through a friend, I just couldn't resist, so I took them both."

Logan looked at the animals with a keen eye, and for the first time noticed the thin scars that streaked their flanks. "You've done a great job getting them healthy. I would have never known their history if you hadn't told me. How long have you had them?"

As they rode back toward the stables, Madison leaned down and tenderly stroked Mercy's neck, cooing when Mercy whinnied back in response to her affections. "I've had them for almost three years now. They were both about a year old when I got them. I lived in the city at the time and had to find a place where I could keep them, so I rented a small farm about five miles from where I live now. The house was practically in shambles, but it had a great barn for the kids and a large fenced-in area for them to exercise."

She glanced over at Logan and decided to reveal all. "I actually ended up sectioning off a corner of the barn and making it into a bedroom. God knows it was probably safer than living in the house. I would shower, change, and eat most of my meals at the hospital. I think most of my associates thought I had lost my mind. Of course, the ones that knew me well took it all in stride."

A grin lit Logan's face. "Somehow I find it hard to get a visual of you living in a barn, Doctor."

Madison laughed. "Yeah, me too sometimes. I tried to get them boarded here at the stables to begin with, but the waiting list was long and they require their boarders have a one-year record of good health as well as a variety of shots and tests prior to their acceptance."

The doctor patted her horse's neck. "After eight months of living in the barn, I decided I couldn't handle it anymore, so I bought the property that my house is on and built. By the time the house was completed, Mercy and Steeler were accepted here, and the rest is history."

"I guess after practically living with them for a year, you really miss spending time with them, don't you?"

A sad smile crossed the doctor's face. "Yes, I do. The time we spent together was a growing time for both of us. They needed so much attention medically and emotionally, and being there allowed me the chance to give them that. I think that is one reason they responded so well, because they knew I wasn't going to beat them or leave them." Looking at the detective, she tilted her head to one side and smiled shyly. "You know, people aren't the only beings with feelings and emotions. Animals have them, too. They have their own way of showing love, devotion, and even appreciation for what we do for them."

They rode along in silence for a while, enjoying what was left of their day, the shelter of the wooded trail providing a barrier against the quickly cooling wind. They were less than a mile from the stable when Mercy suddenly shied and reared up, hurling Madison off backward to land with a thud on the hard dirt path.

Logan jumped off Steeler's back and rushed over to the doctor. "Hey, are you all right? Lie still. Let's make sure nothing's broken." As she knelt beside Madison, Logan looked up to see Steeler snorting, backing up in the direction from which they had come. Looking ahead, the detective spotted the source of their fear and agitation: a rattlesnake lying in the middle of the path. In a low whisper, she said, "Don't move."

Easing to her feet, Logan walked back toward Steeler. When she reached him, she gently stroked his neck while fumbling with the strap on the saddlebag. Finding her gun, she moved forward a few feet toward the doctor, but before she could get any closer, the snake slithered toward the fallen woman. In a lightning-quick movement, Logan raised her revolver and fired one shot, striking the snake in the head, before quickly returning to Madison's side.

Madison sat up, wincing as a sharp pain seared her hip. "Go see about the horses. I'm fine, but they don't know what's going on."

Seeing that Madison was relatively uninjured, Logan returned to the animals and stroked their necks, whispering soothing words and reassuring them of their safety. They soon calmed under her gentle touch and she walked them back toward their owner.

Madison was astonished at how quickly the detective was able to calm Mercy and Steeler. "You're good with them. They trust you."

Logan regarded the horses. "Well, I always have gotten along better with animals than I have people, I guess." She held out a hand for Madison to grasp, and once she was on her feet and convinced nothing was broken, they remounted the horses and resumed their journey. They had only ridden a short distance when the sound of galloping hooves broke the silence of the woods, and seconds later the doctor spotted Sam racing toward them.

Sam slowed his horse as he neared them. "I heard shots. Are you two okay?"

Nodding, Madison glanced over toward Logan, then back at the weather-worn stable master. "Yes, Sam, we're fine. Seems like there was a wandering rattler out in the path as we were riding in, and it spooked Mercy. Detective McGregor took care of things. Believe me, she has a darn good aim. I don't think you'll have to worry about it again."

The stable master gave Logan a long studious look, then smiled. "It seems odd that there would be a rattler out this time of year." Scratching his head, he looked back and forth between the two women. Realizing his help wasn't needed, the cowboy reset the Stetson low on his head and nodded toward the women. "Well, as long as you're all right, I'll just be on my way."

"We'll see you in a few minutes Sam, and thanks." Madison laughed as she watched the stable master's retreating back, then turned to her companion. "I think you hurt his feelings."

With a smirk, Logan lifted her hands in the air. "What? What did I do?"

Chuckling, Madison heeled Mercy onward before glancing back over her shoulder at Logan, still sitting on Steeler with a confused look on her face. "I'm thinking ole Sam there was running to the rescue and you just took the wind out of his sails, Detective."

Rolling her eyes, Logan trotted Steeler beside Mercy. "Yeah, well, I don't remember seeing you too concerned with ole Sam's feelings while you were sitting on your ass in the middle of the path, Doctor."

Madison bit back a smile. She was enjoying teasing the detective and suddenly realized how much fun she'd had that weekend. As they rounded the last bend and the stables came into view, an empty feeling shrouded her at the thought that her day with the alluring woman would soon come to an end.

Once the horses were comfortably back in the stable, Logan walked outside and stood by the truck while Madison whispered her good-byes to the horses, pulling the last of the treats from her pocket. She noticed how tender and caring the doctor was with Mercy and Steeler and wondered if the same gentleness carried over to her patients. *Of course it does. That's why she is one of the most sought-after surgeons in the city.*

Limping out of the stable a few minutes later, Madison tossed Logan the keys and headed for the passenger side of the truck. "Do you mind driving?"

Logan unlocked the door and held on to the doctor's arm as she eased herself up into the seat. "Are you sure you're okay? Do we need to go to Mercy and get some x-rays of your, um, butt?"

Scowling at her companion, Madison winced as she settled herself into the seat. "No, Detective, I'm fine. I am a doctor after all."

Logan walked around the truck and climbed in the driver's seat, then turned toward Madison. "I know you're a doctor. That's what concerns me. I don't think you people make very good patients, do you?"

Madison waved her hand in the air, dismissing the detective's remark as she tried to find a comfortable position, and growled, "Just drive, McGregor. I didn't tell you how to shoot the snake today, don't you start telling me how to treat myself."

Trying to hide a grin, Logan started the truck and turned out onto the highway. "My, my, we get a little grumpy when we don't feel too good, don't we?"

Madison didn't reply, just growled as she leaned against the door, willing the pain in her buttocks away.

As they drove toward Bridgeville, the easy banter they had shared earlier gave way to a reflective silence. As if their thoughts were synchronized, both women spoke at once. An uncomfortable silence filled the air as neither knew whether to speak or listen, with Logan ultimately deferring to Madison.

"I was, um, wondering if you'd like to stay for dinner." Sneaking a sidelong glance at the detective, she noticed her eyebrows furrow. "Of course, I know you're probably tired, so I underst—"

"No, not at all. I was just thinking that I probably need to check in with the precinct." Turning her head, she smiled at the doctor. "I'd love to stay, but on two, no, three conditions."

"Okay."

Logan enjoyed seeing the curious look on the doctor's face. "You let me borrow your phone to call in, *and* you let me borrow your shower." The detective grinned as she sniffed the air. "From the looks of where you're sitting, I must not smell too good. If you're not careful, you just may fall out of the truck."

Curling her lip up in a snarl, Madison shifted her weight to her other side. "You don't smell bad, McGregor, I'm just propping."

Patting the seat, Logan glanced over toward the doctor. "Well, why don't you lie down in the seat and put your head on my lap. Maybe that will take some of the pain out of your a—"

"Don't even say it." Growling, Madison rolled her eyes as she eased her way across the seat and laid her head on Logan's lap, looking up into her smiling face. "A rattlesnake killer and a comedian to boot. You could be rich, Detective."

Logan's hand dropped and lay comfortably along Madison's side as they drove toward Bridgeville. *Careful, McGregor, the water is getting deep.*

"Now what's the third condition, Detective?" Madison closed her eyes.

"Well, this one is a little more risky. I'll stay if you agree to ice your, um, butt while I cook dinner."

The doctor landed a light slap on Logan's leg before laying her hand on the detective's firm quads. "Okay, okay, you win. Just make sure it's something good. If I have to put ice on my ass, you have to suffer too."

Chuckling, Logan eased her hand down Madison's side, gently caressing the bruised hip. "Anything you want, Doctor."

They rode along in silence as the truck filled with the soft melodic sounds from the stereo. The last thing the small blonde remembered before falling asleep was the sound of the detective's voice humming along with the music and how at peace she felt lying on Logan's lap.

CHAPTER THIRTEEN

Logan turned the Pathfinder into Madison's drive just as the sun was setting behind the trees. Gently shaking the sleeping woman's shoulder, she reached over to retrieve Madison's backpack from the floorboard. "Hey there, sleepyhead, we're home." *Damn, I like the sound of that.*

Slowly opening her eyes, Madison blinked several times to get her bearings and realized she was staring at the steering column. Her eyes lifted and she focused on Logan's smiling face. "I'm sorry. I didn't mean to fall asleep on you."

Tracing the strong line of Madison's jaw with her finger, Logan couldn't help but reflect on how comfortable she felt with her. "You obviously needed a nap. You fell asleep not long after we left the ranch."

When she pushed herself up in the seat, Madison winced as a searing pain shot through her hip. "I know I'll definitely be going to see my chiropractor in the morning." She took Logan's hand in her own. "Thanks for driving home. I really don't think I could have done it."

Logan knew the pain must be bad for Madison to so readily admit she couldn't function properly. "Are you sure you don't want to have your hip checked out tonight?"

"Nope. If I remember correctly, you're cooking dinner and I'm icing my, um, bruise." She gingerly slid across the seat and eased out of the truck, then stood for a moment before slowly making her way toward the house, the detective following close behind.

Logan unlocked and pushed open the door for Madison and then took her hand, leading her into the den and onto the couch. "You sit and try to make yourself comfortable. Just tell me where I can find an ice pack and I'll bring it to you."

Femur trotted into the room and stopped short at seeing his mistress lying on the couch, obviously in pain. Easing beside her, he gently licked her cheek and whined. Madison mussed his fur and whispered, "Hey, baby. Mama's fine, she just got her ass kicked today." Satisfied that his mistress was all right, Femur looked up at Logan, whining and licking his lips.

Bending down, Logan scratched Femur's back, reassuring him that everything was in order. "Hey there, big guy, are you hungry?" Femur's bark echoed through the house as he frolicked around the den. "Okay, okay, hold your horses a minute." Looking back at Madison, she chuckled. "Where's the ice pack and the dog food?"

Madison lay face down on the couch after giving the detective the instructions. As she climbed the stairs, Logan felt a strange but exciting flutter in her stomach. *Chill, McGregor, you're getting an ice pack, not taking her to bed.*

Upon entering the master bedroom, the detective looked around, seeing Madison's personal touch on everything in the room. The walls were painted light beige, with a vaulted ceiling sloping down toward a window trimmed with a burgundy-and-beige valance. Sheers covered the window, allowing the early morning light in as the sun slid over the distant horizon. An arrangement of dried flowers hung above the bed, and the scent of eucalyptus drifted through the room. The king-size bed was covered with a burgundy-and-beige comforter, with matching sheets that she felt an overpowering temptation to run her hands across.

Logan looked to her right, eyeing the doorway leading into the master bath. She walked across the thick carpet, and on entering the bathroom, once again saw Madison's personal style reflected in the décor. Walls painted a shade lighter than the bedroom walls set off the Italian marble floors. A custom-built dressing table stretched the length of an entire wall and held twin marble basins at each end.

On the opposite wall was the largest Jacuzzi Logan had ever seen, surrounded on three sides by a marble ledge that held numerous plants and several bottles of bath oils. Stepping closer, the detective peered out the window that stretched the length of the Jacuzzi and saw a myriad of swirling colors paint the sky as the sun began its nightly descent. Her eyes trailed a path further down, and she spotted a hot tub tucked discreetly inside a gazebo and surrounded by a small copse of trees. *You really like your comfort, Doctor.*

Realizing she had been away for too long, Logan shook herself out of the daydream and quickly retrieved the ice pack from beneath the sink before walking back down the stairs and into the kitchen. After filling Femur's bowl with food and the pack with crushed ice, she went back into the den and found the doctor asleep on the couch. Kneeling down beside the slumbering woman, she placed a hand on her shoulder and gently nudged her until sleepy eyes blinked open. "Hey there."

Groaning, Madison tried to sit up but was stopped by a firm hand to her back. "No, just lie still."

Logan knew she couldn't get the ice pack in place without some assistance. "Um, could you, ah, maybe undo your jeans so I can put this on your, ah, bruise?"

Smiling at the detective's obvious discomfort, Madison reached under her body, releasing the snap on her jeans and lowering the zipper before easing back down onto the couch.

With trembling, yet gentle hands, Logan eased the jeans down until she saw the bruise that covered most of the doctor's left buttock. "Jesus, Madison, this is terrible. I really think we should drive into the city and have you looked at tonight."

Madison twisted her head around until she saw the dark contusion. "Damn. I knew it was bruised, but I didn't know I fell that hard." She sighed. "I promise, if it's not better by the morning, I'll have one of my associates take a look at it, but I'm sure it's only a bad contusion." She smiled shyly into the Logan's scowling eyes. "Nothing a little ice and dinner won't fix right up."

Shaking her head in defeat, Logan glared at Madison. "Fine, all right, you win." As she walked out of the den and into the foyer, she called back over her shoulder, "You leave that ice on until I come back, Doctor, and that's an order. Don't make me cuff you."

Madison's attempt to block the images that flashed through her brain was for naught. Burying her head in the pillow, she released a frustrated breath. *Now, I just might like that treatment.*

Picking up the phone in the kitchen, Logan called the precinct. "Hey, McGregor here. Have the labs come back on the Richardson or Cavanaugh cases yet?" She listened quietly as the officer recited the reports. When he was finished, she hung up the phone, assimilating the information. *Finally, a little break.*

Fifteen minutes later, she eased back into the den and removed the ice pack from the doctor's hip. Taking a light blanket from the back of the couch, she placed it gently over Madison and returned to the kitchen to cook dinner.

Madison awoke to the seductive sounds of Enya playing in the background and the alluring aroma of what had to be spaghetti cooking. Tentatively turning over, she smiled as she felt the blanket against her back, knowing the detective had placed it there. She stood and padded down the hall to the guest bathroom.

After brushing her teeth and combing her hair, she walked to the kitchen door and spied the detective at the stove, stirring the delicious-smelling sauce. Unnoticed, she stood there for a few moments, studying Logan's profile. Her eyes lingered on the outline of the small but perfectly round breasts before rising higher to a long, slender neck and a strong jaw line that angled sharply into a perfect dimpled chin, which was offset by the most tempting lips Madison had ever tasted. *I could get used to you, Logan McGregor.*

Feeling an odd sensation throughout her body, Logan turned to see Madison watching her, her eyes hungry and needy with lust. Their eyes held each other captive for a long moment before the blonde self-consciously broke the intent look. "I have a feeling I've been snookered."

Cocking her head to the side, Logan grinned at Madison, her face looking innocent yet teasing. "Well. Whatever do you mean by snookered, Doctor?"

Madison walked over to the stove and lifted the lid of the saucepan after playfully snatching the potholder from the detective's hand. She leaned over the steaming sauce, taking in the aroma of olives, garlic, oregano, and other assorted spices, then turned to the smiling detective. "I think you've been holding out on me. This smells delicious."

Logan snatched the potholder from Madison's hand, lifted the boiling pot of pasta from the stove, and poured the contents into a colander. Glancing back over her shoulder, she revealed one of her most seductive grins. "Doctor, if you stick around, you'll find out I have all kinds of surprises up my sleeve."

Swallowing hard, Madison attempted to hide the heat racing through her body but knew the warmth in her face revealed her true emotions. Stepping closer to Logan, she leaned in close, her eyes locking with deep pools of blue. "I'm sure you do, Detective, and if you stick with me, I'll show you a few of my own."

As if by its own volition, Logan's head lowered, bringing their faces closer. She could feel the heat radiating off the doctor's body and her lips parted slightly as she gently brushed them across Madison's. She hadn't intended the kiss to awaken her emotions, nor had she expected her physical responses to be so powerful, and soon she found herself pulling the doctor closer, hungry and aching for more.

Madison's arm slid around a trim waist and her hands fell to cup firm, taut muscles, drawing the detective closer. She gasped as a long, slender leg slid between hers, making contact with her hard, aching clitoris. Her tongue challenged Logan's as their breathing became ragged and harsh. She could feel the detective's hard nipples pressing against her chest and knew her passion was matched with that of the tall, dark woman before her.

Logan's hands feathered down Madison's cheek, tracing a thin line down to the small vee in her neck. She could feel the rapid rise and fall of the blonde's chest and released a primal moan as she felt a strong leg slip between her own. She knew she needed to slow down, but her body refused to yield as the hunger she had kept locked away for the past few days overtook her senses. Her hands slipped farther down, and she heard as much as felt the sharp intake of breath as her fingers brushed lightly across the doctor's erect nipples.

Madison grasped Logan's hips, demanding the intimate closeness as her tongue invaded Logan's warm mouth, seeking solace from the hunger burning in her gut. She slid her hands around her slender waist, feeling the detective's taut abdominal muscles quiver in response to her delicate touch.

Tugging Logan's shirt from the waistband of her jeans, Madison slipped her hands beneath the thin material and traced her fingers across the smooth skin of the detective's stomach, smiling when she heard her sharp gasp. She outlined the tall woman's ribs beneath her fingers, and her thumbs traced the swell of Logan's breasts.

A low moan escaped the detective's throat as Madison continued higher, searching, seeking, until finally she gently cupped the firm, aching breasts in her hands.

"Oh my God, Madi." Logan's mind reeled from the gentle caresses and her hips, responding to the onslaught of sensations, pressed harder against Madison's thigh. "Do you have any idea what you do to me?"

A seductive grin crossed Madison's face as she focused her eyes on Logan's swollen, ready lips. "No, but give me a few more minutes and I intend to find out."

Growling an incomprehensible reply, Logan captured the doctor's tantalizing lips with her own as a fire raged out of control in her body. She turned off the stove, took Madison in her arms, and in one swift movement lifted her onto the island in the center of the kitchen, ever mindful of her bruised hips. As she stepped between the doctor's open thighs, she felt strong legs wrapping around her waist, pressing her closer, harder against the heat that radiated from the blonde's center.

Logan's hands were trembling as she fumbled with the buttons on Madison's oxford shirt, releasing one and then another until at last soft, smooth, silky skin was revealed to her hands. She dropped her head, feathering kisses along the soft, delicious neck as she unclasped the satin bra. The detective lifted her head and peered into half-closed eyes, dark with desire, that became even darker and filled with lust as her fingers slipped beneath the straps of the bra, sliding the garment off the blonde's shoulders.

Logan's breath was ragged with desire, her chest rising and falling in a rapid cadence with her heart. "You are so beautiful." She could feel the wetness between her own legs as she gazed upon Madison's erect dark nipples. Slowly, almost reverently, she traced the outline of the small breasts with her fingers, never touching the hard, aching nipples as she once again captured warm lips with her own.

Madison's grip became firmer, more demanding as the sensual ministrations continued, and the detective could feel the rhythmic thrust of the doctor's hips against her own. Logan knew she was lost, knew there was no stopping for either of them until the fire that burned within was quenched.

As she lowered her head, tracing the surging pulse in Madison's neck with her lips, she came to the shallow vee of throat. Bending lower, she followed the line of the blonde's sternum until she reached the valley between the small breasts and turned her head slightly to nip the soft skin.

Madison's fingers intertwined with Logan's dark hair as she urged her closer, needing to feel the detective's warm lips on her aching nipples. "Oh God, please."

The pleading voice in her ear was all Logan needed as her lips gently seized the hard nipple. She gasped as Madison urgently pulled her shirt higher and searching hands made contact with her burning skin. She felt Madison tenderly push against her shoulders, forcing her to relinquish her hold on the hard nipple as the doctor pulled the shirt and sports bra over her head.

Before Logan could resume her sensual attack, Madison's hand pressed against the back of her head, pulling her down to warm lips and a demanding tongue that consumed her. The detective felt as if she were in a vortex, spiraling out of control as bare skin pressed against bare skin and breast met breast.

Madison's hands were searching, exploring, aching to feel every inch of the detective's body as her hunger raged. She released the button and lowered the zipper of Logan's jeans. Easing her hands beneath the waistband, she began sliding the jeans down slender hips when a shrill beep echoed throughout the kitchen and she immediately felt the dark-haired woman tense.

Logan released an angry groan as she tore her lips from Madison's. She pulled the pager from her waistband and pressed a small button to silence the instrument. Without looking at the display, she tossed the offending device across the island before once again seizing Madison's lips.

Amassing all of her resolve, Madison pressed against Logan's shoulders, breaking the kiss. "You know you have to answer that."

Logan bent to resume the kiss but was held away by strong, determined arms. Releasing a frustrated breath, she raked her hand through her hair, then stepped back. "Damn, this better be good, or someone is definitely going to get hurt."

Releasing her own frustrated groan as the warmth of the detective's body vanished, Madison watched as Logan retrieved the pager from where it had landed on the floor beneath the table. Suddenly feeling self-conscious, she picked up the oxford shirt from behind her and draped it over her shoulders, pulling it over her exposed breasts. Hearing a menacing growl, she turned to see the same dark expression on the detective's face that she had seen in the parking lot of the hospital two days before when her truck had been vandalized. "What is it?"

Logan explained as she punched in the number to the precinct. "It's the lieutenant, which means it can't be good news."

Knowing the night was over, Madison slid off the counter and readied the coffeemaker. She knew Logan was already tired and would more than likely be awake the rest of the night and that she herself would probably not get much sleep. She listened quietly as Logan spoke to the lieutenant.

"Yes, okay, I'll meet him at his office. I'm about thirty minutes away. I'll be there as soon as I can." As soon as Logan placed the phone in the base, Madison handed her a cup of coffee. "That was quick."

Grinning, Madison turned to get her own cup. "One thing I learned in medical school is that one of the best investments a doctor can make is buying a Bunn coffeemaker. We never know when we'll have to get up in the middle of the night, and believe me when I tell you that you don't want me out on the streets when I'm half asleep."

Nodding, Logan took a long swallow of the fresh coffee, then looked back into dark green eyes that were still hungry with desire. "I'm really sorry, but I have to go." Setting the mug on the counter, she pulled Madison into her arms and tenderly kissed her warm lips. "I promise I'll make it up to you." *Right, McGregor. How many times did you say that to Diane?*

Madison held the detective tight against her body, already missing the warm contact. "Can you tell me what happened? Is it the Strip District killer?"

"Yes. There's another victim tonight, but this time it's different." Stepping back from Madison, she ran her hands through her dark, silky hair. "Tonight he killed a Langston Development executive. Thomas Peters, the name on the business card left on his first victim."

Madison's eyes widened. "So this does have something to do with Langston Development, just like you said."

After taking another long drink, Logan began gathering her clothes. "Yes. Unfortunately it took him killing someone within the inner sanctum to finally get me into Langston Development." She quickly put on her bra and shirt. "After I visit the scene, I'm headed into the city to see none other than C.W Langston himself. Maybe now I can finally get some answers."

Madison walked the detective to the door, and as her hand touched the door handle, she was turned around, then the detective's lips captured hers in a long deep kiss, revealing her frustration and regret at having to leave.

"I'm really am sorry about this, and I promise, I will make it up to you." A sudden uncertainly filled Logan's mind as she closely watched Madison's reaction. "That is, if you want me to."

Madison gently caressed Logan's cheek. "If I want you to?" She seductively slid her tongue across the detective's bottom lip, making her groan, then forced herself to back away from Logan, knowing that the close contact was only delaying her departure. "Yes, I definitely want you to. Will you call me when you have time?"

The detective felt an overwhelming urge to kiss Madison again but knew it wasn't a good idea in the presence of the officer guarding the doctor's house, so she simply nodded. "Yes. As soon as I can."

Madison watched as Logan stopped by the police cruiser and spoke to the officer inside before climbing into her truck and driving away. She stood on the front porch watching the taillights fade into the darkness before entering the house and closing the door. Leaning back against it, she blew out a frustrated sigh and raked her hand through her disheveled blond hair before heading to the kitchen for a second cup of coffee, knowing sleep would not be her companion that night.

CHAPTER FOURTEEN

As Logan drove along the interstate back into the city, she replayed the conversation she'd had with the lieutenant. Thomas M. Peters was the chief financial officer of Langston Development, as well as the first executive singled out by the killer. Logan had wracked her brain trying to piece together some connection between the murders and Langston Development. Hopefully, now that one of his own had been claimed, C.W. Langston would become more cooperative with her investigation.

She turned into the gated community where Thomas Peters resided and saw the flashing lights of police cars disrupting the tranquility of the exclusive neighborhood. Stopping at the gate, she displayed her badge to the ashen-faced guard, then drove down the well-manicured street. Peters's neighbors, dressed only in robes, stood on their lawns, stunned, as they watched uniformed officers milling around his million-dollar home.

Pulling in behind a police cruiser, she turned off the engine and sat for a moment, taking in her surroundings. It struck her as odd that someone could enter such a well-protected neighborhood unnoticed. The blink of the motion detector lights on the side of the residence caught her eye as an officer broke the electric beam. Climbing down from the truck, she nodded to a uniformed officer as he held up the yellow crime scene tape for her to pass.

As she stepped into the foyer, Logan's first reaction was amazement; every nook and cranny exuded the wealth of its owner. Spotting her partner, Phil Dvorak, and Aaron Rodgers in the far corner of the living room, the detective made her way across the room as members of the CSI team worked nearby.

She nodded as she approached her partner and noticed the dark circles under his eyes as well as the lines that creased his face from lack of sleep and too much stress. "Hey, Dove, what ya got?"

Eyeing Logan with tired eyes, Phil Dvorak tipped his head toward the stairs. "We got a dead rich guy, a shitload of blood, and vultures that call themselves the press outside chomping at the bit to get the scoop for the early edition."

Logan frowned at her partner and laid her hand on his shoulder. "Hey, big guy, you okay?"

Massaging the back of his neck, Dove nodded, giving Logan an apologetic smile. "Sorry, Mac. Yeah, I'm just tired, same as you, and frustrated that we can't seem to catch a break on this case. Come on, let's go upstairs. I wouldn't let them move the body until you got here, and the M.E. is chomping at the bit to get back home to the wife that's half his age."

Snickering under her breath, Logan climbed the stairs to the master bedroom. The first thing she noticed was the blood splattered across the room. Dove stood silently beside her, accustomed to the methods his partner implemented when investigating a crime scene. Logan never asked a lot of preliminary questions, preferring to form her own opinions, and Dove watched as her eyes focused in the near corner of the room, then slowly panned around the perimeter, taking in every small detail of the room.

Once she had her bearings, Logan slowly walked across the thick beige carpeting. She knelt beside the body of Thomas Peters, her hands tucked into the pockets of her jeans. She began at the victim's head, noting the large indentation in the skull. Her examination continued as she looked at the soulless eyes staring into space and the dried blood streaking his face. As her eyes moved lower, she saw that every finger had been broken in what had to be a long, drawn-out struggle for control between the murderer and the victim. She paused as she absorbed the information, deciding the killer had been either excessively violent just for the hell of it or desperate for some information the man held. For the time being, she chose to believe the latter.

As her eyes followed the path of violence down Thomas Peters's naked torso, her stomach lurched when she saw his severed testicles lying between spread legs. Her assessment continued as her eyes fell upon his shattered kneecaps and the bare and broken feet lying at odd angles to the rest of his body. The only comforting thought she had, if it could be called comforting, was that she now had an idea of who the next victim would be. The real test was about to begin: finding the killer before he had a chance to find the director of human resources, Phillip R. Crafton.

Standing, Logan walked back toward Dove and raised her eyebrows while tipping her head toward the door. Harold Simons, the medical examiner, called out to her as she was leaving the room. "Detective, I really need to get a move on here. Are you finished with the body?"

Hearing Dove's snicker, Logan shot a scowling look his way before turning back toward the M.E. "Yeah, sure, Doc, you can bag him."

Logan and Dove walked the length of the hallway and down the stairs in silence. She raked a hand through her hair as they cleared the doorway and took in a deep breath of fresh air. In all her years on the force, she had never gotten use to the sweet but pungent smell of fresh human blood.

Quietly she led her partner to a cruiser far away from the keen hearing of the reporters standing on the other side of the police line. Glancing into the crowd, she spotted Jennifer Phillips standing in the crowd. She knew Jennifer would come after her the minute she crossed the tape, but for the moment, she had other things to worry about. "Dove, what are your thoughts on this victim thus far?"

Taking a moment to sort his thoughts, he took a looked around, wondering if Logan was truly interested in his ideas or just testing him as she often did on cases. "From the looks of the body and the violence involved, I believe the killer is making a statement to C.W. Langston that he is really pissed. From the apparent injuries, the killer tortured the victim for quite some time and obviously thought Peters had information that he wanted." Looking at Logan, he saw her intense but thoughtful eyes upon him, taking in everything he was saying. "As for the testicles, who knows? Maybe it was a personal message."

Nodding, Logan absorbed her partner's opinion. "What about his next victim? Do you think he's going to follow the path back up to old man C.W. himself?"

"You'd think so, but then again, he should know we'll have Phillip Crafton under constant surveillance."

Logan smiled at her partner before nodding in agreement. "My thoughts exactly. I'm putting my money on Lester Donovan being his next target. This guy is smart but he's beginning to screw up. His last intended victim survived, and we have her and the only other person that can identify him under lock and key." Logan felt a knot beginning to form in her stomach as her next thought hit home. "He's either going after Donovan, *or* he's going to try to get to Susan Richardson or Dr. Cavanaugh while we run in the other direction."

Pushing off from the side of the car, Logan regarded her partner sympathetically. "Why don't you check in with the hospital and make sure Ms. Richardson is all right? Wake Donovan up, if he isn't already, and put a uniform on him, and then go home and get some sleep while you still have a few hours before your next shift."

Walking away before her partner could argue, she made a beeline to her truck, hoping to avoid Jennifer for the time being.

Sitting in a leather wingback chair, C.W. Langston sipped on his third scotch since being disturbed a little after nine o'clock with the news of Thomas Peters's murder. He had immediately come to his office on Penn Avenue and called in his best political ally, Herbert Whittaker. Across from him, also on his third scotch, Herbert Whittaker couldn't help but feel partially guilty for Thomas Peters's death. *If I hadn't buckled under C.W.'s demands and had allowed the police to question the Langston executives earlier, Peters might still be alive, as well as several other innocent victims.*

The mayor took a healthy swig from his glass and let the scotch go down slowly, burning away his cowardice along the way. "C.W., you know that avoiding the police is out of the question. There isn't anything else I can do to keep them from questioning all of you now that he has killed one of your own."

Scowling, Langston stood up and paced the floor, swirling the amber liquid in his glass. "I need a little more time, Herbert, and I'm expecting you to get it for me." Feeling not a twinge of guilt, C.W. Langston turned toward his friend. "Herbert, you have an election coming up soon; I would really hate to have to break in a new mayor, because I kind of like you."

To Langston, *friend* was just another way of describing a puppet in his high-stakes game of life. As long as people played by C.W. Langston's rules, their lives and careers were safe and secure. However, if they decided not to follow Langston's directives, they often found themselves out on the streets looking for a new life far away from Pittsburgh and Langston.

Langston's influence was far reaching, and he had often seen powerful men and women reduced to floundering outcasts at the snap of his fingers. He had never had the desire to become involved in politics himself but had found a much better, more economical way of getting what he wanted by either buying a politician off or uncovering information that would destroy that politician if the information ever reached the wrong hands. C.W. Langston much preferred the latter method because it gave him so much more control over his puppets. Smiling, he turned back toward the mayor and was about to speak when a sharp knock came through the door. Walking over, he pulled the heavy oak door open and stared into the face he had seen a few days prior in the newspaper—Logan McGregor.

Tossing the medical journal aside, Madison gently pushed herself off the couch and padded into the kitchen to get more ice for her aching hip, regretting her decision not to go into the city to have it x-rayed. As she eased her body back onto the couch, she spied Femur lying in the corner and instantly regretted her brooding behavior. Patting her thigh, she whistled for the pup, and he trotted over, laying his head in her lap. Scratching his ears, she looked into his sad eyes and knew she had frightened and confused him. She reassured him that everything was okay. "Baby boy, it's not you. I'm just one frustrated and hurting woman tonight."

Madison lay back on the ice pack and stroked Femur's head as she thought about the wonderful day she had spent with Logan McGregor. Femur watched her intently, turning his head sideways as she spoke to him. "What am I going to do about that woman, Femur? God knows, I don't need anyone complicating my life right now, especially a cop, for God's sake."

Whining, Femur jumped onto the couch and settled his body next to Madison's in an attempt to provide her the same comfort she had given him during his recovery. Smiling, the doctor continued her musing. *So, what's so bad about cops? Nothing! Surely they aren't all like Loraine Osborne; at least Logan doesn't seem to be.*

Deciding nothing would come of her contemplations, Madison returned to the kitchen, placed the ice pack in the freezer, and headed to bed. Sliding beneath the fresh sheets, she became aware of how much she already missed the warmth of Logan's body next to hers. She turned on her side and hugged the extra pillow to her chest in a weak attempt to find comfort in the large, lonely bed.

Her slumber was restless as visions of Logan McGregor filled her dreams—long arms, warm lips, and an even warmer body pressing urgently against hers. She was pulled from the sensuous dream as an annoying noise filled the room. Her first thought was of the detective's pager, and she sat up quickly thinking that the night had somehow played a cruel trick on her and that Logan was still there, in the house, with her. It took a moment for her to realize that the sound was her doorbell.

Wincing at the sharp pain in her hip, she threw back the covers. Madison couldn't imagine who would be at her door at 6:30 on a Sunday morning. Slipping her arms into her robe, she padded down the hallway, Femur at her side. She panicked as she looked through the peephole and saw Logan standing on her doorstep. She ran trembling fingers through her hair and straightened her robe before opening the door to the very tired-looking but still beautiful detective. "Good morning."

Even through the savaging fatigue, Logan felt the now-familiar warmth spread through her body, the same warmth she felt each time her eyes rested on the doctor. "Good morning to you." Madison's face revealed her lack of sleep and she instantly regretted her decision to bring the doctor breakfast. "I didn't mean to wake you. Um, I was just in the neighborhood, and..."

Grabbing the detective's hand, Madison tugged her into a warm embrace. "I was worried about you. Are you all right?"

Logan didn't speak for a moment, wanting—needing—to feel the comfort of the doctor's arms around her waist, wishing her hands were free to return the embrace. After a long moment, she leaned back slightly and nodded. "I was worried about you too." After taking a good look at Madison's tired eyes, she tenderly kissed her forehead. "It doesn't look like you got much sleep."

Madison snagged a cup of coffee out of Logan's hand and turned, heading for the kitchen, leaving the detective in the foyer with a confused look on her face. "What? What's so funny?"

"I'm glad I don't need you to feed my ego, Detective, and no, I didn't get much sleep. Actually, I was up most of the night, icing my ass and wishing I had taken you up on the offer to drive me to Mercy last night."

Raising an eyebrow at the doctor's admission, Logan took a long swallow of coffee and willed the caffeine into her bloodstream. "I'm free until around one o'clock. Why don't you go get dressed and we'll do just that."

"It's much better now, thank you. What I'd really like to do is sit down and eat this wonderful breakfast with you and hear whatever you can tell me about this latest murder."

Logan knew the next few minutes would not be easy for either of them. "Okay, but first I want to ask a favor of you." She purposely looked away from the doctor, not wanting her eyes to betray her intentions.

"Okay." Madison eyed the woman suspiciously, remembering the last request the tall, dark detective had made of her.

Logan walked to the table and spread out their breakfast, her back to the guarded doctor. Taking a deep breath, she decided an honest, forthright approach might just convince the doctor to go along with her plan. "I'd like for you to come into the city and stay with me for the next few days."

The room was silent for a few moments, and Logan noticed Femur even sat pensively in the corner of the room. She was surprised that when at last Madison spoke, there was fear instead of anger in her voice. "You think he's coming after me, don't you."

"Yes, I think it's a good possibility." The detective quickly lessened the distance between them. Taking the doctor in her arms, she held her close, wanting to provide some semblance of protection. They stood quietly for a few moments, each silently absorbing the strength and courage of the other.

With a single finger, Logan lifted the doctor's chin. "I have no idea what his next move will be, but I don't want to take any chances where you're concerned. I can protect Susan easily while she's in the hospital, but you aren't as easy. I would never forgive myself if anything happened to you." Her heart was racing, blue eyes pleading. "I've just found you, Madi, and I'll be damned if anything is going to happen to prevent us having a chance to explore what we've found."

Madison's heart leapt as she listened to Logan's words, and she couldn't remember why she had questioned her feelings the previous night. She nodded almost imperceptibly and stretched up to place a light kiss on the detective's lips. "Okay. I'll do it, but only on one condition."

Releasing a breath she hadn't realized she was holding, Logan smiled and raised a questioning eyebrow. "And the condition would be what, Dr. Cavanaugh?"

Suddenly embarrassed, Madison laid her head on Logan's chest. "I'll go but first, since you have a few hours off, you have to come upstairs with me to take a nap. You look like shit, Detective." The blonde frowned at the evil grin that crossed the detective's face and slapped her playfully on the arm. "No fooling around either, Sport. I'm tired, you're tired, and we are both *sleeping.*"

Logan attempted her best hurt look. "You're no fun, Doctor."

Taking her protector by the hand, Madison led her through the house and up the stairs. "I never said I was a fun doctor, Detective, and right now the *doctor* is prescribing rest for two sleep-deprived women. Now come on and play nice before I have to get mean and bring out my needles."

Logan followed along behind and upon entering the bedroom for the second time in less than twenty-four hours, she again became aware of the doctor's personal touches. She could scarcely control the heat rising in her body as she watched Madison shed her robe, revealing a lean muscular body barely covered by blue satin boxers and a white T-shirt that was cut off at the waist.

Madison quickly slid between the sheets and patted the mattress, smiling at the ravenous look on Logan's face. "Remember you have to play nice, Detective."

Watching Logan undress, Madison could barely contain her desire as the detective stripped off her jeans and stood beside the bed clad only in her underwear. Closing her eyes, the struggling blonde stretched an arm across the bed, attempting to block out the seductive image of the muscular body she knew would be lying against hers in a few moments. Groaning lightly as Logan slid under the sheets beside her, the doctor pulled the warm, seductive body against hers, tucking the tired woman's head in the crook of her neck.

Their bodies settled together in a perfect fit. Fatigue won over desire, claiming both women in a matter of minutes, and for the first time in days, they slept soundly, each knowing the other was nearby and safe from the evil that lurked just around the corner.

CHAPTER FIFTEEN

Madison woke to Logan's long arm wrapped around her waist and the detective's rhythmic breathing on the back of her neck. The warmth of the body stretched behind hers was almost more than the blonde could stand and she felt a warm rush of desire spread throughout her body. Enticing as it was to lie beside the slumbering woman, she knew her willpower was diminishing by the minute and if she stayed in the bed much longer, sleep would not be on either of their minds for long.

She gently lifted Logan's arm and slid from the tender embrace before tucking the covers back around the still-sleeping woman. Madison noticed that the lines on the detective's forehead remained, a reminder of the constant stress of the investigation. Quietly, she slipped into the bathroom and started the shower, thinking how much she wished the detective would be sharing it with her. *Jesus, Cavanaugh, you need a cold one this morning.* Stepping under the warm spray, she turned the temperature of the water down, hoping to extinguish the desire surging through her veins.

When she walked out of the bathroom ten minutes later, Madison spotted Femur curled up on the bed, head resting protectively on the detective's stomach. The blonde playfully bared her teeth and scratched the dog's head, wishing they could switch places. "I see you like tall, dark, and handsome too." She ruffled his fur, then dressed in a pair of faded jeans and a sweatshirt. Turning at the door, she called out in a whisper for Femur to follow, but he only stretched his lanky body and yawned before dropping his head once again onto Logan's stomach. "Traitor dog."

She padded barefoot to the front porch to get the morning newspaper and then headed to the kitchen to start a pot of coffee. She eyed their discarded breakfast on the table, and her stomach growled its displeasure. *Well, you're just going to have to wait a while.* After retrieving the ice pack from the freezer, she took her mug of coffee into the den and sat gingerly on the couch to read the morning edition of the *Post-Gazette.* Her eyes focused on the full-color picture that flanked the front page.

The photographer had captured the image of a very tired, very irritable detective, the same one now sleeping peacefully in Madison's bed upstairs. As Madison read the article, the full brunt of the previous evening's murder hit home and she understood the pleading look she had seen in Logan's eyes. The article described the grisly murder in detail, citing a reliable source. Madison knew that such a detailed account could only come from someone inside the police department and that her houseguest's reaction to the news was not going to be pleasant.

The reporter also quoted a prominent psychologist in the city as saying the murderer was becoming unstable and unpredictable. Madison could only imagine the gruesomeness of the scene and the toll the investigation must have been taking on the detective. The doctor witnessed pain, destruction, and death on a daily basis, but at least, more often than not, she gained some satisfaction from the fact that she was able to help with the healing process. Most of what Logan saw was just the opposite, as her job entailed cleaning up the results of violence and destruction.

Tossing the paper aside, Madison went back into the kitchen, her stomach once again offering its opinion on her neglect. After pouring another cup of coffee for herself, she pulled an assortment of ingredients from the refrigerator and began preparing breakfast. A few minutes later, Femur strolled into the kitchen and offered a quiet bark in greeting.

"Oh, I see how you are. You don't want anything to do with me until you smell food cooking." Licking his lips, Femur looked up innocently at his mistress and repeated the hushed bark. "Shh, okay, okay, just be quiet." Madison poured Femur's dry food in his bowl and refilled his water dish before walking to the laundry room to unlock the pet door. She glared at the munching canine as she reentered the kitchen. "Fine. You want to play two-timer, fine. So can I."

After pouring a second cup of hot coffee and refreshing her own, Madison climbed the stairs to the second floor. Entering the bedroom, she stopped and silently watched as Logan still slept peacefully, regretting that she had to wake the detective. She set the coffee cups on the nightstand before bending down to lightly kiss her soft cheek and she smiled as Logan stirred under the warm covers, cracking her eyes and groaning as the sunlight beamed through the window. "Wake up, sleepyhead."

Madison grinned as Logan rubbed her eyes with balled fists, reminding her of a small child upon waking. Sitting on the side of the bed, she held out a cup of coffee to the groggy woman. "Here, maybe this will help."

Sliding her long frame up against the headboard, Logan took the mug from the doctor and took a long swallow before speaking. "Morning."

Madison bit her lip to keep from laughing at the very disheveled but cute woman in her bed. "Hmm, I take it you're not much of a morning person?"

Logan left the rhetorical observation unanswered as she sipped her coffee and stretched. "If you bring me coffee like this every morning, I could become a morning person."

Rolling her eyes, Madison swatted the detective on the arm. "Jeez, I think I've released the monster in you."

Logan kissed Madison's lips lightly and smiled. "No, more like liberated me." She noted the almost shy look on the doctor's face and sat back, regarding her seriously. "So, how did you sleep?"

"Well, thanks to you." Madison rested her hand on Logan's leg. "I'm sorry I had to wake you. You seemed to be sleeping soundly, but I knew you said you had something to do at one o'clock."

Nodding, Logan took another sip of coffee. "Yes. I met C.W. Langston last night and believe it or not he wasn't very cooperative." The detective closed her eyes as she raked a hand through her mussed hair. "I don't know what his problem is with us, but I intend to find out. He wouldn't allow us access to any of the company records, so I pulled a few strings of my own and with the help of Loraine Osborne and a judge that despises Langston, I was able to obtain a search warrant." Twitching her eyebrows, the detective grinned. "I'm about to show Mr. High And Mighty C.W. Langston that he can't rule the entire world."

She noticed Madison's strained look, and her smile faded. Sitting up in the bed, she dipped her head to catch the doctor's evasive eyes. "Hey, are you all right?"

An insincere smile crossed over Madison's tight lips and Logan knew she was holding something back. "Tell me what's wrong. When I mentioned Commander Osborne's name you closed up. Added to your reaction at seeing her the other day, I'm guessing there is some bad blood between you two."

Knowing she'd been busted, Madison attempted to deflect the question. "Nah, nothing much."

Logan caught Madison's gaze with her own and knew, without a doubt, that she was attempting to contain her true feelings. "It can't be half as bad as what I've already told you."

The doctor could feel tears welling up in her eyes and quickly turned away from Logan, focusing on Femur. "It's a long story." She swiped the tears from her eyes with the back of her hand. "I'll tell you, but not now. You don't have time and breakfast is about ready."

Deciding to drop the subject for the moment, Logan tried to lighten the mood. "What? You cooked breakfast?" Her hand touched her chest and she playfully fell back onto the pillows. "Jeez, I think I'm having a heart attack."

The doctor stood and walked to the door. "I'll have you know I'm a wonderful cook." She pointed toward the bathroom. "Now get up and take your shower. I washed your clothes and I'll bring them to you. I, um, couldn't wash your underwear, so you'll have to wear your dirty ones or borrow some of mine."

Swallowing hard, Logan felt the heat rise between her legs. "I, ah, well...I guess I could, um, go commando."

"Well, yes, I guess that is an option, Detective." Madison had to bite her lip to keep from laughing aloud. "Hurry up; I would hate to have to eat without you." She walked back toward the kitchen wondering just long she was going to be able to hold back with Logan McGregor.

She was removing a quiche from the oven moments later and looked up just in time to see the detective's dark face. "When I said hurry, I didn't mean you had to break any speed records."

Recovering quickly and shrugging her shoulders, Logan leaned against the island and snagged a piece of bacon from the plate in Madison's hand. "Cops are sort of like doctors. We never know when we'll get called out in the middle of the night, so I've had to learn to shower and dress quickly."

"You have a point there, Detective."

Logan looked around the room. "Do you have the morning paper? I want to see what the vultures wrote last night."

Feeling a cold chill run up her spine, Madison nodded and went to the den to get the *Post-Gazette*. After handing the newspaper to the detective with an apprehensive look, she sat at the table. "I'd rather you didn't read it until you've eaten. I really don't think you'll have much of an appetite if you look at it now."

Lines formed in Logan's forehead as she frowned. "Damn, it must be bad, then." Tossing the paper on the table, she sat beside the doctor and took a long drink of her orange juice. "Maybe you're right about the appetite. I'd better take advantage of it while I can. I'm starving."

Madison tried not to show her surprise, hoping Logan stayed calm when she finally did read the article and found out there was a leak in her department.

Breakfast was relaxing and refreshing, and after depositing the empty plates in the sink, Madison slid behind Logan and wrapped her arms around her waist, pulling her close and trying to ignore the feel of the bulky holster strapped to the detective's side. "Mmm, you smell good."

Logan turned bent her head to capture Madison's lips, savoring the long morning kiss. She smiled into the doctor's eyes. "Mmm, you taste good."

Madison lightly nipped Logan's chin. "You do, too, but unfortunately we'll have to wait awhile. I do believe you have a search warrant to serve, Detective." Hearing a deep growl escape Logan's throat, she eased back, putting a safe distance between them, unsure if she could resist any further temptation.

"Do I at least have time to read the trash?"

Madison regarded the detective speculatively as she sipped her coffee. "Yes, but while you do that I think I'll be a coward and take Officer Freeman a cup of coffee."

Logan spread the paper on the table in front of her, instantly seeing her own image scowling back at the camera. "Jesus, you'd think they could take pictures of something more interesting."

Madison made her escape, knowing that when she returned, the detective's mood would be foul. Opening the front door, she noticed the unusual silence around her. Very few people traveled the road in front of the house, but she noticed that even the subtle sounds of nature were absent. She saw Freeman sitting in the front seat of the cruiser and said good morning as she neared.

Logan was reading the article when she heard Madison frantically calling her name. Bolting through the front door, she saw the blonde's rigid stance and the shattered cup on the ground beside her. She ran to Madison's side, and on seeing the bloody body of the officer inside the car, led the doctor back to the front steps.

"Stay here and don't move." Logan released the snap on her shoulder holster and carefully eased her way back toward the police cruiser, knowing in her gut that the officer was dead and the killer long gone. All she could do at that point was call in the incident and hope the CSI team could find some evidence.

She stepped back from the car and returned to the pale, shaking woman sitting on the front steps. As she knelt before Madison and grasped her hands, she could feel the cold, clammy signs of shock. Logan slipped an arm behind Madison's neck and the other under her legs, lifting her up and carrying her into the den. After settling her on the couch, she wrapped a blanket around her shoulders. Madison sat silently, her hands icy cold and her face deathly pale, while Logan called her precinct.

The detective knew she was taking a risk calling in her own team before notifying the Bridgeville police, but she had to make sure the scene remained clean for the CSI team. Surprisingly, her lieutenant agreed with her judgment call and informed her that he was on his way.

Logan turned to Madison and saw that her eyes were still glassy, but the trembling in her hands had subsided. Logan whispered softly as she held her close. "It's okay, baby. I'm here, no one is going to hurt you, I promise." After several minutes, Madison started to stir and her eyes began to focus. The detective leaned back on her haunches, wanting the doctor to see her face as she pulled herself back to reality.

Madison blinked several times. The uncontrollable shaking returned as tears welled up in her eyes, and she felt the detective's protective arms draw her close. "It's okay, just let it go, you're safe now." Tears flowed down her cheeks and the detective tightened her embrace.

In a trembling voice broken with harsh sobs, the doctor asked the question she already knew the answer to. "She's dead, isn't she?"

Not trusting her voice any longer as the anger welled up inside her, Logan nodded. The murder of the officer, not thirty feet away from where the detective was sleeping, was a clear message the killer was taunting Logan's skills as an investigator.

Suddenly, Madison's body tensed and she pushed Logan's arms away as she frantically tried to get up. "Femur, oh my God, where is Femur?"

Logan pressed Madison back into the cushions with a firm hand. "I'll find him. You stay here and listen for the CSI team."

With a sick feeling in the pit of her stomach, she pulled open the back door and jogged out into the yard, whistling and calling for the Lab, each unanswered call tying one more knot in her belly. She searched the large backyard, and as she cleared the arbor, a dark form lying in the grass came into her line of view. Kneeling down beside the dog, she felt for a pulse, then picked up the limp form and walked toward the house. Logan caught a movement in the doorway, and her eyes locked with Madison's. She felt a lump in her throat as the doctor lifted a hand to her mouth to stifle her anguished cry.

The trembling blonde raced down the steps and took the limp animal from the detective's arms and walked back into the house, cradling the dog's body.

Logan could only watch helplessly, tears streaking her face, as Madison kicked the door closed, shutting her out and leaving her standing in the cold morning air alone and, for the first time in as long as she could remember, afraid.

CHAPTER SIXTEEN

The CSI team spent most of the morning going over Madison's property with a fine-tooth comb, searching for anything that could provide a lead on the case. Logan knew the rookie's death had come at the hands of the Strip District killer and she mentally chastised herself for allowing the inexperienced officer to take part in the surveillance.

Torn as to what to do, Logan swore under her breath and glanced at her watch, realizing she had to leave soon in order to meet the other investigators at the Langston building to serve the search warrant. She didn't want to leave the scene but knew there was nothing further she could do.

The detective hesitated before walking up the steps to the front door and ringing the bell. She didn't recognize the resounding footsteps that crossed the marble floor of the foyer and knew that someone other than Madison would greet her. After a few moments, the door opened and Logan was met by a very attractive strawberry-blonde whose eyes expressed an almost palpable resentment for the intrusion. "May I help you, Officer?"

"May I speak to Dr. Cavanaugh, please?"

"I'm sorry, but the doctor is resting at the moment. Is there something I can do for you?"

Taken by surprise, the detective raised a solitary dark eyebrow. "Well, no, I'm sorry there isn't, Ms., ah, I didn't catch your name."

The gatekeeper remained unmoved. "I don't recall giving you my name, Officer, so if you'll excuse me, I have more important things to attend to."

Logan moved with lightning speed, placing her foot over the threshold, effectively preventing the woman from shutting her out of the house. "Really, I'd like to see Madison, *and now, please.*"

An icy glare passed between the two women as they dueled for control before the smaller woman finally released a low growl and stepped out of the way, opening the door for the detective to enter. Logan's eyes darted about in an attempt to locate the doctor, as she listened for sounds that would reveal her whereabouts, but she saw and heard nothing. "Would you mind getting the doctor for me?"

"Actually, I would, but I can see that you aren't going to leave until I do." The woman turned quickly and retreated up the stairs, leaving Logan alone in the foyer. Several minutes later, she reappeared at the top of the stairs and called out, "You may come up, Detective."

Logan took the steps two at a time, only to have her progress hindered once again. "Only a few minutes, she needs her rest." Nodding, Logan watched as the woman descended the stairs, apparently very familiar with the layout of the house, and wondered what role she played in Madison's life.

Upon entering the master suite, Logan stood silently in the doorway until she heard a soft, gentle voice coming from the oversized walk-in closet. She stepped lightly across the deep pile carpet, stopping in the doorway of the closet when she spotted Madison sitting on a pillow on the floor beside Femur. Easing her tall frame into the cramped space, she knelt beside the doctor and gently placed a hand on her shoulder. "How's he doing?"

A tear slid down Madison's cheek, and she quickly wiped it away with the back of her hand. "He's going to be all right. Nicole said he has what equates to a concussion in humans and should be up and around soon."

"Why the closet?"

A smile crossed Madison's face as she gently stroked the dog's head. "He always comes here when he doesn't feel well." Her eyes swept the contents of the closet before focusing on the detective. "I don't know if it's the scent from my clothes or the security of a small place, but whatever it is, he feels safe here."

Understanding dawned on the detective as she dropped her hand to caress the short, dark fur along Femur's flank. "I see. How are you holding up, and, um, how's the, ah, bruise?"

"I'm okay now that I know Femur will be all right." Frightened, pain-filled eyes searched Logan's face. "He's been through so much already. I was afraid I had lost him."

Logan caressed the doctor's tense shoulders as she sat on the floor, sliding closer to Madison, and encircled her in a warm embrace. "I know. I was scared too."

The small blonde leaned in to Logan as she absently stroked Femur's back. "Did you find anything of any use outside?"

Releasing a frustrated sigh, the detective shook her head. "No. Nothing so far. I'm leaving in a few minutes to go back into the city. Maybe the search warrant we're serving on Langston will provide some useful information."

A noise from the bedroom startled both women, and Logan's arm tensed around the doctor's shoulder. They looked up to see Nicole standing in the doorway, a frown on her face. "Time's up, Detective."

Shrugging, the detective unfolded her muscular body from the floor and stood. "Yes, ma'am, I'm going."

Satisfied that the intruder was preparing to leave, Nicole turned and walked out of the room leaving an angry detective and a sore, but grinning doctor in the closet. "She can be a little overbearing sometimes, but she means well."

"Hmmph. Overbearing isn't quite the word I would use for that woman, Doctor."

Madison held out her hand to the detective, deciding she could leave the recuperating dog for a few minutes. "Help me up and I'll walk you to the door."

A strong arm lifted her into a warm embrace. "Can I call you later?"

The doctor gently nipped Logan's chin. "You'd better. I believe we're staying with you for a while and I'll need some directions to your house."

A smile crossed Logan's face as she gazed down into the doctor's swollen, tear-reddened eyes, and a warm heat spread throughout her body. "That's right, you are staying with me. I'll call you when I've finished at Langston's and I'll come back out to get you and Femur."

The doctor brushed her lips across Logan's and then took her hand, leading her from the room and down the staircase. As they reached the foyer, a knot formed in Madison's stomach. Choosing not to cross the threshold, Madison said good-bye at the door and watched as the detective made her way across the lawn, avoiding the small red flags that peppered the grass.

Only after Logan had disappeared around the corner of the house did Madison shut the door and turn to rejoin Femur, holding her still-tender hip. As she climbed the steps to the second floor, a sudden surge of fear ripped through the doctor's body at the thought that her tall, dark protector would soon be leaving her alone in what she would never again refer to as her safe haven.

Lieutenant Beaudry arrived just as Logan climbed into her truck to drive back into the city. She waited as he walked toward her vehicle, noticing that his limp had progressively worsened over the last few weeks. Making what could have been a fatal error, her supervisor had intervened in a domestic dispute he had witnessed on the drive home from work the previous fall. After calling for backup, he had approached an arguing couple in front of their dilapidated brownstone. The female, wielding a baseball bat, was attempting to fend off her drunken husband, heedless of the growing crowd. The lieutenant had attempted to subdue the man, only to have the blade of a four-inch switchblade imbedded deeply into his thigh.

As one of the officers providing backup in the incident, Logan had sat beside Beaudry on the sidewalk, holding his hand and whispering reassuringly into an unhearing ear, applying pressure to his wound, silently praying to a god to whom she seldom spoke as she pleaded for the life of the man whose pulse she could feel under her fingertips, hoping he wouldn't bleed out...all the while listening impatiently for the approaching sirens.

During the lieutenant's recovery from the stab wound, broken arm and leg, a bond that neither of them truly understood sealed their lives together. Logan had felt a kinship, a duty to protect her commanding officer until he had healed, and she wore that responsibility proudly as she visited and pushed him hard to fight his way back.

During that time, the lieutenant had also taken an interest in Logan, both personal and professional, always pushing her to be more than she thought herself capable of at times. The detective knew she wouldn't be heading up the Strip District task force if it weren't for her lieutenant, and as she watched his approach, she couldn't decide if she wanted to hug him or punch him in the face. "Morning, Lieutenant."

"McGregor." The graying man leaned heavily against the side of the truck, unsuccessfully trying to hide a pain-induced frown. "Fill me in on what you have so far."

She reached over, opening the passenger door. "Take a load off, Pop, and I'll do just that."

The truck dipped as the lieutenant's heavy frame settled on the seat. Growling, he turned to the detective, giving her his best intimidating glare. "If you ever call me that around the squad room I'll buck you down to meter maid, you punk."

"Yeah, right. You couldn't live without me and you know it."

"Whatever, Mac. You give me more heartburn than all my ex-wives put together." The corners of his mouth turned up. "So get on with it, I don't have all day to fart around with you."

C.W. Langston sat in a leather wingback chair at the head of a long mahogany conference table glaring at three men and a woman. Even though Langston had personally overseen the electronics sweep of the conference room a few minutes earlier, he still hesitated at speaking of Thomas Peters's murder. Fear was an emotion C.W Langston elicited in others, not one he himself was accustomed to. As he looked toward his daughter, he realized that even with all of his power and influence, protecting Christine might not be possible.

"I have arranged to have a personal bodyguard assigned to each of you until this madness is over."

"C.W., exactly what is it we are supposed to do now, just sit and wait to be slaughtered like Peters?" Christine Langston, although powerful in her own right, had never once confronted the almighty czar of Langston Development. *Maybe someone should have. Then we wouldn't be sitting here fearing for our lives.*

"I have no doubt you will be well protected with the guards I have arranged for you. Don't do anything stupid and you'll be safe." Making eye contact with his daughter, C.W. Langston raised a graying eyebrow in challenge. "I think our time would be best spent trying to contain this situation before it gets any more complicated."

Running a hand through thinning hair, the CEO released a frustrated sigh. "The police and one particularly unruly detective are currently downstairs in my office rummaging through the acquisition records for the last five years." Lips curled in a smirk as he regarded Lester Donovan. "These people are cops and have no idea what they are looking at, so I wouldn't worry too much about them."

Hard eyes turned toward Christine Langston. "What I do worry about is the McGregor woman. I have no persuasive evidence to use as a means of convincing her to go away. She is one of the hard ones, clean and honest. Find something, anything, and if there is nothing to find, well then, create a little persuasion for me."

Years of being moved around the corporate chessboard as a pawn to further her father's career had forced Christine Langston to hide her emotions well. No one knew her true thoughts and feelings regarding the development corporation and the man she called her father, and no one would until she was ready to let them see the real Christine, the woman that she herself had thought for years was buried away, never to be rediscovered.

Logan looked around the room at cases upon cases of records stacked along the wall of the accounting department. She had no idea what she was looking for but knew in her gut the answer would be found within those walls. Somehow, the Strip District killer and Langston Development were connected, and the detective vowed not to leave until she found the link.

The judge signing the search warrant had given her a broad scope, allowing the search and seizure of past and current records, computers, and financial statements, along with any personal property or information included in the personnel files pertaining to any of the involved executives.

Logan had used the animosity between the two powerful men as her own weapon to fight the hidden powers within the police force that bent under C.W. Langston's pressure to hinder her investigation. A longtime adversary of Langston, the judge had relished the thought of being able to fight him in the legal arena.

The powerful man himself walked into the room and bellowed orders to uninterested officers as they made their way through the hallways with corporate records toward a line of waiting vans below. Blazing eyes pierced Logan's as Langston stormed toward her, his face red and his nostrils flaring in uncontrolled anger.

"You will not come into my offices and disrupt my business. I want every one of those cases placed back where you found them and not a single record disturbed. Am I making myself clear, Officer?"

Logan listened patiently as Langston ranted. "I understand your concerns, Mr. Langston. However, I have a murder investigation to lead, and part of that investigation includes having our financial advisors audit these files in an attempt to locate any clue that will lead us to the murderer." A self-satisfied smile crossed her lips as she watched the CEO's face pale. *Gotcha, you son of a bitch. Now I know there is something here.* "As soon as we have completed the investigation, I'll be happy to return the records." She pressed past the irate man and heard him swear as she headed toward the door.

"You cannot just come in here and disrupt my office. I will see to it personally that you and your superior are reprimanded for this outrageous behavior, young lady."

The detective stopped and turned toward Langston. "You go right ahead and try, Mr. Langston, and I promise you, I will have you and your cronies arrested for hindering my investigation, withholding and tampering with evidence in a felony investigation, as well as any thing else I can come up with." She held the executive's gaze until he finally looked away. "I suggest you cooperate, Mr. Langston, or else you may find yourself in less than accommodating quarters."

Langston stood frozen as the detective disappeared through the doorway, his mind spinning through the different possible scenarios. Quickly walking behind the desk, he lifted the phone to his ear and punched in a familiar number. After several rings, a voice broke into his thoughts. "This woman is going to be harder to contain than I previously thought. Come up with something on your end and put it in motion. If we can't stop her outright, maybe we can throw enough bullshit at her that she won't have time to concern herself with us."

After slamming the phone down, Langston made his way down the hall and toward the elevators on his way to the one person he knew would never let him down. As the elegant private car ascended to the penthouse, C.W. Langston's thoughts traveled back to the events of the last five years. One of the brightest moments in his career had been when the Strip District restoration project had become a reality, but he realized it would all be for naught if the nosy detective poking through the corporate files stumbled across his darkest secrets.

Without knocking, he entered a plush office and sat uninvited in a chair before a petite blonde, impatiently waiting for her to complete her phone call. The instant she hung up, he snapped, "It's time we made some other arrangements in regards to the problem at hand, my dear."

Christine sighed as she regarded her father. "I wish there was some other way, C.W."

"There isn't. I can't afford these distractions, Christine, and neither can you. It's time to cut our losses and move on."

The senior Langston stood as his daughter sadly watched the slow and unsure movements of the man she had always admired and emulated. The once mighty and powerful C.W. Langston was now a fading nova, slowly withering away after long years of being the brightest, richest, and most powerful man in the city. "I know, Daddy. I'll take care of everything, I promise." She watched as her father quietly closed the door, contemplating her options before reaching into her briefcase for her personal cell phone. *Some things you just don't need to know, Daddy.*

Walking quickly toward the door, she slipped the slim phone into the pocket of her blazer and made her way out of the building. Several blocks later, after finding a quiet, secluded place to sit, she removed the phone from her pocket and glanced around once more before dialing a number she knew from memory. "Hey, baby, it's me. I need you to set up that meeting we've been discussing—and make it as soon as possible. This is getting out of hand."

KatLyn

126

CHAPTER SEVENTEEN

Madison occupied her time by caring for Femur and preparing to close the house. Her resentment at having to flee her home was further aggravated as she watched the uniformed officers and the CSI team milling around her lawn. The coroner had long ago removed Patty Freeman's body, but Madison knew she would never again be able to walk up the driveway without seeing the lifeless, open-eyed face of the murdered officer in the patrol car. With a sense of urgency that she didn't fully understand, the doctor started to pack a large suitcase, thankful that Logan would arrive soon and take her away to a safer, less volatile location.

With some reluctance and a friendly shove out the door, Nicole had returned to the clinic to check in with her assistants and close the office for the day. The two doctors had attended high school together, and Madison found that Nicole was the closest thing to family that she'd known in a long time. She recalled confusion and anger that had played across Logan's face when Nicole had exercised her self-appointed right as Madison's protector and defender. She knew the dynamics of their relationship would be interesting and would probably at times be volatile, given their need to be her protectors. However, she also knew that, given time, the two women would work out their differences and come to accept each other and the important roles each played in her life.

As she continued to pack, Femur eased his way from the safety of the closet to curl up on the bed. "Hey, big guy. You don't think I'm leaving without you, do ya?" Dropping the jeans onto the bed, Madison slid down beside the still-frightened canine as a warm wet tongue slashed across her face with lightning speed. "Yuck-o. I love you, my friend, but that breath of yours needs some serious attention." The staccato thumping of Femur's tail on the bed told Madison that her companion was indeed feeling better.

The only light in the room came from the computer monitor as a solitary figure surfed the pages of Mercy Hospital's Web site in search of information on Dr. Madison Cavanaugh. Discovering the identity of the woman hadn't been as difficult as he expected. Once he had determined the name of the dyke cop, the rest had been easy. A deep laugh filled the darkened room as the monitor flickered onto page after page. Suddenly, the laughter ceased and an eerie quiet settled back into the room as a photograph of the attractive blonde appeared on the screen.

The man leaned in, reverently brushing his fingers across the smiling face of the blond doctor. "Soon, Doctor. You won't be smiling, I promise." After searching impatiently for a pen in the unorganized belly-drawer of the desk, he started to write down the information he would need to locate Operation Safety Net.

As Logan sped toward Bridgeville, her mind wandered back over the events of the day. There were still so many loose ends to tie up, so many unknowns yet to be discovered. Knowing the answers were buried somewhere in the massive file rooms of Langston Development, she decided to focus more of her time on that aspect of the investigation and leave the grunt work for the uniformed officers. "I'm going to find your secrets, old man, and when I do you'd better hope Madison hasn't been hurt or you may never see the inside of a courtroom."

Turning into the drive a few minutes later, she saw not one, but two uniformed officers leaning against the police cruiser. She dropped from the cab of the Durango and strolled over toward the officers, noticing their nervous and watchful eyes and their hands moving slowly closer toward the guns holstered at their sides. "Good evening, Officers. I'm Detective Sergeant Logan McGregor."

Both officers relaxed noticeably, smiling nervously as they returned her greeting. "Um, sorry, Detective, but I, ah, guess everyone's a little jumpy after this morning and Patty. I mean Officer Freeman."

Nodding, Logan moved a little closer to the pair, her eyes revealing the sadness and guilt she felt in her heart. "That is certainly understandable. I'm truly sorry about what happened. Although I know there is nothing I can say to make what you're feeling any easier, I will promise you that we are going to catch this guy."

Just then a car pulled into the drive and the three officers tensed in nervous anticipation. The strawberry-blonde smiled as she slipped from behind the wheel of her Jeep and strolled past Logan, slowing only long enough to whisper, "Ah, Detective, you're working late tonight. Wouldn't be trying to work a little pleasure into your business, now, would you?"

Logan felt her pulse rise considerably. The three officers watched as Nicole unlocked the door and entered the house, quickly glancing back at Logan and winking before the door closed.

The detective took a deep breath in an attempt to calm her rising temper and turned back toward the two officers. "You have a good evening, Officers, and keep your eyes open. I will be driving Dr. Cavanaugh into the city in a few minutes, so there will be no need to remain here. However, I would appreciate it if you would drive by several times throughout the night to check on the house."

Both officers nodded, visibly relaxing at the revelation that they would not have to sit vigil in the driveway all night. After saying good night, Logan slowly walked toward the front door, unsure if she was ready to face Madison in the company of Nicole. As she lifted her hand to knock, the front door swung open, revealing a very relieved and smiling blond doctor.

"Hey, there you are. I'm glad you're here. I was beginning to get worried." Stepping back from the door, Madison motioned Logan to enter and quickly closed the door. Before the detective could turn around, warm arms wrapped around her waist. "I missed you today."

Turning in the firm embrace, Logan placed a tender kiss on Madison's warm, inviting lips. "I missed you too. I thought we could stop off for some take-out on the way into the city. If that's okay with you."

The young doctor scowled as she glared at the tall detective. "Hey, I'm not some cheap date, Detective." Still, she couldn't hide the smile teasing her lips as she lightly punched Logan's arm. "If you expect me to accompany you, then I need more than just take-out. I need a movie, too."

Logan felt her heart flutter as Madison grinned up into her face. Before she realized what she was doing, the detective leaned in and gently nibbled the doctor's lips. "Hmm, you taste good. Is this dessert?"

She watched, mesmerized, as the doctor's eyes turned dark with lust. She could almost feel the heat radiating from Madison's body as the sexual tension between them grew stronger. Leaning in, Logan captured the warm lips again, although this time with more passion. Their breathing became ragged as Logan explored the warm cocoon of Madison's mouth and heard her groan with the same passion in return.

Lost to all else except each other, they were both startled by the sound of Nicole coughing and quickly moved apart. Biting her lip shyly,

Madison turned toward Nicole. "Um, Nicki, you met Detect—I mean, Logan earlier this afternoon, didn't you?"

Nicole's eyes moved toward Logan's and for a moment, the detective thought she saw a look of utter disgust. "Yes, we met earlier in the afternoon. How are you, Detective? Any leads on the case yet?"

The detective felt uncomfortable. Unaccustomed to being scrutinized by others, she became defensive. "Yes, fine, and we're working on it." Logan could see the small upturn of the vet's lips as Madison gave her a shocked look and knew the response she had just given was exactly what the vet had anticipated. Placing a hand on the small of Madison's back, Logan turned toward her. "I'm sorry. I didn't mean to snap, it's just been a really long day and I'm a bit stressed."

Walking a few steps toward Nicole and out of Madison's line of view, Logan allowed her eyes to bore into the vet's as she reached out her hand. "Maybe I should begin again. Logan McGregor."

A smile flashed across Nicole's face as she realized the detective had bested her. "Hi, I'm Nicole Adams. It's nice to meet you." The words were light and friendly, although a silent war was being waged as the determined women shook hands.

"The *pleasure* is all mine, believe me." Logan watched as the vet absorbed the hidden meaning of her words and felt the other woman's grip loosen, then release completely.

Uncomfortable seconds of silence filled the foyer before Nicole pulled her gaze from Logan's and gathered her coat and keys. "Madi, I'll call you in the morning to see how you are, okay?"

A confused look crossed Madison's face as she looked from one woman to the other. "Um, yeah, right." Watching as Logan turned and walked into the kitchen, Madison suddenly remembered where she would be the next morning. "No, call me at the office after nine. I'm, um, staying with Logan for a few days. Just as a precaution, that's all." Suddenly the doctor asked herself why she was explaining things. "Look, just don't ask any questions, okay? Because answers are one thing I'm in short supply of right now."

Their eyes held until after a long moment Nicole broke the contact. "Okay. Well, just let me know how you are doing tomorrow. Gina and I are worried about you, you know."

After Nicole's departure, Logan and Madison called in their dinner order and set off for the city with Femur in the back of the Durango, happily hassling as he hung his head over the seat. Logan couldn't help but laugh when he released a long excited whine as they drove along the interstate. "Hey, big guy, are you excited about seeing Clancy again?"

If Madison hadn't thrown her arm up, the canine would have been in the front seat between them. The blonde gently pushed Femur back into the rear of the Durango and laughed, settling back down onto the ice pack she had brought along for the ride. "I can see we need to get you out more often."

Logan joined in the laughter until a frightening thought crossed her mind. "Um, he isn't likely to pee in the seat, is he?"

"No, of course not." Giving the dog a stern look, she shrugged her shoulders and quietly said, "Well, I hope not, anyway."

For a moment, Logan wondered what she was getting herself into bringing these two into her home. Before the thought had left her mind, she was again smiling at the realization that she hadn't been so happy in a long time. She quickly glanced at the pensive woman beside her. "Well, what's a little pee between friends? Just remember though, if he does, you get to clean it up."

Logan stopped at a Chinese restaurant a few blocks from her house and went in to pick up their dinner while Madison sat with Femur in the truck. The doctor hadn't expected the wave of fear to sweep over her as she watched the detective disappear into the building. In an attempt to distract herself, she stroked Femur's head and whispered softly to him when she noticed a beat-up truck pull into a parking space a few cars down.

Her senses went on alert when the man sat alone in the truck, not moving to enter the restaurant. A surge of panic swept over her as she thought about the incident in the bookstore a few days earlier and the man who had followed them during their lunch outing. Although she couldn't be sure in the darkness, the doctor's gut told her the man sitting in the truck was the same man.

Her eyes panned over the parking lot looking for other people and her heart sank as she realized she was alone with only a few cars between her and the suspicious man. She quickly pressed the button to lock the doors and patted the seat beside her, inviting Femur to join her in the hope that if the man was who she suspected, the sight of the large dog would scare him off.

Logan exited the restaurant and a strange feeling crept up her spine. She had learned to respect those nagging feelings in her early days as a cop on the street. Too many times, she had seen other cops ignore their sixth sense only to walk into trouble. Her eyes locked on Madison's, and upon noting the fearful look in her eyes she quickened her pace. Sliding into the front seat, she turned toward the doctor. "What's wrong? You look like you've seen a ghost."

Madison had watched as the man's gaze had tracked Logan's movements toward the car. She had no doubt that the man was following them. "Okay, I'll tell you, but just keep your eyes on me." She picked up one of the bags and pretended to check the contents as she spoke. "A few cars over, there's a man sitting in a blue truck. He drove in right after you went into the restaurant and has been sitting there since."

Logan turned her head toward the windshield, trying to see the vehicle in her peripheral vision. "Yeah, I saw him when I came out, but he doesn't look too threatening to me. Maybe he's waiting on someone who works inside."

"That's what I was thinking, too, until you came out. He watched every step you made and he didn't look happy."

Logan knew the doctor's smile was there to make the man think everything was fine, but even in the darkened truck she could see the fear in her eyes. "Okay, here's what we are going to do. Get Femur in the backseat and turn around and start petting him while I drive, then tell me what the man does when we leave the parking lot."

Madison followed the detective's instructions and watched through the back window as they drove. "He's following us."

"Fuck." The detective followed South Braddock Avenue for a few blocks before turning left onto Race Street. She sped up until she was around a sharp curve and out of sight, then pulled to the curb and waited. The headlights of the speeding car bore down on them, then the truck suddenly slowed as the man went past them, knowing his surveillance had been discovered.

Logan waited until the truck turned right onto Hutchinson Avenue. Making a quick decision, she turned and continued driving until she reached an intersection. Pulling into a vacant parking space, she turned to Madison, who had been unusually quiet. "Hey, are you okay?"

Nodding, Madison stared out the window as a single tear streaked her cheek. The detective knew she shouldn't be making promises she couldn't keep, but as she looked at the frightened doctor, her heart won the internal battle and words simply flowed unimpeded from her lips. "It's going to be all right, Madi. I'm not going to let him hurt you, I promise."

Madison held on tightly, finding comfort in the strength of the woman next to her. Before she realized it, she was being pulled closer to the powerful detective and felt a strong arm circle her shoulders and warm lips on her head. In a trembling voice, she spoke the words that had been a constant companion to her the last few days. "I'm frightened, Logan. What if he comes when you aren't with me? I don't think I could..."

Logan held on to Madison until her sobs subsided, then gently brushed the tears from her cheeks. "Well then, I guess you're stuck with me for a little while." With her free hand, she gently lifted Madison's tear-streaked face toward hers and kissed her before pulling back. "Now, what do you say we head home and have a nice dinner and watch that movie you wanted to see?"

A bobbing head was her only answer Logan as she put the Durango into gear and pulled back into traffic. Making several turns onto little-traveled side streets, Logan drove around until she was certain they were not being followed and turned toward Trenton Avenue and home.

Usually Logan left her truck parked in the driveway, but that night she parked behind the house. She wasn't expecting another incident, but she didn't want to assist the man in finding them either. "It's a beautiful night. Why don't I grab some plates and we can eat on the deck?" Before Madison could answer, her stomach roared its concurrence.

Logan gently nipped the doctor's inviting lips and laughed. "I'll take that as a yes."

Rolling her eyes, Madison grunted. "I hate it when my stomach does that. It's so embarrassing sometimes, especially when I'm in the middle of a board meeting."

Logan gathered the bags of food and climbed from the truck while Madison pulled the front seat forward for Femur to jump out. Entering the house, neither woman was prepared for what happened next. Just as Clancy jumped from the countertop to greet her master, Femur cleared the doorway. The hair on Clancy's back stood up and she took a wide swipe at Femur's nose, making contact and sending the poor dog into a howling fit.

Before Madison could bend down to check his bleeding nose, Femur sped between Logan's legs in hot pursuit, knocking the tall woman off balance, and the bags of food went airborne as Logan reached out to grab hold of the countertop. The doctor unsuccessfully grabbed for the flying food, but all she came away with was the bottom part of the bag. Miscalculating the distance to the counter, Logan grabbed at empty air and fell, and Madison watched in horror as Logan hit the floor with a thud and the ripped bag crashed into her shoulder, spilling a combination of sweet and sour pork and cashew chicken onto her chest and lap.

Logan sat stunned and all Madison could do was watch as their dinner dripped down the detective's chest and a single egg roll tumbled across the floor between her long legs. Logan growled as she attempted to pull herself up, but quickly slid in the slick rice and sauce on the tile floor.

The doctor remained quiet as she pondered the expression on Logan's face, unable to decide if the scowl was anger at the situation or disgust from all the food plastered on her body. Her thoughts were suddenly broken as the commotion continued at the other end of the house. Leaving Logan on the floor to fend for herself, Madison raced down the hallway in search of the offending animals.

Entering the guest bedroom, she found the cat once again perched on top of the window valance and Femur barking relentlessly on the floor beneath. Grabbing the dog by his collar, she led him toward the door, all the while scolding him for his behavior, and then pushed him into the hallway before closing the door behind her. She returned to stand beneath the frightened cat and looked up to find long sharp teeth and a loud ominous hiss greeting her from above.

Knowing the cat wasn't in the mood to have a strange woman climbing up to get her, she moved toward the dresser and cleared a spot for her cat to jump on when she was ready to leave the safety of her perch. The doctor spoke softly to the frightened cat as she moved around the bedroom, but her calming words were rejected and she was met with loud hissing each time she stole a glance her way. Deciding to cut her losses, Madison left the bedroom and headed back toward the kitchen to see about Logan.

The quiet in the house concerned Madison as she quickly made her way back down the hallway to the kitchen, but she realized her fears were unfounded as she turned the corner and took in the sight before her. Logan, still sitting in the middle of the kitchen floor, was laughing while Femur gobbled up the remnants of their dinner. Crossing her arms across her chest, Madison leaned against the doorway, trying to assume her best Mom look. "Hello! Is that my dinner you two are playing with over there?"

Startled, Logan and Femur both looked up to see the piercing eyes. The detective finished chewing a piece of chicken and swallowed before speaking. "Um, well, you see, he was just helping me...clean up...a bit." The detective cocked her head to the side and gave the doctor a bright smile. Femur's tail was doing double time, drumming on the adjacent counter as he happily gobbled the food in Logan's lap while trying not to slip on the tile floor.

Madison's serious glare finally broke as she watched the happy canine stretch his neck toward the messy detective and lick a large spot of sauce from her cheek. Rolling her eyes, she walked toward the happy pair and surveyed the damage. She regarded her two favorite friends, one with most of their dinner on her body and the other with rice and sauce squishing between his toes. "You two are disgusting."

Popping another piece of chicken into her mouth, Logan eased herself from the floor and looked down at the sticky medley of food and then at Madison. Before she could speak, the doctor raised her hands. "To the shower with both of you. Now." Snagging a roll of paper towels, the doctor moved toward what was once their dinner.

The detective moved in for a kiss and for a moment was tempted to draw the doctor tightly against her chest and share the mess, but quickly decided against it as she thought of the food fight that would surely follow.

Leaning in for a quick kiss, Madison quickly stepped back with a look of revulsion on her face. "Out, both of you."

Logan bent down and gingerly picked Femur up, careful not to aggravate his earlier injuries, and looked at the doctor with a look of hurt. "Well, I see how you are—only want me around when things are nice and neat and, um, clean."

Laughing, Madison watched as Logan carried Femur out of the kitchen and toward the bathroom, then yelled after the two adorable creatures, "And don't come back until you have the rice out of your ears." *Hmm, I'll give her one thing. She sure knows how to lighten the mood.* She kneeled down on the sticky floor.

Having managed to rescue one unopened container of sweet and sour pork and two egg rolls from the disaster, she set to work cleaning up the remaining mess. After mopping the floor twice, Madison decided to see what she could prepare to go with the remnants of their meal, and after surveying the scant offerings, settled on the frozen spaghetti sauce she had found in the freezer. She was busy pouring out noodles when Logan and Femur returned and felt her pulse quicken as the she saw the detective in a pair of old, faded jeans and a T-shirt cut off just below the breast line. She didn't bother hiding her lustful look as Logan walked toward her with hair still damp from the recent shower. Stepping into the warm open arms, Madison inhaled the spicy scent of soap and what could only be the detective's own essence. "You smell good."

As she held the doctor, Logan felt a rush of emotion course through her body and mind. *This feels so right.* Resisting the urge to tell the doctor how she felt, she placed a small kiss on the top of her head. "Thanks, you do too." She could feel the pounding of Madison's heart against her own and was amazed and frightened over the feelings she was quickly developing for the woman in her arms. Putting some distance between them, she surveyed the kitchen. "Wow, this place looks better now than it did before the circus."

Madison had felt the detective tense just before she moved away. Confused by the sudden change in Logan's demeanor, she turned back to the stove and slowly stirred the bubbling sauce as the detective looked on from across the room. Glancing down at Femur, Madison tried to lighten the mood by changing the subject. "How did his bath go?"

"He was fine. Actually, I think he enjoyed it." Opening the cupboard and removing two plates, she moved to the end of the bar. "I think we should eat inside. It's getting dark out, the floodlight on the deck is blown and I haven't had time to replace it. Sorry it took us so long. I had to soap him up twice to get all the sauce out of his fur."

Madison could feel the heat in her face as she thought of Femur's shower with the tall detective and how much she would have enjoyed the soapy adventure. *Damn, Cavanaugh. Are you becoming jealous of the dog?* She bit her lip and stared into the bubbling red sauce. *Yep, that's exactly what I'm doing. Damn lucky dog.* She poured out the sauce and finished preparing their dinner.

After they ate their hodgepodge meal, Logan insisted on cleaning the kitchen and sent the doctor into the den to relax. She continued to mull over her feelings for Madison, knowing she was sending out conflicting signals. After spending an inordinate amount of time wiping off the countertops, she finally decided that her absence in the den would soon be called into question.

Grabbing a small container of ice cream and two spoons, she headed for the den and the science fiction movie Madison had insisted on watching, but on rounding the corner, she spotted the blonde stretched out asleep on the dark green leather. Dropping into the matching recliner, Logan tossed aside the extra spoon, picked up the remote control, and flipped through the channels as she dug into the chocolate chip ice cream.

CHAPTER EIGHTEEN

The shadowed figure in the Camaro across the street watched as lights turned on in one of the front rooms of the house. Not wanting to press his luck, he patiently waited. *You have to sleep sometime, ladies, and when you do, I'll be there to wish you pleasant dreams...long, eternal dreams.* He silently cursed himself for his sloppiness earlier in the evening. Logan McGregor was proving to be harder to handle than he had anticipated. Now, since she had appointed herself the doctor's personal bodyguard, he was finding it difficult to catch Madison alone.

McGregor has to be first. If I get her out of my way, the rest will be a piece of cake.

Waiting is always the hardest part. Isn't that what Dad always used to say? He sat and he watched, and the smoke from his cigarette slowly curled out the window like a snake slithering through the night in search of prey.

Madison observed Logan through half-closed eyes. She felt a warm stirring in her body as the desire she had held at bay for so long resurfaced with a vengeance. "Are you going to eat all of that by yourself?"

Logan didn't flinch when Madison's voice filled the room. Instead, she slowly turned her head and shrugged, ice cream smudging her lips. "Well, I brought it for you, but since you were asleep—well, I couldn't let it just melt, now, could I?"

A well-groomed eyebrow rose in question as the blonde held her mouth open like a small bird begging for food. Laughing, Logan kicked down the leg rest and moved over to the couch as Madison moved one leg to the floor, leaving the other to rest snugly behind the detective's back. Once the detective sat down, Madison swung her leg up onto the inviting lap and locked her ankles together. With an impressive display of strength, she quickly pulled the detective's body on top of hers.

The movement took Logan by surprise. With the ice cream in one hand and a spoon in the other, she could do nothing to stop her fall. The resulting position was one she couldn't ignore as the heat between the doctor's legs radiated against her rib cage. Reaching out blindly, she set the ice cream container on the glass coffee table as Madison's lips captured hers in a torrent of desire and need.

The doctor heard the spoons falling to the floor and inwardly smiled as she pulled Logan closer. Hands searched to find warm skin and tongues battled for entrance as their passion erupted from the depths of their souls. Heat-filled minutes passed as the fervor continued, both women ravenous for more. Logan pulled back to gasp for air and Madison's arms tightened around her. "No, don't stop, please...I need you."

Looking down into the dark green pools of Madison's eyes, Logan felt her resolve fading. There was an insistent throbbing between her legs and she knew her fantasy of their first time together, alone in the cottage at Conneaut Lake, was quickly being pushed aside in the heat of the evening. Taking a deep breath and a moment to compose herself, she gently caressed the doctor's soft cheek, concern creasing her forehead. "I don't want our first time together to be something you regret, Madi. Are you sure this is what you want?"

Logan's answer came as the doctor captured her lips in a passionate kiss. She trembled uncontrollably as warm hands slipped beneath her half T-shirt, and a primal growl came from deep within her throat when Madison's long fingernails trailed a path along her spine. Breaking the kiss, Logan stood, pulling the doctor with her. Cupping warm cheeks between her hands, she leaned in and nipped at an inviting lip. "Come with me." As a soft finger played across soft cheeks, the hunger in Logan intensified tenfold. "I want to do this right. I want to make love to you in my bed."

Without a word being spoken, the women made their way down the long hallway to the back of the house. As they reached the bedroom door, Madison suddenly hesitated. Peering into questioning eyes, she asked, "Why don't you go make sure the house is locked up and I'll meet you back here in a few minutes? I want to freshen up a little."

Logan turned and walked toward the kitchen, the shaking in her legs revealing the nervousness swarming in her gut. After checking the doors and activating the alarm, she walked back to the guest bedroom with Clancy's food and water bowls. Entering the darkened room, she heard the cat purring and knew she had settled down happily in the middle of the bed.

After placing the bowls beside the dresser, she walked over to stroke her hand along the cat's back, smiling as she felt her lean into her touch. "Well, girl, I guess you're stuck here for the night." Clancy looked up lovingly with half-closed eyes and continued to purr as Logan scratched under her chin. "Wish me luck, kitty, and here's hoping I haven't forgotten how to do this."

"Oh, I don't think you've forgotten, Detective. You may be out of practice, but I think it will all come back to you after a few minutes." Madison leaned against the open door to the bathroom, grinning at her soon-to-be lover.

Logan was captivated by the luminescent green eyes watching her. She had forgotten that Madison had put her clothes in the guest room and had obviously returned there to freshen up instead of the bath off the master bedroom.

Her mouth became an arid cavern as she looked at the blond woman standing before her in a dark green negligee. Her tongue was a paralyzed bundle of muscle, completely useless and unable to swallow the lump that had risen like molten lava deep in her throat. She couldn't find a way to articulate the words in her head as she simply continued to kneel beside the bed, her mouth agape and her stomach churning, delighting in the beauty of the woman before her.

Madison chuckled at the shocked, somewhat terror-stricken look on Logan's face as she drew closer. For the first time since their first meeting, Madison watched Logan transform from a strong, powerful detective to a frightened, vulnerable woman. She took Logan's hand in hers, pulling the distressed woman to her feet, and led them across the hall.

Logan followed along silently, certain the neuropathways in her brain were short-circuiting. As they reached the master bedroom, Madison hesitated and turned toward Logan, looking up into dark pools of blue. Stretching onto her toes, the doctor placed a tender kiss on quivering lips. "I guess I should ask you if you're sure about this as well." When Logan didn't reply, only continued to stand in shocked silence, Madison took a step back. "Maybe we should—"

Logan heard the first question, but with her mind still reeling, couldn't respond. Only when the warm heat of Madison's body disappeared did she finally pull herself out of her trancelike state. "No!"

Realizing that she had shouted, Logan caressed Madison's soft cheek. "I mean no, I don't want to stop." She bent her head to taste the sweetness of the blonde's lips before backing them further into the bedroom. It took a few moments before she noticed the burning candles sitting along the edge of the dresser and on the nightstand. She turned back toward the suddenly shy-looking blonde. "Looks like you were busy while I was gone."

Madison's slender arms wrapped around Logan's neck and confident fingers ran through the long, silky hair that cascaded across her broad, muscular shoulders. As her hands moved lower, Madison could feel the detective's heart beating furiously. She gently placed a single kiss on the throbbing artery and felt a tremble beneath her lips.

"Do you know how much I've wanted you?" Madison gently nipped Logan's earlobe. "How much I've wanted to taste you?" Her lips traveled down the side of Logan's neck and her tongue left a warm, moist trail along the hot skin. "Feel you?" Her hands lowered until the hard muscles in Logan's chest twitched at the sensual touch. "Make love to you?" Her lips followed the pathway of her hands as her tongue traced the line of Logan's clavicles toward the deep vee in her neck.

The overload of sensations had Logan's mind spiraling. She entwined her fingers in Madison's hair, urging the warm lips to open as a soft groan escaped from deep within her throat. Feeling the unmistakable wetness between her legs, she knew there was no backing out—not now, not ever. No words were necessary as gentle caresses spoke their own language, relaying volumes as the women stood among the flickering candles feeling the fire that raged within their souls while they continued their sensual exploration.

Madison heard a quick gasp as her fingers slid across the taut muscles of Logan's stomach. The rapid rise and fall of the ribs beneath her hands and the warm breath caressing her cheek told her the detective was quickly losing control. With sure hands, the doctor tugged the T-shirt over Logan's head before leaning back in to kiss her chest. The spicy scent that she had come to love attacked her senses and she felt her passion rise almost beyond her control when the usually guarded Logan shuddered as Madison pressed one leg snugly into the hot dampness between her legs.

Growling moans escaped both women as Logan thrust forward, pressing her throbbing clitoris harder against the doctor's thigh. Looking into the green pools once again, Logan gently tugged the silk negligee up and off Madison's body, then stood back to admire the muscular, yet very feminine physique of her lover. "You are so beautiful."

As strong, sure hands slid up her rib cage, Logan's mind whirled in a flurry of emotions. Never before had she felt so out of control, so vulnerable, so free. Commanding all of her strength, she pulled away, feeling her pulse quicken all the more as dark, lust-filled eyes peered into hers. Bending her head, she gently sucked an open lip between hers, lightly tracing the smooth skin with the tip of her tongue as she backed the doctor toward the bed. When Madison's legs pressed into the mattress, she slowly lowered the blonde onto the bed and knelt on the floor between her open, inviting legs.

Logan allowed herself a moment to marvel at the beautiful woman before her as she sat on her heels. Madison's long, silky blond hair fell across her bare shoulders, and the flickering candles made it appear as if golden threads were woven into the honey-colored tresses. Even in the darkened room, Logan could see the sparkle of green eyes as she once again fell under the spell of the doctor's lustful gaze. With trembling hands, she caressed the soft skin of Madison's legs, her fingertips feathering gently along the sensitive skin of creamy thighs. Reaching the taut musculature of the doctor's hips, she gently pulled her closer, immediately feeling a warm, silky wetness against her stomach.

Cradling her lover's face between her hands, Madison kissed her inviting lips, and as a moan escaped from somewhere deep within the detective, pressed her tongue deeper, demanding access to the treasure within. Tongues battled for control as hands reached out for possession, each needing to find release, yet wanting to savor every touch, every taste. Long moments passed as they lost themselves in the exploration of each other's bodies with soothing touches from reverent hands.

With a tenderness she didn't know she possessed, Logan slowly kissed a trail down Madison's neck along the soft, sensuous curves of her throat. Her long fingers feathered over the doctor's sensitive skin, slowly dropping to become still beside green pleading eyes that locked with passion-filled blue. The only sound in the room was ragged breathing and the electrified air flowing between the women as they fell into the chasm of each other's eyes.

Madison pulled Logan closer, the yearning in her soul quickly overwhelming the control she had vowed to maintain. Drowning in deep pools of blue, she relinquished control to the need, the hunger, she had been able to contain, and as Logan's thumbs brushed across her hardened nipples, a desperate cry echoed through the silence as she wrapped her legs around the detective's waist. "Oh my God, Logan, yes."

When Logan slowly, deliberately captured a hard nipple between her lips, Madison threw her head back, shutting out everything except the sweet, tortuous sensations flowing through her body. She felt herself being pressed backward as a strong arm circled her waist, gently lowering her onto the mattress.

Madison's body immediately ached as Logan moved away, missing the touch of her lover's skin. Long slender fingers dipped into the waistband band of her panties and lowered the silky garment along her legs, and then, finally, she felt a welcome blanket of warmth as the long length of Logan's body covered hers. Looking into blue eyes, she pleaded, "Make love to me, now. Please...I need you."

Pressed against the swollen nerves between Madison's legs, Logan felt a sweet wetness soak through her jeans. The detective's aching need was relentless, and she struggled not to satisfy her own cravings by ravishing the woman beneath her. Denying her body's demands, she yielded to the passionate need to savor each taste, every touch, and continued along the journey that she knew would soon drive her insane.

A predatory growl formed deep within her belly as long nails raked over her back, completely dissolving her vow to luxuriate in the sensual feast before her. As her body reclaimed control, she thrust her hips hard against the firm thigh between her legs, crying out as a wave of tremors washed over her. Logan bit down gently on the doctor's nipple, then caressed the swollen peak with the tip of her tongue as Madison urgently thrust her hips higher and harder.

The rest of the world ceased to exist as Madison focused on the warm tongue teasing her nipple and the insistent throbbing of her aching clitoris. Every fiber of her being screamed for release as Logan's lips left a warm, moist trail along her stomach. She slipped demanding fingers into her lover's long dark tresses, pressing her lower, urging the warm tongue to satiate her ferocious need. "Please, baby, I need you."

Savoring every inch of Madison's body, Logan slowly made her way to the only oasis she knew could quench her burning thirst, the aching need in her own swollen flesh sending a tidal wave of sensations along her spine. Her body begged for relief, but Logan refused to stop and remove her jeans and bra, needing only at that moment to fulfill her hunger and the burning desire of her lover. She ached to feel and taste the essence of the women beneath her, and when Madison urged her lower, encouraging, hastening the moment when warm lips would meet soft curls, Logan felt a spasm deep within her core.

Logan watched as Madison's head pressed into the mattress, her back arching and her breasts thrusting into the darkness, the hard nipples pleading to be devoured. Logan gently took one of the prominent peaks between her fingers and gently pinched the tender flesh at the same moment her tongue slid ever so slowly along the warm, glistening length of Madison's hard, swollen clit.

"Oh my God, Logan, yes." Madison pressed Logan closer as her clitoris throbbed under the gentle assault of the detective's warm, soft tongue. "I need you so bad, baby." Her body was hot and the air was thick as she gasped for breath. The heat in the room was intense as she rode the first wave of her orgasm. Opening her eyes, she peered down at the raven-haired woman between her legs and cried out, "No!"

Logan fell backward as Madison scrambled further onto the bed. In her confusion, she simply stared at the doctor. "Madi? What's—"

All Madison could manage was a feral moan as she pointed toward the hallway, completely paralyzed with fear. Logan turned and saw the reason for Madison's panic. Flames scorched the walls and the air around them was thick with smoke. The detective immediately assessed the situation, the emotions and feelings she had felt only moments ago shoved into the background as years of training took over, propelling her body into action.

She grabbed the blanket from the bed, hurriedly wrapped it around the terror-stricken doctor, and led her toward the window. After raising the sash with one hand and knocking out the screen, she pushed the doctor through the window. "Go!"

"Come on, Logan, hurry."

Logan pried the doctor's fingers from around her forearm. "I have to get Clancy and Femur. I hear the sirens. Make sure they come to the back of the house. Femur's in the sunroom." She quickly kissed Madison and then ducked back inside the house. The open window was creating a chimney effect, quickly bringing the flames deeper into the room, so she hastily turned and shut the window, locking herself in the raging inferno.

Seizing the sheet, still warm from their bodies, Logan dodged the ever-rising, flickering tongues of the flames and bolted across the hallway to the guest room. Clancy, frightened and frantically crying, instantly jumped into Logan's arms, seeking refuge from the heat and flames. Wrapping the cat inside the sheet, Logan ran into the bathroom and wet the sheet in the shower, hoping it would be enough to prevent the cat's fur from igniting as they tried to escape the blaze. She ducked her own head under the cold water, thankful that she still had on her jeans and shoes and hoping her sports bra would provide at least some protection from the heat and flames.

Tucking the wet bundle under her arm, Logan once again ducked into the hallway, trying to stay beneath the toxic cloud of smoke billowing along the ceiling. Dodging the flames that were quickly engulfing her home, she headed toward what she thought was the opposite end of the house, only to slam into a blackened wall. The smoke was dense and acrid as she groped along the wall. *Dammit, there should be a door here somewhere. Fuck!* Bits and pieces of the ceiling cascaded around her, burning the naked skin as they ricocheted off her shoulders.

Disoriented in the smoke-filled house, she knew she had to find a way out soon or it would be too late. Covering her face with part of the dampened sheet, she continued to feel her way along the walls. The heat scorched her skin and the greedy tentacles of the flames consumed the oxygen she so desperately needed. Frantically groping along the wall, her hand met open space. *The bedroom. I've been in my fucking bedroom.* She blindly stumbled into the hallway, concentrating as one outstretched arm steered her along and the other clutched Clancy. As the smoke grew thicker, she knew she should drop to her knees and crawl along the floor, but in her haste to reach Femur she chose to take a chance and push on.

Venturing deeper into the burning structure, she felt the beginning symptoms of oxygen deprivation as the smoke became unbearable and her head began to spin. As she stumbled over burning debris, her only thought was getting to Femur and Madison and keeping Clancy safe. The roar of the fire was deafening, and at first, she didn't hear the thunderous rumbling echo through the room. As she looked up, the ceiling came crashing down around her. Unable to pull herself from under the heavy weight that pinned her to the floor, she instantly thought of the blond woman she had so recently made love to, hoping she had at least been able to save Madison, and then her world went dark.

Madison frantically ran to the curb, waving as the fire engines sped toward the burning house. As the first firefighter jumped from the truck, she grabbed his arm. "She's in there. You have to get her out."

The firefighter yelled to his comrades, informing them of Logan's presence in the house, then turned back to the hysterical doctor. "Where did you last see her inside the house?" His voice was calm and controlled, but the look in his eyes revealed the urgency of the moment.

Madison had seen that look a thousand times in the eyes of her fellow doctors as the seconds ticked by in an emergency. She pulled him toward the burning structure. "She's trying to get the animals." Raking a hand through her hair, she tried frantically to remember Logan's last words. "The sunroom, that's it. She said meet her at the sunroom at the back of the house."

Waving his team on, the firefighter headed toward the back of the house. Two additional fire engines arrived, and the yard was instantly a scene of organized mayhem as hoses were unreeled and the fire teams scrambled to their assigned positions.

Madison felt a strong arm around her shoulders as a uniformed police officer led her away. "Miss, you need to come with me." She tried to free herself from the officer's hold, and when strong arms tightened around her waist, she spun around. "I have to find her. Please, let me go!" She screamed at the man, pounding his chest as tears streamed down her face. "You can't just leave her in there. Please, God, no!"

Surprised by the strength of the small blonde, the officer literally picked her up and moved quickly away from the firefighters. Gently but firmly he pinned Madison between his body and the squad car and held her as she cried and called out for the woman they both feared was trapped inside the burning building.

Madison fought to regain her composure as the firefighters rained thousands of gallons of water onto the roof and into broken windows, constantly watching the side of the house for any sign of Logan. Suddenly, one of the firefighters yelled, and she watched horrified as he disappeared into the flames through a hole in the roof. Tearing herself from the officer's hold, she ran toward the house just as a massive explosion erupted through the plate-glass windows in what used to be the den.

The doctor flew backward as the force of the explosion knocked her to the ground and shards of glass rained down upon her. Scrambling to her feet, she ran toward the flames, her mind on nothing but Logan, but was tackled by the officer. He held her, pinning her body beneath his as the entire roof collapsed into the house, and tried to comfort her as she screamed. "Logan! Oh my God, Logan, no!"

A crowd had gathered across the street and watched in shocked silence as the house disintegrated into charred coals. A dark figure stood several feet behind the group, watching as the scene played out before him and desperately trying to hide the smile that played across his lips as the explosion ripped through the structure. The smell of gas hung heavily in the air, and he knew it would not be long before they discovered the gas cans he had placed along the perimeter of the house.

Flush with pride at his first experience with arson, he felt the adrenaline rush through his system and filed the information away for later use. *Damn, that felt good.* He watched as the firefighters continued to spray water on the burning house. He knew it was too late to save the woman or the man who had fallen through the roof and momentarily felt a twinge of guilt for harming the innocent firefighter. Shrugging, he thought to himself, *Well, I guess that comes with the job.*

He watched as paramedics attended to the doctor lying on the front lawn. She appeared to be unconscious. *I guess that was just too much excitement for the little woman.* He kept an eye on the paramedics while attempting to look nonchalant and watched as they placed her onto a gurney, then into the waiting ambulance. As the flashing lights disappeared into the darkness, he turned back toward the house and stood watching for a few more moments before tossing his cigarette butt on the ground and slowly walking to his car, whistling as acrid smoke hung in the night air.

CHAPTER NINETEEN

Madison argued as the paramedics fastened a cervical collar around her neck and straps around her waist and legs. Her head was completely immobilized, having been strapped to the spinal board as well, and she could only look into the darkened sky as the paramedics placed her into the back of the waiting ambulance. "I'm fine, Steve, really. It's just a few scratches. Please let me up."

Her head throbbed, and although the doctor suspected that she had sustained a mild concussion when a piece of debris from the explosion hit her in the head, she was more concerned with finding out what had happened to Logan. *Dammit, I don't even know if she is alive.*

The doors slammed and her favorite paramedic slid into the jump seat to begin his evaluation and call in the report to Mercy. Frantically searching his eyes, she took hold of his wrist. "Steve, the other woman, where is she?"

Steve looked at the doctor and shrugged. "You were the only one we were dispatched to, Doc. As far as I know there wasn't another victim."

Struggling against the restraints, Madison felt his hand on her shoulder as a blinding pain wracked through her head. "Doc, come on now, be still, you know the rules." Tears streaked down Madison's face as she stared at the ceiling of the speeding ambulance.

Sighing heavily, Steve patted her shoulder. "Okay, settle down. I'll radio dispatch and see if there was another call, but damn it, Doc, you have to be still for me. You have a knot on your head and probably a concussion to go with it."

Madison cut her eyes toward him and pain tore through her head. "Thanks, Steve." *God, Logan, please be okay. Please, baby, I just found you. Don't leave me now.* She listened as Steve called into dispatch. A few moments later, he hooked the mike back onto the radio.

"Sorry, Doc. There wasn't another call for a woman, just a man—a firefighter from the same scene, and he's being transported to General."

Fighting frustration, she cooperated as Steve asked her a series of questions, trying to evaluate her level of awareness. "That board that hit your head knocked you for a loop there, Doc. Can you tell me what day it is?"

Although she had difficulty concentrating and it took some time, Madison answered all of his questions. Her vision was still slightly blurred and the ringing in her ears was becoming maddening. Finally, her patience running out, she tried to lift her hand to grab his collar but the restraints held her solidly to the backboard. She glared at the paramedic and growled, "I swear, Steve, if you ask me one more stupid question, I'll slug you as soon as I get up from here."

Shocked, Steve watched Madison, trying to evaluate her condition more thoroughly. Never having known the doctor to raise her voice to anyone, he decided the concussion was worse than he had initially thought. "Doc Madi, don't make me have to restrain you any more than I already have. You just calm down and we'll be at Mercy in a few minutes."

She tried to relax as a wave of nausea washed over her. "I'll tell you one thing, Stevie boy, if old Doc Ferguson is on call tonight, I'm going to see to it that you suffer dearly." The paramedic sat back and radioed his preliminary report into the hospital ER as Madison lay quietly on the gurney, a single tear streaking her face.

Madison knew she had a slight concussion. She was still having trouble concentrating and her vision was blurry. Closing her eyes, she tried to concentrate, focusing on the events that had just occurred. *The fire, the fire engines...No, no, no. Logan pushed me out the window first, and then the fire engines came. Okay, what next? The police officer.* She couldn't think; the memory was jumbled somewhere in her brain. *Wait, I remember. The firefighter fell through the roof, then—oh God, the explosion.* The doctor moaned as she remembered the fiery explosion, realizing there was no way anyone inside could have survived.

An insistent beeping resounded in Madison's head as the ambulance backed into the ER bay at Mercy Hospital. The door flew open and in a flurry of motion, she was wheeled into a brightly lit exam room and immediately saw old Doc Ferguson standing patiently, awaiting her arrival.

"Well, Doctor, it looks like you got yourself into a little mishap tonight." Even as Madison argued, he continued, "Now, now, Doctor, don't cause me any trouble. It won't hurt for me to do a simple exam just to make sure."

The blonde resigned herself to the inevitable and allowed the cursory exam, swearing to herself the entire time. *If he cops a feel, I swear I'll deck him right where he stands.* It was common knowledge around Mercy that Dr. Henry Ferguson had roaming hands during an exam. Several lawsuits had been filed by patients over the years, but the hospital administration had always found a way to make the cases disappear.

Now as she lay in the ER, a patient of the letch himself, Madison fought back the nausea that rolled in her stomach. Dr. Ferguson quickly examined Madison, diagnosing a Grade 2 concussion and a few minor scrapes and lacerations. After the technician completed a quick cervical spine x-ray and the doctor received an all-clear, he removed the spine board and cervical collar. "I'm ordering a CT Scan as well, just to make sure everything is all right, Doctor. When the report comes back, if everything is clear, then we will talk. Nancy will get you all cleaned up and I'll be back in a little while to check on you."

The attending nurse began to clean and apply bandages to the wounds when Madison suddenly covered her mouth and frantically looked around the room. Nancy grabbed a nearby basin and held it under the doctor's chin as she vomited. After wiping Madison's mouth with a damp cloth, the nurse eased her back onto the stretcher and refocused her attention on dressing the wounds. A few moments later, she placed the call button in Madison's hand and left to check the status of the CT scan the ER physician had ordered.

Closing her eyes to the throbbing headache, Madison moaned as another wave of nausea washed over her. The ringing in her ears intensified and the voices beyond the curtain turned into a jumbled echo. As she reached out for the railing, an arm gently held her up, turning her toward the basin while she once again violently vomited. When she no longer had the strength to sit, the warm arm held her up and a soothing voice whispered in her ear until she had expelled everything she could. Lying down, Madison opened her eyes and looked into the familiar face of Julie Ellison.

"I heard you were coming in and thought I'd come down and say hello, although I didn't expect this kind of greeting." Julie flashed her penlight into each of Madison's eyes. "Well, kiddo, from what I hear, you have a concussion. The nukes are going to get a CT scan just to make sure there's nothing going on in that brain of yours, but we all know the answer to that one, right?"

Seeing the tears flow down the doctor's soot-smudged face, Julie took hold of her trembling hand. "Hey, Madi, are you okay? Tell me what hurts."

The tender voice only made Madison's sobs worsen, and she dropped her head into her hands. "I've lost her, Julie, I just know it."

Confused, Julie tried to discern what her friend was talking about. She hadn't spoken to Madison in a few days, but she knew there was no one in her life at the moment. *It's probably just the concussion.* She asked one of the nurses to tell the doctor about Madison's continued confusion and asked that the CT team respond stat. "Madi, who are you talking about?"

Madison knew she was confusing Julie, but she couldn't form the correct sequence of sentences. "The fire. Logan. I've lost her."

Julie was glad Madison couldn't see the shock on her face as the reality of what her friend had just said hit her. *The detective, that must be the person that was DOA.* She held Madison's hand as she cried, not knowing how to respond to her friend's obvious pain.

The CT team came in about an hour later and wheeled Madison out, and Julie released a long sigh. Walking quickly from the room, she found the nearest phone and dialed, waiting impatiently for the voice on the other end to answer. "Hey. Yeah, sorry I woke you, but I just heard that the detective you were asking about the other day got killed tonight in a fire."

She listened for a few moments, glancing around to make sure no one could overhear the conversation. "Yes, I know. Me too. Okay, I have to run, but I'll let you know if I hear anything else. I love you too, baby, talk to you tomorrow." After ending the call, the doctor quickly left the emergency department, walking swiftly toward the elevators.

George Schneider picked up the charred remains of one of a dozen small gas cans he'd found around the perimeter of the house. The latex gloves he had put on an hour earlier were covered with soot and mud. Blowing out a low whistle as he turned to his assistant, he tilted his head to the side, trying to stretch out the tensed muscles. "Someone wanted this place down, and fast. Sweet Mary, there was enough fuel here to burn down city hall, and with this old house being nothing but good kindling, I'm surprised it stood as long as it did." He walked toward the minivan he used as an office and dug the cell phone from the glove compartment.

After looking around to make sure no one was within hearing range, he punched in a number. As he waited, small beads of sweat dotted his forehead. *Jesus, I hate reporting to this asshole.* His thoughts were interrupted as an impatient voice echoed in his ear.

"Yes, Mr. Langston...Yes, sir...No, but...I know." Wiping his brow, he waited until he was given a chance to respond. "I know, sir. My preliminary finding will be arson. Yes, sir. No, I don't have any information on the two victims as of yet. Yes, sir, I will, but you have to remember, I'll have no power if this turns into a murder investigation." Hearing the distinctive click on the other end of the line, the fire inspector closed the phone and tossed it back onto the seat before sighing heavily and returning to the smoldering ashes of the house.

Phil Dvorak stood close by as a technician examined the phone cable leading to the house. They'd already concluded that the alarm had been disarmed prior to the fire, and by the looks of the wires hanging from the side of the house, the phone line had been cut as well. Luckily, a neighbor had noticed the flames and called the fire department, but had been unable to get through to Logan.

As Dove knelt down beside a confused dog, he wondered whose it was. He knew Logan had Clancy but had never heard her mention any other animals. He stood when the volunteer from the animal shelter approached. "Hey, um, I think we know who this guy belongs to now. I'm sorry we got you out here for nothing, but he won't be going with you."

Frustration swept the woman's face. "Well, thanks for calling so I wouldn't have to drive all the way into the city, asshole."

As Dove watched her storm away, he smiled down at the Labrador. "Jeez, I'm glad you're sticking with me, fella. She doesn't seem like a great choice for a late-night date."

Taking hold of his collar, Dove led the dog to his car and put him in the backseat, wondering what he was going to do with the dog. "I'll figure out something, boy. If Logan had you, then that's all that matters. You're not going to the shelter." Rolling down the windows, he spoke to the panting canine. "Stay, sit, or whatever the hell you're supposed to do. Just don't leave."

Moving gingerly through the scattered debris, he walked over to the temporary command post set up by the CSI team. "I have the dog in the car. Are you ready to go?"

The soot-smudged face that lifted bored through him like a knife. "In a minute."

Throwing up his hands, Dove stalked back to the car, leaning impatiently against the fender as his foot tapped an angry cadence on the sidewalk.

After having the CT scan, Madison waited impatiently for the results. The nurses hadn't allowed her to dress in case there were other tests to be ordered, so she sat on the stretcher drumming her fingers on the railing. After another hour, she had reached her limit and decided she wasn't waiting any longer for the letch to return. *Jesus, remind me never to make my ERs wait again while I finish my paperwork.* As she had sat alone in the room, her fear had turned to anger and she threw back the starched sheet. She was slipping into an oversized pair of scrubs when Julie came into the room.

"Whoa, sorry there, kiddo." Walking further into the exam room, she eyed her friend with suspicion. "So I guess old Doc Ferguson decided to spring you, huh? I figured he would want to keep you overnight for observation."

As Madison rolled up the legs of the scrub pants, she growled, "Well, I wouldn't know. I haven't seen him in over an hour and I'm not sitting around here any longer." She headed toward the door, then stopped and turned back toward her friend. "Um, I just remembered, I don't have a car. Can you drive me to..." Madison began to sob. "Damn, I don't know where to go. What to do."

Julie caught her as her legs weakened and her knees buckled. "Hey, come on. You're going home with me." Holding the blonde tightly in her arms, she stood, rocking her until the sobs turned to weak whimpers. "Come on, Madi. Let's get out of here."

Against Dr. Ferguson's protests, Julie signed Madison out under her care, promising she would return with her the next morning for a comprehensive follow-up. As they crossed the ambulance bay, she jerked back quickly on the wheelchair when a blue sedan with a flashing red light on the roof sped into the bay and screeched to a halt. "Freaking cops. Bet they cause half the accidents in this city."

Rolling the wheelchair to the car without further incident, she assisted Madison into the car and the magnitude of what she was doing hit her. After closing the door, she walked around to the other side and climbed inside, glancing at Madison. *Jesus, I hope this works.* As she slowly drove toward her apartment, she wondered just what she had gotten herself mixed up in this time.

Femur was frantic as Dove stopped inside the ambulance bay. With no time to comfort the animal, Dove bolted out of the car and ran through the sliding doors. "I have an officer down in the parking lot! I need help now!"

He was pushed aside as a nurse commandeered a gurney from a passing orderly and raced out the door. Moments later he stood, watching as the gurney reappeared with Logan lying motionless on it. The nurse was riding on top of her, her feet on the bottom rails as she pumped air into his friend's lungs.

Logan had refused to leave the scene until she had some solid evidence, and her breathing became more and more labored as the minutes passed until finally Lieutenant Beaudry had ordered her to report to Mercy for a full examination. Two blocks away from the house, Logan had rolled down the window, gasping for air, and all Dove could do was speed up and watch in panicked silence as his friend passed out on the seat next to him.

If it hadn't been for the heroic efforts of the fireman who had fallen through the roof, Logan would probably have been at the city morgue instead of the hospital. Having sustaining a broken leg and multiple lacerations, the fireman had remained conscious and radioed their location to the firefighters. Once he was clear of the house, he was immediately loaded into an ambulance. Logan, obviously in pain and having difficulty breathing, refused to be taken away from the scene, demanding to be allowed to stay and help with the investigation. Once she'd been assured that Madison was being take care of, she had searched through the smoldering remains of her house.

After a few strong words and finally an order from the primary investigator on the case, Logan had reluctantly inhaled the oxygen the paramedics offered. She handed Clancy over to her neighbors after giving the frightened cat a thorough examination to make sure she was okay. Femur had fared better than any of them; his rescue had come as soon as the firefighters reached the back of the house. His frantic barking had alerted them to his location and he was immediately extracted from the burning structure and tied to a tree far away from danger.

Dove couldn't help but feel guilty for Logan's condition. *Damn it, Logan, why are you so stubborn?* Pacing the floor, he waited for what seemed like an eternity until a doctor walked through the automatic doors.

"Are you with the officer that was just brought in?"

"Yes, how is she?"

"I need to see her family. Do you know where I can find them?"

Dove fought the urge to back the man against the wall and focused on retaining some measure of control. "She doesn't have any family. I guess I'm as good as you're going to get." He glared at the doctor. "Listen, look in her wallet if you don't believe me. My name is in it as an emergency contact. Now tell me how she is before I go in there and find out for myself."

The doctor led Dove to an adjoining consultation room and sat down as he detailed the detective's injuries. "She has first- and second-degree burns on her arms and shoulders, but what I'm more concerned about at the moment is her pulmonary distress. There is a significant amount of edema, which was causing her labored breathing. We have her on a ventilator and will be transferring her up to ICU in a few minutes."

Dove felt like he had just been sucker-punched. Only an hour ago, Logan was barking orders to everyone around her; now she was on her way to ICU. "I'm sorry, Doctor, but I don't understand all this medical talk. Could you please just tell me how she is, in simple words?"

The doctor took a deep breath, resigning himself to a lengthy consultation. "Okay, it's like this. Your friend inhaled a lot of smoke that damaged her bronchial passages, her airway. The cells in her airway became leaky, and that is what caused the edema, or a buildup of fluid in her lungs. There is nothing we can do to stop the edema, but we can help with her distressed respirations—ah, breathing, by placing her on a ventilator."

Holding up a hand, Dove stopped the doctor. "You mean she can't breathe on her own. Is she going to die?"

"No, I didn't say that. What I said was she was having a difficult time breathing and we placed her on the ventilator to assist her respirations so that her body can rest and use its energy to begin the healing progress. At this time, I can't tell how much damage was done to her lungs. The next twenty-four hours and how her body responds to treatment will give me a better idea of what to expect. For now, I suggest you go home and get some rest. I have Detective McGregor sedated so the ventilator can do its job, and she will be asleep the rest of the night." Standing up, the doctor moved toward the door. "Come back tomorrow morning and if she is doing better, I'll let you in to see her, okay?"

Dove sat in the empty consultation room for a long while after the doctor left. He and Logan had been through a lot together in the past, but this was worse than anything they had ever faced. He stood and stretched the tired muscles in his back before leaving the quiet space and returning to the car.

As he slid into the front seat, he met the expectant eyes of the Labrador. Scratching the dog under the chin, he released a frustrated sigh. "Well, kid, I guess we better get back to work." He was about to start the engine when he remembered the woman who had been inside the house with Logan. She had been brought to Mercy by ambulance and Dove knew they would have her contact information at the desk.

After a lengthy debate during which he'd been assisted by Logan's doctor, Dove returned to the car with the information. He pulled his cell phone from between the seats, dialed the number, and waited. After a few rings, the answering machine picked up and he listened to the confident and strong voice of Dr. Madison Cavanaugh. When the beep prompted his reply, Dove left a brief message and his phone number, asked her to return his call as soon as possible, then pressed the off button and tossed the phone on the seat. The detective decided to head home for a long, hot shower before returning to Logan's house to help with the investigation.

Riding off into the early morning, neither the detective nor the dog knew what the future would hold for them.

CHAPTER TWENTY

Madison woke to the subtle aroma of coffee drifting into the bedroom. For a moment she looked around, confused, until the events of the previous evening came crashing down upon her. Tears stung her eyes as she recalled the fiery explosion that ripped through Logan's house, finally accepting that no one inside the structure could have survived the blast.

She tossed back the covers and sat up on the side of the bed. Her head pounded, but she ignored the pain. Walking toward the bathroom, she could hear Julie talking to someone in the other room but couldn't discern if her friend was on the phone or had a visitor. Deciding not to interrupt, she took a shower and dressed in a clean pair of scrubs Julie had placed on the dressing table. When she walked into the kitchen a few minutes later, she saw Julie and another woman sitting on the back porch holding hands, drinking coffee and talking quietly.

Julie noticed the movement out of the corner of her eye and quickly returned to the kitchen. After giving Madison a gentle hug, she leaned back and looked into her friend's eyes. "Good morning. How are you feeling?"

Shrugging, Madison turned to pour herself a cup of coffee so Julie wouldn't see the tears stinging her eyes. "I'm okay."

"Well, if you're up to it, come on out to the porch. There's someone I want you to meet."

Blinking away her tears, Madison looked out at the porch and the blond woman who sat alone. "Thanks, but I think I'm going to just call a taxi to take me to get my car and I'll be out of your way. I, um, probably need to see about, um, locating Logan's CO to find out if I can make the arrangements for her..."

Madison allowed Julie to hold her as the tears flowed unheeded, the emotions of the previous twelve hours finally breaking through the barriers she had erected. After a few long moments, she stepped back, wiping the tears from her cheeks. "I need to call in, get my messages, cancel my appointments for the next few days, and go by to check on Susan before I can do anything else." She attempted a smile. "You go on out and visit your friend and I'll see you later, okay?"

Hesitantly, Julie nodded and stepped back toward the door. "Call me later, okay? I need to know that you're all right, and if you need somewhere to stay tonight, you know you're welcome here."

The morning had been long and tiring. Dove still hadn't heard from the doctor who had treated Logan the previous night, and as he rode to the third floor in the hospital elevator, a thought ran through his mind. *This woman probably thinks Logan is dead. Okay, think, what did Logan tell me about her?*

Not waiting for the nurse to look in his direction, Dove almost shouted his question. "Where is the patient that was injured the other night at the Strip? Has she been moved?"

He heard a sound and turned to see a uniformed officer standing behind him. Realizing how his sudden appearance seemed, he pulled the detective's shield from his pocket. After introducing himself, he asked his questions calmly, and a few minutes later continued down the hall toward Logan's cubicle with Susan's new room number written in his notebook.

The fluorescent lights flooding the room surprised Dove; he had somehow always envisioned the ICU as a dark, quiet place to rest. He could hear the rhythmic sounds of the ventilator as it forced oxygen deep into Logan's lungs and the insistent beeping of the monitor hanging from the ceiling. As he eased toward the bed, an unbridled fear overtook him and he had to fight to keep from turning and running from the room.

Logan's arms lay limply by her side and a thin white sheet was tucked loosely underneath them. Numerous bandages covered the burns on her torso and upper extremities, and her breasts were covered only by a small white towel. Dove felt a myriad of emotions as he observed her, the muscles in her stomach and arms at odds with the helpless, vulnerable woman who lay in the bed. If it weren't for the constant reminder of the machines, he thought, she looked as if she could simply sit up and talk, yet her closed eyes and the pallor of her cheeks told him that was only an illusion. The woman before him was in deep trouble and he felt an overwhelming sense of impotence at not being able to help her.

She was sleeping, and although he ached to see her open those penetrating blue eyes, he knew the induced slumber was what she needed. As his eyes panned over her injuries, his heart ached knowing the pain she would endure when she woke. Thin wires disappeared under the white towel that rose and fell with the timing of the ventilator and he watched in silence, knowing the machine was breathing for his friend. Tape stretched in an X across her lips, holding the tube in place. An intravenous line snaked from beneath a layer of tape on Logan's arm across her body, and as he followed its path to the plastic bag hanging from a stand beside her, a lump formed in his throat.

Taking a seat beside the bed, he gently took her index finger in his massive hands. For the first time since meeting Logan, Dove saw her in a different light. She had always presented herself as a tough, street-wise cop, never the frail and vulnerable woman before him. He sat there for over an hour, holding her finger, hoping that in some way she would know he was with her and silently praying she would have the strength to fight her way back. Finally, releasing his hold, Dove rose and, dodging the many tubes and wires, carefully bent down to place a kiss on her forehead, thankful that her beautiful face had been spared.

Slowly he headed for the elevators as anger rose like bile in his throat. *I'll find you, and when I do you will suffer for what you've done.* As he pressed the button for the fourth floor, Dove was lost in thought when his pager broke through the silence. Stepping off the elevator, he located a pay phone and dialed the squad room, then waited for the lieutenant to come on the line.

"Bad news. Phillip Crafton, vice president and director of human resources at Langston Development, was murdered in the parking garage of the corporate offices." The lieutenant instructed Dove to stay at the hospital and was about to end the call when he hesitated before asking, "Um, how's McGregor?"

After updating the lieutenant and ending the conversation, Dove lightly tapped on the half-closed door and stepped into Susan Richardson's room, surprised to see the bed empty. He was just about to turn around and leave when a voice called out from the bathroom.

"Well, Madi, it's about damn time you got here." Susan stopped short when she saw the stranger standing in her doorway. "How did you get in here?"

Realizing he had frightened her, he pulled his shield from his breast pocket and held it out for her to see. "Um, I'm Detective Dvorak, Logan McGregor's sometimes-partner and friend. I didn't mean to frighten you, Ms. Richardson."

Releasing a pent-up breath, Susan eased toward the bed, gently lowering herself onto the mattress, relieved that she had decided to put on her robe before going into the bathroom. After sliding the sheets over her legs, she asked, "How can I help you, Detective?"

Motioning toward the adjacent chair, he glanced up as the most alluring eyes he had ever seen watched him intently. "May I?"

She smiled. "I'm sorry. Of course. Have a seat, Detective."

Sitting down, Dove looked back at his notes to give his pounding heart a moment to recover. "Ah, yes. Well, I was told that you work for a Dr. Madison Cavanaugh, is that right?"

"Yes, I do. Actually, she should be here any moment." As her curiosity and interest in the detective began to rise, she smiled at his flushed face. "May I ask why you are looking for Madison—I mean, Dr. Cavanaugh?"

Dove tried to regain his professional demeanor as he reined in his attraction to the blonde. "I just need to ask her a few questions." He stood, wanting to quickly make his exit before making a fool of himself. Placing his card on the rollaway table, he smiled at Susan. "When you see the doctor, if you would give her my card and ask her to call me as soon as possible, I would appreciate it very much."

"If I may ask, where's Logan? I thought she was heading up this investigation."

Turning to face the blonde once again, Dove didn't miss the way Susan referred to his partner. *Logan, huh?* "I'm sorry, I guess I should have explained. Detective McGregor is indisposed for the time being and I'll be taking over the case until she returns."

Both heard the quick intake of breath as Madison entered the room. A small hand grasped Dove's arm, and in response, he quickly moved to help the shaking woman sit. Kneeling beside her, Dove spoke gently. "Are you Dr. Cavanaugh?"

Madison's pleading eyes bored into the detective's. She held his hand in a death grip in an effort to maintain some semblance of control. "Yes, I'm Dr. Cavanaugh. Please tell me she's alive."

Dove smiled, knowing the news he was about to give her would be a pleasant surprise. "Yes, she's alive. I've been trying to find you since last night."

Madison could only stare blankly, knowing she couldn't have heard the man correctly. "But I—I saw the house explode. No one—no one could live through that." Suddenly, Madison shrank back. "Where...what...how did she...damn it."

Dove gently soothed the doctor as she struggled for words, finally pressing on her shoulder until she sat back in the chair. "Just listen to me and I'll explain everything." He waited for her acknowledgment and then continued, "Logan was in the house, but she got very lucky. The firefighter that fell through the roof practically fell on top of her. They were both rescued, but I have to tell you, Logan is in pretty serious condition."

He held up a hand to forestall her questions. "She's here in the ICU." Grasping her arm, he eased her back into her chair. "Now, let me tell you what to expect before you go up. I know you're a doctor and will certainly understand all the mumbo jumbo better than I, but I'll tell you as much as I know right now."

He stood and leaned against the desk as he filled Madison in. As he was about to escort her to the ICU, he stopped and asked, "Do you own a Labrador retriever?"

Looking up with expectant eyes, she nodded, too afraid to ask.

"Well, he's been drooling all over my car. Do ya think you could come and get him?" Strong arms wrapped around Dove's neck and he was pulled into an excited embrace. He couldn't tell if the doctor was laughing or crying until she released him and he saw that she was doing both.

Quietly the doctor looked up. "What about Clancy?"

Snorting, Dove rolled his eyes. "Doc, I've tried to get rid of that devil cat for the last three years. Hell, that fire probably just pissed her off more and she's sitting at the neighbors waiting for her next shot at me." Seeing the relief on the doctor's face, he turned toward the door. "Come on, let's go see Logan."

Madison quickly gathered her coat, then turned back toward Susan. "I'll be back after I check on Logan. Are you going to be all right?"

"Of course. Get out of here, I'll be fine."

Dove decided to take a chance. "Um, I'll be happy to come back and keep you company after I take the doctor upstairs. I, um, do have a few more questions I need to ask you."

Madison looked from one to the other and turned toward the door so neither would see the smile that creased her face. "I think that would be wonderful, Detective. That way I won't have to worry about both of them."

Dove stood nervously as Susan watched her friend's retreating shadow. "Would that be okay with you, Ms. Richardson? If you're tired, I, ah, could come back anoth—"

Biting her bottom lip, the blonde smiled at the blushing man and interrupted his stammering. "It's Susan, Detective, and yes, that would be just fine." She couldn't help but laugh as the anxious detective backed into the door, then quickly recovered and made a hasty exit.

When she reached Logan's bed, Madison quickly reviewed her chart. It had been almost twenty-four hours since Logan's admission to

Mercy. She remained sedated, her breathing assisted by the ventilator. During the night, the respiratory therapist had attempted to wean her from the machine but when her oxygen saturation level dropped to 88 percent, had kept her on the ventilator.

Madison read the moment-by-moment record of Logan's treatment in the ER the previous night. The physician's notes reported Logan's initial appearance as cyanotic, her lips and nail beds blue from the lack of oxygen in her bloodstream. She had ordered supplemental oxygen and begun her initial assessment of the detective's injuries while a nurse systematically measured and called out the results for the stat nurse to log. Madison knew the tempo in the trauma room had been quick, yet purposeful, as everyone carried out their assignments with the sure, confident movements required to care for the critically ill.

Logan had been in trouble. Her heart rate was 155, blood pressure 105/62, with an oxygen saturation rate of 83 percent. The attending physician had noted the diminished bilateral sounds in her lungs due to the swelling of the damaged tissues and building edema, and as Madison read on, she wasn't surprised to find that the attending physician had immediately intubated the detective in an attempt to get her blood oxygen level back to at least 94 percent before resuming the examination.

A shiver ran up Madison's spine. So much had changed in the last few hours, and she didn't even know where to begin to sort through all of her emotions. She chose to appreciate the moment and the simple fact that Logan was still hanging on and fighting to come back to her. She stretched and placed a tender kiss on the detective's forehead before dropping into the chair beside the bed once again.

Dove moved closer and looked over her shoulder at the chart, furrowing his brow as he tried to read the medical jargon. "I guess you know how to translate all of that. How's she doing?"

Wiping a tear from her cheek, Madison turned toward him with a tired smile. "She's holding her own. Her blood pressure is a little low, but manageable. She's still being sedated so that she won't fight the ventilator, otherwise she would be awake but in a lot of pain."

Dove nodded in understanding and watched the slim figure lying in the bed, the only movement the rise and fall of her chest as the ventilator breathed for her. "Is there a chance...I mean, can she..."

Madison placed her hand on his shoulder. "Hey, she's doing okay right now, and you have to keep a positive attitude for her. The next couple of days will be the worst for her. There is between a 20 and 50 percent chance that she'll develop pneumonia, but I'm hoping that won't happen." Looking at him sternly, she took a deep breath. "And if it does, we'll deal with it then."

Dove gave Madison a weak smile, then turned back toward the bed. Lifting Logan's hand in his own, he brought it to his lips and placed a gentle kiss on her knuckles. "I'll see you later, Mac." He eased out the door and pulled it shut behind him.

Looking toward Logan, Madison quietly whispered, "What were you thinking, staying at the house instead of going to the hospital right away? Damn, you're hard-headed, but I guess that's one reason I'm falling in love with you, Detective McGregor."

As the sun broke through the sheer drapes, Christine Langston stretched beneath the cool, crisp sheets and turned over to wrap her arms around the warm body beside her. Her lover had arrived a little after three in the morning and immediately crawled into the bed, curled her cool body around Christine's, and fallen fast asleep. The executive knew she should allow her to sleep a while longer, but the slowly rising heat in her body demanded a reprieve from the long lonely nights apart. As she slid her hand over taut stomach muscles and around a small breast, she felt her lover stir, then release a low breathless moan, urging her on. Easing her body on top of her lover's, Christine captured an already erect nipple between her lips and gently sucked the sensitive peak as one of her long slender legs pressed hard between her legs.

Opening sleepy eyes, Jennifer looked up into the ice blue eyes of her lover, suddenly feeling the heat between her own legs. Interweaving her fingers in her lover's short, spiky blond hair, she pressed Christine's lips closer, silently pleading for more as the movement of her hips relayed the depth of her quickening desire.

There were no words as the two women fell into each other's warm embrace, both focusing only on the release they desperately craved.

C.W. Langston paced the thick beige carpeting of his office on the twenty-ninth floor, sipping his third scotch and water of the morning. Sitting in the adjacent chair, Herbert Whittaker felt a sense of déjà vu, remembering his previous visit. The sound of Langston's eerily calm voice shook him from the thoughts tangled in his mind, and a chill coursed through his veins.

"Herb, what is the last thing I asked of you the other night?"

Whittaker self-consciously wiped the perspiration from his brow before speaking. "C.W., I told you there is only so much I can do at this point. I can't bring undue attention to my office concerning this case. You're on your own this time. I will not allow my name or the reputation of my office to be connected with a murder investigation."

A small smile edged into Langston's otherwise blank stare. The line had just been drawn, and to a degree, Langston was relieved that the time had come to cut Whittaker loose. Placing his glass on the coffee table, Langston sat in the chair across from the mayor. "I guess you understand what this means, Herbert."

The mayor stood and walked slowly to the door, fully aware that Langston was analyzing his every step. "Yes, C.W., I do, and to be honest with you, for the first time in many years I feel like a free man." Quietly closing the door, leaving a somewhat surprised Langston staring after him, Herbert Whittaker made his way to the elevator.

CHAPTER TWENTY-ONE

Loraine Osborne sat and stared at the drab gray walls of her office. The phone call from Herbert Whittaker had taken her by surprise. She admired the courage it took for the mayor to admit his long-standing association with C.W. Langston, but it angered her that the only reason he had done so was the threat against his thus far unblemished political career. He had displayed no remorse, only fear at being caught up in the middle of a murder investigation. She could only hope that he had a vast reserve of that courage, because she knew from experience that C.W. Langston did not give up without a fight, and more often than not, he won.

The commander knew all too well how determined Langston could be when he set his mind to something. She would have most likely still been the assistant chief of investigations had she not had the backbone to deny Langston his demands. She pushed away from her desk and slipped on her jacket before locking the filing cabinet and walking quietly from her office.

Riding down in the elevator to the garage level, she relived the tension-filled days leading up to her face-off with Langston. Until that time, she wasn't even aware he knew who she was, but then she had realized that a man as powerful as C.W. Langston didn't get where he was without knowing everything that could affect his business and long-term plans.

She and an old friend had been dining at Primanti Brothers when C.W. Langston and his entourage had entered the deli. Even in 1993, before his illustrious career made national headlines, C.W. Langston's presence drew everyone's attention around the streets of Pittsburgh. The manager had scampered across the room to attend to his needs but was brushed off as Langston's attention focused on Loraine.

She had calmly looked at the man towering above her and denied his request to meet with him. *Sorry, Mr. Langston, but I'm off duty. Since I don't know you personally, I can only assume you are here in an official capacity, so if you would like to discuss anything with me, please contact me on Tuesday, I'll be on duty then, and we can chat.* After a few uncomfortable moments, Langston had abruptly waved his hand at the men accompanying him and stormed out of the restaurant.

He had tried to sideline her career more than once, but she had stood strong and held her ground against him. Ten years after Malcolm Cavanaugh had died in her bed, Loraine's life had changed in numerous ways. Earning the gold detective's shield had been an accomplishment she alone had brought about, without any assistance from anyone. C.W. Langston had threatened to take all of that away in a flash if she didn't cooperate and conveniently lose some vital evidence in a case involving his son, Chris. Out of fear, she had gone along with his demands up until the day before the trial, when she allowed the missing items to suddenly reappear on the back shelves in the evidence room. Langston had been livid and met her unspoken challenge with a vengeful assault on her reputation.

What Langston didn't count on was the loyalty and resources of her fellow officers. Many times over the years small legal matters disappeared due to lack of paperwork or some other inconsistency within the vast and overworked legal system. Such favors happened all the time within police departments across the country, and were tallied and filed away for future reference. Loraine had been overwhelmed by the response of her fellow officers as they called in their marks, and she watched with amusement as Langston was hit with code infractions on his new buildings, lost applications for zone changes, delays in construction permits, and numerous other inconvenient technicalities. After a week, Langston had called off his bulldogs and called a truce, but she had always feared that he would one day return and bring more havoc into her life.

Making her way to the car, she ignored the people passing her by as she remembered the first few weeks after Malcolm Cavanaugh's death. The department had spent a few harrowing days trying to keep her identity quiet, and after the gossip died down, she had been promoted to sergeant in return for her loyalty and silence in the case. She had taken the promotion with a promise to Malcolm's memory never to forget what they had shared together. She had genuinely loved him, caring nothing for his position as district attorney or his money. Her only regret was the resultant publicity and the embarrassment suffered by his daughter, Madison. Marissa Cavanaugh had gotten what she wanted: a mansion, money, and the sympathy of all the young available bachelors in the city.

Slipping into a nondescript sedan, Loraine took a deep breath before starting the engine. What she was about to do could alter the course of her career for a second time, but once again, she wasn't going to allow C.W. Langston to get away with his devious and intimidating methods. Merging with the traffic on Grant Street, she guided the government-issued vehicle through the late afternoon traffic toward Penn Circle and the investigative headquarters Logan McGregor called home.

Charles Thornton, assistant chief of investigations, slid from behind the wheel of his car. The investigation into the Strip District murders had all but come to a standstill with Logan's accident. Although the task force had kept detailed records of the interviews and information gathered thus far, he knew the integrity of the case was threatened by her absence. No matter how well prepared the task force was, he knew the primary investigator on any case had an advantage in solving the case. With Logan out of the picture, at least for the time being, Thornton had decided to take a more active role.

Walking toward the uniformed officers hovering about a blue Porsche, he looked around the parking garage, noticing the many shadowed nooks and crannies in which the killer could have lain in wait for Phillip Crafton. When they noticed his arrival, the group of officers dispersed and went back to the meticulous task of gathering evidence. Thornton looked into the car, and his stomach lurched at the sight of the eviscerated human resources director.

With each murder, the killer was getting bolder and more violent. In less than twenty-four hours, the primary investigator's residence had been destroyed by fire and the seventh murder had been committed. The assistant chief had a feeling that the fire at Logan's house had been started to serve two purposes: to get rid of the primary investigator, and to act as a diversion for the murder of Phillip Crafton. Thornton made a mental note to speak with the department psychologist and get her input on the recent events.

Several years had passed since he had actively investigated a case, and he didn't harbor any egotistical ideas that his input would sway the investigation. The task force was composed of the best investigators the police department had to offer. His role was merely to make sure the department, the public, and most importantly the murderer knew the investigation was in full swing.

"You know, Thornton, I'm not one of your high-class investigators, but in my opinion, for a murder like this to occur, the victim had to know the killer." Harold Simons strolled over and stood beside Thornton as his assistants removed and bagged the body.

Thornton concurred. The first six victims had been attacked in the shadowed alleyways within the Strip. Thomas Peters had been murdered inside his own home, but that in and of itself hadn't given them a solid clue. However, the passenger door of the Porsche had been standing open when the first officers arrived on the scene, indicating the murderer could have possibly been sitting inside the car with Crafton. With the sequence of murders being predictable and knowing he was logically the next victim, Crafton would have been especially wary of anyone he didn't know and trust.

Turning slowly, Thornton glanced at the crowd assembled beyond the yellow crime scene tape. He didn't see the department's photographer on the scene and cursed under his breath until he spotted the spunky crime reporter from the *Post-Gazette* among the throng of newspaper and television personnel. He called out, "Ms. Phillips, can I see you for a moment?"

Ducking under the thin barrier of tape, Jennifer hurriedly walked toward him, silently smiling at the complaints and insults thrown her way by the other reporters. "Hello, Chief Thornton."

Thornton led Jennifer far enough away from the crowd so that they could not be overheard. "You're a good friend of Log—I mean, Detective McGregor's, am I right?"

"Yes, sir, I am."

"Well, I was wondering if you could do me a small favor?" He waited but only received an expectant look. Releasing a haggard sigh, he growled at the young reporter. "You do want the man responsible for putting your friend in the hospital to pay, don't you?"

Standing to her full five-foot four-inch height, Jennifer looked up into the glaring eyes of Logan's superior. "Yes, I certainly do, Assistant Chief Thornton. However, one issue Logan and I never, and I mean never breach is our professional ethics. I won't do it for her and I certainly won't do it for you." Returning his icy stare, she continued, "Now, if you care to explain exactly what it is you need, then and only then will I tell you if I'm interested."

Thornton chewed on his lip, quietly admiring her spunk. "Okay, Ms. Phillips, I'll offer you a deal instead. I know you've been present at all the murder scenes, and I also know you have had that camera with you." He smiled as her hand protectively covered her Nikon. "Here's my deal. I'm asking you to take as many photos as you can of that crowd over there, then go back to your office and round up any other photos you have of the other scenes and bring them to me later this afternoon." Holding up his hand to delay her protests, he continued, "In return, I promise that you will have the exclusive when this thing breaks."

Jennifer held Thornton's eyes as she weighed his offer. *Logan would do this. She would make a deal, something ethical yet productive for both of us.* "Okay, you've got a deal. However, I warn you, if you cross me on this, I'll personally see to it that the only press coverage you ever get from me is bad. Got it?"

"I've got it." He handed Jennifer his card and turned to walk away, then stopped and called out to her once again. "Ms. Phillips, I have Logan under twenty-four-hour guard, no visitors, but I'll leave your name with the officer on duty in case you have some time and want to go by and see her."

Dove returned to Susan's room and found her asleep. He quietly sat in the chair adjacent to her bed, taking in the smooth curves of her face. A strand of long blond hair had fallen across her forehead and he had to restrain himself from reaching out and tucking it behind her ear. *How could anyone hurt someone as beautiful as you?*

His thoughts moved to the recent events and the Strip District killer. *What was it that made him select those women? What event or nonevent set him off? Why target Langston Development? Why were only the high-ranking executives targeted?* Dove was startled when a soft voice shattered his musings.

"Hey there. Have you been here long?" Susan watched as the detective gathered his composure, thinking how cute the slight blush looked on his face.

Clearing his throat, Dove hesitantly smiled. "No, I haven't. I, ah, didn't want to disturb you, so I just decided to sit down." For the first time in many years, Dove couldn't figure out where to put his hands. One minute they were on his knees, the next crossed in front of his chest, then on the armrests in the ready position so he could quickly push himself out of the chair and bolt from the room.

Susan watched his nervous mannerisms, trying to bite back a playful smile. She couldn't believe she was sitting in a hospital room with a broken arm and ankle, a fractured skull, and a seven-inch incision across her stomach flirting with a man she had just met two hours earlier. *For God's sake, he's probably married with two kids and a dog at home. Dammit, why are all the good-looking ones taken?*

Regaining some semblance of composure, she tried to sit straighter in the bed, but cried out in pain. Almost at once, she felt a strong arm around her shoulder as Dove leaned over her. As their eyes met, Susan inhaled the spicy scent of his cologne and felt light-headed by his nearness. Unable to find her voice, she allowed him to help her sit up in the bed.

Backing away nervously, Dove shoved his hands into the pockets of his chinos as his eyes darted first to the woman before him, then to the window, then back again. The detective was suddenly without words. *Jeez, Logan would bust a rib laughing if she could see me now.* He suddenly realized Susan had asked him a question. "I'm sorry, what did you say?"

"I asked if your wife knew that baby-sitting women in the hospital was in your job description." Cutting a quick glance his way, she waited for his reply.

"Well, I don't think so, but come to think of it I'm really not sure. See, there hasn't been a wife for the last two years, so I'm not sure how current she is on my job description."

One eyebrow rose skyward as Susan shot a smile toward the detective. "Oh. Well, um, I just assumed that..."

Dropping into the chair, Dove returned her smile. "Well, it appears that while I was out saving the world from crime and corruption, Libby, my ex-wife, was playing doctor with one of the residents here."

"Oh, damn, I'm sorry. I didn't mean to bring up painful memories." Susan chastised herself, suddenly self-conscious.

"No problem. Ben is a great person and he's a good stepfather to my daughter. He, Libby, and Rachel now live in Philly."

Hmmm, no ex-wife nearby. A kid, but that's okay. "Well, I'm glad it turned out okay for you, then." Suddenly needing to get back to safer ground, she changed course. "So, you said earlier that you needed to ask me some more questions."

Taking the cue, Dove nodded and extracted the small flip pad from the back pocket of his chinos. "Well, yes, but if you're too tired?"

Susan weighed her options, but decided to get the questioning out of the way. *I can always call him back if I remember something else, right?*

CHAPTER TWENTY-TWO

Loraine Osborne knocked on the heavy oak doors and waited until she heard a baritone voice grant her entrance. She took a seat in front of the desk and placed her briefcase beside her. "Good morning, Chief."

Len Youngblood wasn't what anyone would call handsome. His graying hair and creased, broad forehead were telltale signs of his stressful years serving as the Pittsburgh chief of police. His eyes could be cold and piercing when dealing with the men and women that served under him, yet Loraine knew from experience that those same eyes could be gentle and kind when the situation warranted.

After working alongside the chief for fifteen years, she had learned to read the small, almost hidden, signs that indicated his mood. Today she saw fatigue, not from long hours of working a case, but from long years of leading the battle against crime—and losing. Shifting in her chair, she cocked her head sideways, indicating the ever-present tape recorder. "I think you may want to make sure that thing is off for what I'm about to tell you."

Templing his hands in front of his face, the chief regarded his commander for a long moment before speaking. "Before I do that, can I assume this is about the Strip District case?"

"Yes, and I just had a long conversation with one of our esteemed politicians who is in way over his head with Langston." She waited while the chief turned in his chair and removed the cassette from the tape recorder.

Youngblood listened without interrupting for almost twenty minutes as Loraine confirmed what he had suspected for several years. When she finally fell silent, he stood and looked out the window at the Pittsburgh skyline, wondering how much longer he could remain at the helm. "How long have we worked together, Loraine?"

Startled by his question, she looked at the back of his head, knowing the reason he had turned away was so she wouldn't see the disappointment in his face. "A little over fifteen years, Len. Why?"

"In all that time, how many people do you think we have put in prison that had connections with Langston?" His back was still turned, but he knew exactly how his commander was reacting to his questions.

"I couldn't say, Len, probably well into the hundreds."

Finally turning from the window, he moved back toward his chair and sat heavily. "Because in all that time, I've dreamed of putting that bastard away once and for all. This time he has gone too far, Loraine. I don't care what we have to do; he's going down this time."

A small smile creased her face as she silently applauded her decision to come to Youngblood. "We have a good opportunity before us right now to gain access to his records. In fact, he was served a search warrant Sunday afternoon."

Youngblood's eyes were closed and his head rested heavily on the high leather back of the chair as he contemplated his options. Finally, after several minutes had passed, he broke the silence. "The warrant that was issued for Langston Development, what did it include?"

It had taken Jennifer less than an hour to take the photographs of the crowd and drive back to the office. After handing the film off to the darkroom manager, she walked back down the hall to the newsroom. She stepped through the wide double doors that led into the bowels of the *Pittsburgh Post-Gazette*; it was there in that noisy room with its high ceiling and peeling paint that she felt most comfortable.

The smell of still-damp ink from freshly printed newspapers hung in the air and to Jen, it smelled like home. Just as some kids grew up smelling Mom's apple pie, Jennifer had grown up smelling newspaper ink. Before she was old enough to charm her father into taking her to the newsroom with him, she could remember the scent of ink that remained on his clothes each night when he would come in to tuck her in and kiss her good night.

Her father, Carlton Phillips, and her uncle, Jack Silverstein, were co-owners of the Lexington newspaper, the *Herald-Leader*, having inherited the thriving business from their father. Jennifer had loved hearing her father tell stories of his younger days as a struggling reporter, enough that she too wanted to make it on her own merits and not on the coattails of her family name.

As she sat down at her desk, she thought about the Strip District case. It was just the story that could send her into the ranks with the best. She also knew the story came second to her loyalty to Logan. Nothing could make her jeopardize their friendship, not even a career-rocketing story such as this one. She dialed the information desk at Mercy. After speaking with Logan's guard and finding that Thornton had cleared her to visit, she grabbed her coat and headed back out to see her friend. She would get her story, but she would do it her way, in her own time, for Logan and for all of the victims of the deranged Strip District killer.

Madison stood silently watching the rain and the slowly darkening sky as another day came to an end. A feeling of helplessness shrouded her, and for the first time in her career, she truly understood the anguish of having a loved one confined within the sterile, uncertain walls of a hospital. She hadn't experienced those feelings and emotions with her father; his death had come quickly with no need for a hospital stay.

As she watched the droplets of rain slide down the window, it struck her how oddly they resembled life. Each began separately on its journey downward, then some merged with others to be swallowed up into large rivulets, their individual identity disappearing as they became one large mass. Others somehow managed to survive as they traveled down the glass, avoiding the call of the easy course and retaining their individuality as they followed their own paths. The doctor knew that somewhere on the pane of life, Logan was one of the single droplets fighting for survival, trying to avoid the force that at that very moment was trying to suck her into the massive void.

As Madison turned to watch the slow, rhythmic rise and fall of her lover's chest, an overwhelming anger took hold of her. *I will not let you be swallowed up into this madman's chasm. He will pay for what he has done to you.* She picked up the phone, hesitantly dialing the one number she never thought she would have a reason to call.

A brusque voice answered on the other end. "Major Crimes, Olsen speaking."

Struck by the abrupt salutation, Madison resisted the urge to hang up, but instead took a deep breath and spoke into the handset. "Yes, this is Dr. Madison Cavanaugh, and I'm trying to contact Commander Loraine Osborne."

The gruff voice answered, "The commander is out of the office for the rest of the day. Try calling back tomorrow."

Madison silently cursed. "Can you give her a message, then? Ask her to call me at her earliest convenience at 555-1836." A quick "will do" and then a click was all she heard as the officer hung up, breaking the connection. Madison turned back toward Logan and placed a tender kiss on her forehead. "I'll be back soon, baby. I'm going home to shower and grab a bite to eat."

Madison suddenly stopped just outside the room, afraid that if she left, Logan would not be there when she returned. Realizing the guard beside the door was staring at her, she gave him a quick smile. "Sorry, I'm a little tired."

As he nodded, Madison turned and walked through the ICU, passing other patients and their families on the way. She waited at the elevator and stepped aside as the doors parted, allowing the occupants to exit. As she stepped into the car and turned to punch the button for the garage level, her eyes trailed to the retreating backs of the previous occupants. A tall, dark-haired woman turned and momentarily looked back toward the elevator, her eyes locking with Madison's for only a second, before once again turning and walking away.

An apprehensive feeling washed over the doctor as the stranger passed through the double doors. The woman looked familiar but she couldn't place the face. Shaking off her uneasiness, she rode the elevator down to the first floor, fully aware that for the first time in her life she felt out of control, afraid and uncertain.

Through the fog of sleep, Dove faintly heard the insistent ringing of the doorbell as a pleading whine came from the excited Lab bouncing on the bed beside him. Rising slowly, he pulled on a pair of sweatpants and a T-shirt and padded barefoot out of the bedroom, Femur enthusiastically running to the door and back to dance around his legs. "Okay, kiddo, I'm coming."

Yawning and raking a hand through his tousled hair, he pulled open the door and immediately had to grab for the jamb to keep from falling as Femur shoved him aside to get to his mistress. He couldn't help but smile when he saw the excitement on both Madison's and Femur's faces at being reunited.

Madison, on her knees hugging and kissing her furry friend, practically shrieked with excitement. "Oh, baby, I've missed you so much. Come here and give Mama a kiss."

"Hey, hey, hey, you're going to kill my reputation as a hardass with the neighbors if you keep carrying on like that. Get in here before they think you're talking to me."

The doctor lifted her head to see Dove's grinning face, then stood and walked into the apartment as Femur pranced around their feet. "Well, Detective, I certainly wouldn't want to be the cause of your reputation being harmed." She allowed Dove to take her coat, and as he hung it in the closet, she took a moment to take in her surroundings.

The living room was immaculately kept. The furniture looked relatively new and Madison wondered if he had recently moved into the apartment. On the far wall a large entertainment center held a wide-screen television and a state-of-the-art stereo system. In almost every available nook stood small photographs of a young girl with a woman. She lifted one off the shelf. "Is this your wife and child?"

Dove turned back toward the doctor. "Yes. Well, my ex-wife and child, to be correct." Padding over to Madison, he took the frame and touched the image of his child's face. "She's a beauty, isn't she? She was lucky and got her mother's eyes."

Madison noticed the melancholy look in his eyes. "You miss her a lot."

It wasn't a question, and Dove simply nodded while replacing the frame on the shelf. "Libby, my ex-wife, and Rachel live in Philly with her new husband. He's a doctor, too. You may even know him—Ben Wainright. He used to have a practice here in Pittsburgh. I think he's a surgeon."

Madison recognized the name, but she didn't tell Dove of the doctor's long-term reputation for being a playboy. "Yes, I remember him. I didn't have an occasion to work with him, but I hear he is an excellent doctor." In an attempt to change the subject, Madison moved toward the couch and sat down. Femur nudged her hand and she scratched his head while looking back at the detective. "Thank you so much for keeping him for me. I really don't know what I would have done with him the last couple of days."

Dove dropped into the adjacent recliner and ran a hand over his two-day-old beard. "You're not planning to go back to your house in Bridgeville, are you? I really don't think that would be a wise decision with this madman still out there."

"No, I'm not exactly sure what my plans are. I spent the night at the hospital, but I guess I do need to make some plans. I really don't want to go back to Bridgeville, not with what has happened in the last few days."

Dove noticed Madison's pallor. Knowing the last few days had been horrendous for her, he wanted to do something to ease her mind. "Look, Madison, I know you don't know me very well, but Logan is my best friend. We not only cover each other's backs at work, we care deeply for each other."

He noticed the faint rise in the doctor's eyebrow as he spoke and felt a warm heat cross his face when he realized that she had misunderstood his last statement. "Let me rephrase that. I care about her as I do my sister and, well, anyway, what I'm trying to say is, I have an extra bedroom here and you're welcome to use it for as long as you like."

Madison felt her shoulders relax and suddenly felt embarrassed. *I don't have any reason to feel jealous. It's not like we're an item.* "I really don't want to impose on you, Dove. You've done so much just by taking care of Femur."

Dove lifted a hand to interrupt. "Really, it's no imposition. Actually, I would prefer it. One good thing about having nosy neighbors is that, on occasion, it works to my advantage. There is a state-of-the-art alarm system here, and Mrs. Arrington next door will catch anything that happens to slip by the sensors." His lips pressed together tightly as he observed his guest for a moment. "You'll be safe here, Madison. Please, I want to do this for you and Logan."

Madison smiled as she thanked Dove for his kindness. "I can see why Logan thinks so highly of you, Detective. She's really lucky to have you in her life."

She saw what looked like tears fill his eyes as he quickly rose and walked across the room. "No, Madison, I'm the lucky one." He returned with a small key ring and a slip of paper. "These will get you in the door, and here's the alarm code. I'm in and out at all hours, so just come on in and make yourself at home." He laughed. "Mrs. Arrington and Femur have bonded. She has been taking him for walks two or three times a day. I'll let her know you'll be staying here for a while so just let her know if you need her to watch him. Just don't yell at me when he's spoiled rotten."

The blonde rolled her eyes. "Sorry, Dove, but he's already spoiled rotten. I really don't think he can get any worse." She grinned as a bright grin crossed Dove's face, realizing that this was the first time since she'd met him that he had really laughed. *Maybe this will be good for both of us...to have someone to talk to, be afraid with.*

Scratching Femur's head, Dove said lovingly, "Say, Femur, what say we go out to your house and let your mom pack up a few things?" His eyes lifted to Madison's. "I'm sorry, but there was nothing left to salvage from the house. I really hate to tell Logan. She loved that place."

CHAPTER TWENTY-THREE

Christine Langston gazed out the window of her penthouse office. Her mood was somber, the events of the last few weeks convincing her that the time had come for change in Langston Development. Gone were the days when her father had the power and the influence to control the destiny of the company. His dictatorial leadership was coming to a sudden and shocking halt, and she could only pray that she would survive the aftershocks of his tyranny.

Moving from the window, she sat behind the large mahogany desk that had for many years protected her from the onslaught of disgruntled employees that came through her door on a regular basis. Her role in Langston Development entailed much more than her responsibilities as vice president of architectural design and construction. She was also the peacekeeper within the corporation, often sifting through the entanglements and aftereffects of her father's oppressive leadership. More often than not, Christine found herself providing moral support to her father's many underlings. She knew all too well what it felt like to be the focus of her father's indignation, and she strived to counterbalance his power-hungry destruction.

She recoiled as the sudden shrill of the phone shattered the peaceful quiet of her office. She picked up the phone and asked her secretary to show her visitor in. After replacing the handset, she walked quickly around the desk. The pulse drummed in her neck as the door opened and she stood face to face with the man she knew would play a lead role in her plans for Langston Development.

She grasped his hand in a firm handshake. "Detective Dvorak, I'm Christine Langston. Please come in and have a seat." She motioned to the white leather couch at the far end of the room. Taking a moment to organize her thoughts, she walked quickly to a panel on the wall, pressed a button, and waited as two dark panels on the adjacent wall slid back to reveal a built-in bar. "May I get you something to drink?"

"Water would be fine, thank you." Glancing around the spacious office, Dove sank into the soft cushions of the couch. A quick calculation revealed that this one room was nearly the size of his entire apartment, yet the furnishings and personal touches made the cavernous room feel warm and inviting.

His eyes wandered toward the bar where the executive stood, her back to him as she prepared their drinks. Her chic suit fit perfectly over the flowing curves of her slender body. Christine Langston always presented herself as the strong and capable executive that she was while maintaining and emphasizing the feminine qualities that her genes had so generously bestowed upon her. Short, spiky blond hair and smooth tanned skin complemented icy blue eyes set within the chiseled structure of her face, and Dove suspected that those eyes were capable of not only seducing but slaying the beneficiary of her gaze.

Christine held out a water goblet. Dove took it from her hand, noticing a slight tremble as the clear liquid danced, almost imperceptibly, within the confines of the Waterford crystal. To his surprise, she sat down beside him on the couch instead of moving to the safety of the wingback chair on the other side of the coffee table. He turned slightly toward the executive, and taking a drink of the ice-cold water, watched as her curious blue eyes focused on his face.

"Now, Detective, what is it that I can do for you today?" Feeling more in control, Christine lifted the glass to her lips and took a sip of her wine.

Dove put down his glass and removed a small writing pad from his pocket and flipped to a clean page. He could not discern if Christine Langston was mentally preparing to seduce or slay him.

Madison spent the rest of the morning unpacking the small suitcase she and Dove had brought from the house in Bridgeville, her mind constantly replaying the unusual message left on her answering machine. The last time she remembered speaking to her mother was well over a year earlier, distance and time allowing them very little in common of which to speak.

She moved around the apartment, wondering what had prompted the call. Her mother had not mentioned the recent murders, but then Madison knew all too well that Marissa Cavanaugh was not one to speak of such events. For most of her adult life, her mother had hidden behind the protective shroud of high society, never having to address life's shocking reality. It wasn't until the thin façade of her existence was shattered that she truly saw the world as it was for most. Her solution to the unforgivable predicament created by her husband's untimely—and unfashionable—death was to pack up and run to the safety of a new life, in a new country, where no one knew of her unpleasant past.

"Rome? Did she say she was in Rome?" Femur's ears lifted as Madison spoke, his head tilted to the side as he curiously eyed his mistress. "Yeah, I know, you think I have totally lost it, don't ya, boy?" She shoved the dresser drawer closed and walked to the bed. Lying on her back, she stared at the ceiling as a single tear etched its way down her cheek. Femur hesitated momentarily before jumping on the bed and stretched out beside her, his head resting protectively on her stomach.

"We have one hell of a family, don't we, big guy? A mother I can't even begin to keep track of and a brother I haven't seen in so many years I'd probably not even recognize him." Fighting the urge for self-pity, Madison crawled from the bed. Femur danced across the floor as she picked up his leash from the nightstand. "Come on, boy, let's go see if Mrs. Arrington wants to take a walk."

Loraine Osborne sat in the opulent reception area of C.W. Langston's penthouse office suite. Beside her, Len Youngblood twisted his thin gold wedding band. Loraine knew he was contemplating his future, thinking about the implications of confronting the powerful C.W. Langston.

The commander wasn't sure the chief's idea of confronting Langston was a good one, but just as she turned her head to put voice to her concerns, the massive oak doors to Langston's inner sanctum opened and the man himself stood in the threshold. Loraine watched as Langston's eyes settled first on Youngblood, then swept toward her, and she silently delighted at the almost infinitesimal slumping of his shoulders.

"Come." It was more a demand than an invitation, and after a quick glace at each other they stood and walked silently into the office. Langston, already settled behind the massive desk with his hands resting casually on the blotter, waited until the unwelcome guests were seated before speaking. "Well, Len, it's been a long time. How have you been, and how's Martha and the kids?"

Youngblood bristled at the mention of his family and sat straighter in his chair. "This isn't a social call, Langston, and I don't believe for a minute you give a damn about the welfare of my family, so just cut the bullshit and let's get on with this."

A sinister smile flashed across Langston's face. "Now, come on, Len, we go way back. There's no need to get defensive, but if that's the way you want to play this out, then so be it." His eyes momentarily flashed over to Loraine. "What's with the backup, Len? Has the city finally come to its senses and put you back on the street handing out tickets and training rookies?"

Loraine knew, without a doubt, that C.W. Langston recognized her, but she was also keenly aware that the two men were jostling like two lions fighting for terrain they felt rightly belonged to them. She used the time to study the executive's face. The years of scheming and conquering had proven costly. His once handsome face was now worn and haggard from playing hardball with the constant influx of younger executives and politicians. Langston's reign was coming to and end. She knew it, he knew it, and so did everyone else in the city. The time had come to move the progression along, to once and for all put an end to Langston's reign of terror and intimidation.

Loraine was shaken out of her musing by Youngblood's low, barely controlled voice. Looking from one man to the other, she realized she had missed part of the conversation. Youngblood's hands gripped the arms of his chair as if he were fighting to remain seated. "I'm telling you once and for all, C.W., your days of playing games in this town are over."

Langston, his hands flat on the desk blotter, leaned forward, his eyes boring into the chief's. "And I'm telling you, Len, it's over when I say it's over and not before." Calmly leaning back in his chair, he removed one of his trademark cigars from a wooden box on his desk. "Now get the hell out of my office."

After her walk with Mrs. Arrington, Madison showered and returned to the hospital. Madison, concerned not only about Susan's health but her safety as well, had pulled a few strings to keep her as an inpatient for as long as possible, but the insurance provider had taken notice and demanded her discharge, and Susan was becoming impatient with the confinement. Madison's first concern was finding a safe place for her friend to stay. She had pondered the idea of taking Susan to her home in Bridgeville, but now that she was temporarily in exile at Dove's it wasn't an option. *Damn, what am I going to do with Susan? I can't simply let her go home; there's been too much publicity about her attack.*

Distracted, when she stepped from the elevator she collided with Dove. "Damn, sorry about that. I was off in another world. Are you okay?"

He pensively studied the frazzled doctor, "Yes, I'm fine, but what about you? You look a little upset. Is there anything I can help you with?"

"Um, no, thanks. I'm just worried about Susan. I know she is being discharged in the morning, and I'm concerned about her."

A gleaming smile swept across his face and he playfully bowed to Madison. "Well, your white knight has struck again, my dear. That problem has been all worked out."

Madison took Dove's arm, pulling him away from the busy elevator. "What do you mean all worked out?"

"Ha! Never underestimate me, Doctor. I am full of surprises and solutions. As of tomorrow morning, we are getting a new roommate."

Madison's jaw dropped at the surprise revelation. "But—but there—I mean, you only have two bedrooms."

Dove winked mischievously. "Well, Doctor, Susan and I have that little problem all worked out."

"Dove, I know you like Susan, that's apparent, and she likes you too, but, ah, I mean, do you think it's a good idea for the two of you to, um, you know."

He bit his lip to keep from smiling. "Well, yeah, I like her a lot. What better way to see if we get along than to live together for a while? I mean, what if we were to date for six months and then I find out she doesn't like my snoring? That would be just a waste of time, don't you think?"

"Well, what does Susan think?" Madison visualized the two of them together and a blush crept across her face.

"What's wrong, Madison? Don't you think it's a good idea? Sort of like killing two birds with one stone, if you ask me. This way, Susan and I can see if we are attracted to one another and she will be safe and secure. Plus, she will have you there with her as well. Anyway, Susan is all for it. I'm picking her up in the morning and taking her to the apartment to get her settled."

Madison sighed heavily. "Well, I just hope you both know what you're doing. Far be it for me to interfere."

"Oh, by the way, I forgot to mention Mrs. Arrington will be letting some delivery people into the apartment this afternoon, so don't let them startle you if you should be there when they arrive. I'm having a daybed set up in the office for Susan." Stepping into the elevator, he grinned as Madison looked at him in shock. "Have a nice day, Doctor. I'll see you later."

"You little—" The doors closed before Madison could complete her sentence. She laughed, realizing Dove had played her and played her well during their conversation. *I'll remember that, Dvorak. Paybacks are hell and I can play with the best of them.*

Her step became lighter as she continued toward Susan's room. Now she had to figure out what she could do to get Logan to wake up and come back to her. Thinking into the future, she mused over Dove's inventive solutions. *Hmm, well, he doesn't have another bedroom, so that leaves only one solution. One I certainly wouldn't mind!*

Loraine Osborne studied the short handwritten message the desk sergeant handed her when she returned to the office. *So, Madison Cavanaugh wants to talk to me.* She toyed with the pink slip in her hand, wondering what had prompted the call. *It must be something serious for her to call and request me.*

Punching in the numbers, she waited until the cool, professional voice of Dr. Madison Cavanaugh's voice came on the line requesting that she leave a message. "Ah yes, Doctor, this is Loraine Osborne returning your call." She hesitated only a moment before continuing, her curiosity increasing by the second. "I will be out of the office most of the day, but you can reach me on my cell phone at 555-4986. Please, feel free to contact me at your earliest convenience."

After replacing the receiver, she stared at the black institutional phone. For years, Madison Cavanaugh had gone out of her way to avoid any contact with her father's lover. Now, after all this time, she had contacted Loraine. *No doubt the call is about the case, but what interest could she have in it other than the fact that her assistant was one of the victims? Surely that isn't enough to force the doctor to contact me personally.*

Returning to her messages, she noticed that Detective Dvorak had requested to see her immediately. She set the other messages aside and quickly strolled out of the office in search of the detective, wondering what other surprises were in store for her.

CHAPTER TWENTY-FOUR

Madison eased into the quiet space of the hospital room and was pleasantly surprised to find Logan's face unobscured by the ventilator tubes. She walked quickly to the bed, and for the first time since Sunday evening, kissed Logan's lips. Although they were parched from the ventilator, the warm lips twitched under hers, making Madison's heart swell with excitement. She jerked upright as the door opened behind her and a nurse strolled in with a wide grin on her face.

"Well, I see you got here before I could call you with the good news, Doctor." Her eyes gleamed as she fussed over Logan. "Dr. Black was here just a few minutes ago and removed the tubes." She was surprised to see tears in Madison's eyes but said nothing as she applied a fresh dressing to one of the more severe burns on Logan's arm.

"Has she been awake at all?" Madison's heart pounded in her chest. Although she hoped for an affirmative answer, she also wanted to be at Logan's side when she first opened her eyes.

The nurse shook her head. "No, not yet, but Dr. Black did sedate her again just prior to removing the tubes. He didn't want her struggling and wanted to give her body time to adjust to being without it." Her eyes lifted to Madison's. "I'm sure she'll be around shortly. From what I've heard about this woman, nothing can keep her down for long."

Madison sat beside the bed waiting until the nurse finished her tasks and left the room before reaching through the railing and lacing her fingers with Logan's. "Get your ass back here, McGregor. I'm lonely and I need you, damn it."

She watched the rhythmic rise and fall of Logan's chest as she breathed on her own for the first time since late Sunday evening. Startled by her pager vibrating against her side, she released Logan's hand, quietly stepped from the room, then picked up the phone at the nurses' station across the hall, punching in the number for her office on the fifth floor. "Hello, Rebecca. You paged?"

Rebecca, the assistant to another orthopedic surgeon at Mercy, had graciously offered to fill in for Susan. Madison jumped at the offer, having more or less abandoned her practice since Susan had been attacked the previous Wednesday evening. Madison had instructed Rebecca to refer all of her immediate patients to other physicians and reschedule the other less urgent cases for the following week. She hadn't been into the office since the previous Thursday except to collect her messages and return a few phone calls, and she knew the backlog she would face when she returned would surely need the expert hands of an efficient assistant.

She listened as Rebecca delivered several messages, but interrupted as she sped through the fourth one. "Rebecca, hold up. Who was that last message from?" *Oh great, just what I need, a visit from Mother.* "Okay, when is her flight? Yes. Got it. Thank you, Rebecca. Thanks, you have a good evening too. Yes. Bye."

Madison sat down and dropped her face into her hands. *What next!* She jumped as a hand fell onto her shoulder and swung around to face Dove. "Jesus, man, you scared the hell out of me."

The detective's face reddened. "Sorry, Doc, I didn't mean to scare you. I just wanted to say hello. How's Logan?"

A smile slipped across her face as she stood. "As a matter of fact, she is doing much better. They took the vent away a little while ago. Go on in and see for yourself."

Dove's eyes widened, reminding Madison of a little boy getting a new bike for his birthday. He practically ran to the door, but stopped short remembering that he was in a hospital and tentatively pushed on the door and disappeared into the room.

Pushing away from the desk, Madison headed for the elevator, deciding to visit Susan so Dove could have a few minutes alone with Logan. The thought her mother's impending visit set her mind in turmoil. *Damn, why is she coming back? She hasn't been here in six years, and I can't think of a single reason that could be important enough to bring her back to the one place she loathes most in the world.*

The ride to the fourth floor was quick, and she breezed into Susan's room with a light step, feeling better than she had in days. She was surprised to see her assistant sitting patiently next to the window. "Hey there, kiddo, how are you feeling?"

"I'm super. Ready to get out of here, that's for sure." Susan didn't miss Madison's jovial air. "And just what brings you here in such a good mood? It has to be good news about the tall, dark detective. So tell me, how is Logan?"

"She's doing much better. Dr. Black removed the vent this morning and she's holding her own." Tipping her head toward Susan's bags sitting by the door, Madison smiled. "I see you're all ready to join us at the bachelor pad, but if you'll remember, you aren't being released until morning." She crawled into the empty bed and stretched out her legs. "Dove is visiting with Logan, but I'm sure he'll be along soon."

"Yeah, I know I can't leave until tomorrow, but I just want to be ready to go when the doctor gives me the go-ahead." A grin flashed across Susan's face at the mention of Dove's name. "He dropped by on his way in to let me know he was going to the ICU. He's such a sweetheart, isn't he?"

"Yep, a real sweetie, all right." Madison thought back to their conversation earlier in the day. *Yeah, a real smart-ass sweetheart.*

Susan eyed her boss suspiciously. "What? Why are you frowning?"

Madison shook herself from her daydream and waved a hand in the air. "Um, nothing, just thinking about a conversation I had earlier in the day." She quickly changed the subject and told Susan about her mother's message.

"What is she coming here for? I thought she hated Pittsburgh."

Madison shrugged and rolled her eyes. "I have no idea, and yes, she does." She rose from the bed and impatiently paced the floor. "She's up to something, I can feel it. The only way Marissa Cavanaugh would step foot back in this town is if her life depended on it."

Outside in the hall, a man in a white lab coat pretended to study a patient chart and smiled as he listened to the conversation on the other side of the half-opened door. He whistled as he sauntered down the hallway toward the stairs. *If you only knew, Doctor, if you only knew.*

Susan finally calmed Madison enough to get her to sit. Something about her mother ripped to Madison's core, and she felt useless to help. The more she tried, the more she realized there was nothing she could do except listen and be there if and when Madison ever needed her. *Hell, Madison herself doesn't even know what it is that baffles her so much about her mother.*

They were surprised as the door flew open and Julie Ellison sauntered into the room. She stopped, eyeing Madison closely, crossing her arms over her chest. "*Dr.* Cavanaugh, you of all people should know the hospital rules about lounging in the patient's bed."

Madison sheepishly raised an eyebrow. "We're in the middle of a consultation, Dr. Ellison. We're playing psychiatrist and I *am* the patient, so I need to lie down."

"A consultation, huh?" Julie's gaze flicked from Madison to Susan and back. "Remind me if I ever have a compound fracture *not* to let you cut on me. You're a strange one, Cavanaugh, very strange, but God help me, I love you anyway. Now get out of here so I can examine my patient."

She pointed at Susan, who was staring intently at the ceiling. "And you, *Dr. Richardson*, in the bed. Until tomorrow morning, I'm still your worst nightmare. Jeez, what did I do to deserve you two?"

Madison pulled herself from the bed and shot Julie a smile as she leaned in to plant a light kiss on Susan's forehead. "I'll be downstairs in Logan's room. Come and get me when you're finished and we can grab a bite to eat."

Julie distractedly waved over her shoulder as she helped Susan onto the bed. "Yeah, yeah, sure, but you're buying or I'm reporting this little infraction to the suits."

Madison growled, "Sure you will, Doctor, but just remember I know what really happened last year in the x-ray." She smiled as Julie's back slightly tensed, knowing she had made her point, and strolled out the door. Still, she knew she shouldn't have teased Julie and decided to take her to Mr. Ribs, her favorite restaurant, for lunch.

A smile played across Madison's face as she returned to Logan's room, but it vanished as she passed through the door and her eyes locked on the surprised face of Loraine Osborne.

Loraine regarded the doctor cautiously, not wanting to upset her in Logan's hospital room. "Dr. Cavanaugh, it's good to see you again. How are you holding up?"

Even though Madison's first impulse was to be defensive, she fought the urge, remembering that she herself had called the commander requesting a meeting. She hadn't been prepared for an unannounced visit, but then realized that the commander was probably there to see Logan and not her. "I'm fine, Commander, and you?"

Loraine noticed the strain in the doctor's words, but knew if she were in the same position she would probably react much in the same fashion. "I'm well, thank you." She glanced quickly at Dove and then back to Madison, wondering if she should broach the subject of the doctor's request to speak with her. "I would like to speak with you if I may. Ask you a few more questions."

Dove watched the two women regard each other nervously. His senses told him there was a history between the commander and the doctor, but he didn't dare intrude on the conversation. Madison noticed his discomfort and rescued him by asking that he relay a message for Julie to meet her in the cafeteria when she was finished with Susan, then walked to the bed and took Logan's limp hand in hers.

Setting her jaw, she looked steadfastly into the eyes of the commander. It was difficult asking for her help, especially after she had almost single-handedly destroyed Madison's family, but there was nowhere else for her to turn. She knew Loraine was a good cop—one of the best, as was Logan—and she also knew the commander would spare no effort to find out who had done this to her detective. She took a deep breath and lowered the walls of her pride for Logan. "How much progress has been made on the case?"

Loraine struggled for an answer that would satisfy Madison. There was very little she was free to divulge to the public, but she also noticed the possessive hold the woman had on her detective's hand, a hold that in its own way made the doctor family. "I can't tell you everything, Doctor, but I will tell you I won't stop until I find who did this, not only to Detective McGregor but the others as well."

Madison looked at the peaceful rise and fall of Logan's chest for a moment and then raised her eyes back to Loraine's, a new strength shining through the pain. "I want you to find this monster, and I think I have an idea of how I can help."

Loraine opened her mouth to speak, but the door swung open behind her and a lab tech walked in. "Good afternoon, ladies. Sorry to disturb your visit, but I need to draw some vials for the lab. If you'll step outside, I won't be but a minute."

Madison released Logan's hand and stepped around the bed. "Why don't I buy you a cup of coffee in the cafeteria and fill you in on my idea."

Something was puzzling Loraine, but she couldn't put her finger on exactly what it was. Finally shrugging off the foreboding feeling, she got onto the elevator with Madison and they both took a few moments to get used to the idea of being in each other's company.

From deep within Logan's mind, she heard someone speak her name but couldn't quite place the voice. It was familiar, but strange all at once. She struggled to open her eyes as a needle pierced her skin, but her lids were heavy, as were her arms and legs. It was as if she were being restrained, but in the diminishing fog, she didn't understand why. Her heart raced as she fought to break free of the weighty sensation, panicking as her breathing became labored and constricted.

In the distance there was a noise, then the footsteps quickly retreated into the hallway and a few seconds later she heard the shrill sound of an alarm. Her eyes opened for an instant as she realized the blaring alarm was just above her head. She frantically struggled against the restraints that held her arms to the bed and felt a crushing pain in her chest just before her world fell once again into darkness.

Julie had finished her examination of Susan when Dove pushed through the door. The doctor was about to reprimand the detective for bursting in unannounced when she saw the sparkle in her patient's eyes.

Dove looked anxiously at Susan, then at Julie's serious expression. "Is everything all right?"

"Yes, I'm fine, Dove; the doctor was just giving me a final checkup before I go home tomorrow. Come on in."

Julie excused herself and was halfway out the door when Dove remembered the message from Madison. "Hey, Dr. Ellison, Madison wanted me to tell you to meet her in the cafeteria in case she wasn't in Logan's room when you got there."

"Thanks, Detective." Julie went into the dictation room at the nurses' station to finish her notes and sign Susan's release papers for the morning. Ten minutes later, she was on her way to the third floor to meet Madison. She heard a code 99 called to the ICU as she stepped from the elevator and fell into a sprint along with a group of other white coats responding to the emergency.

In the hallway, nurses pushed carts into the room and the attending yelled orders over the controlled chaos. To the untrained eye, the hubbub of activity would appear as massive pandemonium, but to Julie it was a textbook example of a code response. She stopped when she realized the code was well under way and her presence would be more of a hindrance than a help. As she turned to leave, she stopped short and spun around, realizing the code call was in Logan McGregor's room.

She ran into the room and watched Logan's body jerk off the bed as the attending physician pressed the button on the defibrillator, sending 360 joules of current through her lifeless body in an attempt to restart her heart. Julie's eyes danced between the second hand on the clock and the figure in the bed as the doctor snapped out orders, his voice becoming more demanding and more frustrated by the second. Each attempt thus far had failed and with each passing minute, everyone knew the chances of resuscitation were lessening. Finally, pulling herself out of her trancelike state, Julie thought of Madison and bolted from the room, sprinting in the direction of the cafeteria.

CHAPTER TWENTY-FIVE

C.W. Langston sat, fingers laced behind his head, listening to Christine's update on the latest developments in the case. He noticed the fatigue in her eyes but resisted the urge to comfort her. *It will make her stronger.* "Why did that cop come to see you this morning, Christine?"

She'd known one of her father's cronies would inform him the minute Dove Dvorak entered the building and she was ready for the questions. "He just dropped by with more questions, C.W. There's nothing to worry about. I got rid of him quickly."

Langston dropped his hands and impatiently fingered a cigar. "Exactly what did he want?"

Christine sighed heavily, knowing her father would drill her unmercifully about the detective's visit. "He wanted background information on Peters and Crafton. He's concerned with Donovan's safety as well and wants to put a guard on him, but Lester is staunchly refusing."

Langston clipped the end of the cigar with a sterling silver guillotine and then lit it with the matching lighter and exhaled a cloud of blue smoke into the air. "And just how much background did you supply the cop with?"

"Very little, only enough to satisfy his meager brain and get him out of the way." She glanced at her watch and stood before he could question her further. "Look, I have a lunch appointment. Why don't I meet you back here afterward?" She had checked his appointment schedule before entering and knew that the rest of his day was booked. If she could just get out of his office, she would be free at least for a while from his probing questions.

He stood and walked her to the elevator. "Sorry, I'm booked solid for the rest of the day. Come by the house tonight at seven for dinner and we will talk more. I have a guest arriving in town Thursday and need some help getting everything in order."

It wasn't a request but a directive, one that was not to be debated or questioned. "Sure. I'll see you then."

Christine pressed the button for the private elevator and felt the burning eyes of her father boring into her back. As she entered the car and turned, she saw him standing beside his office door studying her with a cold, hard look on his face. It wasn't until the door closed that she released a pent-up breath and slumped against the polished oak panel wall, then immediately straightened again, remembering the camera perched stealthy in the corner.

C.W. Langston's brow furrowed as he watched his daughter—and senior vice president—slump against the wall of the elevator. He walked to the floor-to-ceiling windows that made up the north wall of the office and took in the Strip District a few short blocks away. The area lying parallel to the Allegheny River made up a modest portion of the city; however, as the rejuvenation project progressed, it was quickly becoming one of the more popular areas for young, affluent executives. The condominiums had filled almost as soon as they were listed on the open market, and currently there were over 230 names on a waiting list.

The area was a thriving Mecca that he was not about to relinquish. No one, not even his daughter, would interfere with his vision for the Strip District. This was a culmination of years of hard work and planning—his mark on the world, and he would stop at nothing to make sure his dream became a reality.

"What are you up to, Christine?" He dropped into the leather executive chair behind his desk and snatched up the private phone. A few seconds later the call was answered and his voice, harsh and abrupt, barked into the phone. "What the hell are you doing, Watson? I want answers and I want them now." The pen holder tumbled across the desk as his fist slammed against the oak desktop. "I don't give a fuck what you're up against, I want you to find him, and soon. You have twenty-four hours, then we do it my way."

The chair crashed into the credenza as he stood, tossing papers and folders into his Armani briefcase. Striding to the door, he wrestled with his anger; his frustration, he knew, was apparent on his face. Hand on the doorknob, he took a deep breath before opening the door and walking out into the reception area. "I'll be out the rest of the day. Call me if anything important comes up."

The receptionist, a temp sent to fill in for his assistant, stared fearfully at Langston's retreating back. She waited until the elevator doors closed before picking up the phone and placing a call. "Yes, he just left...No, he won't be back today...Okay, I know the plan...Fine."

She hung up and turned to the monitor hidden inside a cabinet against the wall behind her and watched as C.W. Langston exited the elevator on the first floor, walked out of the building, and entered a waiting limo. She quickly walked to the door of the executive offices, placed a note on the heavy oak door saying she would return in fifteen minutes, and headed to the CEO's private office.

She locked the door behind her, then hastily thumbed through the filing cabinet, knowing there would be nothing of interest in the main vertical files. Moving to the massive desk, she located the small filing drawer on the right side and sat down, her lips curling into a smile when the drawer rolled out effortlessly. "You're losing it, old man. Rule number one: never forget to lock up the secrets."

Her eyes swept the office, as she suddenly realized that the paranoid old man might have his office bugged or wired for video surveillance, and she made a mental note to check the video hub in the outer office before she left. Moments later her eyes fell on the files she was searching for. With the folders tucked discreetly under her arm, she made her way to the outer office, thankful that the executive suite didn't share a copy machine with the other offices on the floor. Careful to keep the documents in order, she meticulously copied the pages, then returned the folders to Langston's desk.

After removing the handwritten sign from the outer door, she phoned Christine's secretary and told her she was leaving for the day, feigning a stomach virus. She quickly stuffed the still-warm copies into her shoulder bag and was halfway out the door when she remembered the surveillance equipment. Returning to her desk, she flipped through the video camera stations. She was relieved when she didn't see a camera monitoring Langston's office, although she acknowledged that if one did exist, Langston might not have it tied into the master monitoring station.

She reset the program and rode the elevator to the garage, haphazardly tossing her bag into her trunk before sliding behind the wheel. She waited until the gate lifted and then merged into the traffic along Lexington Avenue, driving for several blocks and intently studying the traffic around her before reaching for her cell phone. A wave of relief washed over her as a confident voice answered on the other end.

"Jennifer Phillips, how can I help you?"

"Hi, Jen, it's me. Want to meet me for dinner tonight? I have something you may be interested in seeing."

Loraine Osborne studied Madison from across the table. She knew that Madison held her solely responsible for her father's tragic and untimely death, although they both knew that she was not the only one to blame. Years had eased the raw emotions, yet Loraine knew Madison Cavanaugh would never have allowed herself to be in this position were it not for Logan McGregor's current condition.

Without thinking of the repercussions, she spoke from her heart. "Love has a way of making us do things we'd rather not, and I know talking to me is the last thing you want to be doing right now, Dr. Cavanaugh. However, because we currently share a common interest in this case and undoubtedly great concern for Detective McGregor, here we are."

She watched the nervous flitter of Madison's normally steadfast eyes sweep from her face to the window, then to the other patrons in the small cafeteria before she continued. "I'm willing to listen to your plan, Doctor, but remember this, if I don't agree it's worthwhile, it's a no-go, period. No debate." She took a breath, focusing her thoughts and allowing Madison a moment to absorb her words.

"I know you think I have a lot to make up to you—maybe I do, in a sense, but I *will not* be manipulated into agreeing to a plan that will place you or anyone on the police force in any more danger than you already are in." With the ground rules laid out, she sat back and offered a cautious smile. "So tell me about this plan you've come up with and how you think I can help."

For the next ten minutes, Madison laid out the groundwork for the trap she thought would bring the Strip District killer to his knees. "What better way to get him, Commander? He knows I frequent the Strip as part of my work for Operation Safety Net, and he won't be able to resist the opportunity to attempt a hit on me while I'm in the alley, knowing Logan is here in the hospital."

Loraine leaned back on the hard booth seat, studying the doctor and seeing, not for the first time, the same determined look that had been ever-present in Malcolm's face so many years before. Father and daughter were very much alike and she knew that with or without her approval, Madison Cavanaugh was going to do whatever she could to stop the man responsible for Logan's injuries.

"I'll need to think about this overnight, talk to my superiors and see what they think before I can give you an answer." She raked a hand through her already disheveled hair. "I'll also need to check out this Toby fellow to make sure he's being straight with you. Just how—"

Madison's color drained to a frightened pallor. "Madison?" Loraine's eyes traced the path of the doctor's and saw a woman, presumably another doctor, race across the room in their direction. Her training took over and she stood, placing her body between Madison and the approaching woman as she raised an arm in warning.

Madison pushed her way from behind. "Julie, what's the matter?"

"Logan—upstairs—now."

Before Madison could react, Loraine was halfway out the door, her cell phone pressed to her ear. Bypassing the elevators, the three women raced up the stairs to the ICU with the commander leading the way as she took the steps three at a time. Rounding the corner to the unit, they fought through the mass of nurses filing out of the room, their faces grave and unrevealing.

Madison pressed ahead, forcing her way into the brightly lit room and her eyes fell on the still form in the bed. "No."

Dr. Black stood on the other side of the room, his eyes glued to the monitor over Logan's head as a nurse adjusted the IV tubing. Madison's eyes swept the readings: heart rate 95 and steady, blood pressure 100/64. The reinserted ventilator obliterated much of Logan's face, but Madison could see the massive swelling. "What the hell happened here?"

The doctor stopped writing and closed the chart, regarding Madison closely. "Dr. Cavanaugh—Madison, your friend here is one lucky lady." He slipped his hand into the wide pocket of his lab coat and pulled out a small vial. "Someone doesn't like our patient." He studied the vial closely before handing it to the commander. "You'll not likely find any fingerprints of use; too many people have handled it since its discovery. However, I can tell you that it's one of ours and came from the pharmacy downstairs."

Dr. Black pointed to a syringe lying in the corner of the room. "That, on the other hand, doesn't appear to come from Mercy and is most likely the syringe used to inject the detective with a near-fatal dose of penicillin." All eyes focused on the discarded syringe as Loraine knelt and carefully lifted it up by the needle end. "Luckily for Detective McGregor, the guy must have been spooked, because he didn't finish his job. There's still half the vial left in the syringe."

He turned back to Madison. "Detective McGregor is going to be okay. She went into anaphylactic shock, but luckily, the nurse came in and called the code immediately. There's a considerable amount of swelling, and as you well know, we can only treat the symptoms and flush out her system, but I think we caught it early enough to prevent any long-term effects."

"The lab technician." Madison's and the commander's eyes met.

Dr. Black's forehead creased at the comment. "What lab tech? I didn't order any tests for Detective McGregor."

"Exactly." Loraine stood, carefully placing the syringe on the desk. "When we were here earlier, a lab tech came in to draw some blood—asked us to leave. Dr. Cavanaugh and I went to the cafeteria for coffee and that must have been when he injected the penicillin." She placed a comforting hand on Madison's arm. "I'm going to call this in. Please don't touch anything until we've had time to sweep the room."

"Commander?" Madison waited until Loraine turned around. "Where was the guard that was supposed to be on duty?"

"That, Doctor, is the first thing I intend to find out."

After calling Dove and telling him to come back to the hospital, Loraine spent the next thirty minutes coordinating the investigative team called in to sweep Logan's room. The detective, having been moved in a room directly adjacent to the nurses' station, was resting peacefully with a new guard standing sentry outside the door.

Loraine had claimed an empty consultation room at the end of the corridor as a temporary headquarters. Charles Thornton and Len Youngblood had come to the hospital upon hearing of the latest attack on Logan, and all agreed that Madison's plan might work and approved the commander's recommendation to place a guard with Dr. Cavanaugh.

"I know she isn't going to be happy, Len, but she's too visible and mobile for us to protect her any other way. Hell, McGregor is lying in hospital surrounded by hundreds of people and this psycho sauntered right in and took a shot at her."

After walking Youngblood out to the parking lot, she took a long look around, searching for anything remotely out of place. *Jesus, everything is out of place. With so many people, all shapes and sizes, he can blend in with little or no effort.*

Retracing her steps, she punched the call button for the elevator and stood waiting for the car to descend to the ground floor. *Well, Dr. Cavanaugh, you want a frontal attack, you've got one. I just hope you and I both survive the repercussions when Detective McGregor finds out what we're up to.*

Jennifer stepped into the restaurant. Spotting Stephanie in the far corner, she waved away the hostess and walked toward the table, studying her face as she neared. Lines of fatigue and stress etched her face and although she knew Stephanie's job was demanding, there was something more—something almost fearful about her appearance. Suddenly Stephanie looked up and the façade dropped into place, hiding the raw emotions Jennifer had seen only seconds earlier.

"Hiya, kiddo." Stephanie's voice was cheerful.

Jennifer sat opposite Stephanie and dropped her bag into the adjacent chair. "Hiya, yourself. How have you been, Steph? I haven't heard from you in what, months, I guess."

"I know, Jen, and I'm sorry. I've been working on a lead for the last few weeks and just haven't had time for anything other than work."

Jennifer decided to let Stephanie set the pace and divulge what she wanted to in her own time. The call earlier in the day had surprised and intrigued her, but she didn't want to push too hard.

They spent the next hour catching up on the happenings in their lives while enjoying a nice dinner. During their after-dinner coffee, the conversation faded, and Jennifer noticed Stephanie's eyes nervously flittering around the room. "So, you want to tell me why you're so edgy tonight, or do I have to guess?"

Stephanie waved for the waiter and asked for the check. "Look, I'm really not comfortable going over this here. I thought I would feel safer somehow in a crowded restaurant, but now that we're here, I'm not. Let's drive over to my place and I'll show you what I have."

The last thing Jennifer wanted to do was spend the rest of the evening following Stephanie across town, but the reporter in her took over as she grabbed for her bag and followed Stephanie from the restaurant.

CHAPTER TWENTY-SIX

Two days had passed since the attempted murder, and Madison was exhausted when she went to Logan's room directly from her office. The monotonous cadence of the ventilator was gone, once again leaving the room eerily quiet as thick clouds moved in and the sunlight faded beyond the window. Madison was lulled into a deep, yet restless slumber as she sat in the chair beside Logan's bed, swirls of color flashing behind her eyelids as dreams, vivid and horrifying, ran through her brain, the synapses firing off each image in a symphony of heart-racing terror.

A noise somewhere in the distance broke through the nightmare, and she fought desperately to escape the ghastly visions as a familiar smell attacked her senses. It took all of her strength to resist the magnetic influence of the dream as she forced herself back into the conscious world, opened her eyes, and frantically turned toward Logan. What she saw sent a ripple of sheer terror down her spine. On Logan's stomach lay a wilted white rose, its petals spattered with what appeared to be blood.

Bolting from the chair and into the hall, Madison searched in both directions for anything out of the ordinary or anyone close enough to have recently exited the room. Spotting Logan's guard leaning against the nurses' station chatting with a petite blond aide, she stormed over and shouted, "Why the hell are you not beside the door?"

The officer turned toward Madison, his eyes flittering between the startled aide and the doctor's angry face. "I've been right here, Doc."

She glared at the young officer as her temper threatened to override her professionalism. "Get Commander Osborne here *now*. While you were busy flirting, someone was in Detective McGregor's room." She turned her icy gaze to the aide. "And *you*, get back to work and let this man do his job."

The guard jumped into action. He tugged the radio from his belt and stepped toward the door to Logan's room only to feel a firm grasp on his arm. "I don't want you anywhere near her. Just call Commander Osborne and do it fast, before *I* call your lieutenant."

Torn between feeling intimidated and angry, he didn't budge.

"Now!"

She turned and disappeared into Logan's room and the officer radioed the incident into dispatch. Within minutes, footsteps and muffled voices filled the quiet space of the ICU, and she moved to the door to see Dove shoving his way through the crowd in her direction, his face awash in apparent fear.

"What the hell happened?"

"Maybe you should ask the irresponsible officer that was *supposed* to be guarding the door." Her eyes bored into the guard's back as she watched him talking to another officer. "While he was at the nurses' station flirting with one of the aides, someone walked right into the room and left us a little gift—a wilted rose, left on her stomach and spattered with what appears to be blood."

Dove looked at the closed door. "Jesus Christ."

The mass of uniformed bodies parted as Loraine Osborne entered the ICU. The officer assigned to guard Logan shrank back as her eyes bored through him. "In the conference room, now, and don't move, don't talk, don't breathe until I get there. Got it?"

The young officer, his face glistening with sweat, paled noticeably and nodded as he made his way through the sea of bodies to the small conference room. A room he knew would prove to be uncomfortably small and inescapable in only a few moments.

The commander walked directly to Dove and Madison and focused on the doctor. Her voice was clipped, almost angry, as she fought to hide the emotions welling up inside her. "Tell me what you know."

Madison recounted the story. "It's the same man that injected Logan with the penicillin. His cologne is the same. It's very familiar, yet I can't place it."

The CSI team stood ready beside the door, waiting for their orders, yielding as the commander entered the room. The faint, yet obvious odor of an outdated, once-expensive cologne still wafted through the air, and it struck Loraine like a slap in the face. "British Sterling. It was popular about twenty years ago. You probably remember it because your father wore it."

Taken aback at the mention of her father, Madison glared at the commander as they stood facing each other, separated only by Logan's bed. The memory of her father's nightly embraces, the comforting scent that had lulled her to sleep each night as a child, returned like an electric shock. Her psyche screamed for an escape from the presence of the woman who had destroyed her childhood, yet another part demanded that she remain—the part that knew Loraine was her only hope for preserving a future she so desperately wanted with Logan.

With eyes closed and fingertips pressing against the pain pounding in her temples, she tried to block out the pounding of her heart and the bile rising in her throat. She took a deep breath, focusing on Logan, her anchor. "What are you saying, Commander? Do you think this has something to do with my father, just because you smell the same cologne he wore twenty years ago?"

"In and of itself, no. Although it's not just this incident, Dr. Cavanaugh; this entire case seems to be connected with you in some obscure way." Lorain's eyes softened as she watched Madison shrink back. "He's focused on you and Detective McGregor now. Which one of you is his real target? I can't say, but you are somehow connected. You or someone close to you."

Anger flashed from Madison's eyes and tears streaked down her cheeks. "Well, Commander, you'd damn well better find some answers and do it quick."

Breaking his silence, Dove said, "Madison, do you know of any ties that your family has with the Langstons? Business ventures, old grudges, anything?"

"No. Until recently, I've only heard of Langston Development through the newspapers. Of course, I knew who they were—hell, everyone does—but I've never had any association with them whatsoever."

"What about your mother? Your parents were well-known public figures in Pittsburgh. Did they have any investments in Langston Development? Did they socialize in the same circles? Have any mutual friends?"

The questions came from all directions and Madison threw her hands in the air, frustrated, angry, and frightened. "How the hell do I know? For Christ's sake, I was only a kid when my father died, how am I supposed to know the answers to those questions? Only my moth—" It struck her like a bolt of lightning. "*Mother.*" Madison slumped into the chair beside Logan's bed, raking a hand through her hair.

Kneeling, Dove gently took her hand in his. "Madison, what about your mother?"

Tears streamed in a continuous flow down her cheeks as she focused on Dove's calming voice. "My mother, she's returning to Pittsburgh today."

Loraine stood back, allowing Dove to probe for the answers they desperately needed, her chest tightening with every response. Time and time again, she had thought about coming face to face with her lover's wife, finding out once and for all if she was the hard, cold woman Malcolm had portrayed her to be. For years she had lived with the guilt of destroying a family by accepting his description as fact, and after all that time, she was about to find if he had been honest or simply playing her for a fool. She tore her thoughts from the past and concentrated on Dove and Madison.

"She hates Pittsburgh and vowed never to return when she moved to Europe. We haven't spoken in ages, so needless to say, I was surprised when I received a phone call from her a couple of days ago practically ordering me to pick her up at the airport later today."

"What time is her flight?"

"Two o'clock. We're to meet at the baggage claim, that's all I know. She left a message on my machine and all she said was that I should pick her up and that she was staying with a friend while she was in town."

"What friend?" Loraine's voice was curt and to the point.

"She didn't say."

The commander started to pace, her mind racing with different scenarios as she processed the information. "I'm assigning a guard to you, and she will accompany you to the airport. She'll be undercover so you can pass her off as a friend."

Madison's eyes danced between Dove, the commander, and Logan. "I don't want to leave. Someone else can pick her up, and I can use the excuse of having an emergency case to deal with."

"No, Madi, it has to be you." Dove's fingers gently interlaced with Madison's. "We don't know right now why your mother is returning. Hopefully it's just a coincidence, but if it isn't you need to act as if everything is normal."

"I agree." Loraine stopped pacing long enough to look at Logan's helpless form. "I will personally stay here while you're gone." She turned toward Madison. "I promise Logan will be safe with me until you return."

Every cell within Madison wanted to hate Loraine. However, during the last few days the commander and Dove had proven to be the only two people she could truly depend on. Pushing aside years of pain, she stood and walked to the bed. "Okay Commander, we'll play it your way."

Then with cold, hard eyes, she stared at the other woman. "I'm holding you personally responsible if anything happens to her. I don't intend to lose anyone else because of your lack of good judgment, and I'm depending on you to see that I don't."

Dove watched the exchange and knew by the look on both of their faces that there was a deeper meaning to the words Madison spoke. His main priority was protecting Logan and ultimately finding the killer, but he knew all too well how easily biased and unfocused minds could destroy a case. Making a mental note to dig deeper into both women's pasts to find the connection, he moved toward the door and broke the strained silence. "Well, I guess that's settled, then. I'm going to locate Anderson and fill her in on what's going down while the CSI team is working the room."

During the emotional turmoil, Loraine had forgotten about the CSI team outside the door waiting to sweep the room for any evidence. She knew it was unlikely they would discover anything useful, although she still hoped that they might. Waving them into the room, she turned back to Madison. "I need to speak with the guard. Why don't you wait for me at the nurses' station and I'll buy you a cup of coffee while we wait for the team to finish up?"

"Ah, sure, I'll wait for a while."

The commander disappeared into the crowded hallway, leaving Madison alone with Logan and the two CSI techs. The doctor studied Logan and felt her heart tear at having to leave her alone, even for a moment, even though Commander Loraine Osborne would be personally watching over her while she was away.

Sighing in resignation, she stepped aside to give the team room to work and moved toward the desk at the nurses' station down the hall. Most of the officers who had been milling around had gone, leaving the ICU once again shrouded in a heavy veil of quiet apprehension. She sat at the desk and dialed her home number to retrieve the messages from her answering machine. Deleting the first few hang-ups and messages from telemarketers, she was only half listening when she heard Julie's excited voice over the line.

"Hey, Madi, I have to talk to you, and soon. Didn't you say Logan and that reporter, what's her name, Jennifer something or other were good friends? Anyway, I saw her and Christine Langston all chummy together at lunch today. Isn't that strange? Oh hell, just call me when you get this."

Hanging up the phone without listening to her other messages, stunned and confused by Julie's call, Madison was digging through her backpack trying to locate Julie's cell number when a presence cast a shadow over her.

"Dr. Cavanaugh, I'm sorry but I have to go. I'll make sure I'm back before you have to leave for the airport."

Madison tried to read the commander's stoic mask with little success. "Why? I mean, what's so important that you have to leave before the CSI team is finished?"

Loraine glanced around to make sure no one was within hearing distance, then leaned closer to Madison. "He's struck again. Another Langston executive, Lester Donovan." She watched as the realization struck home and grasped Madison's arm as she wavered in the small chair. "Easy now. Come on, let's get you back inside with Logan."

The two CSI techs were closing their cases as the commander guided Madison through the door to Logan's room. "Sorry, Commander, but I don't think there is anything useful here. We lifted a few prints from the railing, but I suspect the lab will find that they belong to some of the hospital workers."

Tipping his head toward the box sitting on the desk, the tech added, "Hopefully we'll get something from the rose, but it will take a day or two for the report to come back."

"Thanks." Loraine eyed the wilted rose. "Get a type on that blood as soon as possible and send the report directly to me."

"But, Commander, we don't even know for sure that it is blood."

"Just do it." She suspected that the preliminary report would match the blood type with Donovan's and further testing would identify it as his. *This is one sick pervert. Killing a man, then bringing a blood-splattered rose to Logan as a gift.*

"It's his blood, isn't it?"

"I don't kn—"

"Yes, you do, and we both know it." Madison caressed Logan's hand. "He murdered that man and then brought that rose here as a sign to let us know that he's aware that Logan is still alive."

"I know, but he isn't getting anywhere near her again."

Madison scoffed, "Yeah, right, Commander. Just how are you going to prevent that? You haven't been able to stop him the last two times he's been inside this room."

A tense silence permeated the void between the two women and was broken only when the door was quietly pushed open from the hallway. Instantly Loraine's right hand dipped into the folds of her blazer and her fingers wrapped around the cold steel of her service weapon. "Hello?"

Moving quickly, Madison placed her body between the door and Logan's bed as a small form eased past the shadows of the doorway. She only relaxed when she saw the look of recognition on Loraine's face.

"Christ, Anderson, knock next time." Loraine released the hold on her weapon and moved toward the door. "Dr. Cavanaugh, meet your new friend Detective Liz Anderson. She'll be accompanying you to the airport this afternoon."

The two women shook hands as the commander stepped closer to the door. "You two get acquainted. I want anyone who sees you together to think you two have been friends for years." She turned to regard Madison, a softness returning to her voice. "I'll be back before one o'clock to give you plenty of time to get to the airport."

Madison watched Loraine walk out, her emotions in turmoil, realizing that if the commander hadn't been responsible for the collapse of her family, she would truly like and admire her. *How could I ever feel those things for her when she is the one who took my father away?*

Jennifer Phillips scanned the crowd for a familiar face. Her position at the far end of the winding drive gave her a perfect view of the crowd across the street as she lifted the camera to her eye and focused on single faces, snapping frame after frame of the unsuspecting individuals. She was halfway through the crowd when the automatic rewind mechanism whirred and she quickly switched the roll of film with a fresh one and began again. After they were developed, she would compare the new photos with the ones she had taken at the underground garage where Phillip Crafton's body had been discovered.

She had just completed the second roll when Loraine Osborne and Charles Thornton parked beside the drive. Pressing between two other reporters, she made her way toward them. "Chief Thornton, this must be a big case to get you all the way out here. Is this case connected with the Strip District case?"

"No comment, Ms. Phillips." Thornton lifted the florescent yellow crime tape, allowing Loraine Osborne to duck under the barrier. "Why don't you continue with your photo shoot and maybe we'll talk later."

Resigning herself to waiting out the afternoon with the rest of the crowd, Jennifer slipped the cell phone from her pocket and walked away from the ever-listening ears of her fellow reporters. "Hey there. Yeah, I'm stuck over in Wellington Estates waiting for some information on a developing case. Why don't I meet you at Primanti's around seven for dinner and then we can talk."

Loraine Osborne's eyes took in every detail as she stepped into the foyer of Lester Donovan's residence. Everything appeared to be in perfect order as she moved through the living and dining rooms, then on through the kitchen. It was only after stepping into the dark paneled library that she saw the blood and stopped midstride. "Jesus Christ."

Lester Donovan lay on the floor beside the massive oak desk. Kneeling beside the body was Harold Simons, his pudgy hands gloved in thick blue medical gloves shaking as he reached out to turn the body over. In all the years he had worked crime scenes, he had never witnessed a murder quite like this one. Lester Donovan had not been just murdered; he had been tortured and repeatedly beaten before the killer had allowed him to die. Simons' stomach knotted as he rolled Donovan's body over into a large pool of dark semiliquid blood and saw what remained of his face.

Loraine watched as one of the CSI members bagged and labeled a bloody mass in the far corner of the room, only realizing when she looked back at Donovan's body that the mass must have been one of his ears. Both had been severed from his head as well as several fingers on each hand, and for the first time since becoming personally involved with the case she recognized the anger behind the crimes. "This isn't just a revenge killing, Charles, this guy was pissed with Donovan over something."

With his hands tucked protectively into his pockets, Thornton studied the body from across the room. "You got that right, Commander. This is personal, always has been. I just don't have a fucking clue who it could be."

Simons looked up. "Fancy meeting you here, Commander. I didn't think you lowered yourself to simple crime scene investigation anymore." He didn't attempt to hide his dislike for her.

"Can it, Simons, and just tell me what you have."

He removed the bloody gloves from his thick hands, folding them inside out before tossing them into a red biohazard bag beside the desk. "What we have is another murder, *Commander*." Stabbing a thumb over his shoulder, he looked between Loraine and Thornton. "This guy is pissed. He literally beat Donovan—or at least we think that's Donovan—to a pulp before methodically slicing off his ears and fingers."

"Do you have a time of death yet?"

"Rigor hasn't set in yet and the call to 911 was recorded at 7:35 this morning." Tipping his head toward the doors, he continued, "The housekeeper gets here around 7:30 every morning, and she found him when she came in to bring him his morning coffee. According to her, he was still breathing."

A frown creased Thornton's brow. "Our man may have been interrupted by the housekeeper, then. I don't think he would willingly leave behind a breathing victim."

"True. Then again, maybe he's just getting sloppy. The rose was left at the hospital about 10:00 this morning, so that tells me he planned all of this." Loraine's gaze swept the room and fell on a crystal vase containing an arrangement of white roses. Careful of her step, she walked toward the credenza. "There's only ten roses here. He took two, but only left one at the hospital."

From the foyer a woman's voice, loud and angry, reverberated off the high, vaulted ceilings. "Get the hell out of my fucking way and tell whoever is in charge here that I want some answers, now."

"Ma'am, you can't go in there."

The trio had just turned toward the noise when a furious woman burst through the wide oak doors. "What the hell do you people—" Her ranting stopped midsentence when her eyes fell on Lester Donovan's dead body. "Oh my God. Lester." Trembling fingers swept upward, covering her mouth as a guttural moan escaped from deep within her throat.

Loraine quickly stepped forward, grasped her arm, and turned, leading her from the room and into the formal living area. She eased the woman onto the sofa and then poured her a healthy shot of brandy. "Here, drink this."

With a shaky hand, the woman took the glass and downed the liquor in one swallow. "Who are you?"

"The more important question, ma'am, is who are you?" Loraine already knew, but decided to play the scenario out one step at a time.

"Christine Langston. Lester works—uh, worked for Langston Development as our vice president of real estate and acquisitions." Her eyes brimming with tears, she looked into Loraine's face and read nothing in the stoic expression.

"Why are you here, Ms. Langston? Do you have a habit of dropping by Mr. Donovan's home in the morning?"

Christine lifted the glass. "How about another, and make it a double." She waited until Loraine returned with the drink before answering. "No, I don't. In fact, this is only the second time I've ever been inside Lester's home."

"So why are you here this morning, Ms. Langston?" Loraine sat in the chair opposite the young executive.

"I needed to talk to him. Warn him, if you will, about this madman on the loose killing us all."

"Warn him, Ms. Langston? Are you saying that you might know the man that we are looking for?"

Christine jumped, startled by the sudden voice behind her, and the brandy sloshed over the lip of the glass onto the plush fabric of the sofa. "Christ. Look what you did."

The corners of Thornton's lips curled into a predatory smile. "Well, Ms. Langston, I think I asked you a question."

Sitting the glass on the table, Christine looked between Loraine and Thornton. "No, Detective, I don't know who the murderer is. I came to warn Lester because when I left for work this morning I found a rose on my windshield, and a note."

"What did the note say?" The commander stood and stepped closer to Christine, as if being near her would bring her closer to finding the killer.

"*Only one to go.*" Christine raked a hand through her short blond hair and paced the length of the living room. "Somehow I knew I would be too late."

"Why didn't you call him?" Thornton snapped the question.

"Is he really necessary?"

Loraine waved Thornton out the door and sat beside Christine on the sofa. "I'm sorry, Ms. Langston, but you have to understand how frustrating this has all been for the police as well."

"Frustrating? Sorry, but frustrating isn't quite the word I'd use to describe what we've been feeling." Christine stood and paced once again. "I haven't slept a peaceful night since this thing began. Do you have any idea how it feels to see your co-workers—friends—murdered one by one and know that you're just one more name on the list and the list is getting shorter day by day?"

Loraine released a deep breath. "No, Ms. Langston, I don't. However, I do know how it feels to see it happening. Knowing I'm responsible for catching this man and having one door after another slammed in my face by the people we are supposed to be protecting from him."

She saw that her words struck home when the young executive stopped and turned to face her. "I can't catch him without your help, Ms. Langston, so from this moment on you have a choice. You can be part of the solution or part of the problem. So what's it going to be?"

Their eyes held for what seemed like an eternity before Christine finally broke the stare. "If you want answers, we're doing it my way." She headed for the door, leaving Loraine sitting on the sofa. "Are you coming, Commander?" A faint smile crossed her lips at Loraine's reaction. "Yes, I know who you are, Commander. I haven't gotten where I am by not paying attention."

Loraine glanced at her watch. "I never doubted that you did, Ms. Langston." She pulled the cell phone from her pocket as she followed Christine out of the house. "Dvorak, it's Loraine. I have an appointment that I can't reschedule. If I'm not at the hospital by one o'clock, I want you in McGregor's room until I get there. Make sure Dr. Cavanaugh and Anderson leave on schedule for the airport."

Her mind was racing and she increased her step when Christine dropped into her car and started the engine. "Look, I have to go. Get a guard on Jonathon Wilson ASAP, and don't leave McGregor's room for any reason until you hear from me."

"What's going on, Commander?"

"I'll tell you when I see you. Just don't leave McGregor alone for any reason, and if anyone comes into the room, make sure you see their ID and confirm their orders before you let anyone near her. Got it?"

"Yes, ma'am."

Madison leaned over the railing as she spoke softly into Logan's ear. Twenty minutes before, Logan's hand had tightened around hers. She was certain she had seen her eyelids flutter, and she was optimistic that Logan was about to regain consciousness.

"Come on, baby, open your eyes. I miss you and want you back here with me."

Nothing. Not even a twitch of her fingers. *Damn, Logan, you're so close. Come back to me.*

Dove studied every person he passed in the hallway as he neared Logan's room. A family, obviously distraught, stood just outside room three. The nurses, all familiar to him, quickly moved through the ICU, focused on their tasks. The only person Dove didn't recognize was a maintenance worker on a ladder at the far end of the hallway. The detective was beside Logan's room, heading toward the worker, when he heard a voice from inside Logan's room say "Please."

With one hand on his service revolver and the other holding a cumbersome arrangement of flowers, Dove pressed the door open with his foot and stepped into the room.

Madison jumped and spun around. "Jesus, Dove, you scared the hell out of me."

"Sorry, Doc. I—I just heard, um, never mind. How's she doing?"

Madison smiled. "I think she's getting better. She squeezed my hand a few minutes ago."

Dove sat the flowers he'd been holding on the desk and walked to the opposite side of the bed. Almost reverently, he stroked Logan's forehead. "It's about damn time, McGregor."

CHAPTER TWENTY-SEVEN

Loraine Osborne stood alone in the living room of Christine Langston's home. The sofa, she suspected, was imported and most likely worth more than she made in a month.

She took advantage of her solitary moment to take in the details of the room. She walked to the fireplace mantle where several photographs were displayed, many including Christine. She looked at each in turn and noticed two smaller photos at the end of Christine at about the age of thirteen, her father, and a young man who looked to be about seventeen. Her mind was racing through the pages of files she had reviewed about the Langstons, and she couldn't remember a son ever being mentioned in any of the reports.

"Here you are, Commander." Christine held out a cup of steaming coffee.

Loraine closed the space between them and took the proffered cup. "Thank you, Ms. Langston."

"Please, call me Christine."

Loraine sat in the wingback chair opposite the sofa and sipped her coffee before replying. "I don't meant to be rude, Ms. Langston, but after weeks of being rebuffed by Langston Development, I find it a little difficult to be, um, chummy at this point."

Their eyes held for a moment, then the young executive extended a knowing smile. "Understood, Commander." She slowly turned her head to look at the mantle. "You have to understand that we were only trying to protect the people we care about, not intentionally closing you or the investigative team out."

Loraine's lips twitched as she attempted to hide a smirk. "Unfortunately, in your attempts to protect those people, Ms. Langston, most of them have been murdered." As she followed Christine's gaze to the photos on the mantle, an odd feeling struck her. Was it was possible that she had not been referring to the other Langston Development executives? "Why now, Ms. Langston? Why have you suddenly decided to cooperate with the authorities?"

Christine's eyes met Loraine's with a sound determination that said more than her words. "Because he has to be stopped, Commander. He's ruined enough lives. He has to be stopped now, once and for all."

On the drive to the airport, a tense quiet filled the car. Madison's thoughts shifted between her distress at having to leave Logan in her state of near-wakefulness and the stress of seeing her mother after so many years of estrangement. As Liz Anderson drove, slipping in and out of the congested traffic with relaxed ease, Madison asked, "How did we meet again?"

Liz's eyes flicked toward her passenger, then back to the traffic ahead. "We met while you were lecturing at W&J last spring."

"Oh yeah, sorry. I just can't keep my mind on all of this right now."

Liz felt for her. She had not been active on the case until the week before, but she had heard about the young doctor's involvement with McGregor. "Hey, I don't really know Detective McGregor that well, but I'm sure she would agree that you are doing what you need to do. She'll understand and I'm sure she knows you'll be back as soon as you can." Liz stumbled for something to say to calm Madison and get her focused on what they had to do. "In fact, from what I've heard about her, I think she'd be pissed if you stayed with her instead of doing this."

For the first time since feeling Logan's hand close around hers, Madison smiled. "I guess you're right. She is an independent and stubborn woman." She took a deep breath and released it slowly as the airport terminal came into view. "Just promise me you'll keep me from throttling my mother if she gets too annoying."

An uncomfortable chuckle escaped the detective. "You got it, Doctor."

Marissa Cavanaugh looked out at the Pittsburgh skyline looming just off the tip of the wing, a sight she had sworn she would never see again. *What the hell am I getting myself into, coming back to this place?*

The captain's voice crackled over the intercom, informing them of their approach and instructing the passengers to fasten their seat belts. The flight attendants walked purposefully down the aisle collecting the remains of the light snack they had doled out earlier. Marissa could hear the muted conversations as other passengers woke from their short naps and prepared for landing.

As was her usual practice, she sat quietly, knowing that there would be plenty of time to disembark. *God knows, I'd delay this forever if I could.* With a resigned sigh she fastened her seat belt and watched as the ground grew closer. A few minutes later the plane bounced once, twice, and then braked hard as they touched down on the tarmac and slowed as the pilot steered the plane to the gate.

She quickly wiped beneath her eyes, careful not to smear her mascara as tears threatened to escape and streak the make-up she had carefully applied. *Damn you, Malcolm. Even after all these years, I hate you for taking this away from me.*

Dove sat beside Logan's bed, listening for any sound beyond the doorway. Loraine had not returned and her absence baffled him. She had seemed determined to be here while Madison was at the airport, so the call a few hours earlier ordering him to the hospital had left him surprised and uncertain.

His fingers curled around the cell phone in his pocket just as a soft voice broke the silence in the room. The phone clattered to the floor as he jumped from the chair and leaned over the side rail. To his utter shock, deep blue eyes stared up at him.

"Oh my God, Logan." Dove searched frantically for the call button to no avail, then bent to recover his cell phone from under the bed.

"Dove." Logan's voice was harsh and dry from days of being on the ventilator. She felt a vibration from beneath the bed, then heard a stream of swearing just before Dove's face came back into her line of view.

"Stay. Don't move." He punched at the numbers frantically as his eyes darted between Logan's face and the door. "Yeah, I'm in McGregor's room. Get in here, she's awake."

A few second later, the door opened and Logan's nurse entered the room. "Well, well, it's about time you decided to wake up, Detective."

Logan tried to smile as the nurse leaned over the railing, but she winced at the pain as her lips cracked from the dryness.

Calm and relaxed, the nurse checked Logan's vitals. "Don't try to talk right now. Let me call your doctor and let him know you're awake, then we'll see about giving you a little ice. I'll be right back."

On the other side of the bed, a look of sheer terror swept across Dove's face as he rushed to stop the nurse from leaving. "Wait, isn't there some kind of test you need to run to make sure she's all right?"

The nurse placed a reassuring hand on Dove's arm. "Sir, why don't you have a seat and relax. Detective McGregor's doing fine, but you look like you're about to pass out and I'll not have that on my watch."

Dove watched as the nurse moved to the door and his eyes flicked between her back and Logan. "But—"

The nurse turned and with an authoritative sweep of her hand ordered him into the chair. "Sit and don't move. I don't have time to pick you up off the floor." As she disappeared through the door, she called over her shoulder, "Stay. I'll be back in a few minutes."

Dove sat motionless as a chuckle came from the direction of the bed and then a single low, harsh word. "Coward."

His eyes cut to Logan, but all he could see were her feet. "Bite me, McGregor."

"So this is all you know, Ms. Langston?" Loraine towered over the blonde.

"Yes, that's all I know, Commander."

The door opened and the two women turned to see a startled woman stop just inside the foyer. "Ah, hi. I'm sorry, I didn't realize you had company."

Christine stood and took the packages from Jennifer, then turned back to Loraine. "Jen, I don't think you've met Commander Osborne."

Jennifer's eyes widened. "No, I haven't had the pleasure." She shook Loraine's outreached hand. "It's nice to meet you, Commander." Her eyes darted to Christine's as questions raced through her mind.

Christine sat the packages beside the sofa and held out her hand to Jennifer. "Commander, Jen is the woman I was telling you about." She faced her lover with cool resolve and smiled. "She was the one that gave me the information that I just gave you."

"Christine, what's going on here?"

"Relax, Jen, I just told the commander everything you told me last night. I'll explain how it all came together later, but I suspect the commander here would probably like to speak with you without me in the room." She turned to fully face Jennifer. "She can't force you to talk with her, you know that, but please don't do anything to protect me. I've already told her everything."

"*Christine.* Do you know what you've done?"

Feeling more confident than she had in weeks, Christine squeezed Jennifer's hand and softly kissed her cheek. "Yes, dear, I know exactly what I've done. Now if the two of you will excuse me, I'm going to change into something more comfortable and leave you to chat."

The two women watched as Christine disappeared down a long hallway, then turned back to each other.

"Commander."

"Ms. Phillips."

They sat in silence for a few moments before Loraine spoke. "Ms. Phillips, what Ms. Langston just revealed to me is a little far fetched, don't you think? I don't mean to be rude, but it sounds a little like a story for the *National Enquirer*, not something the *Gazette* would be following."

Jennifer's hands twisted in her lap as she faced the commander from across the glass coffee table. "Believe me, Commander, I understand your reluctance to believe the story. However, the information came from a very dependable source, and although I can't prove it as fact *yet*, I am working on that as we speak."

"I want the name of your source!"

Jennifer chuckled. "Don't try to manhandle me, Commander. You know I won't divulge my sources."

"I can take you in. I doubt you want that."

"You can take me wherever you'd like. You know as well as I do that the our attorneys will have me out before you have time to get a cup of coffee."

The women glared at each other as tempers threatened to flare until Jennifer broke the tense silence. "Look, Commander, obviously Christine felt you would be able to help or she certainly wouldn't have talked to you. What I *will* do is help you prove the information as best I can."

She stood, and with a determined look in her eyes, walked to the bar and poured herself a healthy shot of brandy before turning back to the commander. "However, if you want to make this difficult and demand my source, I won't even help you out the door."

She drained the glass in one swallow, then sat it on the gleaming surface of the bar. "The choice is yours, Commander."

With a resigned sigh, Loraine sat back, studying the reporter. "Okay, Ms. Phillips, we'll play it your way. Now why don't you have a seat and tell me what you know."

Madison paced the area around the baggage claim area, to Liz's growing frustration. "Dr. Cavanaugh, *please* have a seat and try to relax. You're not making my job easy with your constant movement."

The doctor stopped the pacing and dropped into the seat directly beside her. "Sorry, I'm just a little nervous."

Liz scanned the vast area in front of them. "I understand, but the past few days should make you appreciate how dangerous this could be for you *and* your mother. We don't have any idea who we're looking for or what he looks like. Compound that with an environment like this airport and it only makes it more difficult to keep you adequately covered."

Desperate to change the subject, Madison looked down. "What happened to your knee?"

"Cartilage. I tore the cartilage in a foot pursuit a few months back. That's how I got the assignment to homicide—not much running necessary." A nervous chuckle escaped and she shyly looked at Madison.

"Are you going to have it repaired?" Madison watched as the color drained from the detective's face. "Hey, are you all right?"

"No, I mean, yes, I'm fine." The heat was becoming almost unbearable and Liz felt a rivulet of sweat trickle down her back. "I—I don't do knives." With a sudden look of terror, Liz sat straighter in the chair and looked wide-eyed at Madison. "Just what kind of doctor are you anyway?"

Her lips curled into a smile. "A surgeon. I'm an orthopedic surgeon."

"Oh, sweet Jesus." Liz slid into the next seat. "No, don't even think it."

Before Madison could respond, the area around them became crowded with travelers. She stood and scanned the area nervously, and her gaze fell on an elegant woman walking toward her. It had been almost ten years since she had seen her, but she recognized the regal stature of her mother immediately.

With head held high, Marissa Cavanaugh walked with an air of pretentiousness, standing out from the crowd as one not accustomed to being in the habit of traveling with commoners. Their eyes met and Madison thought she saw a moment of hesitation in Marissa's step. She stood frozen and waited for her to approach.

Marissa stopped a few feet from her daughter and looked around self-consciously before leaning in and dropping a light kiss on Madison's cheek. "Darling, it's so good to see you again."

Liz, standing close behind Madison, nodded when Marissa's eyes met hers. "Ma'am."

"Mother, I'd like for you to meet a friend of mine, Liz Anderson."

Madison stepped aside and was mortified to see her mother's eyes sweep over Liz from head to toe and back again.

"Delighted, I'm sure." Her attention then refocused on her daughter, she added, "I certainly hope you brought someone to gather the baggage, dear."

"No, Mother, I didn't. I'm sure Det—um, Liz and I can take care of your luggage." Madison turned toward the carousel and was shocked to see her mother sit in an adjacent chair to wait.

Liz shrugged and led the way toward the luggage carousel, leaning in to whisper in Madison's ear, "I don't think Mom likes me."

Madison couldn't help but smile. "You're right, but then I've never known my mother to like anyone, unless they have money, fame or a sound social status."

They checked luggage tags as the bags passed with no help from Marissa Cavanaugh, who remained sitting against the wall, impatiently waiting. After five minutes and what seemed like several hundred bags, Liz finally located a large floral suitcase with Marissa Cavanaugh's name and easily lifted the heavy bag from the belt. Once they knew what type of bags they were searching for, they soon located the remaining three.

After paying five dollars to rent a luggage carrier, Liz hoisted the heavy bags onto the cart and the trio made their way out into the cold Pittsburgh afternoon.

"Where's the car, darling? Don't tell me you didn't hire a car."

Liz turned away, not wanting the elder Cavanaugh to see the grin that crept across her face, and came face to face with the small blond doctor.

Madison held out her hand as a gleam came into her eyes. "Liz, darling, why don't you stay here with Mother and the luggage and I'll go get the car."

"But—"

"No buts, dear. Your knee has been bothering you lately, so please let me." She waited as Liz dug into her pocket and reluctantly handed over the keys. "We do need to discuss that surgery you've been putting off. I think next week would be a good time, don't you?"

Liz's throat rippled as she gulped and paled noticeably. "No, next week isn't good for me." She waved her on. "Go, let's not keep your mother waiting. We can discuss this later."

Liz watched Madison until she entered the darkened garage. *Damn, she distracted me and now she's alone in the garage.* "Um, maybe I should go and help Madison with the car."

"That's absolutely absurd. You're not leaving me standing here on the curb like a vagrant. My daughter is very capable of driving the car."

"Yes, ma'am." Liz breathed a sigh of relief when she saw her SUV rounding the curve. Madison stopped and Liz tossed the luggage into the back, then walked to the driver's side and scooted Madison over with a wave. "I'll drive, *Madison."*

Liz dropped the gearshift into drive and crept through traffic. Halfway back to Pittsburgh, Marissa leaned forward, thrust a slip of paper into Liz's face, and spoke her first words since leaving the airport. "Just drop me at this address, please."

Madison turned as the paper fluttered to the seat between her and Liz. "Where are you staying while you're in town, Mother?"

Busily powdering her nose, Marissa stopped long enough to lift her chin arrogantly. "I'm staying with a friend. I'm sure you don't know him, though. Christopher Langston, dear, of Langston Development."

"You are one lucky woman, Detective." The doctor tucked his stethoscope into his pocket and sat on the side of the bed. "How are you feeling?"

Logan twisted the sheets in her hands as her eyes darted around the room. All she wanted was for the doctor to leave so she could drill Dove about the case. "I'm fine, Doc, really. When can I get out of here?"

"Four days ago you were near death from smoke inhalation, then someone tries to murder you in your hospital bed, and you want to know when you can go home." Shaking his head, the doctor rose and moved toward the door. "In a few days, Detective, *maybe*. We'll see how you're doing in a few days, and then we'll talk about your going home."

Logan tried her best to snarl, but winced when her lips cracked under the pressure. She glared at Dove. "Get me some ChapStick and ice, then get your ass back here. We have to talk."

Dove dug in his pocket and came up with a tube of ChapStick with an accumulation of pocket fuzz stuck to it. Tossing it in her lap, he poured ice into a plastic glass. "Sorry, kiddo, that will have to do until Osborne gets back. I'm not leaving you here alone."

Logan picked up the tube with two fingers, and even through her continued grogginess thought better of using it. "Jesus, Dvorak, don't tell me you really use that shit." She took the glass from him and dropped the tube into his hand. "Now get me up to speed on what's been going on. Have I really been here for four days? Where is Madison? Is she all right? What's happening with the case?"

"Stop!" Dove threw his hands in the air and sat beside her on the bed. "Madison is fine, Logan. Right now, she's at the airport picking up her mother, and we have Anderson with her. They should be back soon."

Logan listened as Dove filled her in on the events of the last few days. She stopped him occasionally to ask questions but for the most part sat quietly.

The one thing he couldn't tell her was what had detained the commander. "I don't know what's going on, Logan, but something's going down or she would be here. You didn't see the look in her eyes when she made that promise to Madison. It was almost like a vow she was taking." He stood and paced the length of the room. "There's a history there between those two. I don't know what it is, but something is there and I'm going to find out what."

"Leave it, Dove." Her eyes flared with anger she didn't have the strength to show. "Leave it be and just focus on the case."

Dove stopped the pacing and turned to Logan. "You know, don't you?" He could see the battle raging within her. She seldom kept secrets from him, but she was now, and he asked himself why.

Logan's eyes strayed from Dove's for only a second until her decision was made. "Yes, and I'm asking you to leave it alone." Her words were a whisper, a plea for understanding.

Dove held her stare for several seconds, then shrugged away the uneasy feeling tearing at his gut. "Okay, Logan, whatever you say."

CHAPTER TWENTY-EIGHT

Jennifer's thumb nervously traced the rim of the Waterford tumbler she held tightly between her hands. "My source has documents indicating that Chris Langston, Christine's younger brother, is in the country and that he may very well be the man you're looking for."

"Why do you think that, Ms. Phillips?" Loraine struggled not to reveal her surprise. *So C.W. Langston has a son.*

"It's a long story and I'm sure Christine told you most of it, but I'll give you my spin. Chris, from what I've been told, was always a troubled child. I believe he was about six when his mother caught him behind the garage torturing a neighbor's kitten and demanded that C.W. do something with him. Of course, his answer was to rid himself of the burden, and he shipped Chris to a boarding school in Europe."

Loraine eyed the photograph on the mantle. "Actually, Ms. Langston didn't tell me about her brother. I guess she decided to leave the details up to you. Obviously, he's had contact with the family over the years." She gestured toward the photograph. "When was that taken?"

Jennifer gave the picture a fleeting glance before returning to the bar. "I believe Christine said it was taken about eight years ago, when Chris returned to Pittsburgh after graduating from university." Halfway around the bar with her drink in hand, she stopped. "Are you sure I can't get you something to drink, Commander?"

"No, I'm fine, thanks."

Jennifer returned to the sofa and sank heavily into the cushions. "From what I know, Chris returned believing that he would be welcomed into Langston Development with open arms but was sadly disappointed when he discovered his sister had not only made a name for herself as an architect, but also reigned as the heir apparent of Langston Development. From what Christine has told me and what I have compiled through my research, C.W. provided a token position for his son as Thomas Peters's assistant in the financial department, but Chris soon proved to be intellectually incapable for the job. C.W. then moved him into Jonathon Wilson's department in community affairs."

Jennifer stood and paced. "It quickly became apparent that Chris's main priority was to oust Christine and take over her position as vice president, but what he didn't count on was that Christine was not only daddy's little girl, she was also very good at her job." She walked to the fireplace, lifted the frame from the mantle, and studied the innocent smile on the man's face. "A few months later C.W. caught Chris deliberately altering the specs Christine was about to submit for a new office complex being built in the Strip. He had changed the weight-bearing and wind-load calculations, and had he not been caught, the integrity of the steel used in the infrastructure of the new complex would have been far below the required specifications."

Returning the photograph to the mantle, she turned toward the commander. "Christine's reputation would have been sorely damaged had that happened. By this time, he had realized that the only way he could win was to destroy Christine, and he was doing everything in his power to do just that. C.W. finally had enough, fired Chris, and gave him enough money to go back to Europe."

Jennifer looked toward the hallway. "What Chris did hurt Christine terribly. Frankly, if you want to know more about Chris, I'd prefer if you would ask Christine."

The commander had listened intently, trying to put the pieces of the puzzle together, but something was still missing. *There has to be something that set this whole thing off, but what?* "Ms. Phillips, this whole story is very interesting, but it doesn't explain how or why you think Chris Langston is involved with the murders."

Jennifer carefully set the crystal tumbler on the coffee table, then walked to a desk nestled between two floor-to-ceiling windows overlooking the park below. She opened a drawer and removed a brown envelope before returning to stand beside Loraine. "Here, take a look at these and you'll see why."

Loraine took the envelope from Jennifer's hands and slid four eight-by-ten black-and-white photographs out. The photos of Chris Langston and an older woman were clearly taken without their knowledge. His arm was around her waist in a possessive embrace, and the two were looking into each other's eyes with obvious affection. "I'm not sure I understand what these photographs have to do with the murders. From the background, these were taken in Europe, yes?"

"Yes, they were taken in Europe just five months ago." Jennifer moved to the sofa and sat, her elbows resting on trembling knees. "The woman in the photograph is the key, Commander."

Loraine's eyes studied the woman and the strangely familiar angle of her jaw. "Who is she?"

"Her name is Marissa Cavanaugh, none other than Dr. Madison Cavanaugh's mother. Until two months ago, she was living in Europe with Chris Langston. However, from what I've been able to learn through my sources, she is flying to Pittsburgh today to see her newest lover, C.W. Langston."

Loraine felt her gut clench. With this new twist, she knew that a face-off with Marissa Cavanaugh was inevitable. Suddenly, her thoughts turned to Madison and the danger she was facing by meeting her mother at the airport. "Ms. Phillips, excuse me for a moment. I need to make a quick call to my office."

She dug the cell phone from her pocket as she opened the door and stepped outside into the hallway. Quickly punching in Dove's number, she waited impatiently until she heard his voice.

"Dvorak, Osborne here. Call Anderson and place her on full alert. Have her place Dr. Cavanaugh in protective custody ASAP, and then have her page me when the doctor is secure. Also, get on the horn and have additional security placed on Jonathon Wilson, then get a squad car to the Langston estate and tell the officer that I will be there in twenty minutes."

She struggled to get her arms into the sleeves of her jacket as she held the phone between her chin and shoulder. "I'll fill you in later, but don't leave McGregor alone for a minute. Oh, and Dvorak, call in the team. There will be an emergency meeting in my office as soon as I have a handle on things."

Madison struggled to keep her voice from revealing her shock. "Yes, Mother, I know who C.W. Langston is." She saw Liz tense and cut her eyes cut toward the rearview mirror. "I didn't realize you knew the Langstons."

Marissa checked her make-up and impatiently declared, "Darling, the Langstons are known throughout the world. Actually, I met C.W. through his son Chris, and we've developed a nice friendship over the last few months."

The cell phone in Liz's pocket rang, startling both of the women in the front seat. She dug the phone out and answered, all the while trying to listen to the conversation between Madison and her mother. "Anderson." The clipped tone revealed her annoyance.

The sudden straightening of the officer's back diverted Madison's attention from her mother. She listened to the one-sided phone conversation, trying to figure out what had caused the reaction. She also noticed that Liz had sped up and was covertly checking the mirrors.

"I'm on my way now. Yes. I'll let her know. Thanks, Dove." Liz flipped the phone shut and casually dropped it back into her pocket before glancing toward Madison.

"Anything wrong, Liz?" Madison hoped the concern wasn't evident in her voice.

"Ah, no, everything is fine. That was my boss just letting me know there's been a development at work and I need to go in for a meeting."

Marissa Cavanaugh spoke. "What type of business are you in, ah, Liz, right?"

"Right." Liz frantically thought back, trying to remember if Madison had referred to her work in any way during their introduction. From the corner of her eye, she saw Madison's hand spread across the console as she very subtly tapped the leather. She quickly decided the truth was the best avenue. "I'm an investigator with the Pittsburgh Police Department, Mrs. Cavanaugh." A quick glance in the mirror didn't reveal any emotion. *She's good.*

"An investigator. Interesting, I'm sure." The elder Cavanaugh looked bored with the conversation and turned to stare out the window as they sped down the interstate. *How disappointing, Madison. I raised you better than to socialize with mere blue-collar workers.*

"Yes, ma'am, it is. Very."

The rest of the drive to the Langston estate was quiet, with each woman's thoughts focused on the future and what other surprises remained to be uncovered.

"What's going on, Dove?" Logan's eyes were heavy. She forced herself to remain awake despite her body's cry for sleep. Although there was nothing she could physically do to help, she was more informed about the background of the case than anyone, and she was determined to be available for questions.

Dove struggled with his answer. To withhold the truth would be a betrayal both professionally and personally, but he wasn't sure if she was ready to handle the new developments in the case. Rubbing his hand across the rough stubble on his face, he sat on the edge of the bed. "It seems as if we now have a suspect. Chris Langston."

"What? Christine Langston? Who the hell came up with that lame idea?"

"No, no, not Christine. Chris. Her brother. I don't know all the details yet, but he is somehow involved with Madison's mother." He watched Logan's eyes until they widened slightly with understanding.

"She's at the airport now, right?"

"Yes. Anderson is with her and has been informed of the new developments." He placed a reassuring hand on her leg. "She's safe, Logan. They've already left the airport and are en route to the Langston estate." He stood and paced the small space between the window and the bed. "I called in Hennessey, your old buddy, and he's on his way to intercept and escort them in."

He turned to see Logan reaching for the railing. "Oh hell. No, you don't. You're staying put right here." Dove quickly pressed on Logan's shoulders, forcing her onto her back. The struggle was quick and decisive as Logan realized her weakened state and fell back onto the pillow, her voice a mere whisper.

"Damn it, Dove, I need to be there for her."

Dove's heart broke as he watched a thin line of tears, born from the feelings of frustration and impotence, stream from the corner of her eye. With a gentle stroke of his fingers, he pushed back a stray wisp of hair from her forehead and leaned in close. "Mac, you have to focus on getting well. I will see to it that Madison is safe. Until you can, I'll take care of her for you, I promise."

With her eyes shut tightly to stem the flow of tears, Logan offered an almost imperceptible nod and whispered a weak "Thank you."

His lips tenderly brushed her forehead and then dropped to nip her nose before he spoke. "You'd do it for me, kiddo. Now try to get a nap. I'll wake you if I hear anything else." He stood and walked to the door, pausing for a moment to look back at his friend and partner one last time before leaving her to sleep what he knew would be a restless slumber.

Liz turned into the Langston estate and stopped beside the security gate as a tall, well-built guard stepped through the door. Surprisingly, he was not dressed in a uniform but a neatly pressed coat and tie. The fabric pulled tight across his shoulders accentuated his muscular form, and his mere presence would be enough to deter any troublesome visitors.

Liz casually lowered the window and tilted her head out to meet his shaded eyes. "Hey there. I believe Mr. Langston is expecting Ms. Cavanaugh."

The guard bent and peered into the window, taking each of the occupants in with a studied gaze. "Wait here." He straightened, returned to the guardhouse, and lifted the phone on the small desk. Liz watched as he spoke and nodded, periodically glancing out the window in their direction. Before he could finish the phone call, another car stopped behind them, one she instantly recognized as belonging to Loraine Osborne, the commander of the major crimes division.

Madison stared out the front window of the SUV while they waited to be cleared through the security gate. The appearance of the car behind them caught her interest and she turned in her seat to see the stoic face of the commander. Her first thought was for Logan's safety. *Damn it, she promised me she would stay with her until I returned.*

It wasn't until they were driving through the gate that she realized something must have happened to bring the commander herself to the Langston estate. Her second thought, and the one that tightened her gut, was the realization that Loraine Osborne and her mother were about to come face to face.

Jonathon Wilson closed the battered briefcase he had owned since graduating from college and switched off the light on his desk. He walked toward the outer office through the muted shadows cast by the streetlights below. A faint rustling noise brought him to attention as he entered the darkened reception area. Colleen, his secretary, had left hours before, and no one else had access to this suite of offices except the cleaning crew, which he knew would not be around for another few hours.

He shook off the foreboding feeling as he made his way to the bank of elevators at the east end of the hall. His pace quickened, but he didn't look back as a second noise broke the deafening silence. *Jesus, this has got to end soon.* He jabbed the call button beside the elevator door and waited impatiently as the numbers above the doors slowly lit, one by one, as the car ascended to the twenty-fifth floor. Just as the bell sounded announcing the arrival of the elevator, a low, callous voice whispered in his ear.

"Long time no see, Jon Boy."

The executive's skin crawled as he recognized the voice behind him. Without taking time to weigh his options, he quickly turned and brought the briefcase up in the direction of the voice. The clasp broke when it made contact, sending papers billowing through the air. Using the only moment he had, Wilson literally jumped into the elevator and pressed the close button just as his attacker pulled himself from the floor. As the doors slowly closed, the attacker raced toward the elevator and pressed a hand into the narrow opening.

Using the only weapon available, Wilson plunged his gold-plated pen deep into the meaty flesh and fell back against the back wall as the hand jerked away and the doors shut with a resounding thud. Jerking the cell phone from his jacket, he flipped it open and cursed the weak signal when he heard only silence. Praying that the security guard would be at the main desk when he reached the lobby, all he could do was wait, his heart pounding as the elevator descended to the ground floor.

CHAPTER TWENTY-NINE

The SUV came to a stop just in front of the massive oak doors to the Langston home. Although accustomed to wealth, Madison found herself intimidated by the calculated show of power in the design and construction of what appeared to be a fortress and was further unsettled when three men immediately surrounded the vehicle.

The slight bulge under the sleek jackets of the guards did not go unnoticed as Liz rolled the window down once again. "Mrs. Cavanaugh to see Mr. Langston. I believe he is expecting her."

Aware that the guard was standing close enough to prevent her from opening the door, she waited as he spoke into a hand-held radio. After several seconds of silence, he took a step back, allowing Liz to step from the car. As she turned toward the rear of the vehicle, she saw her commander watching the tense interaction.

Loraine acknowledged Liz with only a slight nod of her head, then looked toward the doors leading into the estate before focusing her attention on the guard waiting impatiently beside the car. Flashing her badge, she opened the door only to have the guard firmly grasp the frame to prevent her exit.

"Unless you have a search warrant, I suggest you leave." The guard, towering over the car, openly sneered.

Liz, watching the interaction from a distance, couldn't hear what was said, but knew by the defensive stance of the guard that the conversation was at best unfriendly. She unbuttoned her jacket, allowing quick access to her weapon if needed, and continued to the rear of the vehicle to remove the luggage.

Cold eyes met the hard gaze of the guard as Loraine pressed against the resistant force and tilted her head toward the car ahead. "I don't need a warrant to speak to Ms. Cavanaugh, so unless you're inviting problems for Mr. Langston, I suggest you get the hell out of my way."

The guard, unprepared for the commander's response, released his grip on the door to reach for the radio clipped to his belt, and Loraine took advantage of the moment to shove the door open. The unexpected contact against his legs knocked the guard off balance, and the radio dropped to the ground and shattered.

Stepping from the car, Loraine allowed only a slight smile to cross her lips before she dismissed the guard and walked toward Liz. She noticed the other men tense and step closer to the vehicle, and their hands eased near the weapons she knew were hidden beneath their tailored jackets. "I suggest you think twice about drawing your weapons."

Liz continued to unload the luggage but kept a keen eye and ear on the peripheral activity, ready for any aggressive movement by the guards.

As Loraine closed the distance between them, she spoke quietly to the detective. "Keep the goons at bay while I speak with Ms. Cavanaugh, and get on the radio and have a warrant issued for the Langston estate. I've just been informed that Chris Langston may be our boy and the old man may he harboring him. I want a warrant for the entire estate, the office complex, and the condo in the city."

Madison and her mother stepped hesitantly toward Loraine and Liz, Marissa not yet recognizing the woman dressed in the smartly official uniform standing beside Liz Anderson. "Madison, what's going on here? Do they know each other?"

"Yes, Mother, they do." Madison could feel the pounding in her chest, knowing that within seconds the entire ugly story would roar from the past once again. Before she could continue, the commander's attention turned to them.

"Madison, Mrs. Cavanaugh, if you don't mind, I would like to speak with you for a moment." She was aware of the older woman studying her and the instant recognition when Marissa Cavanaugh's eyes fell on the brass nametag pinned to her chest.

"You." Marissa spoke with contempt as her eyes swept from Loraine to her daughter. "What the hell is going on here, Madison?"

"Mother, please calm down." She looked to Liz, her eyes pleading for support.

Liz stepped closer to her commander, and Madison noticed the slight tensing in her shoulders. "The commander just wants to speak with you for a few moments, Mrs. Cavanaugh."

Under normal conditions, Loraine would have balked at a subordinate speaking for her. However, if the situation couldn't be defused, she wouldn't gain the information she desperately needed, so she held back and allowed Liz to continue.

"Mrs. Cavanaugh, I don't know if you are aware of the recent incidents here in Pittsburgh involving your daughter, but we think you may have information that can help the case, and we would appreciate any information you can provide."

With her head held high, Marissa Cavanaugh regarded Loraine with contempt. "I will not speak with this woman under any condition."

"Mother, please." Madison gently grasped her mother's arm but was quickly shrugged away as Marissa spun around to face her.

"Don't Mother me. You knew about this? How could you, Madison. How could you?" Tears glistened in the angry eyes that bored into her daughter's.

Madison swept a hand through her hair and took a deep breath. "Mother, I wasn't aware that the commander was even here until we stopped at the guard house." She looked questioningly at Loraine. "I don't know what she wants to ask you, but please, if you care anything about me at all, you'll talk to her."

Just as Loraine was about to retake control of the conversation, the massive oak door swung open and C.W. Langston stepped out onto the portico. "What the hell is going on here?"

Loraine swore under her breath and took two steps toward the angry man. "Mr. Langston, this doesn't involve you at the moment. I suggest you go back inside and Mrs. Cavanaugh will join you shortly."

As was his way, Langston bolted from the portico and stopped just short of the commander. "I don't know what kind of games you're playing here, lady, but you will not trespass on my property and harass my guests." He glared at the nearest guard. "Call my attorney and get these hoodlums out of here." Grasping Marissa's arm, he attempted to pull her toward the door, only to have Liz step in front of him.

"Mr. Langston, I don't think I have to remind you that you are a suspect in this case, and interfering with a material witness is a serious offense." She stood her ground. "If you will release Mrs. Cavanaugh, we'll take care of our business here and be on our way as quickly as possible. Otherwise, I'll place you under arrest for hindering an investigation and intimidating a witness."

A smile eased across her lips when she saw the blood rise to his face. "Hell, I may even add on a few other charges as I think of them, like threatening an officer of the law, and by the way, do your guards all have permits for those weapons they're hiding under their jackets?"

Langston's hand fell away from Marissa's. "You won't get away with your intimidation tactics. You'll be hearing from my attorney before the day is out." Langston turned and stormed into the house, slamming the door with a resounding finality.

Liz stepped back. "So, Mrs. Cavanaugh, what's it going to be? Do you want to come downtown voluntarily or are you going to make this more difficult than it already is for everyone?"

Defeated, Marissa Cavanaugh opened the rear door to the Pathfinder before turning back to her daughter. "I'll never forgive you for this, Madison. Never."

Tears stung the doctor's eyes and she brushed them away before facing Liz and Loraine. "Um, sorry about that. Mother tends to be a little dramatic at times."

Loraine felt for the young woman caught in the undercurrents of past sins and felt guilty for the role she had played in the confrontation. "Why don't you ride with me? It will give you both time to calm down, and I'll fill you in on the way."

Madison looked at the determined lift of her mother's head through the rear window of the car before nodding. "Maybe you're right." She got into the commander's car and felt what little strength she had slowly seep out of her body. *God, Logan, I need you now.*

Logan woke from a dreamless sleep with a foreboding feeling in her stomach. Dove was gone, Madison was God knew where, and she lay in the hospital completely useless to anyone. Helpless and alone, she momentarily panicked when the phone beside the bed rang, breaking the eerie silence in the room. Struggling against the pain, she gingerly turned and pulled the phone cord hanging from the bedside table, swearing under her breath as the receiver tumbled to the floor. "Christ almighty." She tugged on the cord as quickly as the painful lesions on her arms would allow and eased the receiver to her ear. "Yeah, hello."

"Hello? Oh my God, Logan, is that you?"

"Hey there, Doc." A wide smile spread across the parched flesh of her face but Logan ignored the pain, thinking only of the melodic voice on the other end of the line.

"It's so good to hear your voice." Suddenly Madison's voice carried a note of panic. "Logan, where's Dove? Isn't he with you?"

"Calm down. He just stepped outside. I'm sure he'll be back in just a minute." Logan could hear the familiar squawk of a police scanner in the background. "Madi, where are you?"

"We're on our way to the precinct. I'll tell you all bout it when I see you. How are you feeling?"

"I miss you, but otherwise I'm doing fine." Logan gave a hoarse chuckle. "After all, we have a little something to finish, don't we?"

"Um, yes, we do. We most certainly do, Detective. Now, there's someone here who wants to talk to you."

"It's about time you decided to wake up, McGregor," Loraine said. "Tell Dvorak to give me a call on my cell phone when he gets back. I need him to head up a search on the Langston estate."

The door opened slightly and an orderly entered with a large basket of flowers. Logan waved him over and pointed to the rolling tray beside the bed. She listened quietly, fighting the urge to try to pull herself out of bed. "Roger, Commander. I'll tell him to call you as soon as he returns." Going with her gut feeling, she plunged ahead. "Um, Commander? Will you keep an eye on the doc for me? She's, um...well..."

"Say no more, Detective. Consider it done. Now get some rest, I have a lot of questions for when I see you next." Flipping the phone closed, Loraine handed it back to Madison. "Here ya go, and thanks."

The doctor took the phone and tucked it into her pocket as the commander slipped the car into a vacant space in the garage. "Ah, what exactly did she ask you to do?"

Loraine gave the doctor a stern look before reaching for the door handle. "If I told you that, Doc, I'd have to shoot ya, and I just really don't have time for all the paperwork right now." She made a quick escape from the car and waited until Madison joined her before leading the way to the elevator.

"You cops are just too weird for words." Crossing her arms across her chest, Madison walked along beside the commander, mumbling to herself.

For the first time in weeks, the commander felt like things were beginning to come together in the case and in a rare break with procedure decided to let her guard down. "What can I say? We're just one big sorority. Next thing you know, we'll be having slumber parties and talking about cute girls."

As if in perfect time, the elevator doors slid open and Loraine never slowed as she entered the car. After pressing the button for the third floor, she turned around and had to bite her lip when she saw Madison staring at her dumbstruck and open mouthed. With a little shrug of her shoulders, she grinned. "What can I say, the other team was a bunch of losers. Now come on and let's get this show on the road."

CHAPTER THIRTY

Jonathon Wilson pressed his body against the side panel of the elevator as it dipped and stopped in the lobby. After the doors slid open, he waited until he felt certain that the lobby was vacant. He slowly slipped from the confines of the car, then stepped quickly toward the revolving door at the far end of the atrium but came up short when an all-too-familiar face came into view.

Panic stricken, he looked for a way to escape, and saw none. "Why? Why couldn't you leave well enough alone?"

An eerie laugh echoed off the marble walls. "Why? Why should I?" With arms outstretched, the bleeding man regarded the building and all it represented. "They have it all and I have nothing." He moved closer, his eyes wild with anger and resentment. "You saw to that, didn't you, Jon Boy. You made sure I was ruined and banished from the great C.W. Langston's empire." His voice rose, getting louder and angrier with each word. "You set me up and now you're going to pay for what you did."

Wilson's eyes darted from the raving man to a slight movement against the far wall, but before he could make a move to escape, the figure moved into the light. "No, Chris, he's not. You are."

Chris Langston turned to face his sister's voice. His mind reeled as he watched her shaky hand aim the .38-caliber gun at his chest. "Chrissy. Long time no see, Sis."

"Stop, Chris. I'm warning you. You've done enough...made your point. Now it's time to end all of this."

He took one step closer. "You're exactly right there, Sis, and that's what I'm going to do."

Wilson watched from the sidelines and moved toward the security station. When he reached the end of the desk, his stomach clenched at the sight of the guard on the floor. "Oh my God."

Christine turned toward the hollow voice, and the distraction was enough to give Chris the chance he had been waiting for. In two steps, he dove toward his sister, knocking her to the ground and the gun from her hand.

Wilson, too far away to make a run for the gun, stood helpless as the two siblings wrestled for control. Reaching for the phone on the desk, he quickly dialed 911 but before the operator could answer, Chris was towering over his sister, the gun pointed at her head.

"Hang up the phone, Jon Boy, or I'll shoot her."

Wilson saw the insane look in Chris's eyes and knew he wasn't bluffing. He moved slowly from behind the desk, his hands raised. "Okay, Chris, whatever you want. Just don't hurt Christine."

Christine lay perfectly still on the cool marble floor, watching her brother and the unmitigated hatred in his eyes. "Chris, go, just leave and don't come back. If you want money, I'll give you all I have, but please don't kill anyone else."

He regarded his sister with disdain. "Get up and quit trying to bribe me. You're no better than the old man. He always thinks he can buy his way out of anything. Well, not this time, dear Sis, not this time." He leveled the gun at Wilson's chest and fired, then calmly turned back toward Christine. "I came here to finish this, and that's exactly what I'm going to do. Now move. I have a little party planned for us, and you've saved me time because I don't have to go hunting for you."

Defeated, Christine took one last look at the lifeless body of Jonathon Wilson before turning toward the door to the private executive garage. She knew once they were alone in the secluded parking area there would be no way to escape, but she was out of options. She moved along slowly and each step was met with a deliberate jab in her back with the muzzle of the gun. "Chris, please, don't do this."

"Forget it, Sis. I've spent my entire life trying to live up to the unrealistic expectations from you and dear Dad, and now I'm going to set a few of my own." With another jab to her back, he emphasized his next words. "Now move it before I have to make you miss the party."

Liz Anderson stood outside the interrogation room facing her commander. "With all due respect, ma'am, I don't think I'm the best one to do this." She felt her palms, damp with nervous perspiration, clench inside the pockets of her trousers.

The commander raised an eyebrow and shook her head. "Sorry, but you're the only one I have that knows enough about this case. McGregor's in the hospital, I can't reach Dvorak, and she refuses to speak with me. Just ask the questions that I gave you and you'll be fine."

Liz's eyes swept to the doorway to the room where Marissa Cavanaugh sat waiting. "Okay, okay. You're right."

Just as she was turning to enter the interrogation room, the desk sergeant called out to the commander.

"Go ahead, I'll be watching from the observation room as soon as I find out what the front desk wants." Loraine watched Liz disappear into the observation room and then turned toward the front desk to see the sergeant waving frantically in her direction.

Liz stepped into the viewing booth and observed Marissa Cavanaugh for a few moments. She was obviously nervous, her eyes darting between the one-way mirror and the door as she waited. For a moment, Liz felt compassion for the frail-looking woman. In less than an hour she had transformed from confident and outspoken to frightened, even childlike. *What secrets do you hold, Ms. Cavanaugh? Or do you even know yourself?*

As Liz exited the observation booth, she met Loraine Osborne, her eyes wide with what the detective thought was fear.

"Keep Dr. Cavanaugh here with you and don't let anyone inside that room. Dispatch just called. Something's going down at the Langston building, shots fired and they can't get a response from the caller. SWAT is on their way and I'm heading over to see what's going on. I'll radio you when I know something."

"Know what?" Neither had heard the door to the waiting room open or Madison come out. She stood, hands on hips, waiting for an answer.

Loraine glanced at the detective, nodded, then turned and headed in the opposite direction. The detective tilted her head toward the open door. "In here." After the door was closed, she said, "Something is going down right now at the Langston building. That's all I can tell you because it's all I know right now. Just sit tight for a few minutes until I'm finished with your mother and then I'll see what I can find out."

As soon as Liz left the room, Madison picked up the phone and called Dove's cell number. After several rings, she heard the detective's voice, and in the background, a mixture of sirens and what sounded like mass confusion.

"Dvorak."

"Dove, what's going on? I just heard something is happening at the Langston building, but I can't get any other information." She waited as Dove yelled orders to someone on the other end.

"Madi, I can't tell you anything right now."

"But Dove, who's with Logan?" Madison felt a wave of panic rise in her chest. *This could be a trick to get to Logan.*

"No one right now. I just talked with her and she's fine. Look, Madi, I gotta go."

She hung up and started pacing as multiple scenarios sped through her mind. "To hell with staying here." She grabbed her backpack and eased the door open just far enough to peer out into the hallway. Seeing that the path to the stairwell was clear, she moved out into the hall and calmly made her way to the exit. Once she was outside, she took a few seconds to get her bearings, then moved in the direction of the busy street and hailed a cab.

After giving the cabbie the address of the hospital, she sat back in the seat, dialed Logan's number on her cell phone, and waited as the ringing continued unanswered.

Logan opened the card that accompanied the huge arrangement of flowers, a smile washing over her face. *Madi, you're so sweet.* The smile faded as she read the words typed on the card.

> *Isn't the game of chess wonderful? With a single move, empires are built or destroyed. It is a game of logic and one I have thoroughly enjoyed playing with you.*
> *My castle is protected. My pawns in place, knights on guard, and my bishops forever loyal. I do believe I have you in check, Detective.*
> *Your turn. Catch me if you can.*
> *Good luck, and may the best mind win.*

Logan stared at the card for a long moment, wondering what it meant, and jumped as the phone rang beside the bed. "McGregor. Dove, where are you and what's going on?"

"No time to talk right now. I just wanted to tell you to stay on your toes. I've called in another guard to double up your security. Something is going down with the Langston case. I'll let you know what I find out as soon as I can."

"But—Hello? Dove?" Logan threw off the bedsheet as she slammed the phone down and had to grab the railing as a wave of dizziness washed over her. "Damn it all to hell."

She sat for a few moments until her equilibrium returned, then eased out of bed and slowly walked to the closet, swearing when she found it empty. She looked around the room and spotted a neatly folded set of scrubs that Madison had left on the windowsill. Gingerly, she eased the scrubs over the healing wounds on her body and made her way to the door.

Peering out, she spotted the guard sitting just outside and knew there was no way she could sneak out without being seen. She decided the only way she could leave would be to use the intimidation factor she was known for within the ranks and swung open the door with a confidence and power she knew she didn't have inside.

The young guard jerked out of his seat with a frightened look on his face. "Detective McGregor, I thought you were asleep. Is there something I can do for you?"

Logan eased out into the hall, one hand ready to grab for the doorjamb in case another wave of dizziness hit her. "Yes, I need you to come with me."

The young officer looked at Logan in confusion. "But, Detective, I can't leave my post. I have orders."

She regarded the officer for a moment, knowing she was going to force him to make a decision that would most likely get them both suspended. "Your orders, Officer, are to guard me, and if I'm not here, the only way you can carry out those orders is to come with me." She started toward the elevator before he had a chance to respond and chuckled to herself when he quickly gathered up his belongings and sped up to walk beside her.

"Detective, I think I should call this in and let command know we're on the move. I—I don't want to get in trouble and I don't think we're suppose to be leaving the hospital without approval."

Logan stopped and turned toward him. "Officer, all the approval you need right now is mine. I'll take the heat for anything the brass doesn't like. Your job is to guard me, and in order to do that you have to be *with* me, so let's get moving."

Within five minutes, Logan and the young officer stepped out into the late-afternoon sun. The heat instantly caused her raw burns to seethe with pain. She took the officer's radio. "I'll call this in. You get the car." She knew he could call in their movements from the car, but she was counting on his inexperience to work in her favor. Within moments they were speeding toward the only place she knew to go—the Langston estate. *That has to be his castle.*

As they drove, Logan rested her head back and wiped the sweat from her forehead. She knew what she was doing could get both her and the young officer killed. Knowing she wasn't capable of a hand-to-hand fight, she was relying on her brains and intellect to get her through this one. She only prayed that Madison and the rest of them wouldn't figure out what was going on and where they were until it was over.

CHAPTER THIRTY-ONE

The ride to Mercy Hospital seemed like it took forever. As the taxi slowed next to the curb across the street from the emergency department, Madison slid a twenty through the security glass separating her from the driver and opened the door.

"Take it easy lady, or *you'll* be in the hospital," the driver yelled out the window as Madison darted between moving cars.

Madison was oblivious to the blaring horns as she raced across the street and into the sterile confines of the hospital. She didn't slow down until she bounded into Logan's room a few minutes later. There, she stopped in her tracks as she faced the empty room. "Damn it, Logan, where are you?" She laid her hand on the wrinkled sheets. "Still warm. You can't be far."

Just as she was turning to leave the room, something on the floor caught her attention. Madison bent to pick up the card and a strangled cry escaped her throat as she read the message. She thought about calling Dove but knew he wouldn't know any more than she did. *Loraine?* "Maybe."

Madison quickly punched in the numbers to the commander's cell phone and waited impatiently as the phone continued to ring unanswered. "Hell, forget it. I know where she went. She has to be at the estate."

C.W. Langston sat with his hands balled into fists watching as Herbert Whittaker spoke to Norman Watson, the chief deputy, on the phone.

"Norm, we go way back. I know you can do something, anything to get this cleared up." Whittaker watched Langston with weary eyes and knew he wouldn't take no for an answer. "But, Norm, Ms. Cavanaugh is a visitor to our city. She hasn't been in Pittsburgh in years. I can't see how anyone would think she knew something about this case. The police department is using Ms. Cavanaugh as a means of harassing Mr. Langston, and I won't tolerate it. I want her released immediately. If you need to question her in the future, she will be staying at the Langston estate and Mr. Langston has assured me of his cooperation."

Impatiently, Langston rose and poured himself a double scotch from the bar as he listened to Whittaker's argument. *He is nothing but a weasel.* Just as he returned to his desk, Whittaker hung up the phone.

"Watson says he'll look into it, but no promises." Whittaker stood and moved toward the door. "Don't call me again C.W. Do whatever you please, but this is the end for us. You're on your own from here on out." With a final look, Whittaker walked out, leaving C.W. Langston staring at his back.

Logan instructed the officer to pull onto a seldom-used truck path about a quarter of a mile from the gates to the Langston estate. She assumed the path was for the gardeners or the numerous other contractors that kept the estate looking pristine.

She looked over to the young officer with some concern. On the ride from the hospital, she had learned that Alonzo Alvarez was the father of two small boys. She hesitated to involve him in such a dangerous situation, knowing his lack of experience would only hinder them both, but she had no choice. She couldn't call Dove, Loraine would go ballistic if she knew what was about to take place, and the lieutenant would have her ass for even thinking about what she was about to do.

"Alonzo, why don't you stay here and call for backup while I check things out?"

Alvarez shot Logan a suspicious glare. "No way, Detective. Pardon my insubordination, but I don't trust you worth a damn not to leave me high and dry. Where you go, I go."

"I could order you to stand down."

"You could, but you won't." He grinned. "You need me and you know it, so let's just cut the bull and get going."

McGregor chewed her lip as she thought over his comments. *Damn hot shot.* "You remind me a lot of myself when I was in your seat." She climbed out of the patrol car, pleased when the dizziness she had experienced at the hospital failed to return. "Let's get rolling. It will be dark soon."

Alvarez opened the trunk of the patrol car, bent to retrieve something Logan couldn't see clearly, then met her at the front of the car. "Here, you'll probably need this." Handing her a well-polished 9mm

Glock, he regarded her solemnly. "It was my father's extra piece until he retired last year. Now it's mine. Write me up if you want, I don't care. It kept him alive. It's kept me alive and will most likely keep your crazy ass alive today too, Detective."

Logan took a moment to regard him. She had been too preoccupied to notice before, but now as she stood beside him in the overgrowth, she appreciated his size. At six foot four and an easy two hundred sixty pounds, Alvarez would be a force to be reckoned with in a one-on-one. She took him in from foot to head and stopped at his curious eyes. "No worries, I'll take care of the paperwork."

With a smirk she tucked the weapon into the waistband of her scrubs. "I guess you'll do, Alvarez." Then she disappeared through the brush and trees.

Taken unaware, Alvarez was left behind and had to jog to keep up with Logan, grinning as the realization set in that he was about to work a case with the renowned Detective McGregor. *The guys at the station will never believe this when I tell them.*

Loraine watched as the morgue slid the last body bag into the back of the van. Seldom was she as stunned by the viciousness of mankind as she had been with this case. The killer, a sadistic murderer, took great care to emphasize his hatred for the Langston executives he had murdered. *Wilson must have been a surprise kill or a hurried one.* Thoughts raced through her mind at mach speed. She knew if Wilson was killed with a single shot to the chest, Chris Langston was either tired of his games or had another, more immediate agenda. *I have to find Christine—and now.*

Dove was barking orders into to his cell phone when Loraine stopped beside him. His face reflected his frustration and fatigue. "I don't give a damn how many people it takes. I want her found, and now!" He ended the call and sat back in the seat of his government-issued car, unaware that his commander was beside him. "Fucking incompetents."

"Not many have your drive, Dvorak." Loraine knew the case had taken a toll on one of her best detectives. Not only had he witnessed the vile and unmerciful work of the murderer, but that same murderer had almost claimed the life of a fellow officer and his best friend. "Have you checked on McGregor lately?"

"She's gone." He climbed out of the car.

Loraine had assumed the phone call between Dove and the station was about Christine Langston. A knot formed in her stomach when she realized that he had been talking about Logan. "What do you mean gone?"

"Gone, as in not at the hospital. Her guard's missing too. That's what the call was about. We have to find her before he does." A look of near-terror filled his eyes, "If he hasn't already." Dove's fist slammed into the hood of the car. "Stupid, I'm so fucking stupid not to think he would go after her."

"Detective Dvorak," Loraine bellowed, "you need to calm down. You'll be no good to her like this. Tell me what you have and we'll figure it out together."

Dove scrubbed a hand across his two-day growth of beard and leaned heavily against the car. "I have a detective on the way to the hospital to seal off the room and see if there are any clues to where she may have gone." He looked at his commander with defeated eyes. "Dr. Cavanaugh is missing too."

"Damn her. I knew I shouldn't have left before I had a guard on her." Loraine released a frustrated sigh. "Okay, we both underestimated those two. Now let's make it right." She turned and double-timed it toward her car, calling over her shoulder. "Well, don't just stand there, Dvorak. Get your ass in gear and get in my car. We're going over to the Langston estate."

Logan knelt, weapon drawn, beneath the shattered window listening for signs of activity inside the Langston mansion. Alvarez, hidden in a gazebo a few yards away with a clear view inside the room, stood ready to provide cover should someone discover her presence. She could only hope a surprise attack on the rookie wouldn't completely bewilder him. She waited for a few moments and when she heard no sounds from inside signaled him to cover her while she made her way to the door.

Alvarez moved to the other side of the gazebo to allow him a better view of the doorway into what appeared to be the kitchen and nodded to Logan when the path was clear for her to advance. He could feel his heart pounding within his chest, and for the first time since joining the force was afraid. Not so much for himself, but for his unexpected partner. McGregor was a legend on the force, and Alvarez knew he didn't have the experience to serve beside the detective. *Jesus, don't let me fuck this up.*

The doorknob turned easily under Logan's touch. *He unlocked it for me.* This was the most dangerous moment. She had no idea where the killer was in the house. He could be standing just inside the door, waiting for the perfect shot as she entered. *No, he likes his games too much for an easy kill.* She looked at Alvarez, who tipped his head in acknowledgment, and with a raised hand counted down from three before swinging open the door and diving inside.

Madison hailed another taxi, giving the driver directions to the Langston estate as she slammed the door. She knew it was a ridiculous thing to do, but she couldn't stay away. Madison had no doubts that if Logan and the killer were both there, neither would leave until one was dead. A knot formed in her stomach as she thought of the possibilities.

"Can't you go any faster?"

The driver glanced impatiently into the rearview mirror. "There *is* a speed limit in this city, lady. Chill out, I'll get you there and in one piece."

Various scenarios played through her mind. What if Logan was already hurt? *Damn, I don't have my bag.* She rode in impatient silence until the estate gates came into view. "Stop here."

"But, lady—"

"No, it's okay; I want to surprise my friends." After passing another large bill through the security glass, Madison quickly got out of the taxi and waved the man away. She waited until he was out of sight before disappearing into the trees beside the stone wall surrounding the property.

Pain tore through Logan's body as she dove onto the hard floor and rolled to a crouch beside the island. She looked down at her arms at the freshly torn wounds that oozed bright red. *No time to deal with that now.* The house was eerily quiet as her eyes swept the perimeter looking for any movement. After surveying the room, she stood and stepped behind the door, her back against the wall as she waved Alvarez to approach.

The large man's agility surprised Logan, and within seconds, he was safely inside and crouching behind the same island where she had been only moments before. She raised a finger to her lips and tipped her head in the direction of the intercom on the wall beside the door. A red light glowed, indicating the room was being monitored from some other location in the house. Alvarez nodded and stealthily eased his way toward the main doorway into the dining room, his back to Logan.

Damn him. What is he doing? She was about to follow when she saw him reach up, grab something from the counter, and quickly make his way back to her. He handed it to her without looking at it. Pushing aside her anger at the rookie, she tore the paper from his hand and read.

Welcome, Detective McGregor,

> *Now the real fun begins. Unlike a boring chess game where we can watch each other's moves in the light of day, this one holds a promise of adventure and the suspense of the unknown. Find me, and you will find the heroine, the fallen princess of the Langston Dynasty.*

> *Here is a small hint. I hope you paid attention in history class. I'm sure given time, which there isn't much of, you can figure it out.*

> *The Empire of the Dead.*

> *Hurry, Detective, time is running out.*

Logan stared at the writing, willing the paper to reveal more, and mouthed a silent curse. She handed the paper over to Alvarez and waited as he read the neat script. To her amazement, he quickly pulled out his notepad, scribbled, and passed the book to her. The page contained one word, *catacomb*, and he pointed toward the floor. Her eyes swept the room, falling on a door that she thought led to the basement, but as she moved forward Alvarez gripped her arm. Taking the notepad from her hand, he scribbled another hurried note and handed it back to Logan.

She took a few seconds to ponder the information, then nodded her agreement. *No, it wouldn't be the basement. That's too easy.* She leaned in close to the large man and whispered, "I have no idea what he is up to, so be alert and expect anything."

With a curt nod, the officer readied himself for the biggest case he had snagged yet. As he and Logan silently made their way through the dining room, each covering the other along the way, Alvarez prayed that he would live to see his next sunrise.

C.W. Langston sat back in the limo and regarded Marissa with sympathetic eyes as he took her trembling hand in his. "I'm terribly sorry that you were forced to endure the police questioning. Believe me, someone will pay for dragging you into this mess unnecessarily."

With a squeeze to his hand, Marissa turned and kissed him. "It's okay, darling. It's over and I'm fine."

"Well, it's not—"

"C.W. Let's just forget about the entire afternoon. I want to have a nice dinner with you and spend the evening catching up on us."

With a grunt he agreed. "Just let me call Rosa and let her know we are on the way so she can have dinner for us when we arrive." He waited as the phone rang ten times before replacing it in its cradle. "That's odd, Rosa isn't answering." With a shrug and a smile he turned back to

Marissa. "She must be in the garden having the nightly sherry that she doesn't know I'm aware of."

He raised the shaded partition, cutting off the driver from their conversation. The drive to the estate would take thirty minutes, and he intended to make the most of the time. "Now tell me about your time in Europe and what convinced you to come back to me."

With a laugh, she gently stroked his cheek. "Darling, you are terribly convincing. I'm sure you aren't surprised by my choice, are you?" She pulled him closer and kissed him. *If you only knew, darling. If you only knew.*

CHAPTER THIRTY-TWO

Logan and Alvarez eased through the expanse of rooms on the first level of the mansion until they came to what they discerned to be C.W. Langston's study. The walls, paneled in dark walnut and embellished with wide decorative moldings, were symbolic of the man. The vanity wall held the usual diplomas and awards as well as numerous photographs of the CEO with some of the most powerful and politically active individuals in the country. Even in her haste to find his son, Logan didn't miss the well-placed photographs of Langston with the last five United States presidents. *No wonder he's been untouchable.*

After securing the room, Alvarez closed the door, shutting them off from the rest of the house. They continued the silent signals, knowing that the study was most likely being monitored as well. The young rookie was looking under Langston's desk, searching for a hidden switch, when a voice echoed through the room.

"You won't find it there. Dear old Dad isn't stupid enough to place the switch in such an obvious place."

Logan's eyes swept the room and spotted the inconspicuous camera mounted just below the ceiling in the far corner. *Damn, I should have known.*

The voice reverberated through the room. "It's nice to see you have recovered from your injuries, Detective. Sorry I didn't send flowers sooner, but you know I've been busy the last few days."

"What exactly is it that you want, Langston?" Logan tried to get a better feel for his mental state. The note left with the flowers and the one Alvarez had found in the kitchen, as well as Langston's behavior the last few days, were an indication that the man was quickly decompensating.

An eerie laugh filled the room. "What do I want, Detective? I want the great and powerful C.W. Langston on his knees. That's what I want. I want the man that tried to destroy me destroyed." Chris Langston's voice rose in volume with each word.

"I can certainly understand that. Your father is one of the most egotistical people I've ever met." She turned to the vanity wall, her back to the camera. "He's untouchable, Chris; I realized that several weeks ago. He has the most powerful men and women in the world wrapped around his little finger." She turned toward the camera and walked closer, trying to connect with the man behind the camera. "Hell, Chris, the PPD hasn't been able to touch him. We need help if we're to bring him down. You know where all the skeletons are hidden. Why don't you come out and let's team up. Together we can get to him."

All she heard was silence. She waited, watching the seconds tick off the clock. "Come on, Chris, team up with me. We all know your father drove you to this point. No one's going to blame you."

She heard shuffling and the sound of a woman's voice cursing in the background. She glanced at Alvarez and waited for what seemed like forever. Finally, Langston's voice echoed in the room once again.

"Well, well, Detective. It seems like we have another visitor."

Logan's eyes shifted to the front windows, giving her a clear view of the circular drive. No one was there. "You must be mistaken, Chris. I don't see anyone out front."

"Not out front, Detective, sneaking around the back. No worries, though, I have her all settled in here with me for the time being."

She? Logan looked at Alvarez, who only shrugged. "Is Christine there with you?"

Chris laughed. "Oh yes, Christine is here with me. It's actually getting a bit crowded down here. Would you like to say hello to our latest arrival?"

"Logan, don't come dow—"

Logan flinched when she heard a slap and then a soft agonized moan. A knot formed in her stomach and her fists balled at her side as realization set in. Chris Langston had Madison and Christine locked away in some underground cave. Had he known her, he would have recognized the almost too calm reply from Logan as a sign of danger. "Langston, if you hurt either of those women, I will have no mercy on you."

"And just what do you think you're going to do about it, Detective?" More shuffling, along with muted voices, followed. Then nothing.

"Langston?" A deafening silence filled the room and Logan stared at the lens of the camera, willing it to reveal Chris Langston's location. A movement outside caught her attention. *Jesus, this is going from bad to worse.* She quickly moved through the living room, opened the front door, and stepped out onto the portico just as C.W. Langston's chauffer opened the door to the limousine.

Christine sat in a straight-backed chair with her hands tied behind her back. She surveyed the room, one she had never known existed before that day. One wall was solid rock, and she surmised she was somewhere beneath the northern end of the property just at the base of Mount Washington. The other three walls were made of concrete block and mortar. Her mind reeled with questions. *Did Grandfather build this? Daddy? And how the hell did Chris know about it and not me?*

She didn't hear her brother's shuffling feet until he was beside her.

"How're you doing, Sis?" His eyes were full of hatred for her. She was always overshadowing him. Always the smartest, fastest. Always the best and always Daddy's little girl. "I guess you're a little surprised to find out about my little hiding place. It isn't the Langston Towers by any means, but it's quiet." His arms swept the expanse of the room. "And it's soundproof, too. Of course, *Daddy* would have nothing but the best."

Her curiosity won out. "What is this place, Chris, and why is it on our property?"

Chris sat on a makeshift cot and leaned against the cold stone wall. "It's about time you understand that you don't know all there is about our father. He's not a very nice man, Chrissy."

"I'm well aware of that, Chris." Deciding to take a different approach, she added, "I've spent the last year gathering evidence against him for the DA. It's time someone put an end to his reign of terror."

Chris smirked. "Sure, Chrissy, sure you have. Just how much do you know about the great and powerful C.W. Langston?" Bounding from the cot, he crossed the room in three long strides and bent close to his sister's face. "Did you know that he used to lock me in this godforsaken cave?"

Christine could feel the heat of his breath, and drops of spittle sprayed her face as he screamed. Her eyes locked with her brother's, and she saw for the first time the agonizing pain he had locked away for so long. "No, I didn't." Her words were a mere whisper.

Regaining his composure, Chris straightened and moved across the room. His fingers outlined the long-forgotten scratches in the stone wall. "When he would lock me in here, the only thing that kept me sane was carving these drawings in the stone." He turned to his sister. "It would take hours sometimes to etch a single line, so this wall can give some idea of how many hours I was locked away while you were free to come and go as you pleased."

Christine studied the massive wall and the etching before her. She suddenly realized the meaning of his words and knew that her brother had been held captive by their father in that damp and dingy cave throughout his life. The etchings along the lower portion of the wall were obviously from his childhood—the lines were ragged and uneven—but as he grew older and taller, the drawings rose higher along the wall, the patterns evened out and became more complex and detailed, filled with anger and hate. "Jesus, Chris, I never knew. I'm so sorry."

"It's a little late for being sorry, Chrissy."

"Why? Why did he do it?" She knew her father was vindictive, verging on the dark side of evil, but she had no idea he was capable of doing something like this to his own son.

"Why? Because I wasn't the pliable little puppet that you were, Sis. He couldn't mold me into the man he wanted me to be, so he decided to break me the only way he knew how by locking me in his cave." He fingered a series of small scars on his arm. "For the first few years there weren't any lights down here. All he gave me was a flashlight. You remember the time he fell and broke his leg and had to spend two days in the hospital?"

"Yes. I was about thirteen, I think."

"Yes, you were. Well, while Daddy was in the hospital, I was locked down here. I had no food, no water, nothing for three days." He walked closer and bent so she could see the scars on his arms. "When he was finally able to drag his sorry ass down here to get me, I was unconscious and the rats had begun to eat at my flesh."

Christine felt a wave of nausea wash over her. "Oh God, Chris."

"Yes. Poor, poor Chris." He pointed to the lighting strung along the ceiling. "It was only after that and having to deal with the questions over my injuries that he installed the lighting and stocked a footlocker with bottled water and old army rations. He's an evil bastard, but one thing's for sure, that episode taught him to plan for any possibility."

Christine watched as he sat down on the cot and began an almost imperceptible rocking, all the while staring at the etching on the wall.

"What the hell are you doing in my home?" Langston stormed up the steps and stood face to face with Logan.

Just as she was about to answer, Alvarez walked out. "I suggest you stand down, sir." When Langston only glared at him, he took a step forward. "Now. And don't make me ask twice."

The executive faced Alvarez. "Do you have any idea who I am, son?"

A smile creased the officer's cheeks. "Well, I can say this for sure. You're not my daddy, so I would suggest you not call me son."

Langston attempted to shove his way between Logan and Alvarez only to have the officer's hand fall heavily on his shoulder.

"Sir, I really couldn't care less who you are, but if you don't stand down, I'm going to throw your ass in lockup, and then when I have some time we can get to know each other up close and personal."

The men held each other's gaze for a long moment until Marissa broke the strained silence. "C.W., why don't we all go inside and see if we can get this straightened out in more comfortable surroundings."

Langston shrugged off Alvarez's hand and stepped back. "Certainly, darling."

Logan held up a hand. "Let's go into your study, Mr. Langston, but before we do, I need to tell you that your son Chris has your daughter Christine and Dr. Madison Cavanaugh locked in a cellar of some type on your property. I need to know where it is and how to access it before anyone else gets hurt."

"Oh God, no." Logan's eyes flashed to the woman standing behind Langston and saw the raw terror in her eyes just before she fainted.

The chauffer caught Marissa as she fell, but before he could lift her, Alvarez scooped her up in his arms. "I'll take her into the study. Are you ready for me to call this in?"

"Yes, and make sure Commander Osborne is briefed as well." Logan looked up as a car came into view at the end of the drive. "On second thought, never mind. She's here." She waited as Dove and Loraine got out of the car before stepping off the portico. "Commander." She looked at Dove and tipped her head. "Dove."

Loraine moved around the car. "McGregor. Looks like you have some explaining to do."

Logan gave Dove a sidelong look. "D, why don't you go inside and see if you can get some information out of Langston about a cellar that is located on the property while I fill the commander in on the situation." He nodded and moved up the steps, but turned when Logan called after him, "Bring him outside and keep all other conversation to a minimum, because the interior of the house is being monitored. Chris Langston has Christine and Madison locked in the cellar. I need to know where it is, and now."

CHAPTER THIRTY-THREE

Madison listened to the conversation between brother and sister, shocked that any man could do to his son what C.W. Langston had done to Chris. *It's no wonder you're full of hate.* She watched as he went from rational thought to near-insanity in a matter of seconds. As a doctor, Madison understood the impact that emotional and physical abuse could have on a child. The sins of a father, more often than not, followed an innocent child into adulthood and created a near-clone of the monster that bore him.

Lost in her thoughts, she was startled when Chris stepped in front of her chair and pulled her head back toward his.

"You'd better listen when I talk to you, bitch." He released her hair and trailed a line down her jaw with his fingers. "You're just like your mother, soft and sweet on the outside and a hard cold bitch on the inside. Does the illustrious Detective McGregor know all your secrets, Madi?"

Madison's eyes never left his as she spoke with an air of defiance. "What do you mean, like my mother? My mother wouldn't give you the time of day."

He leaned close to her face, so close his sour breath assaulted her senses. "No?" He walked to a backpack against the far wall and rummaged through the contents until he found what he was searching for. As he strolled back toward the doctor, very casually, he turned the oval pendant around so she could see the inscription on the back surface. A small scale of justice hanging from the chain sparkled in the unusually dim light.

Stunned, Madison could only stare at the symbol her father had worn until the day he died in the arms of his lover. "Whe—where the hell did you get my father's necklace?"

Langston's eyes gleamed with pleasure as he took in the doctor's shocked expression. "Not where, my dear, but from whom. You see, your mother decided that old men weren't her thing after your dear old Dad died in the arms of his young lover, and a few years later the great C.W. Langston dumped her for another young one." Ominous laughter filled the cave. "It took some doing, but I finally won her over and for the last five years we've been happily residing in Europe."

He paced the length of the cave, stopping occasionally to look into the eyes of his captives as he spoke. "Rissa gave me the necklace as a symbolic gesture of justice served. After all the years she spent suffering the shame our fathers had dumped on her, she had finally found her rightful place with me."

He turned to Christine and screamed, "Until you told him where I was living. Until you ruined it all for me." His knuckles slammed into her face, leaving a gash in her lip and a rivulet of blood streaming down her chin.

"Do you have any idea what you've done, Chrissy?" His arms swept toward Madison. "You just couldn't leave well enough alone, could you? You couldn't leave me in peace. This, all of this is your fault, Chrissy. You're responsible for all of this, just as sure as if you buried the knife in all of their bellies yourself." His eyes were hard and cold as he regarded his sister. "You always had to be the best—Daddy's little girl."

As if on cue, a deep voice echoed through the cold, damp cave. "Christopher, I want you to stop this nonsense right now. Release your sister and the doctor before you make this any worse than it has already become."

"Well, well, well. Dear old Dad, what a surprise. I was wondering when you'd show up." Chris turned to face the intercom. "You just can't keep your hands out of anything, can you?"

Laughter echoed through the intercom as Langston stared at the box on the wall and listened to his son in the cave below the den.

"You thought you broke me years ago, didn't you, Dad? You thought you could run me out of your life. But you were wrong. All those days and nights spent down here waiting for you to let me out of this godforsaken hole. Do you know what I did, Dad? I became strong. I became immune to your hatred."

Chris stopped in front of Christine. "I had finally resolved all of the hatred I had for both of you. It took a long time, but I moved on with my life—made a place for myself in the world that neither of you could soil with your filthy hands." He bent close to her ear, his breath brushing against her damp skin as he spoke in an eerily soft voice. "But you just couldn't let well enough alone, could you?" When he received no answer, Chris grabbed Christine's hair and pulled her face up to meet his. "Could you?"

The scream reverberated through the study, and Langston backed a step away from the wall as the naked hatred poured from his son's mouth. For the first time since the whole nightmare had started, he finally knew the answer to the question he had been asking himself from the start: Why?

Slowly, he turned to Marissa, his face pale and creased with confusion. "Tell me it isn't so, Marissa." He stormed over to her. "Tell me you haven't been sleeping with my son for the last five years."

Marissa stared coldly at Langston's face. "How does the knife feel, C.W., now that it's in your own back?"

Lightning quick, his hands were around her neck. "Damn you to hell." He struggled against the hands pulling him back as all of his anger surged to his hands and his grip tightened. "I'll kill you, bitch."

Loraine entered the study just as Logan slammed Langston against the wall, pinning an arm behind his back. "What the hell is going on in here?"

Marissa sat across the room, holding her throat as Langston struggled against the force of the detective's weight. Taking a position between the two, Loraine stood waiting for someone to answer. "Detective."

Logan tipped her head in the direction of the intercom as she led Langston toward a chair as far away from Marissa as possible. "Sit and don't move," she said, and was somewhat surprised when the CEO did as he was instructed without argument. She motioned for Alvarez to take her place and moved toward the commander.

"It seems as if Mrs. Cavanaugh here has been playing a game of her own, Commander." Turning to Marissa, she regarded her with cold, hard eyes. "Why don't you explain what all this is about and let us all in on your little game, Mrs. Cavanaugh."

Stunned, Christopher listened to the conversation taking place in the room above. His mind reeled with countless questions. His thoughts were broken as Marissa's voice crackled through the intercom. He released the grip he had on Christine's hair and slowly walked the short distance to the speaker as though being closer to Marissa's voice would somehow make things clearer in his mind.

"It's not a game, Detective. Not a game at all." Marissa walked toward the window, looking out over the expanse of the landscape and beyond. "I met Chris several years ago while vacationing in Rome. We were both alone, and we spent two weeks at the same hotel. He went by the name Chris Langsford and claimed to be an investor in Rome on a combination business/pleasure trip. At first I didn't know who he was, even with the family resemblance."

With a shrug, she turned to look Langston in the eye. "I guess I spent as much time trying to wipe the memory of you out of my mind as your son did. So much so, that I didn't recognize him at first. It was only after several weeks of chatting by the pool in the afternoons that I put two and two together."

A whimsical smile broke across her face. "We would talk for hours. However, it was only after speaking of his mother and growing up in Pittsburgh that it all finally fell into place. By that time I was completely taken away by his charm and wit and despite the fact that he was your son, C.W."

Logan watched Langston with a wary eye, half expecting him to pounce at any moment. Surprisingly, he sat heavily on the sofa, shoulders slumped. In a defeated voice he said, "I never meant to hurt him. He needed discipline and I gave it the only way I knew how. The way my father taught me." As if suddenly realizing that he had revealed a weakness to the others, he straightened his shoulders and stood. "The Langston men have to be strong. Many have tried to defeat us, and all have failed."

Shoulders squared, he walked toward the camera, looking directly into the lens. "Beginning with your great-grandfather, we have been tried and tested. No one has ever beaten us and no one ever will. Not as long as I'm alive. Now get your ass in gear and be a man. Release your sister and the doctor. Face up to what you have done and let's move on, Christopher. If I never taught you anything else, I did teach you to compromise when the cards were against you. They are now, son, so let's end this before anyone else gets hurt."

The silence was deafening. The tension was heavy in the study as the seconds ticked by one after another. Logan silently wished her partner were beside her. Dove had always been able to calm her just with his presence, and she needed calming. She couldn't risk initiating any action based on emotions. She had to dig deep to keep Madison's face from clouding her judgment.

Moments passed without a sound from the caverns below. Finally Marissa rose and walked toward the camera. "Oh for God's sake, C.W., get the hell out of his face and go sit down. You're useless. Who do you think drove him to this in the first place?" She turned her back to the man she had once thought she loved. "Chris, please. He isn't worth ruining your life over. Let me come down and tal—"

"No!"

Logan's muscles tensed as Madison's voice reverberated against the walls. Her nails cut into the palms of her hands and balled into fists when she heard the unmistakable sound of a hand slapping the doctor's face. She took two quick steps forward until she was beside Marissa, then consciously took a deep breath. "Chris, I promise if you end this now, I'll do everything I can to help you."

Logan had to keep him talking while Loraine and Dove set up a remote site to coordinate the SWAT team. With cameras everywhere, they all knew a surprise attack wasn't in the game plan. Their only hope was finding some way to gain access to the caverns below without being observed.

During the heated remarks between Chris and their father, Christine had wrestled with the bindings tying her hands behind her back. She froze and held her breath when the cord slipped from her wrist, causing her shoulder to snap forward. Chris hadn't seemed to take notice of her movements so she sat, hands behind her back, and waited. Soon her brother turned from the doctor and faced her. For the first time, he looked haggard and confused.

Grasping at hope, she forced herself to relax and speak quietly. "Chris, just let us help you. If I had had any idea what Daddy did to you, I would never have stood for it." She watched as Chris's eyes closed against the painful memories. "You're my brother, Chris. I don't care about what you've done up to this point. All I care about is what happens now and what I can do to help you through it." A tear streaked down his face. "Please, Chris. I promise he'll never hurt you again. Not as long as I'm here to help you."

"Excellent speech, my dear. If I didn't know better, I'd think you switched sides on me."

Both Langston siblings snapped their heads toward a dark corner of the cavern to see their father standing not ten feet away.

Logan jumped as Langston's voice rang through the intercom. Her eyes swept the room as she spun around, searching for Langston and praying that her ears were playing tricks on her. "Jesus Christ," she whispered as she bolted from the room, leaving Marissa with a bewildered look on her face.

She sped into the kitchen, interrupting the whispered conversation between her partner and Loraine. "Dove, we have to find a way into that cavern. Langston gave us the slip and he's now down there with them."

Loraine dropped her head back in exasperation and swept a hand through her hair. "Oh for God's sake, McGregor, how did he do that? You were supposed to be watching him." She gave her detective a steely look before brushing past her and barking orders at the officers manning the front door.

A reassuring hand came to rest on Logan's shoulder and she lifted her eyes to her partner's, expecting to see a look of disappointment. What she saw was the confidence she needed from him at that moment. "We'll find a way in, I promise. We're not leaving here without Madison alive and well."

Before Logan could respond, shots rang out from somewhere deep in the caverns below, echoing via the sound system throughout the house.

CHAPTER THIRTY-FOUR

As the scene unfolded in front of her, Madison sat stunned, still bound with her hands behind her back. Without warning, Christine jumped out of the chair and hurled herself into Chris' side, her shoulders down like a linebacker's. Chaos ensued and at some point during the struggle the gun fired, breaking the doctor out of her shocked state. Her eyes were fixed on the two wrestling forms in front of her and she held her breath partly out of fear that the gun would discharge again while pointed in her direction and partly afraid that Christine would not overcome the seemingly stronger man.

Somehow, her survival instincts took over and while she watched in horror, she also tried to escape her bindings. The ropes were loosening, but before she could work herself free the struggle had ended. To her dismay, Chris was victorious and stood, albeit shakily, with the gun in hand, aiming it directly at his sister.

"I should blow your fucking brains out right here." His voice was full of venom.

Christine, clothes torn and battered from the struggle, stared directly into her brother's eyes. "Go ahead. You're going to do it anyway." Seconds passed in silence. Finally, she struggled to her feet before brushing off her clothes and glancing toward Madison. "But just remember, if you kill me, you only have one more ace in the hole, and don't think for a minute that the PPD is going to sit around negotiating with you if you start killing off your hostages."

A weak moan from the shadows of the cavern interrupted the tense moment. The others turned to see C.W. Langston lying on the dirt floor, blood soaking his shirt.

Loraine was barking orders as Logan and Dove entered the vaulted entranceway to the Langston mansion. "Tell SWAT to get their asses up here on the double." Pointing to another wide-eyed officer, she continued, "Get me the engineering drawing on this monstrosity, and double-time it, Officer. I want them yesterday."

She turned to Logan, her voice harsh but her eyes displaying a bit of compassion. "You're too close to this, McGregor. I'm not booting you off the case, but I'm taking command."

Logan opened her mouth to argue, but her commander raised a hand in warning before she could utter a word.

"This isn't a debate, McGregor. You're too close. This is personal for you, has been since early in the investigation." Loraine stepped closer in an effort to avoid eavesdropping ears as much as to offer consolation. "We'll get her out of there, Logan, I promise." With that, the commander turned and began to coordinate an offensive with the small crowd of officers and detectives that had congregated in the atrium.

Logan felt a comforting hand on the small of her back as Dove walked away in the direction of a wide-eyed butler standing on the fringes of the crowd.

Mustering all her courage, Madison took a deep breath and broke the silence in the cavern. "Chris, your father is seriously injured. Please, untie me so I can look at him."

"Let him fucking die." He turned toward the doctor and spat, the years of built-up hatred evident in his voice. "Nice and slow, just like he has been killing me all my life."

Years of medical training forced Madison to try to help Langston any way she could. "Chris, you can plead temporary insanity with the other cases, but if you just let him lay there and die, then you'll be dropping a case of premeditated murder in the PPD's lap."

Chris blinked and his eyes darted back and forth between her and his father. Madison knew he was considering his options, and she was not going to let the moment pass. "You can plead self-defense. He snuck up on you, frightened you."

From across the room Christine spoke, knowing the intercom was transmitting their conversation into the house above. "That's what I saw. Chris, at least let her try."

Chris paced the small cavern for a few moments before striding purposefully toward his sister. "Pick up the rope and hand it to me, then sit down and put your hands behind your back."

Christine did as she was told and Chris swiftly bound her hands. This time he made sure the knots were secure, making them so tight that the rope bit into the soft flesh of his sister's wrists. "Don't think for a minute that you're going to get another chance at me." He strode to Madison and stopped close enough for her to get a whiff of sweet cologne and fear. "One wrong move from you and Chrissy's dead. You got that?"

Madison nodded and answered in a whisper. "Yes."

He moved behind her and untied her wrists, then stepped away quickly, training the gun on his sister. "Nothing fancy, or I'll kill her."

Feeling impotent, Logan looked on as the commander organized an offense. Her attention was diverted to the other side of the room when Dove softly cleared his throat. When she looked at him, he subtly tilted his head and began to move. She met him at the far end of a long hallway.

He hesitated only a moment before saying, "We'll probably lose both of our badges over this, but what the hell." He turned and led the way into the spacious sleeping quarters of the master suite.

Logan followed silently, waiting for Dove to explain. She didn't have to wait long as he quickly moved into the small study. To her surprise, Dove moved behind the desk. He opened a drawer and searched for a moment, then she heard a click and the bookcase behind the desk slid into the wall.

For a moment, the detectives just stared at the opening, silently contemplating their discovery and the consequences of stepping into the passageway.

"How did you know?" Logan's eyes darted between the open doorway and her partner.

"The butler. They know everything." Dove turned to face his partner and friend, a questioning look in his eyes. "Are you with me?"

Taking her first confident step in more than an hour, she moved toward the darkened passageway. "Damn straight I am."

He couldn't help but smile, but he shoved aside the adrenaline-induced excitement as he grasped Logan's arm. "No heroics, McGregor. We're in this one together, and I intend for *all* of us to come out of this cave alive."

Logan held his stare, then closed her eyes and took a deep breath. He was right, she knew it, and although her first reaction was to plow ahead, she also knew that getting into the cave undetected would be difficult at best. Ending the standoff without more bloodshed—or even worse, another death—would take finesse and patience. She nodded. "You're the lead."

Dove was momentarily stunned by his partner's response. Logan had always been the lead on their cases. Now, as she forfeited her command, he prayed that he would not let her, or the others held hostage below them, down.

Madison knelt beside Langston, expertly evaluating his condition as she ripped open his blood-drenched shirt. The wound was just above the right nipple, and she prayed that the bullet hadn't hit a lung. His breathing, while shallow, was steady, with none of the familiar rattling sounds indicative of blood in the lungs. She could only hope that the bullet had gone through muscle and had not nicked any of the nearby arteries.

With no equipment available, all she could do was to slow the loss of blood. With luck, he might survive a few hours, but without adequate treatment his chances of survival reduced exponentially by the hour. "He needs to be moved to a hospital immediately." She didn't look up as she checked his vitals.

"Not a chance." Chris's voice was cold and hard. "Do what you can for him here, but no one's leaving."

"Chris—" Christine's comment was cut off by the cold barrel of the gun pressing against the back of her head.

"This isn't up for debate."

To her relief, the gun was removed as her brother moved toward the figures on the dirt floor. "It's ironic, isn't it, Doctor, that you're trying your best to save the man that is responsible for all of this?"

Madison risked a glance up. "No. Unlike you, Chris, I don't play judge and jury. It doesn't matter to me how or why someone comes under my care. My only concern is getting them through it." She pointed to a discarded rope. "Hand me that and take off your shirt."

To her surprise he did as he was asked, first handing her the rope and then moving the gun from one hand to the other as he removed his shirt, never taking his eyes off the doctor as she knelt beside the man who, only by mechanics of biology, called himself a father.

Logan followed Dove into the passageway, then felt along the wall until she located the switch that slid the bookcase closed. She rested one hand on Dove's left shoulder and the other against the cold, damp wall. Their progress was slow as they walked through the pitch-black darkness. Every few minutes they would stop and listen intently for any sounds further ahead, then continue the slow march toward whatever hell they would face at the end of the tunnel.

Logan hoped Loraine would be too busy barking orders to miss them, but she knew their absence would soon be discovered. Her only hesitation in going along with Dove had been the risk to his career. She didn't care about herself, acknowledging almost too confidently that her history and performance on the job would most likely get her through any internal investigation. However, she wasn't so sure about Dove. *Well, fuck them all. If they fire him, I'll quit too.*

After what seemed like hours of walking blindly, a small streak of light sliced through the darkness. Dove stopped and Logan gently squeezed his shoulder, letting him know she saw it too. Moving even slower, they walked closer, ears straining to hear any sounds. As they reached a bend in the passageway, Dove tensed and stopped short, pressing his body back against Logan's. For interminable seconds they stood holding their breath, waiting and watching for any signs that their presence had been noticed. Dove chanced a quick look around the curved wall and into the brightly lit cave. What he saw sent chills running down his spine, and for the first time since their entrance into the passageway, a bead of fear-induced sweat trickled down his back.

Upstairs, Loraine turned to the last place she had seen Logan. Her gaze swept the room, and again coming up empty, she turned to one of the officers. "Where's McGregor?"

He shrugged and stuttered, "I—I don't know, Commander." He shuffled from one foot to the other. "I haven't seen her in quite some time now."

Raking a hand through her hair, Loraine mumbled as she pivoted and made her way toward the study, "If she's gone off on her own, so help me, I'll shoot her myself."

"Excuse me, Commander?"

She was surprised to find the timid officer keeping pace with her. "Um, nothing. Go find Detective Dvorak and get him in here posthaste."

Relieved to have some reason to escape, the officer turned and sped off in the other direction, leaving the commander alone in the room with Marissa Cavanaugh. *Great, just fucking great. I'm going to shoot you just for the pure fun of it, McGregor.*

Madison took the shirt from Chris and turned it inside out, trying to find the cleanest area to place directly against the wound. As she pressed the shirt to Langston's chest she glanced up at Chris. "I need some help here. Can you hold this while I tie the rope?"

The younger man suddenly looked frightened. The last thing he wanted was to touch the man responsible for his pain and suffering.

"Chris, please. I need to get a pressure bandage on this wound to stop the bleeding, otherwise he may die." Madison glanced at Christine, still bound to the chair across the room. "If you don't want to help, then let Christine."

"No!" He waved the gun in his sister's direction. "She lost her chance when she sideswiped me. You're on your own, Doctor. I'm giving you a chance to save the bastard, but I'm not helping you do it."

Inside the darkened passageway, Dove crouched low, hoping to keep his presence from being discovered. The inability to talk or even whisper, he knew, was going to make forming a plan almost impossible. However, he and Logan had worked long enough together that they had an innate feel for how the other would react in any given situation. This was going to be their biggest test and unfortunately, if they miscalculated—or worse yet, lost—the cost would be more than he wanted to contemplate at the moment. As he eased closer his hand landed on something smooth, and he looked down to see a small button. A plan came alive in his mind, but he knew he had to be quick.

Marissa Cavanaugh sat on the plush sofa in C.W. Langston's study, her face hard and cool as she watched the commander walk into the room. Her first instinct was to vent years of anger on the woman who had stolen her husband and her future. However, now that she had the opportunity, she found herself unable and even unwilling to dredge up the past. The most important thing on her mind was getting her daughter out of that cave unharmed. Ironically, the person who was in charge of the operation, one that would either rescue or kill her daughter, was the person she hated most of all.

"Your daughter is one brave woman, Mrs. Cavanaugh. You should be proud of her."

Lifting her chin, Marissa spoke quietly. "I am very proud of her. Fortunately she takes after her father in that she has never run away from a challenge." She stood, walked to the window, and looked out on the organized chaos of activity on the front lawn. "What are the chances of getting them out alive?" She turned and moved a few feet further into the room. "And don't play games with me. I want it straight up and without the political whitewash."

Loraine felt a renewed respect for Marissa and decided to give her the facts. "Honestly? Not good. Only the two Langston men know the way in and out." For the hundredth time that day, she raked a hand through her hair, then sat heavily in the chair beside the sofa. "The best we can hope for is finding an alternative way into the caverns, one that will provide us an element of surprise."

"And what if you don't have that *element* of surprise, Commander? What then?" Marissa dropped onto the sofa, not waiting for a response before adding, "Even I in my untrained state know that you don't want a gun battle inside a room made of stone."

Loraine nodded her agreement. "That is a very astute observation, Mrs. Cavanaugh, and one that I have been struggling with since we became aware of the cave."

"What about tear gas?" Marissa knew she was grasping at straws, but she felt useless and more than partially responsible. Had she turned and walked away when she first realized who Chris Langford really was, the entire nightmare might have been avoided.

Surprised, the commander lifted one eyebrow. *Smart woman.* "It was a consideration, but we think Chris Langston is most likely prepared for that type of attack. It's obvious from the earlier discussions that he has the cave well stocked with food and water, enough to wait us out for however long it takes."

Rising, she walked to the window to check on the progress outside. Her voice revealed her frustration. "He's been one step ahead of us the entire time. Chris Langston's not the usual street thug. He's intelligent and cunning and that, added to his lack of regret for any of the murders, makes him very dangerous." She turned and met Marissa's eyes. "He's the type of criminal that most detectives, myself included, fear most. Not so much because of what they have done, but what they are capable of doing if pushed into a corner with no means of escape."

Both women grew quiet as they contemplated the possibilities, all of which were horrendous and frightening.

CHAPTER THIRTY-FIVE

The execution and the timing had to be perfect, otherwise their cover would be blown and then God only knew what would happen. While slowing taking a deep breath, and drawing forth childhood memories of playing quarters along the street where he grew up, Dove flipped the button with his thumb and watched as it flew through the air. As if in slow motion the small white disk arced and descended, landing perfectly, silently in the center of C.W. Langston's chest and directly in the doctor's line of sight.

Madison moved to swipe the button away, but something made her stop her hand in midair. Slowly, covertly she turned her eyes toward the entrance and was stunned to see Dove kneeling on the stone floor about fifteen feet away. In the next second she almost gasped when she found herself looking into Logan's eyes. She could feel her heart hammering inside her chest and feared that if Chris were to turn toward her at that moment her expression would give the two hidden detectives away. She forced her gaze back to the wounded man as her mind raced through the possibilities of what was to come.

"How's he doing?"

Startled, Madison jumped as Christine's voice broke the silence. "Um, he's...uh, doing okay for now." Panic raced through her veins as Chris turned and began walking toward them.

Chris stopped opposite Madison, his back to the doorway, and nudged his father in the ribs with his foot, eliciting a low moan. "He seems fine to me."

"He's not fine, Chris. I don't know how much longer he can survive down here without proper care. Please, let the paramedics come in and take him out of here. At least then the cops will take it easy on you if you show them you have some compassion."

Chris's laugh bounced off the stone walls. "Yeah right, Doc. He's not going anywhere for two reasons. One, because I say he's not, and two, because no one else knows the way in here and I plan to keep it that way." He sneered, "You lucked out during your little hike through the woods and stumbled across it just after Chrissy and I arrived and before I could close down the hatch. No one will ever find the way in here."

Arms spread wide, he turned around, laughing, then stopped and to Madison's horror pointed the gun at the opening in the stone wall. "And that way there, no one but the great and mighty C.W. Langston and I know where that leads." With another half-hearted kick to his father's ribs, he continued, "And he won't have a chance to tell anyone." He dropped into a chair, exhaustion evident on his face.

That could work in our favor. Madison sat beside Langston, praying for the opportunity to let Christine know that the detectives were in the passageway. As if by telepathy, Christine shifted in her chair.

"Chris, these ropes are cutting into my wrists. Please loosen them just a little."

He bolted from the chair and stood in front of his sister. "You think I'm stupid? I'm not giving you another chance. You blew it."

"*Please*, they hurt. I can tell I'm bleeding."

Chris moved behind his sister and glared down at the bindings around his sister's hands. Her fingers were tinged blue from lack of circulation and blood dripped onto the dirt floor directly beneath her hands. Suddenly, his heart wasn't in hurting Christine any longer. "Hey, Doc. Get over here and take care of this."

Madison rose and slowly moved across the room. The further she was from the passageway, the stronger she felt the loss of connection from Logan. Somehow, knowing she could simply turn her head and see the detective eased her mind. Instead, she focused on the task at hand. *This may be the chance I need to let her know.* She knelt behind Christine and loosened the bindings under Chris's watchful eye.

"Don't do anything foolish, Doc. I'd hate to have to tie you up again too."

Madison worked on loosening the bindings, careful not to do any more damage. The blood had dried around the rope, adhering it to the torn flesh. Each time she pulled the rope away, Christine flinched with the pain. "I need some water to get these loose. Pulling them away like this is just going to make the cuts worse."

Chris's eyes darted from one woman to the other as if he were contemplating, then he bent until Madison could feel his warm breath against her cheek. "Don't try anything funny or I'll have to punish you too."

A shiver ran down Madison's spine as the cold steel of the gun stroked across her cheek. "Nothing funny, I promise."

Chris stood for a moment staring at this sister before turning and walking to a cooler on the opposite side of the room. As he moved away, Madison eased closer to Christine. "They're in the passageway."

Just as he bent to open the cooler, Chris stood. Spinning around, he pointed the gun at Madison. "What did you say to her?"

The two women's heads pivoted and they watched in terror as Chris stormed across the room. "I—I just apologized for hurting her when I tried to loosen the ropes."

Madison was terrified and for a moment thought everything was going to come to a quick end. When Chris pressed the barrel of the gun directly between her eyes, she froze. In a flash of a second, images of Logan, her family, and all that was precious to her flashed before her, and just as quickly as they began, they stopped. To her profound relief, the confused look on Christine's face apparently convinced Chris she was telling the truth.

"Not another word out of either of you." He dropped the gun to his side and backed slowly across the room toward the coolers. His glare sent a chill down Madison's spine. *Jesus, that was close.*

Logan's heart raced when she saw the look on Chris Langston's face. Hidden in the darkened passageway and out of his line of sight, she watched him disappear from view but could clearly hear the ensuing conversation. It was apparent that the gun was trained on one of the women, but she didn't know which one. Logan forced herself to breathe evenly and had to dig deep to find the calmness she had called upon so many times in the past. This time it was impossible to remain disconnected. This time, her life as well as her future and the woman she loved hung in the delicate balance between trained confidence and sheer outright panic. As she unconsciously squeezed Dove's shoulder in a vise grip, she felt his hand cover hers, offering silent reassurance.

Too many times to count he had blindly trusted Logan to make quick life-and-death decisions; now she had to return that trust. They waited for what seemed like endless hours as their limbs cramped from holding still in the darkness. Her patience was growing thin. She had counted at least two times when they could have made a move, yet Dove chose not to. Silently she urged him on with a constant pressure on his shoulder, pleading with him to make a move soon.

"Excuse me, Commander." The young officer was back, and this time he had the butler in tow.

"Yes. What is it?" Her patience was dwindling fast as the events outside moved at an unbelievably slow pace. She had yet to get her hands on the engineering drawing she had ordered one of the other officers to find over an hour ago.

"Um, this is Mr. Langston's butler, ma'am."

The man, obviously overwhelmed by the commotion, peered at the commander from behind the young officer. He wanted to escape to his room and shut the door, but he knew that wouldn't happen any time soon. His eyes locked on the familiar face of Marissa Cavanaugh and he nodded slightly.

"I don't need a butler, Officer. I need the floor plans to this monstrosity." Loraine swept the drapes back with one hand and impatiently glared out the window.

"Um, ma'am, he knows a way into the caverns." The officer planted his feet for what he knew would be an explosion. "Apparently, he told one of the detectives where it was about an hour ago, and no one has seen them since."

You are so dead, McGregor. "Show me." Loraine wasn't sure if the small butler was running from her or just trying to avoid getting bowled over as she angrily sped to the other end of the mansion. He led the way into a small room and pointed to the wall. Slowly she crossed the room and studied the bookcase. An untrained eye would have missed it, but she spotted it immediately.

As she knelt to get a closer look, her gaze fell on something under the desk. She pulled a letter opener from the desk and knelt again. Snagging something with the sharp end of the opener, she stood to get a better look and cursed under her breath as the only explanation came to mind. *McGregor.*

Dropping the bandage on the desk, she glared at the butler. "If my officers get hurt because of this, you're going to have to deal with me." She could almost hear the small man tremble in his shoes.

"I—I was only answering that man's questions, honest."

"Where is the trip switch?" Loraine towered over the butler, intent on getting quick answers.

"The desk. It's somewhere inside the desk." His eyes darted back and forth between the imposing woman and the nervous officer. "Beneath the left drawer."

Just as Loraine turned toward the desk, the bookcase began to move into the wall. Grinning, the young officer stood and opened his mouth to speak, but a raised hand from his commanding officer stopped him. She motioned for him to close the door and then motioned all of them out of the room. Only after closing the doorway to the master suite did she direct her attention toward the butler and speak in a low voice. "How far is it down to the caves?"

He shuffled from one foot to the other. "I don't know. I've never been down there." The thought of going into the dark cave gave him a chill. For years he had watched from a distance as his boss dragged his terrified son down into the caves. Many nights he had sat listening in the quiet house for cries from below, but never heard a sound. He suspected the caves were a good away from the main house or very deep below it.

The intercom had been turned off from somewhere inside the caves over an hour earlier, just after the shots were fired. Logan had no way of contacting Langston or hearing what was going on inside the caves. She now had a way into the caves but was once again forced to stand down because of the unknown whereabouts of her two lead detectives. As she stomped off in toward the atrium, she cursed them once again under her breath while silently cheering them on, knowing full well that at their age, she would have done the same damn thing. *Fucking jocks, you're both out of your minds.*

Madison watched the scene play out in front of her, thinking that she had to be dreaming. As Chris bent over the cooler, Dove appeared from the darkened passageway, followed by Logan. They stealthily eased into the room, guns drawn, and lined up for a kill shot at the slightest sign of aggression from Chris Langston. To Madison's surprise, when he turned, bottle in hand, and spied the weapons pointed at him, she saw what she could only interpret as relief flash across his face before being hidden behind the stoic façade he had learned to display so many years before.

Even though Dove was in the lead, he gave a slight nod to Logan, keeping his eyes and aim directly on Chris. Under his breath he whispered, "It's your show, boss."

"Drop the gun, Chris." Logan eased away, putting some distance between herself and Dove. To her surprise, Chris slowly knelt and placed the gun on the floor, then kicked it in her direction. *This is too easy.* With Dove holding Chris in his sights, Logan focused on the two women. "Are you both all right?"

Both nodded, still shocked by the almost uncomfortable calm in the room. As if taunting them, Chris twisted the cap off the water bottle and took a long drink before calmly sitting down in the chair.

Logan had an uneasy feeling in the pit of her stomach. Something wasn't right. She saw Chris calmly move a hand toward his hip pocket, and almost in unison she and Dove crouched defensively and shouted, "Don't move."

Chris raised his hands in surrender. "Easy, guys, I only want to give you a letter."

Logan moved in closer, her gun aimed at his head. "Put your hands on top of your head." Langston set the bottle on the floor beside him and complied. "Now, stand up and turn around." Once his back was to her, she stepped in, patted him down, and pulled an envelope from his back pocket.

Chris slowly turned around and smiled. "You have no trust, Detective." Smiling, he reached his hand out. "May I?"

The thick envelope was addressed to Commander Loraine Osborne, Pittsburgh Police Department. It had been through a lot of wear and tear and had what appeared to be blood spatters on the back. It was obviously something he kept with him at all times, even during the murders he had committed over the past several weeks. She glanced at her partner, who only shrugged. She handed the benign-looking envelope to Chris and waited as he picked up his water bottle and returned to the chair.

He opened the envelope and removed several sheets of folded paper. "I made this list a long time ago, once I had the goods on him." For a moment he let his eyes wander to the man on the floor.

Madison, again kneeling beside the injured man, said, "We need to get him to the hospital."

Logan asked, "Where is the intercom, Chris?"

He shrugged. "Sorry. I got tired of sharing my thoughts with the yahoos upstairs and in my impatience, I'm sorry to say I broke it."

"Doctor, take Ms. Langston and follow the passageway back to the house. There's a small switch on the right-hand side that will open the door. You'll be in the study off the master suite when you enter the house." As the two women moved toward the passageway, Logan added, "Make a lot of noise before you open the door. I'm sure the commander knows it's there by now, and most likely there will be firepower waiting for you on the other side."

Logan turned her attention back to Chris, who took another long drink from his bottle. "What's in the letter?" She knew she was breaking countless procedural rules by keeping him down in the cavern, but her curiosity won out. *I deserve some answers before his attorney shuts him up.*

"It's a damning list of all the people the great C.W. Langston has in his back pocket." He gave her a faint smile. "As a treat, I kept it in my back pocket throughout my adventures. The game is over now and it's time to—"

Logan watched in shock as Chris's face contorted in pain and he clutched at his stomach. Something was terribly wrong. Their eyes met and she knew instantly why he had been so calm and collected during the last few minutes. *He never intended to leave this fucking cave.* Beads of sweat trickled down his face and his breathing was rapid and labored. She bolted forward and slapped the water bottle from his hand just as he bent over and vomited on the floor. The bitter smell of almonds filled the room as he collapsed onto the floor and began to convulse.

"Madison!" Logan's scream went unanswered and even if the doctor could have heard her, she couldn't have helped. After what seemed like an eternity, the convulsions stopped, as did his heart.

When the paramedics entered the stone room moments later followed by the commander, they immediately stopped as the unmistakable odor of cyanide entered their nostrils. Madison rushed past them to find Logan and Dove beside Chris Langston, their faces ashen. She knelt beside him and checked for a pulse. Finding none, she shook her head at the waiting paramedics, who then turned their attention to Langston.

Within minutes the room was thrown into a state of chaos as the paramedics readied the older man for transport to the hospital, assisted by Madison. Although she wanted to stay with Logan, she knew they both had jobs to do. While the paramedics struggled up the half-rotten wooden steps to the wooded area behind the house, Madison took a moment to search for Logan.

She found her talking to Dove under a stand of trees just outside the hidden doorway. Not wanting to intrude on their conversation, she stood to the side until Dove's eyes met hers. When Logan turned and walked toward her, she could see the exhaustion clearly in the detective's eyes. "You should come with us to the hospital. You wounds have opened up again and you need to have them seen about before they get infected."

"I will, just as soon as I can get away." Logan looked up as the Medevac chopper neared the clearing behind the house and circled overhead. "You're going with him to Mercy?"

Madison's fingers intertwined with Logan's, and the warmth reassured her. "Yes, and I'll be waiting for you when you get there, Detective."

Trapped, Logan could only smile and roll her eyes. "Yeah, yeah, I'll be there, I promise." She quickly leaned in and kissed Madison on the cheek before turning to walk the doctor to the helicopter.

"What the hell are you staring at, Martin?" Alvarez shoved an officer who'd watched the women's display. "This ain't no peep show here, man. Get to work." The officer hurried his pace and moved along, and Alvarez looked innocently back over his shoulder and winked.

Logan couldn't help but grin. "He's a keeper. Did a fantastic job today."

They walked the remaining way to the makeshift helipad and Logan helped Madison into the chopper, then watched as it lifted into the air and disappeared with the woman she loved strapped safely inside.

The events of the day hit her as she once again descended the stairs and entered the stone room. Logan was silently thankful that Christine left with Madison and hadn't witnessed her brother's final moments. *At least she didn't have to see him die like that.*

Loraine stepped in front of her, blocking her path. "You have a lot of explaining to do, McGregor." She looked over Logan's shoulder at the empty stone room and thought about what could have happened had Logan and Dove not happened on the butler and gained access to the cave. When her eyes met Logan's, she could see the pain written on her face—the pain of knowing she'd miscalculated and even through she'd won the war, she'd still lost because someone died. Loraine had gotten close enough to Logan to know that she would beat herself up over it time and time again.

With a reassuring hand on her officer's shoulder, she turned and gently pushed her through the doorway. "The letter explains a lot, and it's likely to get very messy downtown before all of this is sorted out. But first, let's get your wounds attended to, and in a couple of days, we'll talk more."

Logan walked down the passageway and into the cold air. A sound caught her attention, and she turned to see Dove leaning against his car. "What are you still doing around here?"

Shoving off the fender, he went around to the passenger side and opened the door. "Someone told me you'd need a ride to Mercy when you were done here. I thought I'd stick around and make sure you made it there without any problems."

"I'll bet I know exactly who that *someone* was, too, Dvorak. You're a wimp."

He just shook his head and started the engine. "No, McGregor, I'm smart. That is one feisty woman you have there, and I'm not about to get on her bad side."

Feisty. Damn straight she's feisty. She turned her head, pretending to look out the window so he couldn't see her grin. "Just drive, Dvorak."

CHAPTER THIRTY-SIX

D ove delivered Logan to the Mercy ER as promised. It took him a while to locate Madison, but once he knew his partner was in good hands, he made a quick exit. He smiled as he thought about his eagerness to get home. For the first time in longer than he could remember, someone was there waiting and wanting him to come through the door.

Julie, at Madison's request, had given Logan a thorough workup. Her first instinct was to send the detective directly back to the ICU, but Logan wouldn't hear of it. A war of wills erupted, lines were drawn, and the standoff began. Logan refused to be readmitted unless it was absolutely necessary and Julie refused to release her without a thorough exam. For the last seven hours the detective had been sitting in one of the ER exam rooms, getting grumpier by the minute. Julie knew the only reason the detective was still there was the equally stubborn doctor who sat guard beside the bed.

Bracing herself for round two, she pushed through the door. In the instant before the room's occupants noticed her, she got a rare look at the real Logan McGregor: her face was relaxed and a smile that brightened the room was accentuated by the tender look in her eyes. The subject of her gaze was none other than Madison. *Hmm, maybe this won't be so hard after all. You seem to know how to tame the beast.* "Good morning. How are you feeling?"

The eyes hardened. "Depends. When can I leave?"

"If you behave yourself and do what you're told, maybe tomorrow."

"I don't think so, Doc. I'm outta here." Logan gripped the sheet and moved to throw the fabric off but stopped when a small hand cupped her cheek. She looked into Madison's eyes and knew instantly that the fight was over and done.

"Darling, if Julie says you're staying, then you *are* staying." A quick brush of her lips on Logan's took the sting out of her next words. "Don't fight me on this. One thing Mercy is well known for is our *very* large orderlies. Now behave and don't make me get mean."

What sounded like a growl was the only sound the detective made before falling back onto the pillow and staring at the ceiling. Madison couldn't contain a smile as she watched her lover pout. She turned her attention back to Julie. "What did you find?"

Julie moved closer to the stretcher and handed the chart to Madison. "So far, everything is looking good." She regarded the detective cautiously. "However, as you are well aware, some of the more serious burns you have were reopened during your, uh, escape." She waited for a caustic retort, but only received a half-hearted "ha ha" from the still-pouting woman.

"God only knows what was growing inside that cave, so I'm sending you up to the burn unit to have those looked at by one of the specialists. I think the biggest thing we have to worry about right now is infection in the open wounds, so I'm starting you on a broad-spectrum antibiotic, nothing more."

Madison allowed herself to relax for the first time since Logan had arrived at the ER. "Thanks, Julie. Logan and I really appreciate you coming in on your day off to take care of us."

Julie dared a glance at Logan, who still didn't seem too happy or appreciative. "No worries. You'll be out of here in no time." With a stern look at Madison, she continued, "You need some rest yourself. I suggest you go home and crash until morning, then come back and break your outlaw girlfriend out of here." She didn't wait around for an answer. Quickly turning on her heels, she made a beeline for the door and was gone.

Madison chuckled and leaned over Logan. "Aw, is my little outlaw still pouting?"

Dark eyes swept from the ceiling to Madison's face, then back again to stare at the ceiling. "Stop it."

A hand slipped under the covers and found the warm, taut flesh of Logan's stomach. "Come on, baby. I kind of like having an outlaw girlfriend."

A breath caught in Logan's throat and when Madison's hand slowly rose to cup her breast, she completely surrendered. With lightning speed, her fingers tangled in the doctor's hair and drew her close until their lips were pressed together. For countless seconds they were lost, savoring the taste and feel they had longed for.

Breathless, Madison drew back and looked into the dark hungry eyes of her lover. "God, I've missed you."

Logan smiled mischievously. "If you'll give me my clothes, we'll get out of here and I can take care of that."

Eyes closed, Madison shook her head and chuckled. "You're hopeless, McGregor. Absolutely hopeless."

Dove unlocked the door to his apartment and stepped inside. A lamp beside the sofa cast just enough light for him to make his way through the room. As he shrugged out of his jacket he heard a movement and turned to find Susan lying on the sofa watching him. "Sorry, I didn't mean to wake you." He quickly crossed the room, sat on the coffee table, and gently took her hand in his. "Why are you on the sofa? I told you to sleep in the bedroom. I don't mind sleeping here. In fact, I do most nights."

Uncertain, she looked at everything but him. "I was—I was afraid I wouldn't hear you when you came home. How did it go? Is it over yet?"

Suddenly aware that her interest was in the case and not seeing him, he released her hand and moved across the room. Avoiding her eyes, he busied himself by removing his shoulder harness. "It's over. Langston, Chris Langston, is dead. You're safe now."

When he turned, Susan was standing beside him. He couldn't help himself. His eyes slowly lowered and took in the soft flesh of her breasts exposed by the low cut of the nightgown. *Oh Jesus.* He nervously licked his lips and looked over her shoulder at an uninteresting softball trophy on the mantle. "Starting tomorrow you can get back to your old life and hopefully begin to put this behind you."

"Dove?"

His eyes flickered to hers, then back to the trophy. "First thing in the morning, I'll help you get your things back to your place."

"Dove?"

Digging his hands deep into his pockets, he rocked back on his heels and gave his best attempt at a smile. "By this time tomorrow—"

"Dove!"

As if slapped, he stopped. "What?"

Susan could only smile and sigh. "Dove, shut up and kiss me."

He had learned long ago not to argue with the women in his life. So he shut up and did as he was told. Several minutes later, their breathing hard and heavy, Susan pulled back and looked questioningly into his eyes. "Well?"

Instantly confused, he stammered, "Uh, well what?"

"Oh jeez, Dove. What am I going to do with you?" Cupping his face in her hands, Susan kissed him again, then pulled back and grinned. "Come on, you, Take me to bed, I'm starving." She pulled him away from the wall and led him down the hall, unaware of the silly grin on his face as he followed obediently behind.

Logan awoke to the soft light of early morning. She turned her head toward the window and her eyes focused on the woman sleeping in the chair beside the bed. A hospital-issue blanket covered her body and for the first time in days, Logan saw an almost peaceful expression on Madison's face. The doctor's face was beautiful, more so than any other Logan could remember.

Diane had been a beautiful woman as well, but it was different. She knew she was beautiful and that in some way had made her less attractive. Logan had lived with her ego for several years, until that fateful night when she had walked in and found her in the arms of another woman. In their house—in their bed.

Logan had promptly and efficiently shoved the other woman and her clothes out the front door, then returned to the bedroom to face Diane. The argument that followed had been heated and filled with words that could never be taken back. Within minutes, Diane was packing her bags and before an hour had passed had gone, leaving Logan alone with the rumpled sheets and the memories of what she had witnessed.

As if possessed, she'd spent most of the night tearing the house apart, looking for some clue that she had missed along the way, all the while drinking bourbon straight from the bottle. The sheets and mattress had been the first go out into the backyard, followed by every reminder of Diane she could find in the house.

Sometime during the early morning hours, she'd collapsed onto the couch and fallen into a drunken sleep. The pounding on the front door had awakened her at an ungodly hour. As she fought back the nausea, she'd stumbled to the door and groaned when the bright sunlight seared her brain. It was Dove, and he looked as bad as she knew she did. Without a word she walked to the couch and fell back into the cushions, leaving him standing in the doorway.

Little did she know that life could in fact get worse than it had been at that moment.

It had taken Dove hours to clean her up and get her sober enough to go downtown. Even though he had already made the official ID, she still demanded to see the remains of her lover. He had tried to prepare her for what she would see, but nothing could adequately describe the kind of damage resulting from a crash as horrific as the one that had killed Diane.

Dove had used his connections so that just the two of them were present in the room when the attendant, who was also a friend, rolled out the stainless steel drawer. Logan had taken one look at Diane's ghostly white face and bolted to the other side of the room to throw up in the industrial-sized sink. The weeks that followed had been a blur, and every day since she had been on a self-destructive mission, determined to make herself pay.

Every day—until now. As she watched Madison stir, a smile washed across Logan's face and she knew somewhere deep in her gut that the woman sleeping beside her bed would never betray her. She couldn't explain *how* she knew, she just did, and didn't try to overanalyze it. Sleepy eyes peered at her from across the room. "Good morning, sleepyhead."

Madison yawned and stretched, working the kinks out of her back. "Morning. How do you feel?"

With a chuckle, Logan slid over and patted the bed beside her. "Better than you, it appears. Come here." Madison didn't need a second invitation as she climbed into the bed beside Logan, turned onto her side, and draped an arm over her waist.

Nothing was said as each relished the warmth of the other and they both drifted off to sleep again, finally at peace.

Dove woke to the aroma of coffee and bacon wafting through the half-closed doorway, and a smile teased his lips at the thought of Susan and what they had shared throughout the night. She had more or less assumed control and taken him to a place he had only dreamed of sharing with another. He had been consumed by her touch, her taste, and when he slid into her warmth, he knew he was home; knew without a doubt that he had found the woman he wanted to spend the rest of his life beside.

He felt a boiling heat stir in his gut as he remembered her touch and the gentleness of her lips as she kissed her way down his chest. He ached remembering the look in her eyes as she came and the possessiveness of her lips as she claimed his mouth with hers. He was hard—painfully so, and without thought he closed his eyes and threaded a hand beneath the sheets to slowly stroke himself. The scent of her grew stronger as his mind wandered back to the hours they had shared and he wished she were there taking him, claiming him, devouring him.

His eyes flew open as a soft hand pushed his aside, and he looked into questioning eyes. He turned his head away, embarrassed at being caught, but felt another gentle hand cupping his face.

"Are you hungry?"

"Yes." It was a whisper, broken by desire and the heat boiling in his belly.

She untied his robe and let it drop to the floor, then slid her body over his. "Good. I am too. Breakfast can wait."

Loraine spent two hours questioning Christine before Julie finally broke off the interrogation, insisting her patient needed rest. Now, having most of the answers, she returned to Logan's room only to find it empty. Muttering under her breath, she headed to the nurses' station. "If she's escaped again, I'm hauling her ass to lockup."

After an interminable amount of time arguing with the nurse over McGregor's whereabouts and not getting anywhere, Loraine spotted Julie walking through the door. "Finally, someone who can give me an answer." She waited until the doctor was beside her before demanding to know her detective's location.

With a smile and what Loraine could only interpret as a sigh of relief, the doctor pointed to the chart in her hand. "She was just released."

"Released? Did she say where she was going?"

"No, but I assume that Madi took her home." Julie handed the chart to the nurse. "God help her. Madi will have her hands full with that one."

"Yes. I imagine she will. Thanks, Doctor." As the commander walked to the elevator, a smile graced her otherwise stoic face. *You've met your match, McGregor, and I pity you if you try to fight her.* She swallowed a chuckle as she stepped into the elevator.

CHAPTER THIRTY-SEVEN

Three Weeks Later

After an entire week under the watchful eye of Madison the doctor, Logan had been half out of her mind with boredom. Rules—ridiculous rules—had been established as to what she was and was not allowed to do. Daily naps, no physical exertion, no work, *nada*. Most she had decided she could live with, but the no exertion rule had proved almost unbearable for both of them. However, because she had made the rule, Madison was relentless, which meant no sex. By the end of the week, both had been wound tight, so it was a good thing when Logan was cleared to return to work.

For the first time since her return two weeks earlier, Logan sat at her desk in the major crimes division, clearing up the last remnants of paperwork from the Strip District case. Her nerves were raw from the imposed celibacy and she snapped as one of the new young recruits beckoned her from across the room. "What?"

She swiveled in her chair to see Christine Langston standing in the doorway. She rose to meet her halfway, saying, "Good morning. You're looking well."

Christine's eyes darted around the room, falling on nothing in particular. "Thank you. Although after two funerals and the grand jury testimony yesterday, *well* isn't exactly what I feel."

Small talk wasn't something that came easy to the detective, but she forced herself to at least attempt to be conversational. "I expect you are feeling a bit overwhelmed with all that you are dealing with just now." She lifted her mug. "Would you like a cup? Although I have to warn you, the coffee around here has been declared a deadly weapon. It's not for the weak of heart—or stomach."

"Sure, I'd love some."

Logan led the executive into one of the interrogation rooms so that they could have some privacy. She handed Christine a cup of coffee and took a seat directly across from her. "What brings you down here?"

Hands clutched around the mug, Christine avoided eye contact with the detective. "I, um, I wanted to see you, to thank you personally for the way you conducted the investigation." She forced herself to look into Logan's eyes. "I know I wasn't the most cooperative person to deal with and I apologize for that. However, I hope you understand now that I didn't have a clue how extensive or ruthless my father's dealings had been or how many others were tangled in his underhanded activities."

Logan sat back in her chair and studied her. This was a surprise; she hadn't expected her to come all the way to the precinct to thank her personally. "No thanks necessary. I was just doing my job."

Christine stood, leaving the coffee untouched on the table. "Well, just so you know, I'm cleaning up Langston Development. Anything your office may need to put away Whittaker, Schneider, and the rest of the politicians that were in my father's pocket, let me know. As of now, our offices will be cooperating with the PPD in any way we can to close this case once and for all."

As she opened the door to leave, she paused. "I may be out of line, Detective, so if I am, I apologize for that too. As you now know, Jen and I have been close, quite close for some time now. She respects you a lot, and your privacy, and hasn't told me a lot about your past. I can see just by looking at the two of you that you and Madison Cavanaugh have a lot to look forward to in the future. Don't let the past hinder your path. I think you and I know better than most that the past has to be put in its place if we are to move on." She hesitated, waiting for some response. "That's what I'm going to do, and I hope you will, too."

She placed her hand on Logan's shoulder for just a moment, then turned and left, closing the door quietly behind her.

Logan sat for a long time after Christine left, staring at the bare wall in front of her. So much had changed in the last few weeks. Herbert Whittaker, the mayor and a man she had always respected, was in jail, charged the day before with conspiracy, aiding and abetting, and accessory to murder. George Schneider had been booked on charges of withholding evidence after her house had been torched by Chris Langston. But the one that surprised her the most, the one that tore her heart out with each thought, had been the arrest of Lieutenant Allen Beaudry, a man she had looked to as a father figure. She realized should have known, but she had ignored the signs because she didn't want to see that he too was under the thumb of Langston.

A soft knock on the door brought her out of the uneasy thoughts that flashed through her mind. "Come." She turned to see the beaming smile of the one person who could show her light. "Good morning, Doctor. What brings you to the bowels of this morbid place?"

Madison pushed open the door with one finger and tried desperately not to touch anything. "Only you, my dear, could get me into this horrid place." She kicked the door shut before bending to steal a kiss from Logan. "I'm hungry and thought you might like to have lunch with me."

The detective eyed her suspiciously. "Hmm, you think I'm going to believe that you came all the way across town just because you're hungry and want lunch?" She stood and wrapped Madison in her arms. "The detective in me thinks you are lying. Maybe I should sit you in the germy chair over there and interrogate you until you break."

A look of unbridled fear appeared on the doctor's face. "You wouldn't." The look in Logan's eyes told her different. "Okay, all right, I confess. I am hungry, but I missed you too."

Logan's lips softly brushed Madison's. "Well, now, that was easy. I guess I haven't lost my persuasive touch." Then, with a gleam in her eyes, she said, "So, how about we blow this joint and go home. I think I need a nap, or better yet"—a heat rose in her body as desire washed over her and into her eyes—"I need you."

A breath caught in Madison's throat as she felt the same heat racing through her veins. "I think that is an excellent idea, Detective, and just what the doctor ordered."

EPILOGUE

Three Months Later

Madison stood looking out the kitchen window at nothing in particular. After returning to the Bridgeville house, she and Logan had both realized that living together there was not going to work.

For weeks they had avoided the subject, but after a long night tossing and turning, Madison finally sat up in the huge bed they shared and shook Logan awake. "I can't do this anymore, Logan." She ran a hand through her mussed hair. "I don't want to do this anymore."

Logan tossed the covers aside and reached for her robe, then stood beside the bed. "Don't want to do what, Madi?"

Arms extended and tears streaming down her face, Madison said, "This. I can't live like this anymore." She choked back a sob. "Every time I walk outside I see that officer dead in her patrol car. I have to get out of here. I'm putting the house up for sale tomorrow."

Logan sat on the bed, taking Madison's hand in hers. "But sweetie, you love this house."

"No. I love you." Madison's hand caressed Logan's face. "I see what it's doing to you too, baby, and I won't let it destroy us."

Tears burned Logan's eyes as she pulled the woman she loved into her arms. "Whatever you want. We'll do whatever you want."

In that moment they both felt the chasm that had slowly begun to separate them close. Logan, knowing how much Madison loved the house, had not wanted to suggest moving, while Madison didn't want to have Logan think her weak because she couldn't stay. After weeks of silent suffering on both their parts, it was Madison who had finally had the courage to break the silence.

After that night, things had moved quickly. The house had sold in record time and they found themselves practically homeless. After a few desperate calls, Madison had found a contractor, and his first assignment was getting the part of the old stable she had once used as living quarters spruced up enough to live in while a new house was being built some five hundred yards north.

She was lost in thought as she planned their move the next day into what would be their new home as warm arms circled her waist from behind.

"Penny for your thoughts, Doctor."

Turning, Madison nuzzled her face into Logan's neck. "I'm not that cheap, Detective."

Logan squeezed her lover's butt as she moved away. "Okay. How about a cinnamon bagel with that cream cheese you like so much?"

"Okay, so I am easy." Madison moved to the refrigerator and withdrew a pitcher of orange juice. "I was just thinking of tomorrow and how nice it will be to have our own house." She eased her away around Logan to the cupboard. "And more space."

"Ah, so it's space you want. And I thought you liked these cramped quarters with the quaint scent of hay sifting through the air."

"Ha ha. Hay is for horses, which, by the way, we need to go out to Midland and check on Mercy and Steeler sometime this weekend."

"Um, sure." Logan moved toward the door. "I forgot something in the bedroom. I'll be right back."

During breakfast Logan was quiet and distracted, but Madison pretended not to notice. She knew the changes of the past few weeks were taking their toll on the detective, causing her to be a bit off balance. She made small talk so Logan wouldn't have to, then after breakfast decided to check on the contractors.

"I'm going up to the house. Wanna come?"

As she rinsed out her coffee cup, Logan avoided eye contact. "Ah, no thanks. I have some things to do here."

Feeling dejected, Madison gathered a light jacket and left the brooding detective behind. At the new house, she was soon caught up in a conversation with the contractor about the tile she had selected for the master bathroom and didn't hear Logan enter until she looked up and saw her leaning against the door frame of the master bedroom.

Sending the contractor on his way, she walked over to Logan, bewilderment showing on her face. Not thirty minutes ago, she had left the brooding detective at the barn—the same woman who stood before her with an ear-to-ear grin. "What's up?"

Pushing off from the wall, Logan leaned in to brush Madison's lips with hers. "Not much. Just thought I'd come up to say hi."

"Okay." The doctor shook her head. "A few minutes ago, I thought you wanted to be left alone. I'm confused."

Logan took Madison's hand and pulled her toward the back of the house. "Come on, I think this will explain everything."

The doctor followed along behind, but suddenly stopped when she heard a loud noise outside. "What is that?"

Logan tugged harder. "Come on and find out for yourself." She opened the back door and pulled Madison onto the porch, then stood back and grinned as Madison looked toward the barn.

"Oh my God. Logan." Madison bolted down the steps and broke into a full run as she shouted for Logan to follow.

Two sets of dark brown eyes turned toward the rapidly approaching woman. Logan watched fondly as Madison ran toward Mercy and Steeler, laughing and crying with every step. She gave them a moment to greet each other before easing beside her lover. "I hope you don't mind."

Madison pulled Logan into a hard, fierce embrace. "Mind? Are you kidding? I'm—I'm speechless."

After a tender kiss and a gentle stroke to the horse's necks, Logan turned to Madison. "I thought it was time that they came home."

Taking her hand, Madison turned to walk toward the barn, the horses following along close behind them. "We're *all* home."

Other titles from
StarCrossed Productions, Inc.

Above All, Honor **(Revised Edition)**
Radclyffe
0-9724926-2-3 $17.50

Beyond the Breakwater
Radclyffe
0-9724926-5-8 $19.50

Code Blue
KatLyn
0-9724926-0-7 $18.50

Fated Love
Radclyffe
1-932667-14-8 $18.99

Graceful Waters
Verda Foster & B. L. Miller
0-9740922-6-6 $18.50

I Already Know The Silence Of The Storm
Nancy M. Hill
1-932667-13-x $17.50

Incommunicado
N. M. Hill & J. P. Mercer
0-9740922-5-8 $17.50

Justice in the Shadows
Radclyffe
1-932667-02-4 $18.99

Love and Honor
Radclyffe
0-9724926-4-X $17.99

Love's Masquerade
Radclyffe
1-932667-03-2 $17.99

Love's Melody Lost
Radclyffe
0-9724926-9-0 $17.50

Love's Tender Warriors
Radclyffe
0-9724926-1-5 $16.99

Safe Harbor (Revised Edition)
Radclyffe
0-9724926-6-6 $17.50

shadowland
Radclyffe
1-932667-06-7 $17.50

Storm Surge
KatLyn
0-9740922-0-7 $17.50

The Price of Fame
Lynn Ames
1-932667-07-5 $17.99

These Dreams
Verda Foster
1-932667-04-0 $17.50

Threads Of Destiny
J. P. Mercer
1-932667-12-1 $17.50

Tomorrow's Promise
Radclyffe
0-9740922-1-5 $17.50

To find more great books by these authors and many more, visit our Web site at

www.starcrossedproductions.com